RESCUING YOU

WRIGHT HEROES OF MAINE
BOOK 2

ROBIN PATCHEN

JDO PUBLISHING

Cover by Lynnette Bonner.

ISBN-13 Trade Paperback: 9781950029389

ISBN-13 Large Print Paperback: 9781950029419

ISBN-13 Casebound Hard Cover: 9781950029402

had known the news would be bad, but if Stone made the trip to tell him in person...

His feet hit soft grass. He ran to the road that snaked down the hill toward the rocky shore.

Peter Mason, aka Stone, pushed off from the hood of a red sedan.

"What is it?" Michael called from a few yards off, shoving the phone in his pocket. "Why are you here?"

"Leila's alive."

Michael's steps faltered.

She was alive. *Alive.* Thank God.

Hope crashed like a tidal wave of relief and elation. Maybe he hadn't gotten his girlfriend killed after all.

Maybe he could still keep her safe, protect her from his dangerous life.

But Stone added, "Or she was a few days ago."

Just like that, the relief faded. He froze in the middle of the road, swallowed to keep his emotions in check, then continued more slowly toward his teammate and friend. "Tell me what you know."

"We got pictures of her boarding a private jet in Berlin." Stone's words were delivered matter-of-factly. At just over five-ten, his fellow agent was a few years older and a few inches shorter than Michael—but no less powerful. Any enemy who looked into his eyes knew he was not a man to be discounted. His voice was even when he added, "The guy assigned to Vortex after you left caught sight of him at the airport. Your friend was with him."

Leila was with Vortex?

No.

The terrorist had been Michael's primary assignment in Munich for nearly a year, a man whose face he and his team had seen but whose identity they'd never confirmed. His passport

named him Assad Ghafran, but no one by that name who was his age—late fifties, maybe early sixties—seemed to exist anywhere. There were no school records, no birth records, no military records. No matter how long Michael watched him or how many of his allies Michael uncovered, he could never ferret out the man's real identity.

As far as anyone could tell, Assad Ghafran didn't exist.

Vortex did.

They'd dubbed him "Vortex" because he sucked in the weak and vulnerable—often young, fatherless men—used them for his own purposes, and left chaos and destruction in his wake.

Like a tornado, except Vortex wasn't a natural disaster. He planned and executed his tragedies for the highest possible casualty rate.

All in the name of his religion, as if he believed in anything but himself.

Vortex was cooking up something, but Michael hadn't been able to figure out what.

Since he'd been called back to the States when he told his team leader that Leila, the woman he'd been secretly dating, had gone missing, Michael had lost track of Vortex and his movements.

If the terrorist had kidnapped Leila, then he had to know Michael was on his trail. Had he taken her for retribution or leverage or both?

The thought had his hands clenching into fists. Sweet, sweet Leila, captured by that monster.

But she'd been spotted, alive. "Was she all right?" Michael asked. "What did he do to her?"

Stone opened a manila envelope he'd had tucked beneath his arm, then pulled out the contents and laid them across the hood of the car.

Michael studied the glossy photographs.

Sure enough, there was Vortex, an Iraqi, they believed. One of the most dangerous terrorists in the world.

Beside him, Leila Amato. Her long, silky black hair was hidden by a drab brown hijab, her shapely body invisible beneath a black abaya. In the year he'd known her, he'd never seen her don traditional Arabic garb. She was a Christian and seemed eager to put her Islamic roots behind her. She'd never talked about her past, despite Michael's gentle questioning, as if she wanted to pretend she hadn't had a life before she arrived in Germany.

Michael could have found out where she was from if he'd wanted to. He could have done a full background check, run her fingerprints. But she was his girlfriend. Not an asset. Not a suspect.

The agent had gotten a clear shot of Leila's face. Her skin was darker than Michael's and perfectly smooth, making her look closer to twenty than the twenty-nine he knew her to be. She had high cheekbones and full, shapely lips. But it was her eyes that had drawn him in on their first meeting. Gorgeous, almond-shaped, obsidian eyes.

It was Leila, no question about it.

In the hands of a terrorist.

The photographs tracked their progress from an airport terminal, across the tarmac, up the stairs, and into a waiting Gulfstream.

Beautiful Leila, an innocent immigrant, who had nothing to do with Michael's work, nothing to do with all the ugliness he dealt with on a daily basis.

But if Vortex had realized his movements were being watched, then it wouldn't have been difficult for him to have someone tail the watcher.

That someone must've seen Michael and Leila together. That was the only thing that made sense.

Michael had kept his relationship with Leila secret from his team. But he'd failed to keep her secret from his enemy.

Leila would be safe if not for Michael.

Stone said nothing, just stood beside him, arms crossed. Waiting for...what?

Michael studied the photographs again, noting details he'd missed at first. He'd never seen her without makeup before. And the confidence he'd always admired in her expression was gone. She looked afraid.

But Stone didn't know her at all, so that couldn't be what had him wearing that concerned—suspicious?—look.

And then Michael understood.

Leila wasn't being dragged onto that plane. There were no weapons. No guards forcing her. As far as Michael could tell, she climbed aboard willingly.

"That doesn't make sense." He spoke as if Stone had vocalized his thoughts, which he might as well have. "She was snatched off the street. You saw the footage."

Michael had watched the CCTV recording a hundred times or more, trying desperately to see something, anything, that would lead him to her kidnappers. But they'd worn masks. Not a single clue remained in the burned-out van, no indication whatsoever of where her captors had taken her.

After days of frantic searching, Michael had lost hope that she'd be found alive. That was when Toby Brock, their team leader, had called him back to the States, promising that the rest of the team would continue the search for Leila while agents assigned to the embassy in Germany would pick up surveillance of Vortex.

Forcing Michael to trust Brock and the team. Which he should. Of course. They were on his side. But it was killing him to do nothing. Killing him that he couldn't be involved.

"She was kidnapped," Michael said.

"That's what it looked like."

"She's a hotel manager, not a spy. Not a soldier. She doesn't have the skills to escape." He tapped one of the photos. "She's not fighting because she knows it's hopeless. Or they have something on her. She's not going willingly."

"If you say so."

Michael had never had the desire to punch his friend before. He turned to face him fully, squeezing his hands into fists to keep from doing something stupid. "When were these taken?"

"Tuesday."

Four days ago.

"Why did it take that long for us to get them? Or have you had them—?"

"The team watching Vortex was focused on him. They had no idea who she was when they passed along the images. Nobody knew there was a connection."

"There isn't a connection." Not between Vortex and Leila. None except Michael.

Stone said nothing, but his gaze moved to the photos, his eyebrows hiking, the implication clear.

"She's not a soldier. She has no training. Of course she's not fighting." Michael hated to imagine what Vortex and his men had put Leila through. And it had to be something terrible because the only other option was that Leila was involved with Vortex somehow. If that was the case, then... "She's not a terrorist."

"Because she's pretty? Because you like her?"

"Because I *know* her. She's sweet and innocent, and—"

"I assume she would say that she knows you?"

Again, Stone didn't have to explain what he meant.

Leila knew Michael, the machine parts salesman.

She didn't know Michael, the CIA agent.

But it was different. Maybe Michael hadn't shared his true profession, but he'd shared who he was—his personality, his character, his values.

And she'd done the same; he was sure of it. Michael might not be the most skilled spy in the world, but he could smell a liar, and Leila wasn't a liar.

Unless he was losing his edge. Had he been blinded by her beauty and charm?

He wouldn't be the first to be played by a beautiful woman.

Still, what reason could Leila possibly have to deceive him?

Unless she knew who he was.

Unless she'd been working him all along.

No.

Maybe.

There were too many questions, not nearly enough answers, and certainly none that Stone could provide.

"Where'd they go?"

"Vortex flew to Heathrow," Stone said, "but she didn't get off the plane when he did. We're still working on where the jet went after that."

Vortex didn't own a jet, not that Michael knew of. And he knew a lot about the guy. "Charter?" At Stone's nod, he asked, "You're sure she's not in London?"

"She didn't go through customs. The team watching Vortex hasn't seen her."

"Where did he go?"

Stone sighed. "Brock wants you to stand down and trust us to find her."

Of course he did. Brock never stepped a toe out of line, and if he'd ever had any feelings besides intolerance and scorn, Michael had never seen them.

"Vortex left her on the plane, and the plane took off," Stone said. "Wherever she is now, my guess is, she's there willingly."

"You don't know that. Somebody could've met the plane. There could've been someone on it when Vortex and Leila boarded."

Stone lifted one shoulder and let it drop. "Brock wants to know everything you told her."

"I didn't tell her anything." As rage heated him, Michael's words got colder. "We went out a couple of times. That's it."

"You started dating nine months ago." For the first time, Stone's face registered anger. "And lied to us about it."

Michael should have known they'd learn the whole truth. He'd been vague about his relationship with Leila, but they were spies, after all. Even spies deserved a personal life, didn't they? "I didn't lie. I just didn't mention—"

"Same thing and you know it. Was it her idea to keep your relationship secret?"

"No. And it wasn't a secret. I just didn't—"

"She's been seen with a terrorist, a terrorist you were watching. You wouldn't be the first agent to be taken down by pillow talk."

Cold fury stole Michael's voice. He breathed, considering and then discarding a handful of responses, reminding himself that Stone was his friend. This would be going very differently if Brock really believed Michael had shared secrets with Leila. He'd be in custody, or at least brought in for questioning.

Although that might be Brock's next move.

"No pillow talk," Michael said. "No pillows. No sleepovers. Dinners, long walks, mountain hikes, sightseeing. As far as she knows, I'm a salesman."

"And as far as you know, she's..."

"A hotel manager."

"Well, we know you were lying. Maybe she was too."

"That's your assessment, or Brock's?"

Stone's expression softened. "I trust your judgment. We're

still working on locating her. Brock sent me here to remind you that you're sidelined until this is over."

When Leila first went missing, Michael had seen no reason to worry. For all he'd known, she'd had an emergency. Her parents lived outside Munich. He'd never met them, and she rarely talked about them, which had always struck him as strange. But he hadn't delved into that, trying to stay solidly on the boyfriend side of the boyfriend-spy line.

Because of the long-distance nature of Michael's relationship with Leila, they didn't see each other often or consistently. So, at first, he hadn't worried when she didn't answer his phone calls or texts. But when twenty-four hours passed and she still hadn't responded, he flew to Munich and started asking questions. He learned she hadn't shown up for work for a few days.

He got ahold of the CCTV footage around the hotel where she worked and lived.

That was when he saw the recording of her being dragged into the van. At which point, he'd alerted his team.

Maybe if he'd told them sooner, they'd have already found her. His desire to keep his work life away from his personal life...

Talk about an epic fail.

Now they knew a terrorist had taken her, and it might be Michael's fault.

And he was supposed to do nothing?

Stone's gaze flicked to Sam's house, then toward the little cove at the bottom of the hill. "This isn't a bad place to rest."

"I can't sit here and do nothing."

"Take it up with Brock. I'm just the messenger."

"Fine." Michael grabbed his phone and tapped the speed dial.

Stone leaned against the car, arms crossed, patient as ever.

His calm only irritated Michael.

The team leader answered the way he always did. "Brock here."

"I have to find her."

"You've done enough, *Wrong*." Brock made the call sign sound like an indictment. "Stand down."

"She means something to me. If this is my fault—"

"Your *fault* came when you didn't tell me about her. Your *fault* came when you trusted an Arab Muslim—"

"She's a Christian—"

"—and chose to keep your relationship a secret. Did you tell her anything?"

"Of course not."

"She know you're with us?"

"I kept my cover."

"Mmm-hmm. Here's the thing. You take off looking for that woman, and you're going to force me to make assumptions about where your loyalty lies."

The threat stiffened Michael's spine. "You know I'm loyal."

"Here's what I know. You've been cavorting with a woman associated with a terrorist. Maybe you want to save her. But maybe you want to hide her from us. Or join her."

"I would never—"

"I hope that's true." The way Brock's voice lowered and evened out... This wasn't an empty threat and he wasn't just following some procedure laid out in some manual somewhere. "The problem is, I don't *know*. And this is Vortex we're talking about, not some low-level thug. Even if I wanted to give you free rein, you know I can't."

He paused, but Michael didn't voice his thoughts in the silence. Because, God help him, he could see it from Brock's point of view. Brock was wrong about Leila, but Michael's confidence wouldn't be enough to change his mind.

"If you go after her," Brock said, "you'll give me no choice but to assume the worst. You know what that looks like."

Once, a few years past, Michael had questioned a witness at a black site. He'd seen how terrorists were treated. If it was believed Michael betrayed his country, his American citizenship wouldn't garner him *better* treatment. In fact, it would probably earn him far worse treatment from people who believed him a traitor.

"Stand down," Brock said. "We'll find her and take it from there."

Michael kept silent for so long, eventually Brock gave up waiting for the *yes sir* that wasn't coming and ended the call.

In all the years Michael had worked with Brock, he'd never known the man to change his mind about anything. Which meant Michael would be stuck in Maine, twiddling his thumbs while somebody else rescued Leila.

Assuming they did.

Assuming Michael's attraction to her, his desire to get to know the pretty hotel manager, his desire to have a life beyond the CIA...

Didn't get her killed.

CHAPTER TWO

MY NAME IS LEILA AMATO.

Leila mouthed the words silently, first in German, then in English—staring at the image in the mirror and willing herself to remember who she was. Who she *really* was.

It wasn't the name she'd been given at birth. It was the name she'd chosen.

Just like she'd chosen the life she'd been living.

Just like she'd chosen her city, her profession.

Just like she'd chosen her faith.

"Nawra." *That* name was a jab from a sharp knife. "Look at me when I speak to you."

She forced her gaze away from the dirty mirror, over the narrow bed in the tiny room where she'd been locked for days, and onto the father who'd once loved her. "Where is Mama?"

Baba flinched at her demanding tone.

"Where is Yasamin?" She waved her hand toward the room, the compound. "Do they know you're holding me here? Qasim told me my sister was here." Only Qasim's threats to Yasamin had kept Leila from escaping—or at least trying to. But she

hadn't seen her sister or her mother since she'd been locked in this room.

In Iraq, under her father's thumb, in a world of lies and fear and secrets.

She was so tired of secrets.

"You are my responsibility." Baba's words were cold, delivered in Arabic, the language of her youth, and punctuated by his finger jabbing toward her. "You have been deceived."

He was the deceived one, but for once she managed to hold her tongue.

"You will learn to obey." Beneath his commanding tone, there was a hint of pleading, almost fear. She'd once thought of her father as a powerful man. She'd been proud to tell people she was the daughter of Saad Farad Fayad. After all, he'd rubbed shoulders with the most influential people in Baghdad, thriving in the government set up after Saddam Hussein's fall, meeting and dining with leaders from all over the globe. He'd been powerful, hadn't he? Or had that all been an illusion?

Or did the grown-up Leila Amato see what little Nawra Fayad never had? That Baba's power was mere bluster hiding a deep layer of fear. Either that or the father she'd once revered had changed—and not for the better. Because the man who stood in front of her now seemed broken, as if it took all his energy to survive.

"You will remain in this room until you learn to behave properly and respectfully."

"You're going to keep me locked away forever?"

Because she had no intention of subjecting herself to his rule or anyone else's.

He scowled, then swept her tray of food onto the floor. The bowl shattered, broken pieces skittering with the rice and scant vegetables. "You can eat off the floor like a dog—or learn to control your tongue. And obey." He stepped through the open

bobbed on the choppy water of the Atlantic in Shadow Cove as if all were right with the world.

As if Michael hadn't gotten the woman he'd come to care for killed.

Bryan caught his eye from the far side of the seating area on the oversize deck where the family talked and laughed. The second-to-youngest Wright brother was eight years Michael's junior and the most perceptive of the brothers.

Michael wasn't ready to answer Bryan's questions. Even if he wanted to talk about it, he had to keep his mouth shut. He wasn't sorry when his phone vibrated in his pocket.

The name on the screen made his stomach tighten. It was Stone.

Michael had been waiting for this call—and dreading it. Confirmation of what he already knew.

Leila was dead.

Crossing the deck away from the party, he answered. "Wrong here."

"Wrong" because the people on his elite team of CIA agents assigned to the White House for special projects used call signs to protect their identities, and Michael's had gone from Wright to Mr. Wright to Mr. Wrong in about five seconds. Now, he was simply known as Wrong—or sometimes, because his teammates thought they were so clever, Always Wrong.

Michael used to think it was funny, but it was a little too on-the-nose these days.

"You're at Sam's?" Stone asked.

Michael had kept his team apprised of his activities. "Yeah." He hurried down the wooden steps toward the yard. "What'd you learn?"

"Meet me out front."

"You're here?" What was Stone doing in Maine? Michael

CHAPTER ONE

THE WOMAN MICHAEL WRIGHT had given his heart to was gone. Just...gone.

Maybe he should've told his family, but considering he hadn't even told them he was dating someone, it felt a little awkward.

Plus, it wasn't exactly the best day to share tragic news. His parents were celebrating their anniversary. Fifty years, and still so in love.

He'd made the mistake of letting himself believe he could someday have what they had.

Until two weeks before, when Leila had been snatched off the street in Munich by masked men. The van she'd been forced into was later found deserted and burned, all evidence destroyed.

Years of CIA training, years of uncovering the evil deeds of evil men, and Michael had no idea how to find her.

It was a clear, chilly day on the coast of Maine. The sun shone in a royal blue sky, the bright red and yellow leaves shivering in the breeze. Far below his brother Sam's house, boats

To the brainstormers: Hallee, Misty, Lacy, Sharon, and Susie. Like so many of my stories, this book wouldn't exist if not for you. Thank you.

door and turned to face her. "Trust me, Nawra, you would do better to learn under this roof than that of your husband. Waleed won't be nearly as patient." Baba slammed the door.

The ancient lock turned.

While she stood speechless.

Husband?

Baba planned to marry her off?

To Waleed Shehab?

The image of the man floated in her memory. He'd been a student at the international school she and Yasamin had attended, though he was years ahead of them.

A bully, always surrounded by a cadre of hangers-on, he was someone the smart, kind students avoided. She hadn't been sorry when he'd graduated, believing she'd never have to see him again.

And then he showed up at her house with her uncle.

Waleed had tried to charm her, but while his tactics had changed, cruelty still hummed beneath a predatory smile.

She'd fended off his advances, careful to avoid being trapped alone with him.

But whenever she caught him looking at her, the hunger in his eyes made her skin crawl.

Marry him?

She'd die before she submitted to that man.

Besides, Baba had promised Mama that he would not arrange marriages for his daughters. It wasn't legal in Iraq to force a daughter to marry.

That wouldn't matter, though. A little money, a greased palm, and a judge could be convinced to look the other way.

Leila had to get out of there.

She stalked through the small room that held nothing but a narrow bed with dingy blankets, an old end table, the cracked mirror leaning against a wall, and a lamp. A few clothing items hung in a wardrobe, including the abaya and hijab she'd been forced to don after being taken in Munich.

Please, Jesus, get me out of here.

She stalked to the narrow window that overlooked the courtyard between the three-story house and the outbuildings, all of which were surrounded by stone walls. The compound stood isolated in the desert, nothing nearby but scrubby bushes and sand. In the distance, the Tigris meandered toward Baghdad, the Persian Gulf, and freedom.

For some, the Tigris might look like an escape. But the river had nearly taken her life once. She wouldn't give it the opportunity to try again.

The courtyard and buildings on the far side reminded Leila of an old childhood friend's home. But why would Baba be at Heba's house?

It didn't make sense.

Leila's family had a place like this, though it had been comfortable, a place of rest. When she was a child, the scent of jasmine filled the air, flowers blooming in pots and beds all around the courtyard.

Here, all she smelled were smoke and dirt.

When her uncle wasn't visiting, her family's courtyard had been a place of happiness. Children playing, mamas chatting, fathers laughing or discussing the events of the day. Her aunts and uncles and cousins and friends had overflowed the home.

Here, there were no family or friends in sight, just men, most of whom huddled at a table in the shade of the house. She didn't recognize any of them.

Was Waleed here? Or on his way?

When would this wedding take place?

How long did she have before the nightmare began?

In the courtyard, the men's conversation was dark. Their

laughter felt sinister. Or maybe it only seemed that way because of the guns they carried.

At least one guard stood outside the gate. She'd seen him when a car had driven through earlier, delivering someone Leila hadn't been able to see when the doors opened below her.

Was it Waleed?

Or Hasan?

With her grandparents dead, there was nobody to rein in Baba's brother.

Baba would never have chosen Waleed for her, not knowing how much she disliked the man.

Hasan was behind that.

Her uncle was a powerful man. Powerful because he was ruthless and uncompromising. And unaffected by things he deemed irrelevant, like family ties. Like love and affection. Like forgiveness and mercy.

He claimed to be a devout Muslim. But Hasan didn't worship anything or anyone but himself. He wasn't devout. He was devoid...of humanity.

Had Hasan sent those men after her? Or had her father done that?

Leila slumped onto the bed, which she'd hardly crawled out of during her first couple of days here, nursing her wounds and praying Mama or Yasamin would come. But they never did. Her mother and sister either didn't know she was there or were being prevented from visiting. Or perhaps they weren't on the property at all. She hadn't seen them. Perhaps the man who'd kidnapped her had lied.

If they knew she was there, would they help her escape?

Maybe. Maybe not.

Leila hadn't seen or spoken to either of them in over a decade. When she'd left, she'd believed she'd never see them again. Running had been the hardest decision she'd ever made, but the right decision for her. She'd always bucked under Baba's rule, but after she became a believer, it became harder and harder to keep her opinions to herself. It felt like it was only a matter of time before she gave her newfound faith away.

She hadn't wanted to find out what Baba—or his brother—would do if they discovered the truth.

Yasamin had understood.

Leila hadn't told Mama her plan to leave the country. She hadn't said goodbye. Her mother had needed to be shocked that she'd escaped. If Baba—or Hasan—had believed Mama had known, she'd have paid dearly for keeping the secret.

And Leila wasn't sure she'd have kept it.

She longed for Mama or Yasamin to visit, even though seeing them now would make leaving again torture.

Assuming she could find a way out.

She thought of Michael, the sweet, kind, handsome man she'd been dating. He was gentle, tall and strong, but he was no warrior. Even if he wanted to come to her rescue, how would he ever find her?

Aside from Michael and her coworkers, Leila had one true friend in Munich. Sophia was different from Leila in so many ways—an American Christian who worked at an art gallery, she was artistic and educated and connected.

And funny and generous. They'd met at church and become fast friends. Even with all her connections, Sophia wouldn't have any idea how to find her, and if she did, how could she possibly help?

Leila had to face it. Nobody was coming for her. She had to escape on her own.

But first, she'd have to get out of this room.

~

Late that night, Leila watched the men in the courtyard, who were visible only because of the light spilling out of the first-floor windows.

Her bruises and sprains were healing, injuries she'd earned fighting the men who'd snatched her off the street. She was hungry but stronger than she had been.

She wouldn't look at the food she'd brushed into the corner after Baba left her. She wouldn't stoop to that, no matter how her stomach growled.

Unlike their home in Baghdad, this house didn't have glass or screens in the windows, just shutters that opened to let in the breeze.

The day had been sweltering, but the evening air was cool. Cooler, anyway. She'd forgotten how hot the world could be.

And how quiet. She missed the bustle of Munich, the locals and tourists, the cars and buses. It was an orderly city, tidy and clean, so different from Baghdad. Leila was accustomed to city life. She was accustomed to noises and lights and people.

All that felt eons away from this black and silent world.

The men in the courtyard went inside until only one remained. With most of the lights extinguished, she might have believed him gone if not for the glow of his cigarette and the scent of smoke that lifted to her third-floor room.

It was now or never.

If she could be quiet...

Like a mouse, Yasamin would whisper. *Little feet, little moves.*

Today, Leila's feet were a lot bigger than they'd been back then, but she'd been studying the stone ledge that ran the length of the main house. It would hold her.

Above it, another ledge could act as a handhold.

She could do this.

It was her only chance.

She made the mistake of poking her head out and looking down.

Her stomach swooped. She fisted her hands to try to quell their trembling.

It was probably good that she couldn't make out the hard-packed dirt below—or the twenty-plus-foot drop.

What were her choices? Climb out and try to escape or remain a prisoner. Forced to be the wife of a man she despised.

Her life out of her control.

She'd take potential death.

The glow in the courtyard changed colors every few seconds, telling her the man below was scrolling on his phone. Distracted. Now was the time.

She hoisted herself onto the windowsill. She had done something similar a few times when they were children, back at the family compound outside Tikrit. She'd been confined to her room after disobeying Baba. When the sun went down, she'd crawled out her window—second story, not third—and crept along the rough stone to Yasamin's room next door.

Once, cautious Yasamin had come to her.

Like a mouse.

Facing into the room, Leila stuck her feet out one at a time until her stomach was balanced on the thin sill. She lowered her feet slowly, silently, feeling with her toes and wishing for a pair of tennis shoes.

Where was that ledge? She dared not look, but if she went any farther down and missed it, would she be able to get herself back up?

Breathe, Leila.

She lowered herself a little more.

Her toes caught the edge, and she managed to fit the balls of her feet on the narrow space.

Now, to get her hand from the sill to the upper ledge. She

moved one, gripped the ledge, tested her weight. Everything held.

But to move the second hand...

Courage.

Help me, Lord.

She probably should have sought God's leading *before* climbing out a third-floor window.

Seeking counsel wasn't exactly her forte. Or taking it.

She took a breath, shifted her weight to her feet, and released her hold on the sill, reaching for the ledge.

Her grip was loose, her fingers slipping. Her heart jumped into her throat.

She grabbed with her other hand and held on. And didn't plummet to her death.

Not yet, anyway.

She shuffled to her left, her progress painstakingly slow. The stone was rough, scraping her fingers and toes, but she didn't stop. Wouldn't stop. She had to get to the empty room.

At least she hoped it was empty.

There'd been zero noises coming from the room next door, nor had she noticed any light in the window. In fact, she didn't think anybody else was staying on the third floor at all. She hadn't heard footsteps in the hallway that didn't stop at her door.

She was certain the next room was empty. Mostly certain, anyway.

She'd find out soon enough.

Hopefully, she'd get into the empty room, creep out the door and down the stairs. With luck, she'd find a set of car keys. There might be a guard near the garage, but once she found a car, as long as she gunned it, she could get out before the alarm was sounded.

Maybe.

And then head south to Baghdad. Assuming they didn't catch up with her. Or call ahead for someone to head her off. Assuming she didn't get lost or need gasoline. Or get stopped by the authorities.

"Do you see that?"

At the sound of the voice, she startled, her foot slipping. She managed to keep herself from falling and hugged the rough rocky wall, breathing through panic.

Waiting for the men to sound the alarm.

"What?" another man answered.

"It's a UFO." His Arabic was rough and uneducated. "They're everywhere now, haven't you heard?"

They were looking into the sky. Not at her.

She tried to make herself as small as possible. Thank God for the dark T-shirt and sweatpants she'd been given. A little shift, a tiny noise, and they'd see her. *Please, God. Please...*

"That's a satellite, not aliens." The other chuckled. "Go in. I'll take over."

Leila dared not move. She stayed put, fingers so tense they ached, for another minute, two minutes. Then, praying the latest guard had lost interest in the night sky, she continued her slow journey along the wall.

Finally, she reached the open window and transferred her hand from the ledge to the sill. She shifted her second hand, hoisted herself up onto her belly, and got a look inside.

It was dark, not a bedroom but an office.

She lowered herself to the floor silently.

She sat there a long moment, listening to the house. It was quiet. No shouts. No pounding footsteps. Nobody knew she'd escaped.

She didn't know what would happen next, but at least she wouldn't have to do that again.

Once her eyes adjusted to the darkness, she looked around.

A desk had a number of chairs surrounding it. She opened drawers and searched in the darkness, feeling around for a weapon or a set of keys.

She found neither.

She hadn't expected there to be, but it seemed wise to search. Mama had always kept a basket near the garage door for Baba to put his things in when he came home. Maybe these people did the same. Maybe, if she could find the garage, she could find keys.

She had been here before. Her best friend, Heba, had lived about thirty miles south of Tikrit, not far from the country compound Leila's family owned. Was this Heba's father's office? If so, what was she doing there?

What was Baba doing here?

And where was Heba? Obviously, she knew nothing about Leila's capture and imprisonment. If she knew, she'd help her.

The desk drawers held nothing helpful.

She studied what lay across the top of it. Beneath the single lamp, there was a map.

She opened the top drawer again, feeling around for something she thought she'd touched before. Yes. A lighter.

She lit it, keeping her body between the flame and the window, and bent to look.

Why have a paper map? Who used maps anymore when everyone had GPS on their phones? Someone had drawn circles around intersections.

Her breath caught.

It was a map of Munich, the city that had been her home for years.

Had Baba used this to find her?

She hadn't thought about the fact that, even if she did manage to survive a second escape from Iraq, she couldn't go home. She'd need to start over in a different city in a different country, and with a different name.

The life she'd built was gone forever.

The life she'd let herself dream about with Michael...gone forever. How could she renew ties with him after changing her name and disappearing?

Her feelings for him had grown far past friendship, though she hadn't realized that until now, until she knew she'd never see him again.

The thought sucked the air from her lungs.

No. There was no going back. She'd started with nothing before—no money, no name. No Michael. She could do it again.

She left the map of the city she'd loved and hurried to the door.

She turned the knob and pulled.

But it didn't open.

No!

It was locked.

Just like her room, locked from the outside, only this was keeping people out. Why?

She hurried back to the desk, thinking maybe she could find something to pick it. In her haste, she forgot to be careful. Forgot to be silent. She bumped into the desk and knocked the lamp over. It hit the floor. Didn't break, but the sound felt deafening.

"What was that?" The words carried through the window.

Somewhere nearby, a door slammed.

Then footsteps.

They were coming!

She righted the lamp, hoping to get it back in the proper spot, then ran to the window. She jumped on the sill, dropped outside, and hung on by her fingertips.

Her feet dangled, searching for the ledge.

Come on, come on...

Any second, someone would check the office. Or maybe check her room.

Finally, her toes touched the ledge. She shifted her hands to the tiny outcropping of stone and shimmied across, back to her prison, where at least she was safe. Barely remembering to be afraid of a fall. Because she hated to think what would happen if she were caught. Baba would move her to a windowless room for sure. There'd be no fresh air. No opportunity to escape.

And if Hasan found out…

Or Waleed.

Baba wouldn't be able to protect her. Maybe he wouldn't care.

The distance that had taken long, painstaking minutes to cross earlier, she now crossed in seconds. She reached the windowsill of her room and launched herself through.

The room was still dark, the door closed. *Thank You.* She stood, pressed her hand to her chest to calm herself down.

And then the light flicked on.

She was blinded and trapped.

Leila gasped and stepped away from the figure who stood between her and the door, but there was nowhere to go.

CHAPTER THREE

MICHAEL SHOULDN'T BE HERE.

He'd probably lose his job if Brock found out he'd flown to London against orders. And lose it for no good reason, considering this trip had yielded exactly nothing.

Michael had hopped on a plane a few hours after Sam and Eliza's wedding, a small ceremony after church on Sunday. Since he'd arrived at Heathrow Monday morning, he'd been searching for information about where Leila might be.

He'd connected with contacts and discovered whom Vortex had visited while he was there—two men already on the CIA's watch list, people suspected of funneling money to terrorists. Vortex was believed to be connected with a branch of ISIL—the Islamic State of Iraq and the Levant—recruiting followers in Europe. There'd been rumblings that the group was plotting something, but nobody had been able to figure out what.

And this trip hadn't helped. Michael had learned nothing new about Vortex, and nothing about Leila at all. Nobody had seen her, not at the airport, not in the neighborhoods or establishments the terrorist had visited before he'd flown back to Baghdad a few days prior, alone.

Which meant Stone had been right. Leila hadn't gotten off the jet in London. So where was she?

The jet had continued to a small airport in Turkey, where all the occupants disembarked. According to the owner of the charter company, that had been the end of that client's charter.

Leila had been in Turkey. Was she still? Or had she been taken elsewhere?

Was she safe now? Was she still alive?

It was killing him, not knowing, and for the first time, he had an inkling of how Sam had felt all the years Eliza was missing. Of course, Eliza had left willingly.

Leila had been kidnapped. Despite what the photos showed, Michael was sure of it.

And he was going to find her.

Please, Father. Help me find her.

He returned to his hotel and the cookie-cutter room that looked like it could be in any hotel near any major airport in any major city in the world. He flopped onto the bed, frustrated.

It wasn't even nine o'clock, but he was exhausted. Not sleeping for two nights would do that. London had been a waste of time. He ought to head back to Maine and hope Brock never discovered his little jaunt to England. Not that Brock had forbidden him to go to England—or anywhere, for that matter.

He'd only forbidden him from looking for Leila. If he found out where Michael was, of course he'd know why he was there. If Michael were smart, he'd head straight back to the States.

But he wasn't smart. He opened his laptop and booked a flight to Istanbul. Maybe he could pick up Leila's trail there.

At least he'd be doing something.

CHAPTER FOUR

LEILA BLINKED in the bright light, bracing for a blow.

The figure barreled into her.

And wrapped her in a hug.

Leila's body reacted before her brain caught up, her eyes filling with tears.

Yasamin.

"You're alive. Oh, thank God." Leila's twin sister backed away just enough to peer at Leila's face. "All these years I've worried, wondering if you made it. It's been awful, not knowing."

"I'm sorry, I should have—"

"No, no. You couldn't."

Leila studied her twin, taking in the familiar features. They'd once been identical, so alike they could even fool their parents. Sometimes, anyway.

But the years had changed them both. Leila knew she looked older, but Yasamin's once glowing skin was yellowish, her cheeks sunken.

Beneath her sister's tunic and loose pants, she was too thin.

"Are you sick?" Because what else would explain the gaunt appearance?

"It's nothing." Yasamin waved off the words with a flick of her hand. They sat on the bed, side by side, each with one knee bent up so they could face each other. Mirror images, as if nothing had changed. "Did you make that crash I heard earlier? When I saw you, I came straight over. And then the noise...I told Baba it was me. That I'd been looking for something."

"So he's not coming?" In the joy of seeing her sister, Leila had forgotten to worry about the footsteps, the people looking for her. She strained to hear, but the house was quiet again.

"How are you here?" Yasamin squeezed her hands, holding on as if fearing Leila might drift away. "What happened?"

"I was in Munich, and they just..." She didn't describe the moment she'd been grabbed in the alley outside the hotel where she lived and worked, and then shoved into the back of a van. She didn't describe the way she'd been tied up and gagged. She didn't share her terror or the certainty that she was about to die for her sins—or what they would perceive as sins. Converting to Christianity, escaping her family and her country for a life of freedom.

She'd fought her captors, trying desperately to get away, until the man had told her she could either cooperate or Yasamin would pay the price.

She remembered his face from her childhood. He was a friend of her father's, but she'd always been afraid of him.

He didn't seem the type to make idle threats.

No, Leila wouldn't tell her sister any of that. Quiet, kind Yasamin didn't need to feel guilty for something she couldn't control.

"How did you find me?" Obviously, Baba hadn't told her twin she was there, or she would have come sooner. "What did you mean, you saw me?"

"Hanging off the house like Spider-Man." Her lips quirked. "Some things never change."

"Hey, you did it too."

"That one time. But I've grown older and smarter. You're lucky nobody else saw you. And lucky you didn't fall. And they didn't catch you in the office."

"I don't understand. You weren't in the courtyard."

"I've been staying in the guest-house, the old place"—she gestured toward the window—"over there." It was an ancient building on the opposite side of the courtyard, probably the original house. "Baba lets me stay there sometimes."

"Why are we here? Is this Heba's old house?" At her sister's nod, she asked, "Where is she?"

"She and Mostafa live in his home. You remember?"

"Yes, but I don't understand. Why are we here?"

"It doesn't matter."

The lack of answers was frustrating. "Why aren't you in Baghdad with Baba and Mama?"

Yasamin leaned away, blinking. "Baba didn't tell you?"

"Tell me what?" Leila's stomach, already churning from fear and surprise, clenched at the look in her sister's face.

"Mama is gone."

"Is she in the city? Why isn't Baba with her? Why aren't you?"

But Yasamin shook her head. "I'm sorry, Nawra."

"Leila," she corrected automatically. She didn't answer to Nawra anymore.

"I like that name." Yasamin leaned closer. "Leila." She seemed to taste it on her tongue. "Mama passed away the year after you left." She delivered the words with little emotion, as one who'd come to grips with the news. "Cancer. By the time they discovered it, it had spread from her stomach to her bones. She died a few months after she was diagnosed."

What?

No.

Mama was gone? *Dead?*

Leila bent at the waist and covered her head with her hands. Tears filled her eyes and spilled onto her lap, turning to sobs.

All the years since she'd left, she'd longed for her mother. All those years, Mama had been gone. Lost to her. Lost forever.

How could Leila have not known? How could she have not been here?

When she escaped, she'd known Mama would grieve her loss. Had the grief contributed to her death? Would she have survived if Leila hadn't broken her heart?

Yasamin wrapped Leila close and rocked her. "She forgave you. She understood."

Had she, really? Or was Yasamin trying to make her feel better, saying what she wanted to hear?

Leila would never really know how Mama had felt.

Not that anything had changed, not really. She hadn't thought she'd ever see her mother or her sister again, and yet here Yasamin was.

Yasamin, who'd stayed behind because she thought Mama needed her.

As if her sister read her thoughts, she said, "I should have gone with you." She leaned away, her face harder than Leila had ever seen it. "After you disappeared, Mama said as much to me, that I should have run when I had the chance."

"I shouldn't have..." But she couldn't say the words because they'd be a lie, and her sister wouldn't be fooled. She changed direction. "I should have insisted you come."

"I didn't want to leave her. And I was afraid."

By her twin's tone, her fear of running had waned.

"You can help me, help us," Leila said. "You can...call someone or..."

She expected Yasamin to refuse. Yasamin had always been the cautious one, so of course she'd be afraid to step out of line. But her twin surprised her.

"Who should I call?" She stood and looked down at Leila. "Tell me, now. I'll do it as soon as I can."

"You'll come with me?"

"Yes, yes. But we must leave soon. As soon as possible. And when we do, I will be Jasmine again." Jasmine, the name their English-speaking friends had called her at school when they were girls.

"That is a good name," Leila said.

"Give me a number. Hurry. I have to get back before Baba looks for me."

Leila didn't have time to think about why her sister looked sick or why she was so eager to leave when she'd flat-out refused a decade earlier.

Instead, she scrambled for a name. Who could they call?

Her boss at the hotel? She might want to help, but what contacts would a German hotel manager have?

Sophia? Her friend had money, but again, no contacts in Iraq.

There was Michael.

Michael, the man she'd been falling for. As an American man, he had money and power. And he'd told her once that his brother Grant was in the military, in one of their elite forces.

Maybe...maybe Michael could call him. Maybe Grant would have contacts who could help.

Or maybe Michael would hire people, or know someone...

Michael was their best chance.

CHAPTER FIVE

MICHAEL'S FLIGHT was scheduled to leave the following morning, so after setting his alarm, he shut off the light and prayed for Leila until he fell asleep.

The ringing of his cell woke him. It wasn't his work phone but his personal one—meaning it probably wasn't Stone or Brock, and thus not related to Leila. He considered letting it go to voicemail but checked the caller ID, just in case.

An international number beginning with 964. He searched his memory for the country associated with that code.

Iraq?

Vortex was Iraqi. And though she'd never confirmed it, he was almost certain Leila was too.

He bolted upright and snatched the phone. He pulled it from the charger. "Hello?"

"Yes, hello?"

The female voice had his heart hammering.

"Is this Michael?"

"Leila?"

"It is... Yes. Leila. I was hoping—"

"Where are you?" He flicked on the light and searched for a pen and paper. "Whose phone—?"

"Not mine. Do not call me. I am trapped here." She sounded strange, her Arabic accent thicker than it had been. But the voice was definitely Leila's, familiar despite the terror that laced it.

"You're in Iraq?" Because she could have borrowed the phone from an Iraqi. She could be anywhere. "Send me a pin. Are you safe?"

"Hold on."

His phone dinged, and he checked her location, then zoomed out and studied the remote area. "Tell me everything you know about this place."

"A compound near Tikrit." Her voice was surprisingly calm. "It is heavily guarded. I am on the third floor overlooking court-yard, center window."

He snatched his laptop from a side table, opened it up, and searched the coordinates she'd sent. "A military installation, or a business—?"

"No, no. A family home surrounded by a stone wall."

"Okay. Hold on." He found the house on his laptop and zoomed in. He'd need access to a more recent picture, real-time satellite coverage. Which he could get...maybe. "How many guards?"

"Always two at night—one at gate, one in courtyard. During the day, many men, all armed."

"Do they go to mosque? Is there a time—?"

"No, no. They are here always. Sometimes more, sometimes less."

"When are there more? When are there less?"

"I do not...no normal times. Only...inconsistent."

Again, he was struck by Leila's thick accent and her

inability to find the right words. Her English was normally perfect, her diction better than his.

"Sweetheart, are you all right? Are you hurt?"

"Please." He heard tears in her voice, and his insides clenched like a fist. "You must help. Will you?"

"Of course. I'll get you out of there. I've been looking for you. It might take—"

"You must hurry. My life is in danger. I am afraid."

"I'll make a plan. Try to call back tomorrow."

"I cannot. You hurry. Please."

The line went dead.

Michael squeezed the phone in his hand, breathing through panic and the overwhelming desire to call the number back, to ask more questions. But if Leila could've told him more, she would have. If she'd had more time, she'd have taken it.

Had somebody caught her using the phone? Was she being harmed right now?

Father. Please, protect her.

He had to go. He'd contact his team and figure out a plan on the way, but he needed to get in the air, now.

He dressed and shoved his clothes in his suitcase. Five minutes after Leila had broken the connection, he yanked open his hotel room door and headed for the elevator.

It was just dumb luck that he heard a distant ding, and then indistinct voices. He strained to listen.

"You don't think this is overkill?"

Stone?

What was he doing in London?

"I specifically told him not to look for her, and we both know he's not here on vacation." Brock's voice was cool and unaffected.

He hurried in the opposite direction. With Stone and Brock in the hallway, the heavy door to the stairwell would be too loud. Michael slipped into a little room where an ice machine hummed. He listened. And waited.

A knock came from down the hall, knuckles rapping against the door to the room he'd just left. After a moment, another knock was followed by, "Open up, Michael. We know you're here."

Michael considered returning to his room. He could still come back from this. Maybe that was the right play.

Brock had promised to keep searching for Leila. Maybe, now that Michael knew where she was, Brock would send the team in to rescue her.

But what if he didn't? What if he chose to abandon Leila and also prevented Michael from getting to her?

Michael wished he could trust the team leader to do the right thing.

But...but he didn't. It was that simple. He'd promised Leila he'd rescue her, and he was going to keep his promise.

"Last chance to let us in." A door opened, no doubt the one to his room, which told him Brock had used his credentials to get the hotel staff to make him a key.

As soon as he heard the door close, he bolted for the staircase, yanked open the door, pushed through, then closed it carefully, as quietly as he could. Once it clicked, he picked up his suitcase and ran down two flights of stairs to the ground floor. He hurried through the lobby and exited into a chilly, drizzly night.

He was thankful for his waterproof jacket as he jogged away, his suitcase bouncing along behind him. He'd chosen one of the many hotels that ringed the airport, all connected by a four-lane road that was mostly deserted tonight. A sidewalk ran between the hotels. He passed two of them until he reached the third, an international chain. Keeping his head down to avoid CCTV cameras—they were everywhere around here—he loitered near the edge of the drop-off area and opened his Uber app.

Thirty minutes later, he purchased a ticket on the first flight that left for the Continent. From Frankfurt, he'd figure out a way to get to Iraq...and Leila.

Hopefully, Brock wouldn't catch up to him until after he'd rescued her.

God willing, he wouldn't end up at some black site for this. Even if he did, Leila was worth it.

CHAPTER SIX

FIVE DAYS HAD PASSED.

Five days since Yasamin...Jasmine had spoken to Michael.

Leila paced her tiny room from the window to the door and back, trying to pray and trust God.

It wasn't easy.

When her father had come with a small bowl of rice on the third day after their argument, she'd played her part, apologizing and promising to try harder to be the daughter he wanted—not only because she'd been very hungry, but also because she hadn't wanted Baba to think she was planning to escape. She'd been so subservient that she'd feared she overplayed her hand. But he'd accepted it, apparently believing that he'd broken her.

He didn't know her at all. Maybe he never had.

Even so, he was her father. Had Jasmine told Michael that Baba was there? What if Baba were hurt or killed when Michael —or more likely his brother—came to rescue them? Would she be able to live with herself?

All Leila could do was wait and trust that God would do what was best.

Which was more difficult today than it had been, thanks to

the car that had arrived earlier. She'd seen it approaching, seen it stop at the gate. She watched two men step out as her father rushed to greet the visitors.

As usual, she couldn't get a look at their faces from her vantage point.

Until Baba pointed to her window.

One of the men looked her way.

She'd stepped back, but not fast enough.

A slow, cruel smile crossed Waleed Shehab's lips. He didn't wave or nod, just stared at her as if he knew exactly where she was, hiding in the shadows in her locked room. Trapped.

And then the other man followed his gaze. Uncle Hasan wasn't smiling. The look he shot her was filled with contempt.

It was his decision to force her to marry Waleed, payback for believing she could live her own life. Choose her own way.

Waleed was to be her lifelong punishment for defiance.

She couldn't wait any longer. She had to get out of here.

She and Jasmine could do it, together. If they could get to her old friend's house, Heba and her husband would transport them to Baghdad and out of the country. After all, Heba had helped her last time.

She lived with her husband in a little town between here and Baghdad. If Leila and Jasmine could get there, Heba would protect them.

But Leila's twin had only come to see her once since the night they'd talked, and she'd only stayed long enough to report that Michael had promised to rescue them.

Was Michael coming? Would he be able to get into the country? Would Grant, his special forces brother?

Former special forces, but surely he still had contacts.

Would those contacts care about two insignificant Iraqi women?

Get us out of here, Lord. Rescue us.

Leila longed for her Bible. There were promises in there about how God rescued captives, and she needed to know them, all of them. She could only think of one, the one Jesus had recited in His hometown. Something about proclaiming freedom for captives and releasing prisoners from darkness.

Why hadn't she memorized it?

I promise, if I ever get my hands on another Bible, I will read it faithfully. I will memorize verses. I will do whatever You ask. Just get us out of here.

As if God might be swayed by her bargaining, but what else did she have? She needed Him to move.

Please.

She stopped at the window and peered out. It was dark now. The days were too hot and too bright with nothing—no trees, no clouds—to protect the land from the burning sun. The nights were dark as pitch, so black beyond the compound that it seemed as if the rest of the world had disappeared, as if the compound were all alone in the universe.

Iraq was a land of extremes.

Leila longed for Munich, the city she'd made her home, where people of all colors, ethnicities, and faiths coexisted. Yes, she'd dealt with some there who made assumptions about her because of how she looked, but for the most part, she felt accepted, even embraced, by the locals. She could look different and believe different things without fear of persecution.

There were places in Iraq where that was true. Not here.

She had to get out. She was not going to live the rest of her life here. She was not going to become the bride of a madman.

She was not a commodity to be traded for power or influence or wealth.

Please, God.

She'd taken to sleeping during the daylight hours, prowling her room at night, determined to be ready when rescue arrived.

In the courtyard, the guard sat at the table, smoking his cigarette and scrolling his phone. He would be replaced in a couple of hours. They were always the same men. Always complacent as if there were no real cause for worry.

The building Jasmine had called the guest-house was dark. Was her sister asleep? Prowling, like Leila was?

Was she sick?

Based on her pallor, the skin-and-bones feel of her, something was wrong. She needed medical attention. The sooner the better.

Hurry, Michael. Please.

Would he come himself?

Probably not. He had no military experience.

Still, she hoped.

She longed for him. Longed to see him. Longed to feel his arms around her.

Hours later, she'd given up pacing and was seated on her bed, facing the window. Waiting. Praying. The moon outside her window was barely a sliver. Otherwise, all was dark.

All was silent. All was still.

And then a figure appeared in the window.

She gasped and jerked back.

"Shh. It's me, it's me." The man dropped his feet to the floor and crossed toward her.

Even though she'd been hoping for him, she didn't believe it. "Michael?"

Rather than answer, he pulled her up and into his arms.

Just like that, she wasn't alone.

Cheek pressed against his slippery jacket, she wrapped her arms around his back and breathed him in. In Munich, he'd always smelled of sandalwood, a manly scent she'd come to associate with feeling cherished. Here, he smelled of sweat and desert, and still, it made her feel cherished.

Valued.

"Thank God," he said. "Thank God you're all right."

The words were a whisper against her hair, warm breath on her skin. It was surreal that Michael was here, in Iraq, in a compound-turned-prison. So strange that it was almost fantastical, but his arms were strong and sure and altogether solid.

He stepped back, gripping her shoulders. "Are you all right? Are you hurt? What did they do to you?"

"I'm all right." She took in the image of the man she was coming to love. He wore sand-colored camouflage from his long-sleeved T to his cargo pants to his boots and his gloves. He had on a matching helmet with strange eyewear perched on top.

Night vision goggles.

He was suited up like a soldier. Speaking of... "Where is your brother?"

"My...what?"

"Grant. Isn't he with you?"

"Why would he...?" Michael's words faded. Rather than answer, he slipped past her to the doorway, pulled something from his pocket, and crouched in front of the lock.

"Is Grant getting Jasmine?"

Michael stopped what he was doing and turned. "What are you talking about?" His voice was barely audible.

"My sister. We have to save her."

"Your sister is...? How is she...?" He took a breath. "You should have told me about her." Leila had never heard anger in Michael's voice before. Maybe it was just confusion she picked up now. Or frustration. Either way, she didn't understand.

"Jasmine called you. She told you where we were. Didn't she?"

"You called..." And then, "It wasn't you?"

Now Leila was confused. Why wouldn't Jasmine have told

him who she was? "It doesn't matter. I can't leave her here. I won't." Not again. Surely, Michael wouldn't ask her to.

Michael said nothing for a long, terrifying moment. Then he nodded and returned his focus to the door. "What you're wearing works."

She glanced down at the dark sweatpants and T-shirt. Ugly, but it should blend in the darkness.

"If you have a jacket," Michael said, "grab it. It'll get chilly. Do you have an abaya and hijab? We might need them for your sister. I only brought one set."

Michael worked the lock while Leila grabbed the garments from the wardrobe.

A moment later, the lock clicked.

He stood and looked her up and down. "Jacket? Shoes?"

"I have neither."

The faint light coming from the courtyard illuminated his face just enough to see the fierce expression. If she didn't know him, she'd fear him. But she didn't, not really, except... Where was the salesman? Who was this soldier?

He slid his backpack down and opened it, snatched the abaya and hijab she held out, and shoved them in before swinging it back on. Then he lowered his goggles and, from a holster beneath his T-shirt, grabbed a handgun. "You ready?"

Her heart stuttered in her chest.

He must've seen her fear because he said, "I don't want to shoot anybody, but I will if I have to."

"My father is here. Please, don't kill him."

"Your father?" Michael seemed to take in the information, file it away.

"We'll get Jasmine?"

"Where is she exactly?"

Leila pointed out the window to the building across the courtyard.

"Okay. Stay right behind me. If I tell you to do something, do it, no questions. Okay?"

He didn't know the house as well as she did. He didn't know the threats. But now didn't seem the time to argue. He'd gotten this far, after all. Maybe he could get them all the way out.

Surely, he and his team had come up with a plan.

"Leila?" His voice was barely audible, but she heard the urgency in it. "Do you trust me?"

She did. And even if she doubted, what choice did she have? "I'll do as you say."

He started to turn the knob, then turned back again. "You used to drive a moped, right?"

She had, in Baghdad when she was a teenager.

At her nod, he asked, "You ever drive a motorcycle?"

"Once." A friend in school had let her drive his, just for fun.

"You remember how?"

"I think so."

"Good." He opened the door and peeked out, then stepped into the dark hallway. She followed him toward the stairway that would take them to the ground floor and out...to freedom.

She prayed they wouldn't run into anyone along the way. Not guards, not Baba or Hasan. And definitely not Waleed.

CHAPTER SEVEN

MICHAEL DIDN'T UNDERSTAND.

As soon as he got Leila and her sister to safety, he'd ask all the questions ping-ponging in his brain.

Like how both Leila's father and sister were here, but only her sister needed rescuing.

The house was old, though by his guess, not the oldest structure on the property. The other buildings looked more dilapidated. He and Leila crept across the tile floor down the hallway and past closed doors, the only thing separating them from sleeping people—probably more guards. They reached a stairwell that was so narrow his shoulders barely fit.

His plan had been to exit the house on the outside of the walls and run.

He did not want to go back through the courtyard. He hadn't killed the guards he'd encountered, and they'd only sleep another few minutes. If this had been an official CIA operation, he'd have had access to all the tools he'd need. As it was, he'd gone old-school, buying a bottle of chloroform and drenching a rag.

The chemical didn't work as fast in real life as it did in the movies. He'd had to hold the cloth over the first guard's face for a couple of minutes before the man lost consciousness. Fortunately, Michael had done his homework, wearing gloves and a mask to keep himself from inhaling the chemical.

Once the guy had inhaled the first whiff, he'd been too weak to fight back. Michael had just needed to wait until he passed out, at which point, he'd dragged the guy into the garage, tied him up, and gagged him.

The guard in the courtyard took a little less time to lose consciousness—but more time to tie up and gag. Michael wanted him to look awake, which meant tying him in place on his chair. The ropes would be visible in the daylight, but as dark as it was, he felt confident nobody would see them.

He'd scaled the rough stone walls to the center window on the third floor.

This plan would have been perfect, if not for the sister.

He'd never met the woman, but he was already cursing her. No wonder she'd sounded off on the phone. No wonder her English hadn't been good.

He should have known it wasn't Leila. He'd been so grateful and relieved to hear from her that he hadn't asked enough questions.

Stupid. It was that kind of stupid mistake that proved he deserved his call sign. A mistake that could get one of the sisters killed.

It was entirely possible that it'd already gotten him killed.

One obstacle at a time.

At the bottom of the second flight of stairs, he crept through a dark room that he assumed backed to the courtyard, the opposite direction he'd planned to go. A living area, based on the sofas and chairs. He reached a door, hoping it led outside.

Leila gripped his arm, hard, and he turned, eyebrows lifted.

She tipped her head to another door.

Okay.

They moved that direction, and he leaned down to speak in her ear. "This opens into the courtyard?"

She nodded, the silky strands of her hair brushing against his cheek.

"Where is your sister from here?"

"This opens near the wall, so we'll be in shadows. We'll go straight across, then turn at the far edge and pass the first building. The second is the guest-house. Jasmine will be there."

He took a breath, then pulled Leila into his arms. She felt so good there, so perfect. He wanted to relish the moment, knowing it might be his last opportunity to hold her.

She held onto him as if she feared he'd walk away. Or disappear. Or maybe just to remind herself this was real, he was real.

He knew exactly how she felt.

Whatever risks he'd already faced, whatever threats remained, he'd do this again. He'd risk everything to keep Leila safe, no matter the cost.

They'd been growing closer since they started dating. They'd seen each other whenever he was in town. They'd talked on the phone every day, texted multiple times a day.

How had he not realized his feelings for her had expanded? How had he not realized before she disappeared how important she'd become to him?

Her body was too thin, her face, in the greenish glow of the NVGs, nearly gaunt. She didn't smell like perfume and flowers and shampoo like she had back in Germany. She needed a shower, and a good meal, and to be told how very loved she was. She needed to be cherished and pampered.

Protect Leila and her sister, Lord. Help me get them out of here.

He added a prayer for himself but wouldn't dwell on that.

Reluctantly, he let her go, turned the knob, and stepped into the courtyard. His gaze went straight to the guard.

He wasn't in the chair.

He was on the ground, wiggling. Trying to get free of his ropes. In the silence, Michael could hear the man's grunts around the gag.

Staying near the stone wall that lined this end of the compound, Michael led the way across the dirt-covered yard, considering his options.

He could run into the open, risk being seen, to knock the guard out again.

Or grab the sister and hope to get away before the man could raise an alarm.

Michael had dumped the chloroform rag, not wanting the poison anywhere near himself or Leila. To silence the guard now, he'd have to put him in a chokehold and render him unconscious. And he'd have to do it without the man making any noise. Which he could *probably* do.

But Michael would have to risk being seen—and having Leila seen—which would get them captured. Well, her captured. Him killed.

Which meant his only other option if he wanted to silence him—his only *real* option—was to slit the man's throat.

So, kill him, or hope for the best?

He chose the second option. *Let him not get free, Lord. Just a couple more minutes.*

They reached the first outbuilding and turned toward the second. At the door, he turned the knob, expecting it to be locked. It wasn't, but before he could push it open, it swung on its hinges.

A woman stood there.

She wore an abaya and hijab, which hid most of her face. All he saw were wide, frightened eyes. "We go?"

The fact that she was there and ready told him she'd seen him in the courtyard, confirming his decision not to expose himself again.

He whispered, "Shh," and started back the way they'd come. A strong grip on his arm stopped him.

He turned, and the sister—Jasmine, Leila had said—tipped her head into her house. He looked past her but saw nothing but darkness.

Michael glanced at Leila, but she seemed confident in her sister as she slipped past him and into the dark house.

If she had a way out that took them away from the courtyard, he was happy to take it.

The house was dark. His NVGs showed the walls of a long hallway that ended in a door.

Jasmine stopped a few feet in front of the door and stepped aside to give him access. "You pick." Her voice was so low, it took him a second to figure out what she'd said.

"This leads outside the walls?"

"Yes, yes. Hurry." Her gaze flicked to a doorway, telling him someone dangerous was behind that door. Who?

Doesn't matter.

Things had gone remarkably well so far. Another few seconds and they'd be free.

He gripped Jasmine's elbow, then pointed to Leila's bare feet.

She nodded and tiptoed away. Hopefully, she'd return with shoes.

Not enemies.

Michael holstered his gun, yanked his lock-picking kit from his pocket, and went to his knees in front of the door.

This lock wasn't the old-fashioned kind like on Leila's door. This was new, a deadbolt, and took longer to pick. He heard quiet scuffling behind him but didn't look at the sisters.

Within seconds, the lock disengaged with a telltale click. When he turned, Leila was shoving her feet into bright red Nikes. They looked so out of place that he nearly laughed.

Except nothing about this was funny.

When she was finished, she and her sister looked up at him, eyes wide. Leila's face was uncovered, but her sister had her abaya draped across her mouth and chin. He was struck by how similar they were. Same height—barely five feet tall. Thin as fence posts, both of them. Even the way they stood, leaning slightly forward as if ready to run. Holding hands.

Frustrated as he was with Jasmine for not telling him the truth, he could practically feel the love between the sisters.

Help me get them out of here, Father. Rescue them.

And then rescue me.

He turned the knob and pulled the door open.

A siren pierced the silence.

CHAPTER EIGHT

AT THE SHRILL SOUND, Leila's heart, already racing, nearly pounded out of her chest.

Before she could figure out what to do, Michael grabbed her hand and yanked her outside.

The three of them bolted away from the building. The soil was rough and rocky, and she thanked God for the sneakers Jasmine had given her.

Michael ran toward a couple of bushes about fifty yards away.

Above the siren, low-pitched shouts sounded from the compound.

The men were coming.

Where were Michael's people? Were there not soldiers? Special forces? At least his brother? Or a partner?

Were they truly alone?

Truly doomed?

They reached the bushes, and Michael yanked a sand-colored tarp back, revealing a motorcycle.

A motorcycle.

She should have put it together when he'd asked her earlier.

She should have realized...

He lifted it, settled it on its stand. "Get on."

"What? No. You drive. We'll—"

"You promised to do as I say." His words came fast, intent. He pulled her against his chest, pressed a rough kiss to her lips.

So brief, yet she felt in it a flood of emotions she could hardly endure.

"Michael, I won't leave—"

"I did not come this far to lose you now. Go. I'll hold them off."

"But you—"

"As long as you're safe, it doesn't matter."

The siren was silenced.

The guards' shouts carried in the desert night.

"Sister. Hurry!" Jasmine's voice was filled with terror. She'd already climbed onto the back seat of the motorcycle. "Please, we must. He'll kill me."

How could Leila leave Michael?

How could she not save her sister?

"You go!" She spat the words at Jasmine. "I'll stay—"

"I can't drive this. Please, sister. Please!"

"Go, or you'll get us all killed." Michael lifted Leila and settled her on the seat like he might a small child, then he leaned close. "Listen to me," he said. "Memorize this, both of you. Go to Baghdad. South of Victory Square, there's a hotel. Dijlat Al Khair. Across the street, there's a small store with a red awning. Go past the store on the north side to a green door. Inside, second floor, through the first door. Repeat it."

She did.

Behind her, Jasmine said, "We got it. We go."

Michael opened the storage compartment on the back of the bike. Leila didn't know what he was doing, couldn't see beyond her sister. "My friend is coming tomorrow to get us out. If he gets there before me, go with him. I'll find you. There's food and water in here. I'm leaving my cell phone so I can get in touch with you. Don't make any calls but leave it on. It's untraceable."

"Please." She heard the pleading in her voice. "You can fit. We can all—"

"You're too small to pass for a man in the daytime," Michael said. "But at night..." He shoved a baseball cap on her head. "Hide your hair."

Jasmine shoved Leila's hair into the back of her T-shirt. "I'll fix."

"Get to the safe house before daylight," Michael continued. "Maybe nobody will stop you. Go. Now." He reached across her and started the engine. It roared, the sound so loud it sent a fresh shot of panic through her.

The guards knew exactly where to look now.

A map lit up on the dash.

Michael leaned close and spoke over the noise. "The address is already plugged in. Follow the directions. Get there as fast as you can. I'll find you."

"But—"

He kissed her again, then kicked the stand back. "Go."

Before she could protest again, he bolted away, back toward the compound and the men with guns. Disappearing into the darkness.

Behind her, Jasmine yelled, "Hurry, hurry!"

A gunshot sounded over the too-loud engine.

Leila had no choice.

No choice.

She shifted gears, twisted the accelerator, and sped over the rocky ground toward the highway.

Leaving Michael behind.

CHAPTER NINE

MICHAEL HAD ENDURED six months at the CIA's training facility.

He'd considered himself at least a little prepared when he arrived at the Farm. After all, he'd known how to shoot a rifle and a handgun. He'd even been a pretty good shot, having hunted with his father and brothers his whole childhood.

But he hadn't known how to spot booby traps. He hadn't known about dismantling—or building—bombs. He hadn't known how to identify chemicals and known which were used to make weapons of mass destruction.

He hadn't spoken multiple languages.

He hadn't successfully recruited assets.

Fact was, he hadn't known anything, really, that he'd needed to know to become a spy.

He certainly hadn't known evasion techniques—how to escape on foot, in cars, on speedboats.

But he'd learned—and learned well.

Surely, with all that knowledge, he could figure out how to hide from a bunch of guards at a remote compound in Iraq.

Right?

Except he'd somehow missed the alarm on Jasmine's door. None of the other doors had shown signs of a security system. He'd checked, of course.

Yet that one door had been wired with a siren. Hidden wires, considering he hadn't seen them and Leila's sister hadn't known about them. The alarm was intended to keep people in as much as to keep them out.

To alert the guards that someone was trying to escape.

And alert the escapee that she'd never get away.

Jasmine's prison might've looked different from Leila's, but it had been a prison, just the same.

Michael had run from the motorcycle because he'd feared Leila wouldn't leave until she knew there was no other option.

After the women sped toward the highway, he crept back to the low, scrubby bushes and took cover beneath the tarp. He inched his way toward the river a good hundred yards in the distance. Slowly, slowly. So slowly that nobody would notice the lump of sand moving in the darkness.

Or so he prayed.

Shouts sounded from the compound. Michael imagined the men streaming out, guns drawn, searching the barren landscape.

The motorcycle engine had drawn them close. His only hope was to stay hidden until they gave up. He needed them to believe the sisters—and those who'd helped them—were long gone.

The roar of the motorcycle had faded a few moments earlier. There'd been no indication that the guards firing at them had hit their marks.

Please, let them be okay. Get them to Baghdad.

"The house is clear," someone shouted.

"Which sister?" Another voice rose above the rest. He was closer, somewhere between Michael and the walls surrounding the property.

"Yasamin!" This voice came from farther away and belonged to an older man, if Michael's guess was correct. "It was her alarm."

Yasamin. Jasmine, obviously.

But another voice said, "Nawra's gone too!"

Nawra. Not Leila. But of course she'd changed her name.

That information was greeted by silence—for a few beats—and then everybody was shouting.

Michael kept moving away from the noise, hoping he was going in the right direction but unable to make out landmarks through the thin tarp.

In the chaos, he couldn't decipher all the Arabic words, but one was clear.

Motorcycle.

Of course they'd seen how the sisters had escaped.

With the men distracted, Michael risked lifting the tarp the tiniest bit. Ahead, scrubby trees indicated water nearby. He moved a little faster, ignoring the jab of rocks and the hard desert floor.

Another shout from behind. "Why are you not following!" An older man, though not the same as the last who'd yelled. Definitely someone in charge.

The man who answered explained what Michael already knew.

The tires in every car in the garage had been slashed. Michael had done that before he'd found Leila. If he hadn't, he might've considered stealing one. The motorcycle had been a great escape—for two.

The good news was that the guards weren't going anywhere. Did they have people on the outside who'd do their dirty work? Was someone, even now, calling for help to search for two women on a motorcycle?

Leila and Jasmine needed to get to Baghdad as fast as

possible—and try to do so without being stopped. The roads would be quiet this late at night, and two women on a motorcycle would certainly capture attention.

Michael had had no choice but to send them away alone.

"Over here!"

The voice was too loud, too close. Michael stilled beneath his thin tarp.

"The motorcycle was here." This man sounded around Michael's age and rang with authority. His Arabic was smooth and cultured. "Who left it? When? How did you miss it?"

"I don't know how—"

"The tires didn't slash themselves. Where were you?"

"It wasn't my watch—"

"Incompetent. All of you." There was quiet, then the same cultured man called to someone farther away, "You said the women were confined. Someone freed them. I want Nawra back. Tonight. I don't care how you do it, but she will be ready tomorrow, as planned."

Nawra—Leila. Ready for what?

Michael didn't hear the man's voice again, though other men remained close

"Were there two bikes?" one asked. "Two men?"

"Only one drove away, with two people."

"Did he get to the river?"

"We would have seen."

"So he is here. Where are you, little snake?"

Michael shifted his head slowly and, through the thin tarp, saw the glow of flashlights sweeping the ground.

He risked a peek behind. Yup. Just twenty yards back, there were two more lights.

And they were closing in. The tarp should be hidden in darkness, but if they swung the beams his way...

He inched the handgun up, preparing and praying he

wouldn't have to use it. He'd managed not to kill anyone so far tonight, and he'd prefer to keep it that way.

These men had kidnapped and imprisoned the woman he loved. He could admit that, mostly, he didn't want to fire his weapon because doing so would bring the wrath of the whole compound down on him, and he'd have to kill a lot more people in order to survive.

He really wanted to survive.

His parents had just gotten their first son back. They didn't need to lose their second.

And if he didn't survive, Leila would blame herself. And maybe her sister.

He couldn't think about that. *Focus, Wright.*

You got this.

God did, anyway.

A flashlight beam lit the ground beside him. Where was the other man? Had he gone in a different direction?

Or was he still back there? Michael didn't dare move to check.

He watched the beam he could see, estimating where the guard was. If the light hit him, he'd need to act fast.

But the beam, and the man, moved ahead.

Michael exhaled his relief.

And then something bumped his foot.

Michael lifted a leg, pushed himself backward, and kicked.

"Ach, he's—"

Michael's foot connected with something, hard enough that it cut the man's words off.

He braced himself, swung one foot to the side, and brought the man down.

"Oof...Bachir!"

Footsteps, coming fast.

Michael flipped the tarp off, aimed toward the sound of the footsteps, and fired.

The man went down.

Michael swung the gun toward the first man.

Too late.

The guard had his gun up, aimed.

Michael rolled out of the way a second before the bullet flew.

He crouched to attack but his arm got tangled in the stupid tarp. He let the gun go to shake himself free, praying that wouldn't prove to be a fatal mistake.

He launched himself at his attacker and brought him down, knocking his weapon away. Michael kept their momentum going until he was on top, punching. Pummeling.

Taking punches.

His feet still tangled in the stupid tarp, making it impossible to grab the knife sheathed at his ankle.

A sharp jab to the abdomen, but he ignored it.

He was stronger. He could best this guy.

In time, though?

Michael aimed punches for the face, the nose, the eyes. *Disarm, disable. Run.*

Run.

The man's blows weakened.

Michael leaned a forearm against the guy's neck, cutting off his air. When the guy quit fighting, he pushed himself away, shook the tarp off his feet, and scrambled for a handgun. He couldn't see his attacker's. But his was in the tarp, somewhere. He searched. *Where is it?*

Where...?

There! He grabbed it, swiveled, and aimed at his attacker, just in case.

But the guy wasn't moving.

Michael sprinted for the river.

More guards were coming. Shouting. Shooting.

He kept low, trying to make himself a smaller target.

Bullets whizzed by.

He shifted directions, shifted again as the guards followed, firing.

It was dark. And he was fast. Maybe he could disappear in the night. His shoes ate up the rocky soil, then hit vegetation. Meaning the river was...

There.

Dark ground interrupted by a wide black swath.

He holstered his gun. And jumped.

And flashed back to his childhood, leaping from the end of the dock at their family's vacation home off the coast of Maine. His brothers' voices. Mom shouting for them to be careful. Dad egging them on.

The salty water shockingly cold.

But Michael didn't land in the frigid Atlantic.

He landed in warm bathwater. Filthy bathwater.

His feet hit the ground before he went under.

He ducked, dove, swam upstream—away from Baghdad, away from the closest town—keeping low enough that not even his pack would drag along the surface.

His pursuers would assume he'd go with the current.

Do the opposite of what they expect. Never be where you should be.

Always take them by surprise.

He'd almost done that tonight.

He should have shot the men holding the flashlights as soon as they got close. He'd hoped to get away without them confirming he was there.

He hadn't wanted to kill anybody.

Stupid.

Stupid move.

He swam and swam. Underwater. Only surfacing long enough to pull in a breath.

He'd always been a fast swimmer. All those years by the water—and competition with his brothers—had guaranteed that.

After a few minutes, when he surfaced, he didn't hear voices.

But he didn't stop, just kept on.

What was that animated movie?

Just keep swimming, just keep swimming.

And he did. For a long time.

Picturing the fish. He could hear the goofy voice in his head.

He shook off the strange thoughts. Where was his mind going? His strength?

Because suddenly, he couldn't continue. By his watch—a waterproof diving watch he'd had for years—he'd been at it for almost sixty minutes, but that was nothing. He should've been able to swim hours more.

He was weakening. Why?

He poked his head up, heard nothing. Behind him, only quiet meandering river.

Scanning the riverbanks, he searched for a place to shelter. He needed to tuck up until he felt safe enough to get out. In the cold rivers of Maine, there'd be rocky banks, tall trees with webs of roots, brush, branches.

Maine rivers were beautiful.

He could see vegetation, dark trunks and bright green leaves, the occasional white birch breaking up the forest. He could hear the water gurgling over rocks.

He blinked, and the image disappeared.

Focus, Wright. This isn't Maine.

What was wrong with him?

He spotted a place where the bank lifted a foot, maybe

sixteen inches, above the surface. It would do. He swam there, not rising again until he was close enough to blend into the dirty rise of land.

He leaned against it and gazed downstream, looking for any sign of his pursuers.

Far away, on the opposite side of the river, the compound's lights glowed, probably two miles distant. There was nobody between here and there.

A long look at the river proved that, unless someone was also swimming beneath the surface, nobody had followed him. At least not this far.

He kept his body in the warm water, head barely poking out, and watched.

His eyes were heavy. Too heavy. He needed to assess his injuries. As soon as he knew he was safe, he would.

At home, summer nights that at first seemed quiet proved to be the opposite. Crickets and frogs sang from dusk till dawn in the summertime.

But winter, with the critters quiet, snow muffling everything... The silence was soft and comforting, tinged with the scent of wood smoke, the promise of home.

This silence was different.

This wasn't the silence of rest. It felt more like the silence of death.

A quiet splash had Michael's eyes popping open. When had he closed them?

Was something there? Someone?

He blinked, stared at the dark, dark water, glowing green and black in his NVGs. And then saw...

A man's foot broke the surface of the water, just yards away.

Michael dove to the side, head ducking below the surface. His gun would work, even underwater. But a gunshot would reveal his location.

The guard grabbed his foot, yanked him back.

Michael kicked, connected with something hard. Managed to get free.

He yanked his knife from its sheath at his ankle.

His attacker had gone up for air.

Thank God for years competing with his brothers. And his training. He didn't need air yet.

He swam around to the guard's back. The guard's torso twisted this way and that. He didn't know where Michael was.

Michael waited until he was facing away.

He got right behind him.

Stood. Grabbed the guard's face, covered his mouth with his gloved hand. Yanked his head back.

And slit his throat.

CHAPTER TEN

"WHAT ARE YOU DOING? This isn't the way."

Leila ignored her sister's protests as she angled toward a tiny town on the bank of the Tigris.

Yes, Michael had told them to go straight to Baghdad, but he didn't know about Leila's friend.

Or about Jasmine's illness.

Her sister had thrown up twice in the forty minutes they'd traveled. Leila hadn't stopped, had only slowed down so her sister wouldn't fly off the bike as she leaned over, trying to keep her vomit off both of them.

Maybe the problem was the rocky terrain. Once they'd gotten far enough away from the compound that she could no longer see it in the rearview mirror, Leila had left the highway, traveling instead on an old dirt road, far from the river and houses. Anything to evade capture. Because in Iraq, two women, traveling alone at night...

If they were seen, they might be stopped. And if they were stopped, they would not be allowed to continue.

Between that and Jasmine's sickness, Leila didn't dare try to get all the way to Baghdad. She needed to get her someplace safe, now.

Once they got to Heba's house, they'd find another way into Baghdad, preferably not on a motorcycle. Heba and her husband would help. This was the safer play.

If Michael were here, he'd agree with her.

Michael.

Dear Jesus, let him be okay.

But how could he evade all those men? Even if he did, how would he escape? How would he get to Baghdad without a car? Miles between towns, the desert temperatures scorching in the daytime, even this late in the year.

He'd had nothing but weapons. No food and water, as far as she knew. And he'd left his cell phone with her.

That thought was a twist in her heart. He'd left his cell because he'd known they'd need it—and he hadn't believed he would survive long enough to use it again.

If he died, it would be her fault. She should never have had her sister call him.

And Jasmine should have told him who she was, that they both needed rescue.

A mile outside of town, Leila navigated behind an old, crumbling house that would hide the motorcycle from passersby and killed the engine. "We walk from here." She climbed off and helped her sister do the same.

"We should continue to Baghdad like your friend said." Jasmine's voice was weak. "There's a safe house."

"You need rest and water." Leila opened the storage compartment. It was nearly impossible to see in the darkness, but she felt fabric on top.

Her abaya and hijab, and below those, a second set, which Michael must've bought. Since her sister already wore hers, Leila slipped an abaya over her sweatpants and T-shirt, thankful for the warmth after the chilly ride, then covered her head with the hijab.

When she was suitably attired, she searched for Michael's cell phone, which she shoved in the pocket of her sweatpants, then found two bottles of water and handed her sister one. "Drink slowly."

Jasmine twisted off the cap and took a few small sips, and Leila did the same. When they'd both had enough, she returned the bottles to the storage compartment and closed the lid. "Let's go."

As they ambled toward the few houses clustered near the Tigris, Leila struggled to remember where exactly her friend lived. Heba had moved into her husband's house after they'd married when Leila was still in school. Her friend had dreamed of graduating and going on to university. She'd dreamed of becoming a doctor. But her father had decided she needed to marry.

Heba might've fought harder against her father's plans, but she liked the man he'd chosen. Mostafa was kind and gentle, and Heba, almost against her will, fell in love.

The whole thing had terrified Leila.

Her friend had given up her dreams, choosing to please her father rather than fight for what she wanted. While Leila had tried to support Heba's choices, she'd known she would never follow in her footsteps.

If she married, it would be to a man of her choice. A man who did not rule her.

She recognized Mostafa's home, the largest one in this tiny town.

They reached the front door, and Leila lifted her hand to knock.

Jasmine grabbed her arm and whispered, "I do not think this is a good idea. The compound we were in belonged to Heba's family. What if they are looking for us?"

Leila's gaze flicked behind them as if enemies lurked beyond the low wall that surrounded the yard. This property wasn't nearly as large as the one they'd just left, but it was newer. Tidier. There was glass in the windows, and a low hum told her an air conditioner ran somewhere. Shrubs grew near the front door and along the walls. The sweet scent of jasmine filled the air.

"Heba and Mostafa helped me escape. They are friends. We can trust them."

"Things have changed, sister." But Jasmine's words faded as she bent at the waist, her arm pressing against her stomach.

"You need to rest."

"I'll rest when we're out of this country." Her voice was strained. "We must go."

"Heba will help us." Leila pulled her arm out of her sister's grip and knocked.

The sound was startlingly loud in the silent night.

A moment later, a light flicked on through the windows.

And the door swung open.

A man looked down at them from his perch a step higher, eyes narrowed beneath bushy brows. His beard was thick and covered more than half his face. He looked fierce.

"Mostafa?"

He blinked, his gaze flicking from Leila to Jasmine and back. "Nawra?"

"Can we come in, please? Yasamin is ill."

He stepped aside, and Leila helped her sister into the small living area.

"I'm sorry to bother you," Leila said. "I know it's late."

"Please, sit." He indicated a sofa. "I will wake Heba."

After he went up a staircase, Leila took in the space, different in many ways from the last time she'd seen it. Toys filled a chest and overflowed onto the floor. A few framed photos showed smiling children, three of them, at various ages.

When Mostafa returned, his wife was behind him.

Heba's head was uncovered, though she'd thrown on an abaya—probably over pajamas. The loose fabric didn't hide her swelling belly. When she saw her visitors, she rushed across the tile, arms open. "Nawra!"

Leila stood to embrace her old friend. Yes, coming here had been the right decision.

After greeting Jasmine, Heba excused herself into the kitchen, and Leila and Mostafa exchanged small talk. Finally, Heba returned with tea and served it, along with cookies and figs, as if it made perfect sense to entertain at three o'clock in the morning.

There were some things about Middle Eastern culture that Leila missed, and the hospitality was one of them. She tried to imagine how a German neighbor might have greeted her in the middle of the night. Probably not with open arms. Probably not with refreshments and chit-chat.

It wasn't until after they'd finished their tea that Mostafa's mild expression shifted to concern. "What are you doing back in Iraq? Why are you here?"

His questions confirmed what she'd already guessed—that Mostafa had no idea what was going on at his family's home.

Leila related everything that had happened from the time she'd been snatched off the street in Munich to that night.

Heba looked horrified. Mostafa, angry.

"We need to get to Baghdad," Leila said, "but it is not safe for us to travel by motorcycle. And Yasamin is sick."

They all looked at Jasmine, who didn't waste their time arguing the point. Her skin was pale as beach sand, her cheeks gaunt, her eyes sunken, the skin around them dark.

"Is it a flu? A virus?" Mostafa asked.

"It is nothing," Jasmine said.

He studied her a long moment, then shifted his gaze back to Leila. Though she was only a few minutes older than her twin, she'd always been the one in charge.

"You will stay here tonight," he said. "Tomorrow, we will see about getting you to Baghdad."

"Thank you." Leila exhaled anxiety with the words. She'd been sure—nearly sure—her old friends would help her again. But, as Jasmine had said, things had changed since the last time she'd seen them. A decade had passed, after all. Heba and Mostafa had a houseful of children now. They didn't need trouble.

But they would help.

The couple moved their children out of a bedroom to make room for Leila and Jasmine, who crawled beneath the sheets in a twin bed in the air-conditioned space.

Leila let herself relax for the first time in hours.

She needed to sleep. Tomorrow, they would get to Baghdad. Hopefully, Michael would be there, waiting for them.

She closed her eyes, prayed for his safety, and tried to sleep.

CHAPTER ELEVEN

MICHAEL HADN'T BEEN THINKING.

After he'd slit the man's throat, he should have dragged his body out of the river. He should have found a place to hide it.

He absolutely should not have let the body float downstream.

But his brain was slow, his thoughts fuzzy. He stared at the black, gritty water as it streamed past him on its journey to the Persian Gulf, and he considered swimming after it.

But the body was gone.

What would happen when it was spotted?

Leila's captors would know which direction Michael had gone. And they'd search for him.

A problem he'd deal with.

Soon.

He was back against the riverbank, catching his breath. Watching.

Waiting for someone else to pop up. To attack. Or shoot.

He couldn't be stupid again. He wouldn't survive another mistake.

He stared for five minutes. Ten.

Thirty.

When he was sure nobody else was coming, he climbed out of the river and collapsed. Vegetation covered the ground, something softer than dirt.

After allowing himself a few minutes of rest, he sat up, swung the waterproof pack off his back, and dug inside. Everything was dry despite the time it'd been submerged. He found his first-aid kit.

What hurts?

Everything.

No, not everything. *Think, Wright. Don't be Wrong tonight.*

He was sore and bruised. Internal injury? Was that why he was losing energy and focus? Was he slowly bleeding to death?

He was tired, but he didn't feel ill, and wouldn't he, if that was the problem?

What else?

His side ached. Throbbed, now that he thought about it.

He lifted his black T-shirt to look, then bit back a curse word.

Though everything was shades of green and gray in the NVGs, he saw a wound and a dark line streaming from it. A touch confirmed it. He yanked his hand away from the blood.

He thought back to the fight in the water. But no, this injury must've happened before that, outside the compound walls. He remembered now, the pain.

He'd been stabbed.

All this time, he'd been bleeding.

No wonder he couldn't think straight.

Great.

He'd been stabbed, and then he'd gone for a swim in a cesspool.

If the loss of blood didn't kill him, the infection would.

Assuming the enemy didn't find him first.

He lay back, inhaled and exhaled, exhausted. He'd just close his eyes for a second and...

Nope.

He sat back up, paused through the pain and a wave of dizziness. He yanked off the NVGs and dug into his bag for his penlight. Then he unzipped the first-aid kit and dug inside until he found what he was looking for.

A bottle of alcohol.

This was going to hurt.

He got the rest of his supplies ready, taking them out but laying them inside the bag so they didn't get dirty. He lay on his side, opened the antiseptic, took a deep breath, and poured the liquid into the wound.

At the sting—a thousand times worse than the stabbing itself —he managed to bite back a scream, barely.

After setting the bottle down, he pressed gauze treated with a clotting powder over the wound and wrapped an ace bandage around his torso to keep the gauze in place.

Assuming the knife hadn't hit any vital organs—and wouldn't he feel weaker if it had?—that should stop the bleeding.

He leaned back against one hand, afraid to lie down. Afraid he'd fall asleep. Be discovered by bad guys. Or...anyone, really.

After a few moments of rest, he stood, shoved the NVGs back on, hoisted his pack, and started moving.

He'd studied the map enough to know that, if he continued north along the river, he'd eventually run into a town. The main road was just to the west, but he'd steer clear of that.

He needed transportation. He needed to get to Baghdad, to make sure Leila and her sister made it safely.

Mostly, he needed to survive the night.

CHAPTER TWELVE

LEILA DESPERATELY WANTED TO REST. But just a few minutes after they settled beneath the sheets on the narrow bed, Jasmine grabbed a trash can and vomited.

"Sister, what can I do?"

"Don't worry." Jasmine's words were weak and still somehow harsh, so unlike the pliable, docile twin Leila had left behind a decade before. "It is nothing."

It wasn't nothing, and Leila was definitely worried. And the more Jasmine argued the point, the more suspicious Leila became.

Was it cancer? Mama's had been in the stomach. Did Jasmine have the same thing?

Was her sister dying?

Leila wanted to demand answers, but all she could do right now was try to make Jasmine comfortable and get them to Baghdad. And then out of the country.

To where, though?

Her escape to Europe the first time had been terrifying—being smuggled into Turkey, traversing the country while staying out of the clutches of the authorities, trying to remain hidden as her group made their way over mountains and along narrow country roads in Eastern Europe until they finally reached Germany. And then there'd been the months she'd spent in a refugee camp in Berlin.

Jasmine was already so weak. By bringing her sister along, had Leila endangered her life? If she'd left her with Baba, she might not be happy, but at least she'd be alive.

Please, Lord. Please save my sister's life. Please, let it not be cancer.

But it was definitely something.

"What can I do?" she asked in the darkness.

The question was met with silence. Had Jasmine fallen asleep?

"I think bread or crackers would help."

Maybe she should have eaten the cookies Heba had provided. But would sugar make it worse?

"Be right back." Leila opened the door into the hallway. Light rose from the first floor, and she headed that direction and down the stairs. Heba wouldn't mind if she helped herself to something that would calm her sister's stomach.

As Leila neared the door that led to the kitchen, she heard voices, low and vehement. Mostafa and Heba were arguing.

Should she interrupt? Wait until they were finished and then...what? Be caught lurking and listening?

No. She'd come back down after they returned to bed. She started for the staircase.

"...now that Nawra's here..."

She stopped at the sound of her former name.

Mostafa continued. "We cannot risk it again."

Leila crept forward to better hear.

Heba said, "But I can't—"

"It is not your job. Their father will protect them."

"Can he? He's not the one they should fear."

"*They* should fear?" Mostafa's voice pitched lower, angry. "I worry about *us*. I risked everything to save her—for you, because she was your friend. But now we have three children..." His words became tender. "Almost four."

Leila imagined Mostafa touching his wife's swelling belly. Yes, they had a family to protect. But what were they afraid of? Surely, Baba wouldn't blame them for her escape, and even if he did...

"They are more powerful than ever," Mostafa said. "I will not risk this family for her. Not again."

Leila waited for Heba to argue, to take up her cause. The longer the silence stretched, the more her hope slid away.

"In the morning," Heba said. "Let them rest tonight."

Betrayal hit like a blow to the chest.

But Heba had to obey her husband. And protect her children.

It wasn't fair for Leila to expect anything else.

She hurried back to the bedroom. "We must go."

Her sister sat up. Leila expected to see shock, but her sister's expression was resigned as she bent to put on her shoes.

Leila did the same, trying to figure out how to get out of the house without alerting Heba and Mostafa. Would he stand guard all night?

Would Heba alert her husband if she caught them escaping?

With their things gathered, Leila went to the window and raised the pane.

The roof of the attached garage was only a few feet down.

Jasmine bumped her shoulder and whispered, "What are you waiting for? Go."

Leila crawled out and lowered herself gingerly onto the tiles, praying the sound wouldn't carry.

She turned to help Jasmine, but her sister was already climbing out beside her. "Which way?"

Leila led the way toward the front of the property, not wanting to be caught within the walls that enclosed the side and back. It was maybe a ten-foot drop to the gravel driveway.

Was there another way? A ladder would be nice. Even a trellis. But no.

She lowered her body over and dangled by her fingertips from the slick clay tiles. *Please, don't let either of us get injured.*

This escape was going to be hard enough without a sprained ankle.

She dropped to the hard ground, fell back, and landed on her butt.

She stood, and when Jasmine dropped beside her, she grasped her sister and kept her from falling.

They ran back to the motorcycle.

Jasmine had been right. They'd wasted hours and hours.

Leila should have listened to her sister. She should have listened to Michael.

She'd told Mostafa their plans to go to Baghdad. At least she hadn't told him where the safe house was. Even so, if Baba and his guards hadn't guessed already, when Mostafa called them, they would know where to look.

Assuming Leila and Jasmine managed to get all the way to the city. Which, considering the glow on the eastern horizon, wasn't going to happen tonight.

Leila and Jasmine needed to hide. They'd been traveling toward Baghdad since they'd reached the motorcycle thirty minutes before, but the sun was nearly up. Who knew how many men Baba had looking for them? He'd once held a position of power in Baghdad and had friends all over the country.

But Baba wasn't the one Mostafa feared.

Who, then? Qasim, who'd snatched Leila in Munich?

More likely, Hasan was pulling the strings.

Was he telling Baba what to do now?

Had he become so dangerous that Mostafa would rather betray a friend than risk his wrath—and Heba wouldn't disagree?

Leila didn't know anything for sure, only that they wouldn't be safe until they were out of this wretched country.

After that terrifying moment in Germany, the hands that gripped her, the hood over her head, would she ever feel safe again?

At least Jasmine had stopped throwing up. Her arms around Leila's waist were strong, proving she was awake and alert on the back of the motorcycle, probably scanning the surroundings like Leila was.

The highway was deserted in this stretch between villages, but that wouldn't last, especially as they neared the city. Leila had stayed on the paved road, choosing speed over stealth, but now they needed to find a place to hide.

A tap on her shoulder had her easing off the gas.

"There." Jasmine pointed to the right, away from the river and onto a small rise. At the top, a few trees rose. In this barren land, trees usually meant water...or people. There'd be no water that high up, but trees would provide cover and shade.

Leila spied a narrow road and turned onto it. She drove up the slight incline, eyes open for threats and ready to speed away if any appeared.

At the top of the hill, dilapidated structures lined the road. There were no families, no cars, no pets. When Leila cut the engine, she heard nothing but silence.

A gecko darted out of their path, the only sign of life.

Could it still be called a village if the people had abandoned it?

Who had lived here? Where had they gone?

One of the buildings was crumbling, clearly the target of a bombing. In the early morning light, shadows highlighted pock-marks on the exterior cement walls. There'd been a battle here. Very little had escaped the war. Villages. Families. People. All were affected.

Had this been an enemy stronghold? An Al-Qaeda base?

For whatever reason, the people who'd lived in this village had migrated elsewhere—or had all been killed.

They climbed off the motorcycle.

"I think it's safe," Jasmine said.

"Hmm." Leila hoped so as she pushed the motorcycle between two buildings and lowered the kickstand.

Back on the street, nobody peeked to see who'd so noisily arrived. No generators hummed. No dogs barked.

"Sister."

Jasmine stared at one of the small houses. Stone, flat roof, probably only one or two rooms. No glass in the windows, no life at all.

Before Leila could stop her, Jasmine started that direction.

"What are you doing?"

"They are gone," she said. "We need to rest." She reached the doorway and knocked.

The sound seemed thunderous in the creepy silence.

When nobody answered, Jasmine pushed the door open and stepped inside.

Leila followed her into a tiny room with stone floors and stone walls. Everything was covered in dust.

Jasmine crossed to a sofa, sat, and then reclined.

Leila resisted the urge—barely—to snap at her twin to get up, get out of this strange, malevolent place. But where could they go that would be safer than this? An abandoned house, a shady spot, and a sofa?

"I'll hide the motorcycle." Outside, she pushed the bike around to the back of the house where, if Baba or his men—or anyone, really—happened to come this way, Leila and Jasmine would have a chance to escape. Of course, then the desert would claim their lives.

She wouldn't think about that.

She grabbed water, packets of food, and protein bars from the storage compartment, then returned to the house.

Jasmine was already snoring.

"Wake up, sister. First, we eat, then we rest."

Jasmine groaned but reluctantly pushed herself up, and together they shared the food.

What came in the packages—marked on the outside with "MRE. Meals Ready to Eat"—was not good, but it would keep them alive. Jasmine took a few bites before setting the food aside and choosing a protein bar instead.

"Tell me about Michael."

Leila couldn't help but smile. "We've been dating. He lives in the States. Maryland, which is near Washington, DC, but he comes to Munich often for work, a couple of times a month or more. He takes me to dinner and shows and concerts."

The last time she'd seen Michael, a few days before her abduction, she'd had the day off work, and he'd had a day between meetings. He'd rented a car, picked her up early, and driven them to Kitzbühel, Austria, two hours south of Munich. On the way, they'd stopped at a little village for coffee and croissants, then continued to the tourist town, where Michael had planned a day of hiking and sightseeing.

They'd trekked up a mountain, the trail steep but the views amazing. At a little after noon, he'd stopped at the most perfect vista. Rolling hills covered in wildflowers in the foreground, the snow-topped Alps glistening in the distance. He'd pulled a blanket from his backpack, flattened it over a grassy spot, and directed her to sit. Together, they'd eaten lunch and sipped glasses of wine.

He'd told stories about the farmhouse where he grew up. The family camp on an island off the coast. His five brothers. His stories were sometimes sad, sometimes moving, often funny.

Leila had loved every moment—except the guilt of not sharing her own life the way he did his. But she didn't talk about her past. Ever. To anyone.

Maybe, she'd thought. *Maybe, someday, I'll tell him everything.*

The picnic ended with a kiss, which turned into many kisses. For a moment, she wondered if he'd chosen the spot not only because of the view but because it was so private. Maybe he planned for more than a kiss.

She hoped not because that would have ended horribly what had begun so sweetly.

But he'd pushed away and laughed and apologized like the gentleman he was. Then he'd taken her hand, helped her up, and packed the blanket.

Before they started back down the mountain, he took her hands. Lowered his forehead to hers.

"I don't know what we're doing, Leila. I know that I like it. That...it's important for me."

Her heart had nearly burst within her.

She cared for this tall, handsome, strong American. This man who didn't know the truth about her.

In that moment, she'd felt secure.

They'd held hands on the ride back to Munich, quiet but content in each other's company. At least that was how she'd felt. But as they neared her home, he'd broken the silence.

"There are things I need to tell you. Things I should have—"

Her ringing cell interrupted him. Her boss told her there was an emergency at the hotel. She'd spent the rest of the drive on the phone, trying to find a plumber to come out on a weekend to deal with a broken pipe.

Michael hadn't had the chance to finish what he was going to tell her.

And then she'd been kidnapped.

She didn't share any of that with Jasmine, who used to be her closest confidant but now seemed...different. Distant. Leila settled for, "He is...very sweet."

Jasmine lowered the protein bar to her lap, her head tilting to the side. "He did not look sweet. He looked fierce."

Leila thought back to the man who'd rescued them. He had looked fierce wearing the camouflage and the helmet, holding the gun in his hand. Fierce and terrifying.

So different from the gentle man she'd known.

"He's a soldier?" Jasmine asked.

"A salesman."

"But he used to be a soldier." She said the words with confidence.

And Leila understood why her sister assumed. Michael had been experienced and competent when he'd broken them out of the compound. And yet...

"He told me he was never in the military."

Jasmine's eyes narrowed. "You have known him months, you say?"

"I've known him more than a year. We've been dating since January."

"Dating for ten months, and yet you don't know this truth about him?" When Leila couldn't refute that, Jasmine said, "He lied to you. Why?"

"He rescued us. He might have *died* for us." The words were bitter in her mouth. *Please, God.* "We owe him every-thing," Leila snapped.

Jasmine nodded, nibbling on her breakfast. But suspicion

settled in her eyes. "Perhaps. But he did not tell you the truth. Why? And if it's something he feels he can't tell you, then...then can we trust him?"

"Of course we can." Couldn't they?

Leila trusted Michael with her life. Even if she hadn't trusted him with her own secrets.

Jasmine didn't argue. After she finished her protein bar, she lay on the sofa to rest.

When the sun went down, they would continue their trek to Baghdad and find the safe house. Would Michael's friend still be able to get them out of the country?

Was Michael still alive?

A new worry niggled at Leila as she reclined on a chair near her sister.

Had Michael lied to her?

And if so, why? And, even though he had risked his life to rescue her, could she trust him?

There were no answers. Maybe there never would be. All she could do was keep going and pray that God would protect them and keep Baba and his men from catching up with them.

CHAPTER THIRTEEN

MICHAEL WOKE TO A STRANGE SENSATION. A *slithering* sensation.

Only good training kept him from jerking his foot.

He opened his eyes to a brightening world and spied what he'd already feared.

A snake slid over his outstretched legs. Sand-colored. Strange black markings on its back. Horns.

Horns?

Yup.

The flat, triangular head suggested it was a viper.

Poisonous.

As if the desert heat, the lack of potable water, and the armed men out to get him weren't enough...

Snakes.

He didn't move.

Just watched the slithering thing. It wasn't long—maybe eighteen inches—but that was full-grown for many species of viper.

After tending his wound by the river the night before, Michael had spied an outcropping of rock in the distance. It hadn't looked that far away—maybe a mile to a mile and a half. But traversing the distance in the dark with a stab wound had taken all his energy. When he'd reached it, he'd made his way over the rocks into the shallow cave. He'd slid down, propped his pack against the stone wall, and passed out.

Now, the sun was rising. And Michael was dripping with sweat. Which, considering the cool desert nights, didn't make sense.

Did he have a fever?

He didn't feel sick.

He twisted his wrist to check the time. After seven. He'd slept like the dead for hours.

The snake made it to the other side of Michael's body, continued toward the back of the cave—which, in the daylight, was no more than an outcropping of rocks—and disappeared into a crack.

Only when it was out of sight did Michael shift.

The movement was instantly arrested by a sharp pain in his side.

He lifted his shirt and spied the blood-soaked ace bandage. He unwrapped it, lifted away the gauze, and confirmed what he'd already guessed.

The stupid wound was still bleeding. So either the clotting stuff hadn't worked—and it was standard-issue for a reason—or the wound was deeper than Michael had realized.

On the upside, if that knife had hit a major artery, Michael would already be dead. So, something to be thankful for.

He shifted to access his pack, found his first-aid kit, and pulled out the supplies.

Two Tylenol for the pain, washed down by water he tipped from a fresh bottle.

And then superglue.

He worked to keep his hands from shaking as he pinched his

wound closed with the fingers of his left hand and squeezed the superglue onto it with his right.

All the while keeping one eye on the crack in the rock, praying the viper wouldn't reappear. He and the snake were going to have to cohabitate until sunset. God willing, Michael would be strong enough to move by then.

He worked slowly along the two-inch gash, pleased to see the glue holding his skin in place.

See, Dad. I could've been a doctor too.

Except Michael doubted his father or his doctor-brother ever got nauseated at the simple act of gluing a wound. Task completed, he added antibacterial ointment and fresh gauze and wrapped the bandage around his torso again.

When he was done, he settled against the wall, breathing heavily as if he'd just climbed a high summit. Hopefully, he'd gotten the worst part of the day over before breakfast. But he wouldn't count on it.

After scarfing down an MRE and the rest of the water, he stood, stretched—careful of his wound—and looked out of the cave.

Nothing in any direction except sand and, to the east, the river snaking toward Baghdad and the gulf.

"Looks like it's just you and me, Vipe."

Fortunately, the snake didn't answer.

And then...uh-oh.

The river was in front of him, and the sun was behind him.

He thought back to the night before. He'd climbed out of the Tigris on the west bank, right?

Come to think of it, it wasn't getting lighter outside. It was getting darker.

It wasn't seven o'clock in the morning.

Michael had slept all day.

At least that explained why he was so hot.

Obviously, he'd lost more blood than he'd realized. Been more injured than he'd realized. He was lucky he hadn't bled to death. Or been found by a hostile.

God had protected him.

Had He protected Leila and her sister too?

The thought of the two women, alone, running for their lives in the Iraqi desert, sent fear to his churning stomach. But if they hadn't been stopped along the way, they'd reached the safe house before dawn. Michael's old friend would have already collected them. He'd only have brought papers for one, but surely Splat would figure a way to get the sister out of the country.

Much as Michael might not like being dubbed *Wrong* by his buddies, he'd take that over *Splat* any day. Talk was that Splat had taken quite a fall on his first mission, earning him the unfortunate call sign.

Leave it to the SEALs to find the most embarrassing thing a guy ever did and never let him forget it.

If Splat could get the women into Turkey, Michael could catch up with them there. He'd arranged transport for two across the border.

He'd figure out how to add Jasmine to his plans.

One problem at a time.

He prayed for the sisters' safety, then thanked God he'd escaped and survived the night.

A miracle, to be sure.

Much as Michael would like to rest—and probably needed to rest—as soon as the sun set, he hoisted his pack and started moving.

He had to find a way to Baghdad as soon as possible.

~

Michael trekked for an hour before he reached a small town on the bank of the Tigris, where he stayed out of sight and searched for a suitable vehicle.

He hated to steal—especially from such poor people. He chose the only car he could find that was old enough to be easily hot-wired. Fortunately, it was parked on the street, not in a driveway. As he shoved his knife into the ignition and twisted, he prayed the car would be located and returned to its owner after he was finished with it.

He started the aged Volkswagen, cringing as the engine sputtered to life. Nobody came running. No lights came on in the nearby houses.

Breathing a prayer of thanks, he hoisted his pack onto the passenger seat and headed south.

It was after eleven when he abandoned the Volkswagen a mile from the safe house and hoofed it through Baghdad, thankful for the darkness that covered him. Despite the hour, the city was hopping. Music drifted from nightclubs, voices and laughter from restaurants.

He hurried past hotels and gathering places, praying he'd either find Leila and Jasmine asleep in the safe house or find that they'd been there and gone. Maybe Splat had already smuggled them out of the country.

After he climbed the steps of the newish building where he'd secured a fully furnished apartment, he pushed open the door and discovered...

Nothing.

Leila and Jasmine weren't in the kitchen or the living area. He peeked into the bedroom and attached bath. Also empty.

None of the food he'd left in the small refrigerator had been touched, none of the bottles of water emptied. The toothbrush and toiletries and clothing he'd bought remained unopened. The beds un-rumpled.

He stifled a curse word.

Where were they?

In the city? Or still in the desert?

Were they even alive?

Refusing to consider the alternative, he cranked the air conditioner and removed his laptop from where he'd hidden it beneath the cookie sheets in one of the kitchen cabinets. He powered it up and searched for the location of the cell phone he'd left with them.

He got a location—but it was from outside of Tikrit, the city where he'd launched his rescue plan, two days before.

Fine, then.

That didn't mean anything. It didn't mean they were dead. It didn't mean they'd been recaptured. It just meant they hadn't gotten close enough to a cell tower to connect to service.

His gaze flicked to the windows. He knew what lay beyond the buildings.

Desert. And darkness. Miles and miles and miles of darkness.

Where are they, Lord?

He stared at the screen, willing their location to flash.

No deal.

He showered in the bathroom off the living area, leaving the en suite bathroom for the sisters, then checked his wound. No longer bleeding, and he saw no redness or puffiness, so not infected. He changed into clean clothes and holstered his Glock beneath his black T-shirt.

He powered up one of the burner phones he'd brought with him, connected it to the one he'd given the girls, and brought up the tracking app.

Still no sign of the women.

He donned a head scarf—a keffiyeh. That, along with his beard in need of a trim, would help him blend in.

He couldn't sit here and wait. He'd look for them. Maybe the phone had been damaged. Or run out of juice. Maybe they were wandering around, trying to remember the instructions he'd given on where the apartment was.

Besides, he'd only bought enough supplies for one woman. He needed another toothbrush, if nothing else.

Because, yeah. Right now, that was what he was worried about. Toothbrushes.

Before he left the apartment, he found paper and pen and wrote a note.

Do not leave. I'll be back. M

He left it on the counter, upside down, pen angled across it just so. He needed to know if anybody came in while he was gone and assumed the women—and intruders—would read the note.

Outside, he headed toward the river and the hotels and nightclubs that lined it, following the hum of music and the glow of lights. There'd be a store open, somewhere.

He'd look for them. Maybe he'd just happen upon them.

Right. There were more than seven million people in Baghdad. It would take a miracle for him to find them.

He prayed for that miracle.

He'd sent them off, on a motorcycle, on their own, in the middle of a hostile nation. If anything happened to them...

It would be his fault.

He walked, shoulders back, head up, as if he belonged. Nobody paid him any attention as he kept his eyes open for two tiny women in Arab garb. Or a motorcycle.

Cars whizzed past on the busy street as if it were noon, not midnight.

He found a dingy little shop where he purchased a toothbrush. As soon as he'd arrived in Iraq, he'd bought toothpaste, deodorant, a container of lotion because...didn't women like lotions? Along with all the other stuff he'd thought of.

Trying to be thoughtful, anticipating Leila's needs.

He shoved the toothbrush into his jeans pocket and wandered the street, checking his phone often for the sisters' location.

An hour passed with no sign of them.

And then, just like that, their location showed up—only a few blocks away, coming toward him.

Thank You, God!

He'd been wandering near the safe house. Now, he urged his feet to hurry back to the main drag.

As he turned the corner onto the sidewalk, a group of young people exited a nightclub just ahead of him. They were loud, laughing, chatting. Drunk, Michael guessed when one of the women stumbled on heels even sober women shouldn't wear. She was kept from falling by the man nearest her, who took the opportunity to pull her against his side.

The group quieted as they approached a crowd gathered ahead, the guys lifting on tiptoes to see what was going on.

Other voices filled the void, shouts in Arabic—two men, maybe more. Arguing.

Michael scanned the faces of those who'd stopped to witness the fight. Even with his height, he only glimpsed the tops of heads but nothing else.

He glanced at his phone. Leila and Jasmine were close. He dialed the number.

No answer.

Traffic on the sidewalk had ground to a halt in both directions, and people were bunching up.

But cars zoomed past on the road.

The shouts got louder, followed by the thwack of a fist hitting a target.

The young people in front of him backed up, one bumping into him.

Up ahead, someone screamed.

The woman who'd stumbled earlier dashed into the street to avoid the mass of bodies.

A horn blared.

Michael snatched her back an instant before a van whipped by.

She was babbling to him, her breath heavy with the scent of liquor, and he didn't even try to decipher her slurred Arabic.

He caught sight of something on the other side of the scrum.

Red sneakers poking out beneath a black abaya. The short, slender woman wore a brown hijab.

Leila.

But a second after he'd spotted her, the crowd swallowed her up.

Michael passed off the drunk girl to one of her friends, all the while searching for that brown hijab.

He checked the traffic and dashed onto the street, skirting the edge of the crowd.

Where were they?

He was nearly to the far side of the fight. He searched faces, clothes...

There.

Leila and her sister were trying to elbow their way past the gathered lookie-loos to get away from the fight.

On the steps of the building nearest them, a man watched their retreat.

He didn't look familiar, but that didn't matter. Michael hadn't seen most of the guards' faces. He rested his hand on his weapon. He didn't want to shoot anybody, but if that guy went after Leila...

The man on the stairs descended.

Michael pushed his way through the crowd until he was right behind him.

Followed until there was no question the guy was following Leila and Jasmine.

Michael shifted forward, walking right beside the guy.

Without looking, he elbowed him in the stomach. When the man bent forward, Michael jabbed his elbow into his face.

The guy went down.

Michael leaned over him and spoke in Arabic. "Hey, you okay, man? What happened?" Before the guy could catch his breath, Michael shielded his movements with his body and whacked the enemy on the side of the head with his gun.

And then he stood and jogged away, gun tucked beneath his shirt.

A glance behind showed none of the onlookers had noticed the wounded guard yet. Nobody else was following—that he could see, anyway.

He came up behind Leila and Jasmine. Passed Leila on her right, brushing his hand against hers, feeling the comforting warmth.

"Don't react. Follow me."

No need for a reunion scene. No need to draw attention.

Leila's quiet gasp was her only response.

Michael walked ahead, moving quickly but not so fast that they couldn't keep up.

Past the next hotel, he ducked into an alley.

Leila and Jasmine followed.

"Come on." Gun at the ready, he moved through the narrow space, wishing for his NVGs. It was too dark, but there was light at the other end.

They reached the quieter street. Nobody followed.

As far as he knew.

He took Leila's hand and ran.

"Wait," Leila said. "Jasmine."

Turning, he saw that Jasmine had fallen behind. He slowed, biting back the *hurry up* that wanted to escape.

He contemplated picking up the weaker sister and carrying her.

Not exactly the best way *not* to draw attention to themselves.

But he had no doubt the man he'd left unconscious had woken up—and called his buddies.

He had to assume there were enemies everywhere.

Finally, they reached the apartment building. Michael stopped at the corner just inside the mouth of the alley and nodded to the green door behind him. "Go. I'll be right there."

The women passed and went inside.

He waited until the door closed. Waited another minute. Two. Three. Five.

Just in case.

Ten minutes later, certain he'd lost anyone who might have tried to follow, he went inside. Up the stairs, through the door.

In the dim room, Leila stood a few feet beyond the threshold, facing him as if she'd been waiting.

She was alive and well and, as far as he could tell, no worse for the trouble she'd gone through to get there.

He shut the door, closed the space between them, and wrapped her in an embrace. "Thank God. Thank God."

At first, she seemed reluctant, almost stiff. And then she melted in his arms.

And wept against his chest.

CHAPTER FOURTEEN

LEILA HADN'T REALIZED how afraid she'd been until that moment.

She'd feared that she would be captured and returned to the compound.

Feared that Michael hadn't escaped the guards. That his body would lie in the desert forever. That his family would never know what had happened to him.

Those fears bubbled up as she gripped his soft T-shirt, afraid that if she let go, it wouldn't be real. He wouldn't be there, and they wouldn't be safe.

"Sweetheart." His voice was low, a rumble against her ear. "You're okay. You're safe now."

But they weren't safe, were they? It was more like they were in the eye of a storm. Trouble behind, certainly. But more ahead. There was no end to the trouble.

Which only made her cry harder.

"Hey, hey." He gripped her shoulders as if to ease her back, but she tightened her grip on his shirt, not ready to be out of his embrace.

"All right, sweetie." He leaned down, swept her feet out from under her, and lifted her into his arms.

His strength took her breath away. How could he be so strong when she felt so weak?

He carried her into the living area and sat on the sofa, draping her legs over his lap. When she was settled against him, she nestled in as if he could protect her. As if, right there, nothing could harm her.

But she saw pain in his expression. "Are you hurt?"

"I'm fine. Are you?"

She wasn't sure she believed him, but she didn't have it in her to demand the truth. She sniffled, tried to speak, and settled for a shake of her head.

"Is your sister?" He looked over her head, searching the room she'd barely looked at, only watching, hoping he'd come.

She'd been terrified that, seconds after finding him, she'd lose him again.

Concern crinkled the skin around his eyes. "What is it?"

"Jasmine's in the bathroom." Her sister had hurried to the small en suite the minute they'd arrived. She hadn't been back out of the bedroom since. "We're both okay."

"Thank God." He pulled her against his chest again. "When I got here and you weren't here, I feared the worst. What happened?"

"Jasmine was sick after we left the compound. Vomiting. So I went to the home of an old friend and—"

"You what!" He leaned as far away from her as he could get without knocking her off his lap. Again, she saw the hint of pain in his expression. "I told you to come straight to Baghdad."

"I know, but she—"

"There's no 'but,' Leila. You should have done what I said."

At the anger in his voice, she swung her legs to the floor and paced to the other side of the small room.

When men were angry, distance was always a good idea.

"I do not answer to you, Michael Davis."

He flinched, but the expression was gone so fast she wasn't sure she'd seen it.

He pushed to his feet. "I risked everything to... I saved your life. I got you out of there and nearly got myself killed in the process. But *you don't answer to me?* Seriously?"

"I don't answer to anyone." Her voice sounded strong, determined, even as she pressed back against the wall, looking for something to use to defend herself.

Mama had never fought back, but Leila would. She wouldn't allow any man to harm her.

A lamp. She inched toward it, planning to grab it. Just in case.

"Knock it off." His voice was too loud. He took a breath, blew it out. Spoke more quietly when he added, "I'm not going to hurt you. I would never do that. You'd think the fact that I risked my life to save yours would encourage you to at least trust me that much."

"I'm sorry. You're right." The man she'd known in Germany had never been anything but tender and gentle. "Forgive me. I am just...tired and afraid."

He paced to the kitchen, running a hand over his head. He stood there a long moment before turning back to her. "Did it not occur to you that maybe I knew what I was doing?" His anger was gone, replaced by an emotionless tone. "That I knew what was best?"

"I understand that. But also...this is *my* country, after all, so I also know things, perhaps things you don't know."

"Is it? Your country?" There was no surprise in his voice, only a sardonic timbre that hinted at sarcasm. "And I was supposed to know that how?"

Right. She'd never told him where she was from.

On the other hand... "Even if it weren't, I'm obviously more experienced with Arab culture than you are, considering I live here."

"*Lived* here. A long time ago. Things might've changed since then. You should have done what I said."

Obviously, in retrospect. But she couldn't have known what would happen.

Which was probably all the more reason she should've trusted him.

She wasn't good at trusting people. Men, specifically. And she definitely wasn't good at doing what she was told.

"I'm sorry. I will try, next time."

He stared at her—maybe trying to see through her. After a moment, he ground out, "Fine." The word seemed to cost him something. "Will you please tell me what happened?"

"I would like to clean up first, okay?" Not that she needed his approval, but no sense antagonizing him.

At his nod, she stepped into the bedroom.

Based on the scent of soap and the moisture hanging in the air, Jasmine had showered. She must've taken a short one because she was curled up on the king-size bed beneath the covers, apparently sound asleep.

Leila hadn't been allowed to shower in days. She was covered in sweat and dirt and filth. She smelled. Her hair was greasy. She was desperate for soap and shampoo.

Plus, she needed a moment to think. To breathe. To consider how much she should tell Michael. Because her sister was right. He wasn't the salesman he'd claimed to be. Or, if he was, he'd once been in the military. Meaning he'd lied to her.

But why? And did it matter right now? He had nearly died saving her.

She showered, thankful for the soap and shampoo that Michael must've brought.

There was only one towel, damp from her sister's use. She lifted it to dry off and found a plastic shopping bag on the hook underneath filled with two sundresses and a package of ladies' underwear. Jasmine had pulled out a pair, but there were several more.

Thoughtful. Like Germany Michael. As opposed to Iraq Michael, who was short-tempered and terrifying.

As she dressed and pulled a brush through her long hair, she pondered... Which was the real Michael Davis?

CHAPTER FIFTEEN

WITH LEILA in the other room, Michael dialed Splat.

Despite the hour, his old friend answered immediately. "What happened?"

"We were detained. We're here now. And there's another woman with us."

That revelation was followed by a short pause. "Your transport into Europe is gone."

Michael had figured that. "Can you still get us across the border?"

"You have papers for the second one?"

"Not yet."

"Get me a photo first thing tomorrow. I'll see what I can do." The line disconnected, and Michael headed for the kitchen.

He'd bought a box of crackers and a container of hummus when he'd first arrived in Baghdad a few days before. He snacked while he waited.

Finally, Leila stepped out of the bedroom wearing one of the dresses he'd bought. He'd originally planned to buy pants and shirts, but there were so many styles and sizes and cuts, and after a few minutes in the department store, he'd given up in favor of pretty floral dresses, figuring he couldn't screw those up too badly. Leila was small, so he'd grabbed smalls. Seemed pretty straightforward.

He'd had no idea how...shapely the dress would be.

She must've noticed him noticing because she paused after she closed the door, her cheeks turning pink. "It was this or those dirty sweatpants."

"No. Yeah. It's..." Wow. Almost enough to make him forget his irritation. He cleared his throat and shifted gears. "I bought pajamas too. But just the one...set." Set? Pair? He couldn't think straight. Where had his brain gone in the last thirty seconds?

"Jasmine must be wearing them."

"She all right?"

"Sleeping." Leila moved closer and reached for a cracker, then stopped and looked at him like he might deny her.

"Help yourself. There're plenty."

She took one, dipped it into the hummus, and ate.

"Hungry?" he asked, stupidly.

"Those...what are they called? REMs? Ready-to-eat meals?"

"Meals ready-to-eat. Wasn't your favorite?"

She winced as if she could taste the food again. "You remember when you forced me to try haggis?"

"I didn't force you." He pictured her face twisting in disgust after she'd tried the Scottish meat pudding. They'd found a little pub outside the city, and maybe he'd put a *little* pressure on her. He might've used the word "coward." She'd been too prideful to let that moniker stick.

"I had thought nothing could be worse," she said. "Those MREs—is that what you feed criminals in America? I think that is...what is the expression? Cruel and unusual punishment?"

He chuckled, relaxing. He liked this woman. More than *liked* her, despite all the secrets she'd kept from him.

Not that he should be lobbing stones.

He kept his expression neutral even as he remembered what she'd named him.

Michael Davis.

Yeah, he hadn't exactly been a paragon of honesty.

Picking out a cracker, he said, "They're for soldiers. Convicts eat better."

Her smile faded. "You told me you were not a soldier."

He stilled, then forced the cracker into the hummus, into his mouth. He took his time chewing. Swallowing. Swigging some water before he set the bottle down.

He grabbed a second bottle from the refrigerator, twisted the cap off, and set it in front of her.

She looked at it, at him, waiting,

"I'm not a soldier. Never was."

Her eyebrows hiked.

"I'll explain everything, but not right now. Not until we're safe." Because the last thing he needed was Leila or her sister telling anybody who Michael really worked for.

"I'm supposed to trust you, even though you hide things from me?"

"If you want to get out of Iraq, I don't see that you have a choice."

She crossed her arms. "How can I trust you when you lied to me?"

"Gee, *Nawra,* I don't know. Why don't you tell me?"

"I had to change my name."

"You have good reason to keep certain facts about your past secret. I can accept that. You'll have to believe me when I tell you that I do too."

She rubbed her lips together, looked past him. Seemed to be building up to another round of questioning.

"So you went to your friend's house?" He moved the food to

a table in the living room and sat in a chair. "Can you tell me why?"

"Jasmine is ill." She curled up on the corner of the couch, seemed to want to pull her knees up but thought better of it in the dress. By the way she rubbed her arms, she was chilly. Not shocking considering he'd cranked the AC.

He found a blanket and pillow in a closet by the door. He'd need them later, assuming he ever managed to get some rest. He draped the blanket over her.

"Thank you."

He sat again, leaned forward, and rested his forearms on his knees. Waiting.

"There is something wrong with my sister. She's too thin. Drawn and pale. I already thought that, and then she vomited a few times after we escaped the compound."

The way Jasmine wore her hijab, he'd barely gotten a look at her face. But even under the abaya, it was obvious she was skin and bones. "Was she throwing up because of fear?"

"I might think that, except it continued even after we got to Heba's house, when we thought we were safe."

Thought they were safe.

He'd circle back to that if Leila didn't.

"I planned to go straight to Baghdad," she said, "but I thought Heba would help us."

"Who is Heba?"

"An old friend from school. She lives in a village about twenty miles south of the compound."

"Last name? Husband's name?"

She blinked as if surprised by the questions. For a moment, he thought she'd push back, but she didn't.

"Heba Iyad. Her husband is Mustafa Aqeel."

"She didn't take her husband's name?"

"Many don't. Arabs are named for our fathers. Heba Iyad's father is named Iyad Assad."

Oh.

Wait.

Iyad Assad owned the compound where Leila and Jasmine had been held. And yet Leila had believed Heba would help her?

She continued, not reading his thoughts. "Her grandfather would be Assad... something. I do not remember."

Michael had already understood Iraqi naming conventions but allowed her to explain, wanting as much information as he could get. "And you are...?"

"Leila Hura Amato."

A smooth lie. Though, perhaps it wasn't a lie. Perhaps she'd legally changed her name.

Which made sense, really. If she'd left Iraq as a refugee, maybe she'd left without her family's permission.

Things were starting to come together.

He let his silence ask the obvious—what had her name been before she'd left Iraq? Because Amato was an Italian surname. Nobody would believe her to be Italian, certainly not after they heard her accent.

"You do not tell me your secrets," she said, "but I am expected to tell you mine?"

He chewed on the question—and spit it out. "Yes."

"Is that fair?"

"All things considered, yes."

All things being the fact that he'd risked his life to save hers. He not only deserved to know the truth about her, but he *needed* to know everything if he was going to keep her safe.

She glared at him across the room, the furious look almost comical on her small face.

Even angry, she was breathtaking.

Long, silky hair, still wet from the shower. High cheek-bones. Straight nose over full, very kissable lips. But it was her eyes that had first captured his attention. Big, beautiful almond-shaped eyes, black as onyx stones. They didn't falter as he stared.

"I think not," she said.

"Seriously?"

She straightened her shoulders. "I'll tell you mine if you tell me yours."

Close enough to the American idiom that he nearly smiled.

"Fine, *Leila*. What happened when you got to Heba and Mustafa's house?"

She sat back, looked away. "Yasamin was throwing up again."

He listened to the rest of her tale—how she'd overheard her friends talking about calling her father.

Her father.

Her *captor*.

Information she perhaps hadn't meant to share. This was why he'd wanted to question her tonight, when she was tired and her guard was down. Before she had time to consider her words or make up a story.

He could picture it—Leila and her sister, her *ill* sister—climbing out a window, jumping from a roof, and running.

Finding a place to hole up—an empty house that might not have remained that way. A place where they could easily have been discovered as they'd slept. But they hadn't been. They'd survived.

They'd left the abandoned village at nightfall and reached Baghdad.

"But there were soldiers, a roadblock," she said. "We were afraid they were looking for us."

Michael hoped his expression didn't give him away. But the

fact that they believed their father had enough pull to get soldiers involved in the search said a lot.

Who was he?

An itchy feeling crawled up Michael's spine.

How many enemies were out there?

Nobody would be able to find them. Right?

Michael had disabled the guard on the street, but not until after the man had spotted the sisters. Meaning, Leila's father's guards knew the area where they were hiding.

Michael had already known that.

What he hadn't known was that the entire Iraqi army might join the search.

"We turned around before we reached the soldiers," Leila said, "and left the motorcycle on the side of the road in a residential area. We walked in."

"How far?"

She shrugged. "A few miles. We'd been walking a couple of hours when you found us." She tilted her head to the side. "How did you find us?"

"The phone. I was tracking it. It didn't show your location until you were almost here."

"Probably when I opened the map to look for Victory Square." She started to stand. "I'll give the phone back to you."

"Keep it. It's fine." It was a burner. His real phones were powered down and stashed in an air vent.

After she settled back in her spot, he asked, "Did you know you were spotted?"

She sat straighter. "What do you mean?"

"A man was watching you. He started to follow."

Her gaze darted around the apartment as if the guy might materialize out of the walls.

"I took care of it," Michael said.

"But they know where we are."

"I think they'll assume we're in one of the hotels. Don't worry."

"How can I not worry?" Her voice rose as she gestured to the closed bedroom door. "My sister is ill. We barely made it to Baghdad, and still, we are in Iraq. How are we supposed to—?"

"You'd be in Turkey tonight if you'd done what I told you to do." He hadn't meant to sound accusing. Or maybe he had.

"You were not there." She stood, tossing the blanket aside. "You do not understand."

He stood as well but kept his voice even. "I'm just saying, I had a plan. If I'd known about your sister—"

"And where is your brother? The soldier? I never thought you'd attempt to rescue us all by yourself."

He breathed, slowly. Working to staunch the words trying to escape. "I think you need to rest."

"I am only saying, it was foolish to do this alone. You should have asked for help."

"It was foolish to go to your friend's house. You should have done what I said. If you had, you'd already be out of the country."

"And where would you be?"

"Here. Sleeping. Peacefully."

Yeah.

Based on the flush on her face, that was the wrong thing to say.

But seriously. He'd saved her life, and she was criticizing him? Thinking he should've asked Grant for help?

Grant, who had a wife? And a kid on the way, not that she knew that last part, but the point remained.

As if Michael would risk his brother's life.

As if he'd needed help. All he'd really needed was for Leila to listen and do what he said.

Was that really so hard?

Her tiny hands clenched into fists, her gaze furious.

He felt exactly the same way.

They were both tired. Now that he'd gotten the story, this conversation needed to end, before one or both of them said something they couldn't take back.

"I need to rest." He nodded to the sofa, and she stepped out of the way.

He plopped down on it. "We'll talk more tomorrow."

He didn't wait for her to argue. Or respond. Just shoved the pillow under his head—ignoring the pain in his abdomen. He pulled the blanket she'd cast aside up to his shoulder and closed his eyes.

"Okay."

Though he didn't open his eyes, he could feel her watching him.

"Michael?"

He peeked. She was standing a few feet away, her damp hair framing her face, making her eyes look larger. The anger had slid away, replaced by a tender look that gave him a whole new reason for needing her to go into her bedroom and close the door.

"It is an instinct, to argue when someone tells me what to do. To argue or disobey. To mistrust. A friend once told me it was my besotting sin."

He felt his spreading grin. "*Besetting* sin."

She whispered it like he'd seen her do many times on dates, committing a word to memory by repeating it to herself.

"I don't wish to argue with you. We owe you our lives."

"You owe me nothing. Get some sleep."

She flicked the lamp off and returned to her room.

CHAPTER SIXTEEN

LEILA WOKE the next morning to sunlight peeking past the blinds. She had not gotten a good rest.

She'd replayed her conversation with Michael more than once, thankful to him for cutting it off before it turned into an argument. She'd been tired and grumpy and not thinking rationally.

Considering all he'd done to rescue her and her sister, he certainly deserved her trust.

After coming to that rather obvious conclusion, she'd sought the Lord, trying to turn over all her worries and fears to Him.

Finally, she'd drifted off, only to be awakened by her sister's retching in the bathroom. Leila had gone to see if she could do anything, but Jasmine had brushed her away with her typical, "It's nothing."

Leila wasn't stupid. There was something seriously wrong, and the fact that Jasmine adamantly refused to talk about it—or even acknowledge it—infuriated her.

Which led to another hour of fuming and more time in prayer. She probably hadn't gone back to sleep until nearly dawn.

Which explained why she'd slept so late.

"I'm sorry."

Jasmine's voice, coming from the living room through the closed door, had Leila sitting up.

"I did not mean to wake you," Jasmine continued.

"I was just dozing." Michael's voice was rough. He cleared it. "I hope we can start fresh. I don't want to argue with you."

Leila stood and grabbed the dress she'd worn the night before.

A long pause, and then, "Coffee?"

"Sure."

Dressed, Leila used the restroom, brushed her fingers through her hair, and hurried into the living room.

Michael was sitting on the couch. His gaze snapped to her, then to her sister and back.

He got that look she'd witnessed all her life—confusion, followed by surprise. She could see it, the remark forming on his lips before they quirked up at the corners.

"Two weeks ago, I didn't even know you had a sister." He directed the words at Leila. Though she and Jasmine wore their hair the same way, were exactly the same height, and were technically—and practically—identical, he knew immediately which was which.

Which, she had to admit, gave her a little thrill.

"Now I find out you're a twin."

"You did not tell him?" Jasmine spoke from the kitchen. "I think I am insulted."

Before Leila could come up with a defense, Michael said, "Don't be. She hasn't told me anything about her past."

"Whereas you have been nothing but forthright with me." She infused humor into her tone, hoping not to reignite last night's argument.

"Touché."

"What is this, *touché?*" Jasmine asked.

Michael turned to her with a smile. "It's French for 'good point.' Or, more accurately, 'good hit.'" He stood and headed toward the kitchen.

"Ah. I see. It is strange that to learn English, I must also know French. And other languages as well, yes? It is complicated."

"I bet." He stopped a few feet from her and held out his hand. "Michael."

Jasmine slid hers into it, then wrapped her other hand on top. "And I am Yasamin, but now Jasmine."

"Pretty name," he said.

Jasmine took a step closer. "I owe you my life, Michael. Thank you for not leaving me behind, and for giving me your seat on the motorcycle. I am sorry about the alarm. I did not know."

He nodded, seemed unsure what to say. And then, "Wish you'd told me who you were on the phone."

She pulled her hands away and stepped back, her gaze dropping to the floor. "I am sorry about that too."

Leila moved forward, ready to tell Michael to back off.

But her sister didn't need her help.

"I was afraid you would not believe me." Jasmine met his eyes and shook her head. "No, that is not true. I was afraid you would not choose to take me. You would only help my sister, and I needed to get away. I did not want you to come prepared to refuse me. Now I understand you would only have been better prepared to save us all. Because of what I did, you could have been killed. I am very sorry."

Leila waited for Michael to let her have it.

Like Baba would have.

And most of the men she'd known.

But he didn't. Just dipped his head. "Apology accepted.

From now on, please be honest with me." He turned to include Leila in his next remark. "We need to trust each other if we're going to get out of here. Okay?"

Jasmine's answer was immediate. "I promise."

Michael smiled at her, then quirked an eyebrow at Leila.

"You will tell me everything, soon?" she asked.

"When we're safe. And you'll do the same?"

"Yes. Okay."

"Good." Michael returned to the couch and pulled a cell phone from a charger. "You mind if I step into your room to make a quick call?"

"A private call? What is the secret?"

He crossed his arms and smirked. The unspoken words were loud in the quiet room. *Do you trust me, or don't you?*

She did. Mostly.

"Go ahead," Jasmine said.

Michael didn't wait for Leila's agreement, just slipped past her and closed the door.

Leila turned to her sister. "I want to know what's going on."

"If not for him, we'd still be captives." Jasmine took coffee mugs from the cabinets. "I can't find sugar or cream."

"Black is fine." After her sister poured her a cup, she sipped the bitter liquid, not exactly enjoying it but needing the caffeine. "How do you feel this morning?"

"I'm fine." She opened the refrigerator and took out the only food in there—the leftover hummus, which Michael must've stowed after she'd gone to bed the night before. "It's nothing."

"Is it, sister? Have you seen a doctor?"

"I will when we're safe." Jasmine pulled a cracker from the package, dipped it in the hummus, and ate it.

Leila didn't appreciate her sister's cavalier attitude. "It might be something."

The door opened, saving Jasmine from having to answer.

"My friend's working on a plan to get us out of here," Michael said. "I spoke to him a few hours ago, but I wanted to update him on the whole...twin thing."

"That's important?"

Michael shrugged. "Could be. More information is always better than less." He didn't pair that remark with any knowing looks. "He said we should be ready to move around noon. We need to eat and pack our things. Since you two were seen last night, I went out this morning and got you both new abayas and head scarves. There're also shorts and T-shirts to wear under them. It's going to be hot. Is there—?"

"You were seen too," Leila said. "What if they followed you?"

His smile—if it could be called that—was patient. "I was careful. Is there anything you need before we go? It'll be a long journey."

Jasmine shook her head, but Leila said, "Maybe something for nausea?"

"It is nothing," Jasmine said. "Please don't worry."

"It's not nothing." Leila couldn't help the frustration lacing her words.

Michael didn't step into the argument, just lifted a paper shopping bag from the floor near the couch, which he carried to the counter, pulling out a bottle. "I don't know if it'll help. My dad's a doctor, so I texted him this morning. He suggested this."

Jasmine took the medicine and read the label. "It is—"

"Do not say it's nothing," Leila snapped. "It's obviously not."

Jasmine smiled, barely flicking a glance at her. "I was going to say that it is kind of you to worry."

"It's not just that," Michael said. "There are times we'll need to be quiet. We can't have you giving us away."

Her twin's smile faded. "I hadn't thought of that. I'll try it. And also, lemons help when I add the juice to water."

"Good to know. I'll take care of that." Michael shifted to Leila. "How about you? You need anything?"

"Food?" Leila asked.

He pulled more packages out of the bag. "No more MREs, I'm sorry to say."

"Very sad. I was so looking forward to...what was it? Meat, I think?"

He lifted his gaze long enough to smile. "There's no telling what's in those things. I looked for haggis—"

"You wish to poison us?"

He chuckled. "I got more protein bars and bottles of water. Hopefully, this'll tide us over until we're in Turkey."

"And then?"

Michael left a couple of protein bars out, then started transferring what he'd bought into his backpack. "One step at a time."

Leila didn't like that answer. "It is not easy to get from Turkey to Europe, harder now than when I did it ten years ago."

He didn't look up. "I'm aware."

"A long journey. I went through Bulgaria and Serbia, sometimes riding, often walking, always paying, paying everything I had. It took months."

Now, Michael did look up, eyes narrowing as he studied her. "I look forward to hearing that story."

"That is not the point. The point—"

"I understand, Leila. I know what I'm doing."

"Do you?"

His eyebrows shot up. He looked around the apartment, his implication clear. They were here, in Baghdad. Not trapped in the middle of the desert.

He'd somehow managed to get away from all those armed

guards and then travel sixty miles through the desert with no vehicle. And he'd beat them there.

He knew what he was doing.

Even so... "I would like to know the plan," she said. "That's all."

"When I know it, I'll tell you." He resumed stuffing things into his pack.

Her sister grabbed a protein bar, bumping her shoulder. "We must trust him," she whispered, not that Michael wouldn't hear.

"I know that." Leila also knew that escaping from Iraq was one thing, but getting into Europe was entirely different. As an American, Michael didn't need to worry about what would happen if he were caught in Turkey. But if Leila and Jasmine were, they would be detained—and the detention centers were neither clean nor safe. They could be held for months, years, even.

And then they could be sent right back here.

CHAPTER SEVENTEEN

SITTING on the floor beside his pack, Michael could feel Leila's doubt. Or maybe it was disapproval. Either way, he didn't need her input on his plan—which was barely more than a vague idea at this point, anyway.

It wasn't as if there were a plethora of options.

Step one, he had to get the sisters out of Iraq and away from the people trying to recapture them and probably kill him.

He'd figure out step two soon enough.

Which meant not engaging in debate with the woman currently giving him the side-eye.

Or worrying about the other one, who was scrutinizing a protein bar as if it might attack her. Considering the vomiting he'd heard in the middle of the night, it might.

Where would they be the next time she got sick? Because an ill-timed episode could mean the death of all of them. As if they didn't have enough to worry about.

He texted Splat.

> One of the women is throwing up. Bring lemons.

How lemons could help, he couldn't imagine.

His friend's only reply was...

???

No idea.

That got a thumbs-up.

At least somebody didn't feel the need to question his every decision.

He'd bought both sisters a small backpack so they could carry their own things. Everyone was packed now, food eaten and, aside from the one protein bar, stowed. He'd instructed Leila and Jasmine to shove as many bottles of water as they could fit in their backpacks, and he'd gotten most of the rest of them in his.

There was nothing left to do but wait.

Well, maybe one more thing.

He cleared his throat. "Would you mind if I pray for us?"

Leila looked up from her seat on the couch, big eyes blinking. "Yes, that would be...good."

Jasmine dropped the protein bar—still unopened—on the counter and joined them in the living room.

He stood and held out his hands. He and Leila had prayed together over meals. They'd attended church together a few times and joined in corporate prayer, but this was different.

He had no idea if Jasmine was a Christian or a Muslim or if she believed anything at all. So it felt a little awkward, but if Michael had learned anything in the years he'd been with the CIA, he'd learned that things went wrong with even the most perfectly planned missions. Most of his teammates would say they needed luck on their side. Michael didn't believe in luck. He believed in God.

Leila slid her hand into his left one, Jasmine his right. They closed the circle and then looked at him.

"Father," he said, "Your word tells us that You go before us, walk beside us, and rejoice over us. You are our Rear Guard and the Rock beneath our feet. That means we're surrounded by You, by Your love and protection. Lead us on every step of this journey. Hide us from our enemies and deliver us from evil. Take us out of Iraq, through Turkey, and to safety in Your time, on Your path, as only You can."

Yes. God was the one in control. Not Michael.

He would work very hard to remember that and let God keep ahold of the reins.

In the silence, Leila prayed, "Please heal my sister and let her not get sick on this journey."

And then Jasmine added, "Thank You for bringing Michael to us and for bringing us this far. Please, protect us all."

"And protect Splat," Michael added. "Let no harm come to him or anyone who aids us." When he could think of nothing else to add, he said, "In Jesus's name, amen."

"Amen." Leila squeezed his hand, looking up at him with an expression that made his heart thump.

He really liked this woman. Oh, who was he kidding? He'd risked his life—and his career—to save her. He didn't think *like* covered it.

He leaned down and pressed a quick kiss to her lips.

Jasmine stepped back. "You two go ahead and kiss." Her accented words were heavy with sarcasm. "Do not worry about me."

"Sorry," Michael said, but she was grinning.

The low knock—two quick raps—had them turning toward the door.

Walking that way, Michael waited for three more, which

would confirm who was on the other side. When they came, he opened up.

Owing to his Guatemalan roots, Alanzo Gonzales, aka Splat, had dark skin, black eyes, and black hair. When Michael had first met him at the Farm, he'd looked like all the other agents in the specialized training school. Today, he had a thick beard and bushier eyebrows than Michael remembered beneath the keffiyeh wrapped on his head. He pushed a dolly stacked with boxes inside, then closed the door.

Michael wrapped him in a hug. "Long time, man. Thanks for doing this."

Splat slapped his back. "Anytime."

Michael indicated the women. "Meet Leila and Jasmine."

Splat shook their hands, lingering a little too long, then gave Michael a look over his shoulder. "Now I understand why you risked—"

"What's with the boxes?" Michael gave him a pointed look. Splat no doubt knew that Michael was persona non grata with the CIA, but there was no reason for Leila to know.

"Pretty simple," he said. "We're moving furniture." He unloaded the boxes, opened the tallest, and took pieces of wood out. One-by-fours, two-by-fours, and plywood lined with padding.

Michael had a bad feeling about that padding.

While the women looked on, he helped Splat build crates. One was the size of a small wardrobe, not quite as tall as Michael, with a layer of polished mahogany, complete with gold trim, that ran beneath the crate. Meaning, if anybody pried up a side, they'd see furniture, never knowing, God willing, that anything—or anyone—hid behind that false front.

The obvious opening spot was on the front. Nobody would realize there was a hinged side.

Pretty ingenious, actually.

When they finished that, they built a three-foot cube, which had a similar false front.

Michael sat back on his heels. "Am I acting as the second mover?" *Please?*

"Got a guy to help with that. Local. Name's Omar."

Michael flicked his gaze to the cube, then the wardrobe, and he got a sick feeling in his gut. He stood, not daring to look at the women when he asked, "You don't plan to shove three grown adults into those two boxes. Right?"

Splat stood as well, facing the sisters.

They were standing in the living room, side by side, looking so much alike it was almost eerie. Same stance—one leg straight, the other bent. Same crossed arms. Same squinted eyes. Same pressed lips.

Splat gave them a once-over. "I have a nine-year-old nephew bigger than you two. Combined."

Jasmine's lips shifted into an almost-smile.

Leila wasn't amused.

"What they lack in height," Michael said, "I make up for in weight."

"I wasn't gonna say anything about that paunch, but..."

"I'm not kidding, Splat. This is the plan?"

The man leaned back against the kitchen counter, his expression sobering. "Soldiers are swarming the city—along with a bunch of rough-looking men—armed, I'd bet my life. Story is that the twin daughters of a high-ranking official have been kidnapped."

Michael's gaze flicked to Leila. "What official?"

"Above my pay grade." He focused on the women. "We gotta get you out of the city, and we gotta do it without any of you being seen. I got a van downstairs filled with furniture. The story is we're moving it from a city house to a country house. At the border—"

"We can't stay in a box until the border." Michael wasn't claustrophobic, but still...

"Once we're out of the city, you can get out, as long as you can get back in fast." Splat looked between the women. "Which one of you is sick?"

Jasmine said, "It is nothing."

Leila glared at her.

"As soon as we're out of Baghdad," Splat said, "we'll drop off Omar, and then you'll come up and sit with me." To Michael, "You have papers for her?"

"For Leila."

Splat grinned. "Six of one, a half dozen the other, I think."

"What is that?" Jasmine looked from one man to the other as if they'd switched to Swahili.

Leila flicked a hand toward them. "An expression. It means we're interchangeable."

"Not what I mean, ma'am," Splat said. "Just that, since you're identical, papers for one can be papers for the other, right?"

She nodded, but her gaze strayed back to the boxes. "Who will be where?"

Splat smacked the cube. "Jasmine." He spoke to her, eyebrows hiked, ensuring he'd gotten the name right.

When she nodded, he continued.

"Jasmine will travel in this until we're clear of the city. Then I'll break you out, and you'll ride up front with me. How's your English?"

"Not as good as my sister's, but I can speak."

"Perfect. You're my interpreter. I'm a civilian working for the US, and I'm moving furniture for a bigwig colonel. I don't speak Arabic, and that's why you're there, to help me through the checkpoints. Can you do that?"

"A simple task." She flicked her fingers at him and spoke in her native tongue. "I am curious, though. Do you?"

He answered in smooth Arabic, "When it suits me."

Jasmine smiled. "Okay. This will work."

Splat turned to Michael, then included Leila. "You two will be in the big box."

"Together?" The pitch of her voice—too high—revealed her surprise.

How she'd missed the obvious, Michael had no idea. "It's either that or you travel in the cube. I'd offer, but I won't fit." He sent the small box a glare as if that were its fault. "But you'd have to stay in it all the way to Turkey. With no hinged side, it'll take too long to get in and out of. If you were outside and we got stopped..."

It would be fatal.

She swallowed—and seemed to be considering that option anyway. As if she'd prefer to take her chances in the little box rather than be stuck in the wardrobe with him.

He tried not to be offended.

Nobody spoke, and after a few tense seconds, she nodded.

"Good," Splat said. "Hit the head, and then we go."

Michael had known this wouldn't be easy. He'd figured he'd be donning his old-man disguise again, which was how he'd made it to the store that morning. He'd even been considering different disguises for the women. Dressing them up like boys would work.

Never had he thought they'd be leaving the building in boxes.

As long as the boxes weren't coffins, though, he wouldn't complain.

CHAPTER EIGHTEEN

THIS WAS NOT GOING to work.

After Michael backed into the tiny, tiny crate and leaned against the edge farthest from the hinged side, Leila stepped inside.

She felt cramped, and she was much, much smaller than Michael was.

He couldn't even straighten to his full height. He was hunched over, giving her space at his expense.

The plywood was covered with a thin layer of foam, but the boards holding the plywood in place were not. Even with the foam, it was not comfortable.

She was still trying to figure out how they were going to make it work when Michael's friend said, "Scoot forward for a sec."

She scooted nearer to Michael, turning to see what Splat was doing.

He set her backpack on the floor, then dropped Michael's on top. "We gotta hide these, in case we get searched. I'll put them in the cube after your sister's with me."

He closed the narrow door behind her, and the latch clicked.

"Maybe you can sit on mine?" Michael's voice was low, a rumble in the darkness.

After her eyes adjusted to the dim light that shone through tiny cracks—made on purpose so they wouldn't suffocate—she propped his giant pack against the plywood behind her and tried to sit. It was too tall, but she couldn't lay it flat or it would take up the entire floor.

She leaned back onto it, trying to keep her feet out of Michael's way.

"I'm sorry," he said.

"This is not your fault." This had been Splat's idea. And what kind of name was that? Resentment toward the man rose inside her, but she squashed it. He was trying to keep them alive and out of Baba's hands. If this was the only way, then she could do it. She had to do it.

At least she was able to stretch a little. Jasmine couldn't even do that. And Michael was hardly better off.

So she wouldn't complain. She could do this.

But when the box moved, she squeaked, bumping the wood beside her.

"Keep it down, bro," Splat said. "You don't want the lady to think you're scared."

"Haha." Michael's voice was flat.

"Seriously. Omar thinks this is about transporting illegal goods—not people—so you're gonna have to be quiet." Then, almost as an afterthought, "Probably could've passed that off as a mouse, though."

Leila determined that she wouldn't make another noise. She braced her hands against the wood on either side of her.

Again, the box tilted, surprising her. Her hand slipped, and her shoulder rammed into the side.

Again, it settled in its spot. "Brace yourselves." Splat sounded annoyed.

"I'm trying," she snapped.

His voice was more patient when he asked, "Can you sit, Michael?"

"Sure. I'll just pull up a chair in here, flip on the TV." He lowered his voice. "Come here, sweetheart. I'll hold you steady."

Sweetheart.

Everything felt so off, so wrong. Was she still his sweetheart? Did he want her to be?

With all that was going on, did it even matter?

He'd kissed her last night. Kissed her again just a few minutes earlier. And he was here.

So maybe this rescue attempt wouldn't ruin what they'd built. Assuming they survived it.

He inched his feet forward, stretching out his legs on either side of hers until he could rest his back and head against the plywood. That had to be more comfortable than standing straight and bending over. "I think if I just wedge my feet against the pack…"

He did and then tugged her gently toward him, pulling her to his chest with one arm and bracing himself against the wood with his other hand.

Taking his cue, she pushed her hands against the sides of the box.

"You okay?" He mumbled the words in her ear. Despite the cramped quarters, the strangeness of the situation, the danger all around, his warm breath sent tingles over her skin. "Do you feel steady?"

Not even close. But he meant physically, so… "I think this will work."

"If you're ready…?"

At her nod, Michael spoke louder. "Try it now, Splat."

The box tilted.

With Michael holding her tight, his legs bracing her hips, she was able to keep from bumping the side. This time, rather than being set upright again, they stayed angled as Splat rolled them around on the dolly.

Then stood them back up.

"Good job." Splat must've moved away from their crate because his next words, likely spoken to Jasmine, were barely audible. A few moments later, he called, "Getting my buddy. Be quiet, and be prepared to move."

The door closed.

Leaving the three of them boxed up and waiting.

In the months she and Michael had dated, they'd been alone more times than she could count, but never like this. Never trapped, in danger, in silence. With a million questions between them.

And nothing to say.

Michael tipped her chin with his free hand and kissed her, the slightest brush of his lips against hers, but the gesture calmed her. He was here because he cared. And after everything—after finding her in an Iraqi compound, after she'd ignored his directions and nearly gotten herself and Jasmine recaptured, after their disagreement the night before—he still felt something for her.

And she still felt something—more than something—for him.

He trailed his fingers in her hair, raising goose bumps on her flesh.

She pressed her hands against his broad chest, then followed with her cheek, listening to the beat of his heart.

When two voices filtered through the wood, they braced themselves again. The crate angled and bumped against the back of the dolly. They were rolled out of the apartment, into the elevator and back out, and then through a door. No steps this way, apparently. Was there a loading dock maybe?

She had no idea.

The box was rolled up an incline, then straightened again.

Silence followed, but she dared not speak or move.

A few minutes later, the guys were back, talking football, joking around. A thump sounded nearby. A few more strange noises—sliding, bumping, shifting—and then the unmistakable sound of a metal rolling door falling into place.

Doors slammed.

The engine rumbled to life.

And they were moving. The radio came on, the Iraqi pop music familiar if not comforting. Splat and Omar's voices were muted but audible.

Tension seemed to drain from Michael's body. He kept his hand braced against the ceiling but held her close with his other arm.

She gripped him right back, praying that they would all get out of this, safe and healthy. And that she and Michael, when it was all over, would still be together. After all he had done for her to get her here, after all their dates, their long talks, their sweet kisses... After all the ways he'd proved to her he cared, she held onto him and admitted to herself that she never wanted to let him go.

CHAPTER NINETEEN

GET YOUR HEAD ON STRAIGHT.

Michael's brain knew what he should be thinking about. But his body had entirely different ideas. Because Leila was tucked right up against him, snug and comfortable, resting her cheek on his chest. Trusting him. Trusting her life, and her sister's, to him.

The rumble of the van, the hum of the music, the feel of her against him, and... Oh man. He wanted to kiss her. He wanted to kiss her so badly he ached.

He bit his lip. Maybe the pain would redirect him.

It didn't.

But he knew better than to follow his impulses in this cramped space with nothing to distract him from the feel of her in his arms.

Considering the only things between Leila and recapture were the crate and the van—and him—he could not risk losing control.

He was falling in love with this woman. He needed to honor her, and honor God.

Which felt a lot easier when she wasn't so deliciously close.

The van slowed and rounded a corner, and he braced himself against the wood. "Hang on to me." He kept his voice low.

She slid her arms around his back, and despite the wound that ached at her touch, that didn't help his out-of-control thoughts at all.

Conversation. Something to distract. "I'm confused." He kept his hands on the plywood. Safer that way.

She backed away enough to look at him. "About?"

"The place you were held captive was owned by your friend's father, right? Iyad Assad?"

It was dark, but he could see enough to know she blinked, her long eyelashes flicking closed and open a couple of times. "How did you know that?"

"After your sister sent me your location, I did some research. I recognized the name when you mentioned it last night. Did you know it had belonged to Heba's family? Had you been there before?"

"Yes."

Her answer was terse and surprising. "Then why did you go to her house? Didn't you realize they'd work against you?"

"She and Mostafa helped me escape Iraq the first time, even though both of their families would have objected. I thought they would help again."

Wishful thinking, then. Foolish logic that almost got her recaptured.

"You said your father was at the compound?"

She nodded. Her face was angled down, so he couldn't see her expression.

Was she hiding something? "Is your father the one who kidnapped you?"

Was Vortex her father?

The thought churned in his stomach.

"An old friend of our family."

"His name?"

"Qasim. Khalid Qasim"

A spark of hope zinged through him. Finally, he had a name —a real name—to attach to Vortex.

To be sure, he said, "About sixty? Gray hair, clean-shaven? He escorted you onto the plane in Munich, right?"

"How do you know that?"

"I've been looking for you since you disappeared." Not a complete answer, but maybe she'd accept it.

"You got access to video feeds or something? How?"

"I have a few connections. Was that Qasim?"

She bit her lip, then focused on his chest. "That is him."

Okay.

Wow.

Leila's family was associated with Vortex. But how? Were they aware of his links to terrorism? Was Leila?

Was that why she'd been snatched? Did it have nothing to do with Michael?

Or had Qasim discovered that Michael was looking into him and then, in watching him, had found Leila?

Had she been hiding?

Which brought up another question, one that'd hummed in the back of his mind since they'd been escaping the compound.

"I thought your parents lived in Germany."

Her shoulders lifted and fell, but she offered no defense for what had obviously been a lie.

"Can I ask you something else?"

Her nod was her only answer. She still wouldn't quite meet his eyes.

"When you were walking to the plane, Qasim didn't have ahold of you. Did he have a weapon? Why didn't you try to get away? I mean, even in the terminal, you could've tried to run or alert somebody that you were being taken." He didn't actually know she hadn't, but it was a logical guess.

"He threatened Yasamin."

That made sense. Michael would risk everything to protect his brothers.

"How does your father know Qasim?"

"They have known each other as long as I can remember."

"Do they work together?"

"I don't believe so."

"What does your father do for a living?"

She shrugged. "When I left, he was with the government. Now, I do not know."

"What is his name?"

That question was greeted by silence.

"Leila?"

"When we're out of Iraq, I will tell you more about my family."

"What's the big secret?"

"It is not a secret. It is only that...I just want out of this country. You don't need to know who my father is in order to get me out of Iraq. His name will mean nothing to you."

Probably not true, but he didn't say so. "More information is usually better than less."

"What is there to say? I escaped. They found me and brought me back."

By means of a suspected terrorist, one Michael had been surveilling.

She was keeping secrets, but he was too. And he wasn't ready to reveal his.

"You told me you came to Christ through the family of a school friend. Was that friend Heba?"

"No, no. A girl at the international school in Baghdad."

Now that he'd shifted the conversation away from Leila's parentage, she seemed to relax.

"Her family was from Dallas, Texas," Leila added. "She used to speak of a brother who was in the rodeo, with horses and bulls. Does that not sound exotic?"

He laughed. "I've been to Dallas. I wouldn't describe it as exotic."

"But the American West, with ranches and cowboys."

"It isn't exactly like it's portrayed in the movies."

"I suppose not. This family was very wealthy. Her father worked in the oil industry. Jasmine and I went often to their house to play with her. When we were there, her parents talked about Jesus. I don't think they were trying to convert us, though maybe they were. But they talked about Jesus like He was somebody they knew they could depend on. I remember the first time I heard such conversation, I thought they were talking about a regular person. I asked if He was a relative or a friend."

Michael smiled, imagining the innocent question from a little girl. "How old were you?"

"Nine or ten, I think. They told me Jesus was their Savior, and Mr. McLeary explained that He is the same Jesus spoken about in the Quran. Not that I was much of a student of the Quran, but I had heard of Him. What these friends said was very different from what I had learned. Mr. McLeary explained that Jesus forgives sin and that everyone who believes in Him will be saved."

"So your friend's father led you to the Lord?"

"It took many years before I made the decision. It was a frightening thing to reject Allah. To reject Islam was to reject my family—and be rejected by them. Not to mention being sent to hell.

"But Allah felt like an angry dictator, making rules and

demanding we follow. Do his will, he said, and maybe if you do it enough, and well enough, maybe you will be saved. But maybe not. And there was no way to know. He felt...fickle and impossible to please. I wondered what my chances were. How many Muslims would Allah accept? I asked the question of a religious teacher once, and he said we would be lucky if Allah took half."

What a horrible way to live, always hoping your good deeds outweighed your bad, hoping that your god would accept you, but never knowing for sure.

"I looked at myself," Leila said, "and I looked at my twin, and I knew of the two of us, she would be saved, and I would not. Because Yasamin is the good one, and I am the one who stirs up trouble. I do not like to do what I'm told."

"Really?" he deadpanned. "I'd never have guessed."

A smile tipped her lips up. "This is shocking, I know. I am always so sweet and compliant."

He chuckled. "You're definitely sweet."

The van slowed, then came to a stop. Michael kept himself and Leila from jostling as the vehicle inched forward, then sped up again.

He was dripping with sweat and dying for a breeze. He'd be cooler if Leila wasn't so close, but he wasn't about to push her away.

"How old were you when you finally gave your life to Jesus?" he asked.

"Fifteen. Yasamin had a doctor's appointment that day, so Mama took her and I stayed with my friend. We started talking, and I told Bridget that I wanted to know more about Jesus. She called her father, and he came home from work to talk to me. He led me in a prayer, and I was converted and saved."

He kissed her forehead. "I'm so glad you were."

"I didn't tell Jasmine for almost a year. And then God told me that, if I didn't tell her, she could die believing in the wrong thing, and then she would be rejected by Jesus. So, I was very afraid, but I told her."

"Afraid of what?" Michael asked.

"That she would tell our parents. I had no idea what they would do, but it would not be good."

"Did she?"

"She prayed to Jesus with me and accepted Him. But then she wanted to tell our parents the truth. I was very afraid, but Jasmine... She was always the good one. I see as I get older that she was never timid, only meek. Patient and willing to follow and obey. This is meek, yes?"

"My father says meekness is power under control. He says good men are meek men, the kind who can fight enemies with great strength but who also place themselves under the authority of others. Good soldiers are meek, submitting to the authority of those of higher rank. Good fathers are meek, submitting to the authority of God—and pastors and employers."

"This is my sister."

"So, did you? Tell your parents?"

"We told Mama." By the flat tone of the words, the conversation hadn't gone well.

"And?"

"She said she would pretend she'd not heard us, and we should never speak of Jesus again."

"Not the reaction you'd hoped for."

"The one I expected."

Her bitterness surprised him.

"Jasmine was a fool to believe she would listen. Mama could never stand up to Baba. She is...she was..." Her voice trailed.

Was?

"Did something happen to her?"

"She's been gone nine years. Cancer. I didn't know until Jasmine told me."

"Oh, sweetheart." The van was moving at a steady speed now, so Michael risked snaking one arm around her. "I'm so sorry."

She held herself to his chest as if finding comfort there. "I prayed for her all those years, but she was gone. Even before that, I prayed for her—and Baba. From when I first came to know Jesus, I prayed she would be safe. And now she is gone, so there is no hope for her. She is lost to me forever."

He ran his hand down Leila's hair, unsure what to say. It took a moment before words came. "Maybe you and your sister had an impact on her. More than that, we know God heard your prayers. Maybe He reached her, but she was too afraid to tell anyone."

"If that is the case, then is it real? If she was too afraid to admit, then is that not denying Him?"

This was getting a little too theoretical—and theological. "We can only know that our God is never looking for reasons to deny somebody entrance into His presence. From the garden all the way through the scriptures, God demonstrates His desire to be with His people. In fact, there's nothing He wants more. So, if your mother opened a door to Him, I believe He walked through it."

"Do you think she did?" Michael didn't miss the spark of joy in her voice.

"We can't know, Leila. But there's always hope."

She settled her cheek against his chest. The physical desire that had hummed inside him was gone, replaced by a holy desire to protect this courageous woman who'd lost so much.

The van slowed and came to a stop, and this time, the radio's volume went down.

Leila looked up at him with wide eyes.

He shook his head. With no radio and no road noise to cover them, they needed to be silent.

He'd been trying to guess the van's route through the city. By his calculations, they should be nearing the outskirts by now.

A harsh voice barked, "Papers."

"Yeah, okay, man." Splat, speaking English, sounded nervous, as well he should. Any American who didn't feel nervous at the sight of armed Iraqi soldiers would be deemed either arrogant or foolish. Splat would do his best to appear as neither.

Omar spoke in Arabic. "We're transporting furniture for a colonel's wife." He made a joke about American women and all their stuff, but the soldier didn't engage.

"We will search."

"Okay," Omar said. "I'll open up."

Footsteps thumped past them, and then the door in the back of the van rumbled.

Bright light filtered through the narrow openings in the crate.

Michael pulled the handgun from his holster. He had no idea what he'd do if they were discovered.

Shooting a soldier would probably get him killed.

But Splat would try to get them out of there before that happened.

We need You now, Father. Protect us.

The van bounced as the soldier—no, *soldiers*, based on the multiple voices and footsteps—climbed on.

Leila clung to him as if he could protect her. As if holding onto him would make her invisible.

Which was so far from the truth.

If she were discovered in the arms of an American CIA agent...

He didn't want to think about what they'd do to her.

CHAPTER TWENTY

LEILA WAS AFRAID TO BREATHE.

Boots stomped, each footstep pounding inside her.

"Open it!"

Please, God. Please...

The squeak of nails against wood, and she cringed, knowing they would be exposed. Or Jasmine would.

But no additional light filtered into their small compartment.

"It's just furniture." Omar's voice sounded from only inches away. "I think those boxes contain clothes."

More pounding, a *thump*. Tearing.

"No, my friend," Omar said. "Please don't ruin the boxes. You tell me what you want opened, and I'll open it."

"That one."

"Yes, okay." Another loud squeak, meaning it was a crate. Theirs? Jasmine's?

"Only a table," Omar said. "I think all the crates are furniture."

"You think?" The soldier's voice was gruff and commanding. "You do not know?"

Splat spoke in English. "Can I help? I can tell them what's inside."

Omar translated.

A smack sounded so close that Leila gasped.

Michael pressed her face against his chest and held her there, muffling her mouth in his T-shirt.

She'd resent it if she hadn't almost given them away.

"This one," a soldier demanded.

Splat said, "That's a bookshelf," and Omar translated.

The soldier indicated another box, and Splat told them what was in it, adding, "If I remember correctly."

Omar translated.

The sound of tearing cardboard followed.

"Hey, now," Splat said. "You're gonna get me in trouble."

Again, Omar translated.

One of the soldiers laughed.

Scraping. Demands to know what was inside this or that. The opening of more boxes and crates.

"Clothes," Splat said. And a few minutes later, "Pots and pans." After that was confirmed, "Books."

Another smack sounded, this right over her head.

She managed not to gasp this time. Not that it would matter. They were about to be exposed.

"It's a wardrobe," Splat said.

Omar translated.

The soldier barked, "Open it!"

"Aw, man." Splat managed to sound genuinely disappointed. "We gotta move all this—"

"Do it!"

Grunts, the drag of wood against metal.

Michael let up his grip on her and pushed her back, gently.

He aimed a gun toward the soldiers.

She stared at it, at him. Shook her head. Better to be taken than be killed.

But he didn't seem to agree.

The sound of nails coming out.

The wood around them shifted.

Additional light filtered in.

"Like I said"—Splat's voice was flat—"a wardrobe."

Fingertips poked between the two panels that would make up a wardrobe's doors were it truly a wardrobe, not a well-crafted trick.

As soon as the soldier lifted, he would discover them inside.

"Where are the pulls?" he asked.

Omar translated, and Splat said, "We took them off for transport. To protect them. They're in one of these boxes."

"Show me, then."

Did they actually have pulls for the wardrobe? No, of course not. Splat was making his answers up.

Now, he said, "All right. Give me a sec... It was a box of knickknacks, I think."

As Omar translated, more boxes were moved, shifted.

The fingers were pushing through, trying to get a grip.

Michael's weapon was inches from those fingers. If the wood came up, he would shoot.

All hell would break loose. Would they escape? Even if they did, soldiers would hunt them down. They'd all be killed.

Jasmine. Michael. These two men who'd come to help them.

And it would be Leila's fault.

She couldn't look. She covered her face with her hands. *Please, God. Please.*

From farther away, someone shouted, "It's clean. Let's go."

The fingertips disappeared.

Footsteps pounded again, and then the van's floor shifted.

Had they jumped off?

"Go." Omar's voice was low but vehement. "I'll take care of this."

The engine rumbled.

Michael wrapped her in his arms and braced himself a second before the tires rolled.

Just like that, it was over.

She pressed her cheek against his chest and reveled in the sound of his racing heartbeat.

She knew exactly how he felt.

They traveled twenty minutes in silence, the van not slowing at all, which told Leila they were on the highway out of the city.

Splat and his friend had talked about the tense moment, making jokes to cover their own nerves, she thought.

Even after they turned the radio back on, she and Michael were silent. Leila didn't know why he hadn't said anything as he'd holstered his weapon and held her close.

For her part, she couldn't help thinking of all the things that could have happened.

But didn't.

Thank You, Lord. Thank You.

The van slowed and, a moment later, turned. After a few more turns, Splat thanked his friend, and a door opened and closed before the van moved again.

"All clear," Splat called. "Everybody okay?"

"We're good," Michael said. "Is it okay for us to get out?"

"Yup."

He smiled at her. "If you'll shift to one side, I'll try to get that door open."

But she'd seen how it worked. She leaned behind her and flicked the latch.

The door swung open, and sweet, sweet air spilled in.

She hadn't realized how hot she was until the cooler air hit her sweat-covered skin. She climbed over Michael's bag and stepped into the cargo area.

It was filled with boxes and crates, so many that there was barely room to stand. She had to squeeze between stacks in order to make room for Michael to get out.

"You all right?" he asked.

"Better now."

He called, "Jasmine?"

"Here."

The voice came from one of four cube-shaped crates stacked against the side of the van.

Splat called, "She's in the bottom one. You'll need to move the others."

Michael nodded toward the passenger seat. "Sit for now. I'll get her."

Leila wanted to help, but there wasn't room for both of them. She climbed over the console and sat beside the man who'd secured their escape from Baghdad. "Thank you."

"Exciting stuff."

"You call that exciting? I thought I would lose control of my bladder."

He chuckled, checked the rearview. "You find the crowbar?"

"I see it," Michael called. He removed the boxes from atop Jasmine's, then pried open the top.

He held out his hand, and Jasmine stood. She looked wan and wilted. "That was not fun. But..." She looked through the windshield at the passing desert landscape. And smiled. "We are free."

"Not quite," Michael said. "But getting there."

Leila and Jasmine switched places, and then Michael

handed Jasmine her backpack, which he'd pulled from her crate. "Your papers are in there. Be sure you know them inside and out."

"I have memorized already," she said. "I know who I am."

"We got a long ride ahead of us," Splat said. "Five more hours to the border, then a few more to Diyarbakir."

"You're taking us all the way there?"

That Michael hadn't known already pinged anxiety in Leila's heart. "You do not have a plan?"

Michael barely glanced her way and didn't bother responding.

"If those thugs pass into Turkey looking for you," Splat said, "they'll concentrate near the border. I wanna get you guys farther in."

"Thanks, man," Michael said. "I'll arrange a truck."

"Already done." Splat reached into a cubby beneath the radio and handed back a packet of papers. "It's under your alias."

His alias?

The way Splat said it, as if it was normal... Why would Michael have an alias?

He tensed, and did she imagine it, or was he very careful not to look her way? "Perfect. I appreciate your help." To her, he said, "Let's find a place to sit."

She followed him back among the boxes.

After he dug into his pack for bottles of water and protein bars, he settled on one of the cubes he'd moved.

Leila perched on another, contemplating asking all her questions, but he'd already told her he'd explain everything once they were safe. She opened her protein bar. "What is the plan?"

"Get a car in Diyarbakir, drive to Istanbul, and—"

"Drive? But it is so far." Sixteen hundred kilometers from the Iraqi border to the west coast.

The very thought of making the trek again had her heart racing.

"Don't worry." He lowered his voice to a soothing timbre. "I have money and resources. We'll get the car today and reach the border tomorrow."

Could it be done so quickly?

Perhaps. If they weren't stopped along the way.

Michael added, "And then we'll cross into Bulgaria."

That plan could work, assuming... "Then we will get papers for me in Diyarbakir?"

"One of you will have to cross the border in the crate. If I'd known there were two of you, I'd have been prepared. If we want back into Europe, this is the way."

"If we're stopped by authorities..." Leila worked to keep fear out of her voice. "Unless you plan for one of us to be in the crate all the way to Istanbul."

"If we get stopped, I'll deal with it."

"How, by shooting someone?"

Michael's lips flattened. "I'm not going to murder anyone, but I'll do what I have to do."

"You'll get us all killed."

He tipped his head back, facing the roof of the van.

She knew he was frustrated, but he needed to understand the danger. "Even if we're not stopped on the way, the crate will be searched at the border."

He didn't bother to look at her when he asked, "Why do you say that?"

"There are many boxes here. The soldiers couldn't check them all. But if there's only one—"

"There won't be just one." Now, he leveled his gaze on her. "We'll stack the one you or your sister is in underneath others, so—"

"They'll look. They're looking for refugees." Her words

were coming too fast, her voice high and squeaky with fear. "The papers won't pass, and even if they do—"

"Leila." Her name usually sounded sweet on his lips, but not this time. He settled his forearms on his knees, water bottle dangling between them. "Do you really still not trust me?"

"It is not a matter of trust." Was it? No. "It is only that you do not know all that could go wrong."

"Yeah. That's how I broke you out of that compound. That's how I got you out of Baghdad. By not knowing what I'm doing."

"Splat got us out of Baghdad." By the way his face reddened, that was the wrong thing to say. "I didn't mean... I am only saying—"

"I get it." He was angry, no question. "When you come up with plan B, let me know. I'm going to rest." He crawled into the crate where they'd been trapped for hours, shoved his backpack against the far edge, propped himself against it, and closed his eyes.

And somehow, if the rhythmic rise and fall of his chest a few minutes later were to be believed, fell asleep.

Apparently, unconcerned about her worries.

And unaware of the dangers he was leading them into.

CHAPTER TWENTY-ONE

MICHAEL'S FATHER always claimed that the ability to sleep no matter the circumstances was the result of a clear conscience.

Not so in Michael's case. He'd learned how to shut his mind off to rest, despite all his worries and frustrations. Even with his training, it'd taken a few minutes for his irritation with Leila— and yeah, he should call it what it was...

Anger.

It'd taken a few minutes for his anger to fade enough for him to drift off. But he'd hardly slept the night before, and he was still recovering from a stab wound—a wound he hadn't even told her about.

If he did, she'd probably blame it on his incompetence.

Splat got us out.

She assumed Michael had had nothing to do with their getting out of Baghdad. Which, in her defense, he hadn't—aside from asking Splat for help. His friend had come up with the plan, but not because Michael couldn't have. He'd just had his hands full rescuing them and then escaping a bunch of armed guards.

How did Leila figure he'd managed that? Dumb luck?

Michael wanted to go back to sleep, but something had awakened him.

A knock on the wood over his head had him sitting up.

Leila looked in the opening. "Splat says to tell you we'll be at the border in about ten minutes."

The border? Already? That meant he'd slept for hours.

He crawled out of the crate and stretched, restacked the boxes in the cargo area, shoving his backpack into the empty crate where Jasmine had hidden.

When the area looked as it should—the boxes neatly stacked, all remnants of their having been sitting back there stowed—he checked on Jasmine and Splat.

Jasmine had donned an abaya and hijab, which covered much of her face, just in case the border agents were on the lookout for her and Leila.

"All good here," Splat said. "Get hidden back there. We'll see you on the other side."

God willing.

Michael and Leila returned to the crate. Without his backpack, there was plenty of room for both of them to sit—on opposite sides. Which was just as well because the last thing he wanted was to hold her again.

Well, maybe not the *last* thing.

"You are angry," she said.

"Did you come up with plan B?"

Her silence answered the question.

He'd expected crossing into Turkey to be rife with tension. He hadn't believed that most of that tension would be confined to their crate.

The Turkish authorities let them through without incident. As soon as they were on the other side and Splat gave the all-clear, Michael unlatched the door, stepped out, and settled on the floor, his back to a box.

She sat beside him.

"You should rest," he said. "It's going to be a long night."

"It's only that I don't understand how you know the things you know. Maybe if you explained—"

"What's your father's name?"

She clamped her lips shut. A moment later, she said, "I will tell you. Soon."

"When you do, we'll talk." He nodded to the crate. "The padding's not comfortable, but it's better than this." He knocked on the hard metal floor. "Go rest."

"I don't want to argue with you."

"Who's arguing?"

She studied him another few moments, then crawled into the crate.

Maybe she'd be a little less critical after a nap.

He grabbed a couple bottles of water from his pack, then wandered to the front, where Jasmine had reclined in the seat and was trying to sleep as well.

He opened one and handed it to Splat.

"Thanks." He kept his voice barely audible over the engine noise.

Michael did the same. "Need a protein bar?"

"I got some." He nodded to the console. "She all right back there?"

"Resting."

"You do the same. I'll get us there."

Michael had hoped for a distraction, but with both the ladies sleeping, it seemed rude to talk. He settled on the floor and went over his plan.

Not that it was much of a plan. Get the truck, move a bunch of boxes and crates into it—including the empty one that would hide one of the sisters—and drive.

By his calculations, they'd make it to Istanbul the following day, then cross into Bulgaria, where they wouldn't need visas. With Michael's American passport and Leila's German one—it was a forgery, but it would pass—they shouldn't have any trouble.

In Bulgaria, he'd get them on a flight to the US. At that point, Brock would catch up with him. He'd been ordered to stand down, after all. And when Brock showed up at his hotel room, he'd probably planned to detain him to keep him from searching for Leila or even question him.

Once Brock got ahold of Michael, he was going to be in trouble. But maybe the information Leila and Jasmine could supply about Vortex—Qasim—would buy him leeway.

He grabbed his laptop, itching to do some research into Qasim, but the service available through his burner phone's hotspot was patchy at best. His own phone would work, but he had no doubt Brock was waiting for him to power it up so he could use that to track him down.

So fine.

Michael would get his answers soon enough.

It was dark by the time they reached the outskirts of Diyarbakir, a city of nearly two million people in central Turkey about a hundred kilometers north of the Syrian border. Michael had never been there. He stood between the seats to look through the windshield, but it was hard to get a sense of the place. A distant glow told him the city wasn't far, but they seemed to be in the middle of fields.

Jasmine said, "It is so dark."

"Are we skirting the city on purpose?" Michael asked.

Splat flicked his gaze to a phone attached to a holder on the console. "Just following the directions." A few minutes later, he exited the highway toward the airport.

Leila joined Michael, and he stepped aside so she could see. She'd slept—or at least stayed in the crate—for the nearly four-hour drive from the border.

"Did you get some rest?"

"Yes," she said. "Thank you."

Her overly formal response did not bode well.

But she was scared. He understood that. And he didn't want to argue with her. He was about to slip his arm around her waist when she spoke again.

"Did you change your mind about driving?" Her voice was filled with hope as she read a passing sign for the airport. "Are we getting on a flight?"

He dropped his arm and faced her. "How would we do that with only papers for one of you?" He tried to keep his voice level. Tried not to let the fresh annoyance seep out.

"I thought maybe you figured something out."

"There's no forged-passport superstore."

"I know that. I just thought maybe Splat..." Her voice trailed.

Wow.

How much more afraid would she be when her apparent savior left her alone with Michael?

Splat spoke into the heavy silence that followed. "We need an all-night car rental place, and airports are the best bet for that." To Michael, he said, "I'll drop you off and find a place off the grounds and out of sight of cameras where we can transfer the boxes. I'll text you the location."

"That works."

Leila's gaze flicked from Splat to Michael, and he didn't miss the questions in it. She wanted to know every step of their plan.

Which was why he didn't look at her again as they drove to the terminal. He didn't speak to her when he raised the back door and climbed out, just calling to Splat, "See you in a few," before slamming the door back down.

Maybe, once they crossed into Europe, she'd decide he was trustworthy.

CHAPTER TWENTY-TWO

IT ALL HAPPENED SO FAST.

Splat left Michael at the terminal, drove out of the airport, and found a small parking lot beside a restaurant nearby. Everything was closed at that late hour, so there would be nobody to witness them moving boxes once Michael arrived with the pickup.

Splat climbed out of the van, walked around the area, then climbed back in. "No cameras. Let's figure out what we should move."

Leila and Jasmine helped Splat in the cargo area, shuffling boxes. She was pushing one of the four cube-shaped crates toward the back when the rear door jerked up.

Michael, already? That was fast. She turned toward him with a smile.

A gunshot blasted.

The sound ricocheted off the walls, deafening.

She heard a scream, muffled as if from far away, though her sister's mouth was open in horror.

Splat fell. Facedown.

There was blood, so much blood.

Leila scrambled toward the driver's seat, but that door opened. A second man climbed in and started the truck.

Behind her, a man climbed into the van, aiming a gun at them. "Did you really think you could get away from us?"

Waleed.

Terror spread to her limbs, made her hands tremble, her legs weaken.

A slow grin stretched across his face. A grin of triumph and conquest. The grin of a predator anticipating his next meal.

She stepped between Waleed and her sister, though he barely acknowledged Jasmine. His gaze skimmed down Leila's body, and she wished for the ugly pants and shirt she'd worn at the compound. For the first time in her life, she wished for an abaya and hijab. The shorts and T-shirt were modest and breathable but showed more skin than she wanted Waleed to see.

He licked his lips.

He looked past Leila to Jasmine. "You'll be lucky if he doesn't kill you."

Who? Baba wouldn't do that, would he?

Leila glanced back at her sister and watched her face pale, though her expression was stoic, or maybe *resigned* was the word.

To Leila, Waleed said, "You will receive your punishment when you are mine."

"I will never be yours."

His smile didn't waver. "I look forward to proving you wrong. Sit. Both of you."

Jasmine sat on the hard metal floor and dropped her head into her hands.

Leila's pride tempted her to refuse, but this was a battle she would lose—and it was not worth fighting. She sat and focused on the air entering and exiting her lungs.

She was alive. For now, she and Jasmine were alive, and there was hope.

Poor Splat. He was gone, and it was her fault. All of this was her fault.

She shouldn't have gotten complacent in Munich. She should have traveled farther from home.

And then when she was caught, she should have stayed in Iraq. Instead, she'd alerted Michael, putting him in danger. And Jasmine. And now Splat.

The sight of him, face down and unmoving, had her swallowing. She turned away, breathed through her nose, trying desperately not to expel the contents of her stomach.

Another man climbed into the cargo area and dragged Splat to the edge of the metal floor. He kicked him onto the street.

Then the second guard lowered the door with a bang.

Jasmine flinched.

The guard plopped down on the floor, back against the door, arms on his bent knees, gun dangling from his hand.

Waleed sat beside him and shouted in Arabic. "All set back here."

Leila pressed her shoulder into her sister's and whispered. "Do not lose hope. Michael will find us."

Though how, she had no idea.

When Jasmine lifted her head, Leila peered into her eyes and saw...despair.

But Michael knew where they were, right? *Hurry. Please.*

She looked around for something to use to defend herself. There was a crowbar, somewhere. But she didn't see it and wouldn't be able to get to it even if she did, not with Waleed and the guard watching.

She had no way to fight, no way to defend herself or her sister.

The driver hit the gas, and they lurched forward and drove away.

Michael would never find them.

It was all over.

CHAPTER TWENTY-THREE

THE RENTAL WAS AN OLDER model Ford F-150 with four doors and a roomy backseat. Michael stowed his pack and mapped directions to the pin Splat had sent. He was eager to get the boxes loaded and start the trek to Istanbul. Thanks to his long nap—and the refreshingly cool air outside, such a contrast to the Iraqi desert—he shouldn't have any trouble driving through the night.

After connecting his phone to the truck's Bluetooth system, he drove off the airport grounds and headed toward a city street. Buildings rose on his right. Apartments, he guessed, or perhaps offices. It was hard to tell in the dark.

He was a quarter mile from the cargo van when he saw a figure on the sidewalk ahead.

A man. Limping. Holding his arm.

Splat?

He slammed on the brakes, his heart racing.

His friend limped around the front of the truck as Michael opened the door.

"I'm driving."

Michael hopped the console into the passenger seat. "What happened?"

Splat let up the pressure on his arm to grab the wheel as he climbed in. Blood dripped from the wound. More covered his hand. "Give me your phone." Michael did, and Splat tapped the screen, leaving red stains across the glass. "They must've been looking for us at the airport."

Having his fears confirmed sent adrenaline coursing through Michael's veins. "How many?"

"Three, at least. I was an idiot. Moving boxes."

So maybe more than three. "We need to dress that wound."

"Just a scratch."

Right. His friend was already paling.

"You get any of them?"

"I'm lucky the guy had bad aim. He opened the cargo door, took a shot, and I went down."

They didn't call him Splat for nothing.

"I managed to fall on the wound and cover my chest with blood. I think the guy thought he got me in the heart. Incompetence working in our favor."

"Aren't you armed? You didn't fight back?"

"I'm a leftie." Splat didn't look up from the phone. He was typing fast. "Didn't think I'd be able to grab my gun before they saw me move. Better play was to wait for you."

Yeah. Maybe. If the guards didn't kill the women before Michael could find them.

Poorly trained guards, maybe. But they had the sisters, and the CIA agent and the SEAL had lost them.

"Got 'em." A fresh map came up on the truck's screen, and Splat dropped Michael's phone in the console, leaning back, breathing heavily.

The red dot indicating the cargo van's location was already

a mile away and moving fast. Obviously, Splat had left his phone in the van. Small favors.

He shifted into drive, and Michael tried to figure out what they were going to do when the men stopped. Which they would have to do, wouldn't they? Or would they wait until they were back in Iraq?

Michael couldn't let them get that far.

He reached into the backseat, opened his pack, and found his first-aid kit. No time to worry about a bullet, but at least he could staunch the bleeding.

"They stopped." Splat's voice was still strong. A good sign.

According to the map, the van was a little over a mile away.

Probably transferring the women into a different car.

Splat turned at the corner toward them and floored the gas pedal.

A quarter mile out, Michael said, "Stop here. I'll run." He pointed to the map. "Cut them off in front. Can you walk? Shoot?"

"I'm fine."

Sure he was, but Michael needed his help. "Turn toward me and I'll wrap that."

"You gotta go before we lose 'em."

"I need you alive. Give me your arm."

Splat shifted, and Michael reached across him and placed the clotting gauze over the wound. *Wounds*—entry and exit. Good. Then he wrapped a bandage around his biceps, tight. "Okay? You can get your gun?"

He pulled it out with his right hand. "You come from behind. Two minutes."

Michael grabbed a second handgun from his bag and shoved it in his waistband. He checked the knife sheathed at his ankle, looked at the map once more, and noted the time.

"Two minutes."

He got out and ran.

Michael stayed low and crept along the edge of the building toward voices, all male, all speaking Arabic.

A quick peek around the corner showed the cargo van and a few men. They were discussing who would drive in what.

Where was the second car? Vehicles lined the street. Most were dark, but there was a dome light on in one of them.

Michael crept in that direction. Thanks to the light, Michael got a good look. A guard...? Maybe. Maybe not. Impossible to be sure. But if it was, Michael could cut off at least one escape route.

A man sat in the driver's seat, tapping his fingers on the steering wheel impatiently.

Crouching beside the rear door, Michael took a breath, exhaled a prayer. He stood and yanked the door open.

Pulled the driver out, wrapping his arm around the man's neck.

It took precious seconds, and the driver fought. But Michael kept the pressure until the man went limp. Michael dropped him on the ground, sat in the car, and took the keys, only then noticing the laptop bag on the passenger side floor.

He grabbed it and dropped the strap over his shoulder as he jogged back to the mouth of the alley.

The buildings were dark at two in the morning, only a couple of the windows showing light beyond blinds or curtains.

Hopefully, nobody was looking out those windows. Once bullets started flying, they certainly would be.

A light attached to the side of the building illuminated the area enough for Michael to get a decent look at what was happening.

Three men were engaged in conversation in front of the van. Complacent, which would work in his and Splat's favor.

If Leila and Jasmine had already been taken away, Michael would get their whereabouts from one of those thugs. He prayed he could before the twins were whisked over the border.

One of the men had the slightly higher voice and clean-shaven cheeks of a young man. Late teens, maybe early twenties. The second man was nearly bald but overcompensated with a thick beard. The third looked familiar.

It was hard to be sure in the dimness, but Michael thought he'd seen his image before. He knew he'd heard his voice—back at the compound. He was the one who'd insisted the guards find the women, that Leila would be ready for something the following day.

The man was taller than his compatriots, and broad. All the men wore dark pants and long-sleeved tops, but this one had donned a red-and-white keffiyeh, which he'd wrapped around his head and secured with a black cord. He had a round face and a black trimmed beard and mustache.

He was the one in charge.

They were discussing logistics—what route they should take back to the border and where they could fill up the gas tank and who would drive what.

He checked his watch. Thirty seconds to go.

Keffiyeh-guy answered his phone, then barked to the kid something Michael didn't catch.

The kid headed for the back of the van. The door rumbled.

A moment later, Leila and Jasmine walked hand-in-hand into his line of sight.

Michael stifled a curse. This would have been much easier with the women inside.

He willed the time to move faster. When there were ten seconds to go, he aimed at the one in the keffiyeh. Cut off the head, and maybe the body dies. If nothing else, it gets very confused.

Three. Two.

A gunshot split the silence, a second too early.

Michael fired, but Keffiyeh ducked just in time.

Baldie went down.

Good shot, Splat.

Keffiyeh bolted behind the van, and Michael lost his shot. He couldn't see what was happening, but more gunshots were coming, loud and fast, echoing off the brick walls.

The kid yanked the women in front of him and moved toward the cargo doors, using them as a shield. Except he was a foot taller than they were.

Michael took aim...

The kid crouched low. He must've been armed and breathing threats because the women made no attempt to run.

The driver's side door opened.

Michael caught the glint of a gun and ducked behind the building.

A gunshot cracked, the bullet so close Michael was sure he'd felt a breeze.

From the far end of the alley, the gunshots continued. Keffiyeh and Splat battling it out.

Michael dropped low and prayed for a good shot.

But the kid forced the women around the back of the van and out of sight.

Two more men showed themselves. One in the passenger seat, barely visible above the dash.

Another dropped to the asphalt behind the driver's door, scanning for threats. He didn't see Michael in the shadow so low to the ground.

Michael aimed at the man's shin. Fired.

The driver screamed and went down.

As soon as he did, Michael aimed at his head and took him out. Because a shattered leg didn't keep a person from firing a weapon.

The engine started and the van barreled forward.

Michael shot out a front tire and scrambled to his feet.

The van jerked but righted itself and kept coming.

Another gunshot, and another tire was gone.

Splat, thank God! Did that mean Keffiyeh was down?

Splat was coming toward him, limping into the alley, alive and conscious, though he looked like he was about to collapse.

Michael stayed out of sight, waiting for the driver to show himself.

When the man's forehead popped above the dash, Michael aimed.

Fired.

The van slowed, and Michael bolted toward the driver's seat. He opened the door, ducked below the window as another man fired.

Inside, a scream.

A stream of obscenities floated into the night.

Michael swung around the side of the door and looked.

Beyond the deceased driver, Leila struggled with the passenger, holding his arm up, keeping the gun aimed at the ceiling. The man was trying to push her away, but she was behind him—and not letting go.

Giving Michael a clean shot.

Stubborn woman. He loved that about her.

He fired.

The passenger slumped forward, and Leila stumbled back.

Michael pulled the driver out. The car was rolling slowly toward the intersection. He reached across the seat and yanked up the parking brake.

The van lurched.

There was one gunman left. The kid. Where was he?

"Michael!"

His name, screamed in fear, came a second before a volley of gunshots.

But at the warning, he'd jumped to the ground. The kid missed.

"I will kill them!" The shout came in Arabic. "I will kill them both!"

"You don't want to do that." Fury stole over him, but he wrapped his words in a calming cadence as he matched the man's Arabic. "Your boss wants them alive or they'd already be dead."

Splat hobbled to the rear door. Blood dripped from his left arm, more from his leg. Michael had no idea how he was still on his feet.

"You don't have to die today, son. We can work something out."

A gunshot, another scream.

The sounds tore through Michael like shrapnel. "You girls okay?"

"They don't talk!" the man shouted.

"You hurt one of those women"—Michael made his voice deadly cold—"you'll wish you were never born. You hear me?"

"Throw your gun in. I take the women, and I don't kill them."

Yeah. That was gonna happen.

"All right," Michael said. "I don't want them to get hurt. That's the most important thing."

"Toss the gun!"

Splat was steadying himself on the back of the van. When he caught Michael's eyes, he nodded.

"Here it is." Michael threw his gun onto the passenger seat.

A gunshot blasted.

A woman's scream tore a hole clear through to his soul. *Please, God. Not Leila.*

Second gun drawn, Michael launched himself into the van, landing so that his head was in the space between the seats. Ignoring the blood splattered there.

Aimed and ready.

But the sisters were standing, hugging.

On the floor of the van, the kid lay lifeless.

The rear door dropped against the floor with a clatter.

"Are there any more?" Michael asked. At Leila's quick head-shake, he said, "Are you hurt?"

"We're all right."

Michael pushed himself to the ground and bolted to the back of the truck.

Splat was crumpled on the asphalt, unconscious.

CHAPTER TWENTY-FOUR

LEILA HAD THOUGHT the danger was past, so when Michael shouted that he needed help, her stomach plummeted to her toes.

Jasmine raised the rear door, and Michael laid Splat inside. Splat, who'd been dead—hadn't he?

But he must've been the one to raise the rear door and shoot the guard. She hadn't gotten a look because the second the man went down, the door slammed shut again.

And now she saw why.

"Back down the alley," Michael shouted. "The truck is there."

Leila shook out of her stupor and launched herself into the driver's seat. She'd never driven such a big vehicle, but she managed to shift into reverse and hit the gas. It wasn't easy keeping the van straight with two flat tires, and she made no effort to avoid the bodies, just rolled over them. Protecting the living was more important than respecting the dead. Especially *these* dead.

She reached the mouth of the alley. "Which way?" Her voice sounded calm, belying the shock and panic in her body.

"I don't know!" Michael's words were strangled.

She peered in both directions, saw a blue pickup and hoped that was the rental. She drove that way.

The cargo door rose, and Michael said, "Open the tailgate."

Jasmine hopped out and lowered the back of the pickup.

Leila opened the door and, just before she jumped out, caught sight of the backpack on the floor in front of the passenger seat.

She snatched it, praying it held the forged passport. She didn't have time to grab anything else and doubted they'd be back.

She ran to the pickup's driver seat. The truck was running already. She found the lights and flicked them on, then grabbed a phone in the console and searched for a hospital.

The tailgate closed. In the rearview, Jasmine and Michael were bent over Splat.

Cloth ripped. Jasmine said, "He needs a tourniquet."

Leila pressed the button to navigate and hit the gas.

Please, God. Please, don't let him die.

It took ten minutes. Ten precious minutes. And then she pulled toward the ER, honking to alert those inside that they needed help.

A woman in scrubs came out, looked over the edge of the pickup, and ran back inside.

More people came out seconds later, one pushing a gurney.

Splat was lifted onto it.

Michael stayed beside his friend while medical personnel rolled him inside.

Leila shut off the truck and dropped the keys in the console.

But before she could jump out, Jasmine climbed into the passenger seat, shoving a black bag at her feet, a bag Leila had never seen before.

Her hands were covered in blood.

"What are you doing?" Leila asked. "We have to go in!"

"Michael said we must stay in the truck."

"Why?"

"He didn't explain, only that we were to find a dark corner and wait for him."

Leila didn't want to do that, not one bit. But she did what her sister said, backing the truck into a spot at the edge of the lot, its rear to a building, where they could keep an eye on people and cars coming and going,

And waited.

There were so many questions, so many things to say, but all Leila could think was *Please, God. Please don't let him die.*

Splat had been a stranger that very morning. He'd been kind. He'd risked everything for them.

And now it looked like helping them might literally cost his life.

She didn't even know his real name.

How many would have to die because of her desire for freedom?

She hated the fear that tried to edge its way in, but what if more guards were looking for them? Where was Waleed? Had he been killed? Or was he alive, searching for her even now? If he'd seen Splat's injuries, if he'd witnessed their escape, he'd know what they were driving and could guess their destination.

Would he know they'd come to the hospital? And if so, wasn't sitting in the truck a bad idea?

Thirty minutes passed. Then an hour.

No guards came. But Michael didn't return, either.

What if the guards had found him inside? Or what if Michael was injured as well and hadn't told them?

What if something terrible was happening while they sat there and did nothing?

She opened her door.

"What are you doing?" Jasmine grabbed her arm. "Stay here."

"I'm just going to check on him."

Before her sister could argue, Leila slipped out. She hadn't noticed the temperature earlier, and now she took a deep breath of the cool, dry air. What a difference a few hundred miles could make. She fast-walked to the entrance and inside. It was an empty room. Abandoned, like the airport. Like the streets, where evil men attacked.

She visited the restroom, then grabbed a handful of paper towels. She wet some of them, kept others dry. If Jasmine wouldn't come in, at least she could get the blood off her hands.

Back in the entry, Leila tried the only other door.

Locked.

She didn't know what to do. Should she knock? Bang until someone opened it to her?

Or just trust Michael?

She knew what he'd say.

Fine. She'd rejoin her sister and wait a little while longer.

She was stepping outside when the locked door opened behind her.

Michael saw her. By the way his lips pinched closed, he wasn't happy.

"Sorry, I just—"

"Quiet." He grabbed her upper arm and practically dragged her into the cool night. "You were supposed to stay in the truck." Despite the low volume, the words seethed.

"I was worried. Is he all right?"

Michael didn't answer.

When they got to the truck, he opened the rear door. As soon as she was inside, he slammed it and climbed into the driver's seat.

"What is wrong with you?" she asked.

Jasmine's gaze flitted from Leila to Michael and back, then she shook her head. Definitely a *stop talking* look.

Leila held out the paper towels, and Jasmine gave her a tight smile and wiped her hands.

Michael shifted into drive and made his way out of the parking lot onto the street. "Jasmine, will you put in directions to Antalya, please?"

"Sure." Her sister wiped blood off the phone screen and then tapped the map.

"I thought we were going to Istanbul," Leila said.

Michael acted as if he hadn't heard her. "We'll need an all-night convenience store on the way, if you can find one."

"Okay." Jasmine didn't question him, just did what he directed.

But Leila was confused. "Antalya is the wrong—"

"I have my reasons." His tone shut her up. "Just like I had my reasons for leaving you in the truck. There were cameras everywhere. Cameras that have now caught you getting out of this vehicle. If anybody has access to those cameras, they'll know what we're driving."

"But they saw you..." Her words were weak as understanding washed over her. What had she done?

"They didn't know me." Michael's words were measured but angry. "The only time they saw me was in the dark at the compound. I've been hidden through the checkpoints. And maybe they were looking for Splat, and maybe they'd eventually realize he was the injured man brought in tonight, but only if his ID was scanned. Now, though..." He didn't finish his thought. Just drove.

"I'm sorry," Leila said. "I didn't think."

He picked up speed as they angled onto a highway.

Jasmine plugged the phone into the truck's navigation system, and a map came onto the screen.

"Thanks," he said.

"Is he going to be all right?" Jasmine's question was gentle but didn't ease the tension at all.

"He lost a lot of blood," Michael said, "but maybe if they push fluids..."

"We will pray for him," Jasmine said.

"I appreciate that." A few miles passed before he added, "And I appreciate your help. Getting that tourniquet on him might've saved his life."

"Leila drove."

Kind of Jasmine to try to make her feel better—cast her in a good light—but it didn't make a difference. Probably not to Michael. Certainly not to Leila.

Because it was entirely possible that her mistake could cost them their freedom. Or their lives.

The tension between Leila and Michael didn't lessen. About ten minutes after they left the hospital, Jasmine fell asleep in the passenger seat, making the silence in the car feel more oppressive. Leila wanted to say something to get her and Michael back to friendship at least—if not to the close relationship they'd enjoyed before. But she'd already apologized. What else could she say?

If her blunder got Michael killed and Jasmine recaptured, her paltry *I'm sorry* would be less than meaningless. It was no wonder Michael didn't want to talk to her.

It was the middle of the night after a long, pressure-filled, terrifying day. How she wished she could rest, but she couldn't quiet her thoughts. When she managed to take her mind off the foolish thing she'd done, terrifying memories assailed her.

Gunshots.

Guards.

Waleed.

Splat covered in blood, collapsing.

Please, let Michael's friend be okay. Please, let him recover completely.

Get us out of this country and to safety. Please.

She didn't deserve to be rescued. She knew that. But Jasmine did. And Michael had done nothing but help. And Splat...

She squeezed her eyes closed, trying to think of something else, anything else.

You will receive your punishment when you are mine.

Waleed's words felt even darker now than when he'd spoken them. She'd sworn she would never be his, but would she have a choice?

Had she ever, or had the years of freedom only been a mirage? A slight hitch in a life that would never truly belong to her?

Marriage to Waleed would be a fair reward for her foolishness.

She deserved Michael's scorn. She deserved Jasmine's, too, though her sister would never offer anything but kindness.

Leila swiped at her tears and tried to pray as the world passed by the truck windows, pitch black and menacing.

An hour after they left Diyarbakir, a few scant streetlights told her they were approaching civilization, a town if not a city.

Michael said nothing as he turned into a gas station parking lot.

Beside him, Jasmine roused.

"Thought you could use a bathroom." He spoke to Jasmine, then met Leila's eyes in the rearview mirror. "You hungry?"

Was she? She couldn't remember when she'd eaten last. She felt too heartsick to consider food.

Jasmine stretched. "I am."

Michael parked at a pump. "Stay in the truck until I finish fueling." He didn't wait for a response, just climbed out and slammed the door.

Jasmine twisted in the seat to face her. "Are you okay?"

"Not really."

"I believe Splat is going to recover, and you and I are going to reach freedom." Jasmine spoke the words as if she had no doubt. "It is going to be all right."

Leila wasn't sure, but she didn't say so. Nothing felt *all right* at that moment.

"Who was that guard talking about?" Leila asked. "Who would have you killed?"

Jasmine dropped her hand and turned away. "It doesn't matter. We are leaving them behind."

"It does matter, sister."

Jasmine stared forward. In the dim lights from the parking lot, Leila saw a depth of sorrow she'd never seen on her sister's face.

Had Baba really become so cruel that he would murder his own daughter?

No. She couldn't believe that of her father. So, somebody else?

She willed Jasmine to speak the truth, no matter how awful. *Trust me,* she thought. *Tell me..*

Jasmine licked her lips, and they parted. She turned to face her again. "There is some—"

The door swung open. "Thanks for waiting," Michael said. "You two ready?"

Jasmine hurried to climb out and slammed the door, closing Leila in the truck—and her words in her mouth.

Frustrating, but Jasmine would tell her eventually. They'd never been able to keep secrets from each other for long.

A few minutes later, they were on the road, Jasmine in the back, explaining that she wanted to lie down, Leila in the passenger seat beside Michael.

He still wasn't speaking to her—not unless she counted, "Get whatever you want" and "You need to eat."

But after Jasmine fell asleep, Michael reached across the console and took Leila's hand. "I'm sorry."

"You did nothing wrong." They kept their voices low to keep from waking Jasmine.

"I was rude. I was too angry to talk for a few minutes."

A few minutes? Try an hour. More than an hour.

They'd left the streetlights behind again, and only the dim glow from the dashboard lit his face, illuminating the sharp angles in a strange yellow light. But judging by his voice, he didn't sound angry now.

"I wasn't only angry," he added. "I was scared. For my friend."

"I'm sorry."

He gave her hand a squeeze. "That wasn't your fault. None of this is your fault."

Wasn't it? But with Michael holding her hand, a little of the weight that'd settled on her shoulders slipped off.

"There was a man back there." She needed the answer to one question, a question that'd been pricking her thoughts since they'd escaped that murderous alley. One she'd dared not to speak. But she could wait no longer. "He is tall and thick with a beard and mustache. He wore a keffiyeh. He was in the van when we left and then climbed out when it stopped. Is he... Did you kill him?"

Michael turned narrowed eyes toward her. "Who is he?"

She should tell him. She wanted to tell him everything. He deserved to know everything. But she was so tired, and she didn't want to think about it anymore. "There is a long story, and I want only to rest and feel safe for a few minutes. This is so bad? To rest from it?"

"Telling me his name will keep you from resting?"

Maybe, depending on how he reacted. It certainly wouldn't be a short conversation. "Telling you now will be so much better than telling you tomorrow?"

Michael exhaled, loudly. "He took off toward Splat. Your friend shot him in the leg."

"Not my friend."

"If Splat got him back or not"— Michael glanced her way, watching her reaction—"I don't know."

She closed her eyes, fighting emotion. Knowing, *knowing* Waleed had survived. He was too mean to die. Like a rat or a cockroach, he'd squeezed through some impossibly small crack and escaped.

"I can't tell by your reaction," Michael said. "Is that good news or bad?"

"He is a horrible man, and I'm sorry he hurt your friend. You will forgive my foolishness at the hospital? Are we okay, you and me? Or...at least friends?"

"Friends?" His lips ticked higher, genuine amusement. "I hope we're more than friends."

"I feared maybe, after all this—"

"You thought maybe I'd throw you over because you made a mistake?"

"I did not tell you about my past. And Splat could have... could still not survive. And you could have died, and now we're in greater danger because of me. And we might not—"

"Sweetheart."

The single word silenced her rambling and nudged a little more of that pressure from her shoulders.

"Nothing has changed for me." His voice was low and

gentle and serious. "If anything, my feelings for you have only deepened."

"How can that be?"

"You're brave and loyal and strong. I don't know your whole story, but what you've shared... I can't imagine the life you've lived."

Her eyes stung. His words were too kind. Too generous. Too much to take in.

"How about you?" His tone implied that he was unconcerned, but she didn't miss the undercurrent of uncertainty. As if *she* might reject *him*.

"You saved my life."

"I'm not looking for repayment, Leila. You don't owe me anything."

"That is not what I mean. Only, I always knew you were a good man. Now, I have seen it. A man who is willing to risk everything for me—and my sister. How can I not love that?"

His eyebrows hiked at the L-word, but she didn't take it back. She wasn't saying she loved him, only that she loved his heroism.

His heroic heart.

She loved his kindness and selflessness. The way he'd put her and Jasmine on that motorcycle, knowing he might not escape.

She loved the way he'd saved them from Waleed and his men.

She loved the way he cared for his friend.

The way he'd apologized for being unkind, even though she'd deserved his scorn and worse.

She loved his compassion and his competence and his confidence.

She loved...him.

She *loved* him.

Of course she did. Probably had for a long time, though she hadn't realized it. She'd never been in love before, after all.

In the awkward silence that followed her strange, unfinished declaration, he said, "So nothing's changed between us, right? Not for the worse, anyway."

"At the hospital, I should have done what you said."

"Yes." He shot her a look. "You should have. You need to trust me. I know what I'm doing."

Which was clear, but she didn't understand how. "You are not a salesman."

"I *am* a salesman."

Jasmine was asleep. It was just them and darkness in every direction. There was nobody to hear the truth if he were to speak it.

But the silence stretched, raising a barrier between them, transparent but impenetrable.

He blew out a breath. "I'm not *only* a salesman."

And the barrier cracked. "Then what—?"

"Can you trust me for a little while longer?"

Trust him? How could she not?

She lifted his hand in both of hers, bending to press a kiss to the knuckles. "I trust you, Michael."

"If that were true, you'd do as I say."

She lowered his hand, resting it on her knee. "It's not a matter of trust. It's just that, like I told you, I'm not the compliant sister. I like to know the plan. And I don't like to be told what to do—and to be expected to obey without question." Bitterness tinged her voice—enough that Michael glanced her way, squinting as if trying to read her thoughts.

He said nothing, just waited for her to explain.

He deserved that, at least.

"My father made all the decisions, always. If Mama questioned him..." A memory came, no less unpleasant than the ones she'd been battling since they left the hospital. "When I was about eight, my parents got into an argument. Baba told Mama to do something, and she didn't think it was a good idea. She tried to tell him, gently, but also to make her opinion known. It should have been a simple conversation."

He'd backhanded Mama, sending her sprawling across the room.

Which was horrifying enough, but they were at Leila's grandparents' home, surrounded by people. Hasan was there, along with Baba's parents and other cousins and aunts and uncles.

And none of them, not one, went to Mama's aid. None even acted surprised.

The women looked away.

Hasan watched with approval. Approval, as if Baba striking his wife were a perfectly reasonable thing to do.

Which wasn't unusual. Many Iraqi men beat their wives and children. But not Baba, not before that.

He'd grabbed Mama's arm, hauled her to her feet, and marched her like a child up the stairs. He locked her in a room— and left her there.

Though Leila had never shared the story before, she told Michael everything. "During the next few days, Yasamin and I begged Baba to let Mama out of that room, or to let us in to see her. But he refused. And through the door, Mama told us it had been her fault. That she should not have disagreed with her husband. That she'd *made* him do it. As if she had gotten what she deserved." Humiliation burned Leila's cheeks as if Mama's shame were her own.

As if her shame was the shame of every woman who didn't fight back against such treatment.

As if they could.

Michael's jaw hardened. "Nobody deserves to be treated like that."

His reaction cooled her own bitterness. He would never treat his wife that way. She knew that. Intellectually, she knew.

"I will not be dominated, not by my father or a husband or any man. I always asked questions. I always argued. Even when mine was the cheek he slapped. Even when it was my body crumpled on the floor. Because...because how dare he? I would rather fight and suffer the consequences than be someone's servant."

Michael waited, perhaps giving her the space to continue.

When she didn't, he asked, "Was your mother all right?"

"Yes." Leila exhaled her frustration. "Only bruised. And hungry because he didn't let her eat, even though she said she was sorry. Even though she groveled." She swallowed a fresh wave of shame.

"Did your father...these last couple of weeks, did he hurt you?"

"He did not feed me for a few days because I was disrespectful, but he didn't touch me." He hadn't even hugged her when she'd first been presented to him like some sort of battle spoil, just flicked her away like a fly. Ten years absent, and he'd barely spared her a glance.

He was not the father she'd known as a child, the one who'd loved her and Jasmine and Mama, the one who'd never hurt them.

"How long?" Michael asked.

She scrambled to remember what they were talking about.

"How long did he starve you?"

"Three days. And he only fed me then because I promised to try harder to be the daughter he wanted."

That brought raised eyebrows. "Did you? Try harder?"

"I am here, not there, so I think not. I only said it because I knew I would need strength. I can go without food—I have fasted longer than three days. But I would not have the endurance to escape if I didn't eat."

"Wise."

"I can be, if I try very, very hard."

At that, Michael smiled. "You survived. I'd say you did something right." He lifted her hand and kissed her fingertips. "Whatever it takes to stay alive—that's what you need to do." The amusement faded from his expression. He lowered their joined hands and settled them back on her knee. "Which means you need to trust me. If I tell you to do something, you need to do it, without question."

"But—"

"Even if I'm wrong. Even if you think you know better. Hesitation could get us all killed. And sometimes, I know things you don't."

"You could just tell me those things."

"There's not always time."

Like at the hospital. The cameras.

She considered how to respond. Because, the truth was, she could agree to jump when he said to jump. She could. She just knew herself well enough to know that, when the time came, her stubborn feet wouldn't leave the ground.

"I've never been good at that," she finally said.

"Learn. Fast."

She bristled at the command but clamped her lips closed.

Baby steps.

They didn't have time for baby steps, though.

In the backseat, Jasmine gasped. "Pull over." She lowered her window and stuck her head into the cool breeze. "Hurry. Please."

≈

After they got back on the road, Leila twisted to check on her sister.

Jasmine had rested her head in the corner between the backrest and the cool pane of glass, her legs stretched out on the seat beside her. Michael had given her a sweatshirt from his pack, which she'd laid over herself like a blanket.

If Leila wasn't mistaken, her twin had already fallen back asleep after their short stop—just long enough for Jasmine to lean out of the truck and vomit.

Again.

"How is she?"

Leila watched for a reaction from her sister, but Jasmine didn't move.

She faced forward again. "Sleeping, I think."

In his pack, Michael had also found a plastic bag she could use if she got sick again. Not that he minded stopping, he'd been quick to say, but once the sun rose, it would be better if they could remain in the car behind the tinted windows. Out of sight.

The sun was already glowing on the horizon behind them.

Maybe the lemon juice Jasmine had added to her bottle of water would help. Splat had brought a small container, which was almost empty. She swore the bitter juice settled her stomach.

"Any idea what's wrong with her?" he asked.

"Whenever I ask, she says it's nothing."

"How long has she been dealing with it?"

Leila shrugged, not that Michael could see. But her sister wouldn't talk about it.

He took her hand again, squeezing gently. "Has she seen a doctor?"

"I don't know. I don't know anything. Only that..." She was afraid to voice the fears rising inside her. But keeping them inside would give them more power, not less. Fears were like cockroaches—they thrived in darkness. "It was stomach cancer."

Michael's quick intake of breath had Leila hurrying to add, "Mama's cancer. Not... I'm not saying that's what Jasmine has, only that it scares me. Because, what if she does? I mean, I just got her back. I cannot..." She pressed her lips closed, but the emotion she was trying to hide leaked from her eyes.

"Was your mother sick to her stomach like your sister is?"

"I wasn't there. I don't know."

"But your sister was. Does she think—?"

"We haven't spent enough time together. I had only seen her twice before you came, and both times we had to keep the visits short. We didn't want Baba to know she had discovered me. When I ask her, she tells me—"

"It's nothing."

"Right."

"Well, as soon as we get you to the States, we'll take her to my dad. If he can't figure out what's wrong, he'll find someone who can."

Whoa. What?

"The States? We are going to America?"

He shot her a look. "If that's okay. I mean, we don't have to, but I think you'll be safer there, farther from your father and—"

"Yes, yes. I would like... I have tried many times to get a visa, but it is impossible. You really think you can get us into America?"

"I'm pretty sure." His lips tipped up at the corner. Not amusement, though, because his eyes didn't seem to agree.

America.

Her heartbeat quickened. The land of freedom and opportunity, where she could build a new life—without looking over her shoulder, waiting for her father or Waleed or one of Hasan's men to snatch her and yank her back to Iraq.

America.

Where she would be safe, able to attend church wherever she wanted without fear. Without having to explain herself to Muslim refugees who judged her for eschewing Islam for true worship.

"I would like that." Her voice cracked, and her cheeks heated with embarrassment. For Michael, this was nothing, to go to America. But for her, it was...it was life-altering. It was future- and family-altering. It was...so much.

Now, he turned her direction, and the smile he gave her was genuine. "I'm not sure it's everything you're expecting, but the people are kind and welcoming. Most of them, anyway. I can't wait for you to meet my family."

"They will like me, you think? My family is not like yours. Maybe they won't like who I come from." Because in her country, a person's heritage defined who they were. Good people came from good, respectable families.

People who did not come from good and respectable families were not trusted. Not given responsibility. Not able to marry well.

Germany had been different. She hadn't felt judged by her heritage but by her work. Because she was a hard worker, competent and devoted to the hotel she managed, she was accepted and respected. Mostly.

What was the benchmark in America? Was it work? Or money? Or fame?

Would she be judged well? Or scorned?

"Will you tell me about your family?" Michael's words were spoken casually, but she wasn't fooled.

"I have told you much."

"I need to know your father's name and the names of the people trying to find you."

"I will tell you when Jasmine and I are safe."

"Why not now?"

"Why do you not tell me who you really are?"

He shot a look her way. "For your safety."

"And yours, I think." She gave him a moment to correct her, but he didn't. "If they catch us, they will demand to know what we told you. They will use methods to make sure we tell them everything. It would be better if we could honestly say we'd told you nothing."

He nodded slowly, rubbing his lips together. "That makes sense." He sent a small smile her way. "You are not them. You're not your father or your uncle or any of the people he associates with. My parents and brothers will accept you for who you are."

Maybe.

But she'd encountered racism in Germany. Not dissimilar, she assumed, to the racism in Iraq, only in Iraq, she belonged to the acceptable race.

What about America? Some said they hated Arabs, but most Arabs she heard of who'd gone there were happy. Even so, she couldn't put away her fear.

"I am not white. Will they reject me because of that?"

It would be one thing if she were pale, but she was dark like her father. Much, much darker than Michael.

"Whenever talk of race would come up when I was a kid," Michael said, "my parents would tell us that there are only two races. Seed of Adam and Seed of Christ." He lifted her hand and held it to his chest. "You, sweetheart, are in the family of God, which makes you Seed of Christ. Regardless of the color of your skin, you and I *are* the same race."

Could that be true?

Seed of Adam. Seed of Christ.

She'd never thought of it in such simple terms. "Your parents are wise, I think. They are in Maryland?"

The pleasure on Michael's face slipped away. He dropped

her hand to his thigh. Opened his mouth, closed it again. Finally, he said, "I have a lot to tell you. When we're safe."

Which meant...no. Not in Maryland. He'd lied to her about that too.

She tried to pull her hand away, but he held on. "I know I have a lot to explain, but please believe me when I tell you that I had no choice."

"You are a spy, yes? Some sort of secret agent. Like...like Double Oh Seven or Jason Bourne?"

"I promise, I'll tell you everything. But the things that matter, Leila—what I believe, who I am as a person? Those things are true. You know what matters."

She hoped so. She dearly hoped so, because she cared very deeply for the man she thought he was.

She loved him. She could no longer deny that. But what if it was all a lie?

"It also doesn't change how I feel about you," Michael added. "That isn't going to change no matter where we are. No matter what I learn about you or your family. You've been keeping secrets too. But I know *you*, Leila. I trust *you*."

"Even after all of this? Seeing where I come from, you still—?"

"None of that changes who you are."

"Even though I never do what you say and argue with all your plans?"

"Even then."

She didn't know everything about him. But she knew he was kind and gentle. She knew he was heroic and strong and brave. She knew he loved God and was devoted to Him. She could trust him, even if all the things he'd told her weren't true.

"Speaking of your father," Michael said.

Not that they had been, but she didn't say so.

"You said he hit your mother in front of an audience. Did he do things like that when others weren't around?"

"Only when there was an audience. He was more patient when it was just us. He had a temper, but also sometimes, I think he was putting on a show to gain or retain the respect of men. Don't misunderstand. Baba did expect obedience, and if we didn't obey, there were consequences. But he rarely struck us unless someone was watching. It was as if he had to prove something. Last week, he was very angry, but he didn't strike me, only refused to feed me."

"*Only*? As if that's nothing?"

"There are no bruises. It could have been worse."

Michael's jaw clenched.

In the year she'd known this man, she'd come to recognize his facial expressions, but this deep anger, contained but not hidden, as if he were fighting very hard to rein it in—she'd never seen that in Munich. Now, he worked his jaw, mastering his emotions. When the anger dissipated, he continued in an even voice.

"It's interesting that your father doesn't feel"—Michael seemed to grope for a word, finally settling on—"secure in his own skin, as if he has to be something he isn't. Did you get that sense from him?"

She hadn't seen it that way when she was a child, but in retrospect, Michael's assessment seemed true. "It is like he is one person but pretends to be another. He wishes to be a loving husband and father—and a harsh one, when others are looking." She remembered the man she'd once adored. "It is like his job. Baba worked for the government, and he was successful under Saddam Hussein. I was only a little girl, but I thought Baba liked and respected our leader. When the Americans came and Saddam was deposed, we celebrated like everyone else. And then Baba worked for the new government, and he was successful there too. He was happy to put Jasmine and me in the international school, proud that we could speak English and were friends with powerful people.

"But his brother hated Americans, and when he stayed with us, he and Baba would talk for hours about the evil imperialists and how to get them out of the country. Baba would agree with everything. The next day, he would go to work and smile and do his job, mingling with Americans and Europeans and other foreigners. It was like he lived on both sides."

"A fence-sitter," Michael said.

She considered the odd phrase. "What is that, fence-sitter?"

"Oh, just... You know, somebody who doesn't want to commit to one side or the other, so he sits on the fence in between."

"It feels shameful to say, but that is Baba, I think."

"It may be his shame, Leila, but it's not yours. You are definitely *not* the fence-sitting type."

She smiled at the compliment, wishing there wasn't a console between them, wishing she could cuddle up beside him. Maybe she didn't know Michael's real job, but she knew him. She knew who he was.

"I heard a story about a guy like that." Michael's words rumbled, low and soothing. "When he was young, the Lord invited him into His family. But Satan came, too, and told him he'd be happier on his side. The man considered both arguments carefully and decided, after much thought, to choose neither. 'I don't need God or Satan to live a good life,' he said. 'I'll make myself happy and do what I want.'"

Leila had met many such people, those who pretended it didn't matter what they believed. Those who only believed in themselves. Many talked the talk of religion, but it was only talk.

"He lived his life balancing on the fence," Michael said, "never falling to one side or the other. And he was right—he had a good life. He had children and grandchildren. He was prosperous and successful.

"On his deathbed, he congratulated himself for his cleverness, believing he'd outwitted both the devil and God. But when he closed his eyes for the last time, expecting an eternity of peace, he was surprised to find Satan waiting for him, a sinister smile on his face. 'You belong to me now.'

"The man argued. 'No, I never chose you. I stayed on the fence.'

"'Ah,' Satan said. 'You don't understand. I own the fence.'"

Michael's story ended on that note, the fictional man slipping into eternity apart from God.

That would be Baba's future if he didn't repent. And, knowing what she did about her father, he never would. Because of him, Mama had probably never considered Christ either.

"Sorry." Michael spoke into the silence. "I'm not saying your father is that man. It was just a story."

"But he is. He is that man, always trying to be everything to everyone but not really believing anything." She'd seen her father at the call to prayer. In public, he would go down on his knees and perform the ritual. At home, she'd caught him more than once ignoring it. "Even Allah didn't matter to him," she said. "Though Baba claims to serve him, his service is obligation, not worship. It's the reason it was easy for me to reject Islam. Because my father doesn't really believe."

"Huh." The single syllable didn't reveal what Michael was thinking, but his expression was quizzical. After a moment, he said, "If he isn't a true believer, then..." The words trailed. "Do you know...?" He didn't seem to know how to articulate what he was trying to ask. Finally, he said, "Do you know how he found you?"

"No."

"Do you think he'd been looking for you?"

"Once I got out of Iraq, it would be very difficult for him to track me down. He has contacts outside the country, but none, I think, who would help him find me and drag me back. Perhaps Qasim or..." She pinched her lips closed before her uncle's name escaped. When they were free, she would tell Michael all of it.

Even the parts she'd never told anyone.

"Perhaps my uncle wanted me brought back. I don't believe Baba would have tried very hard. Not unless he was pressured or made to feel like he had failed. Perhaps because I had brought him shame, he would try to find me to restore his reputation."

"Do you think, deep down, he wanted you to be free?"

"I think my father worries for himself more than for me. I thought, once I left Iraq, I would be safe."

"I'm sorry you weren't."

A few miles passed in silence, the smooth hum of the engine and the grumbling of the tires on the road lulling her to sleep.

And then she was gripping a wall, her fingers shoved into narrow spaces, her toes on a thin ledge.

She slipped.

And fell.

And jerked awake.

"Hey, hey." Michael squeezed her hand. "You okay?"

"A nightmare."

"You were only asleep for five minutes. What was it about?"

"I was falling. But I remembered something." Not just the futile escape from her room but what she'd seen in the office. "I don't know how he found me or how someone did, but maybe they were doing something else and saw me. Maybe it was an accident. Or maybe...maybe it was the opposite. They knew I was there, and that's what the map was for."

"You lost me. What are we talking about?"

"Yes. Sorry. I climbed out the window in the compound and crept to the next room."

"Wait. You did what?"

"It was fine. The walls were rough stone. I had handholds."

"Fine?" His voice was too loud in the quiet cab. He lowered it and added, "You were on the third floor. If you'd fallen..."

"You came in the same window I went out. How did you get there?"

"It's different. I'm trained. Why didn't you wait for me?"

"It was before Yasamin came. Before she called you. I was trying to escape."

"You could've killed yourself."

"Better dead than married off to some cruel man."

"Married?" Again, his voice rose. "Married to whom?"

Waleed's face filled her vision, that hungry smile. "It doesn't matter now. I would have died before I married him."

By the look on Michael's face, it did matter—very much.

"I am here and alive," she said. "And not married."

He nodded, one quick dip of his head. "Go on."

"The room next to mine was an office, and there was a map on the desk. Of Munich. I thought maybe it was what they used to track me down, but there were things circled. Intersections downtown, in the business district."

The hotel where she'd worked and lived was farther north, on the opposite side of the river.

Michael became very still beside her. His face blanked, but in his eyes, she saw something she didn't recognize.

Something...frightening.

"Do you remember what intersections?" he finally asked.

She closed her eyes and tried to imagine the map in her head. She'd seen the park and the river, a few of the street names. "I only looked at it for a second."

He must have heard something in her voice because he asked, "But?"

"Maybe, if I saw another map, I could remember." She slipped her hand out of his to reach for his phone, but he slid his fingers around her wrist.

"Not right now. We'll get a paper map, one similar to what you were looking at. I think your memory might be more accurate that way. If you try to look at the map on that tiny screen, I'm afraid you'll contaminate the memory."

"Is it important?"

"It might be. It might be very important."

A chill that matched his tone dripped down her spine.

CHAPTER TWENTY-FIVE

MICHAEL LIMPED along the walkway between the park and the coastline, shopping bags looped over one arm, the other hand leaning on a cane.

While annoying, the pebble in his shoe made the limp realistic and consistent. The cane added to the deception.

The makeup he wore—and the gray hair beneath a beat-up fishing cap—didn't hurt.

To all the world, he looked like an old man. In fact, he looked like his grandfather, albeit about four inches too tall.

Nobody gave him a second glance.

He'd been to the resort town of Antalya once before, though he hadn't had time to linger then either. This was one place he wouldn't mind staying awhile. The coastal city in Turkey was as beautiful as any Greek tourist spot he'd ever seen. Lush, green landscape rolling to meet the deep, deep blue of the Mediterranean. Mountains rose on the western horizon beyond the water, adding depth to the breathtaking view.

It was a clear, sunny day, surprisingly warm for October and more humid than Michael had anticipated. Though there were no clouds on the horizon, he inhaled the faintest scent of rain and wondered if there was a storm somewhere off the coast, just out of sight.

People wandered past in all manner of clothing—jeans, shorts, T-shirts. Some women wore abayas and hijabs, some men keffiyehs. But most seemed to be European tourists.

Hardly anyone gave the stooped old man a second glance.

After driving all night and most of the day, Michael, Leila, and Jasmine had arrived the afternoon before. They'd checked into adjoining rooms in a mid-priced hotel and had dinner delivered. The sisters had retired early, though he'd heard them talking quietly for an hour or so through the slightly ajar door.

Now that they had some time alone together where they were safe, he hoped Leila could get some answers about her sister's condition.

In the privacy of his room, he'd opened the laptop he stole from the terrorist's car. Locked, of course. He couldn't get past the password.

But his cousin could.

She picked up on the first ring. "Alyssa Wright."

"It's Michael."

"Burner phone?"

"Long story. Can you help me break into a laptop?"

"Whose is it?"

"Long story."

"Aren't they all?" When he didn't explain, she asked, "Don't you have people who can do that sort of thing?"

"They're not speaking to me at the moment."

"The people, or the whole...? What's going on? Are you in some sort of trouble?"

"Can you help me, or can't you?"

There was a long pause. He pictured her—tall, redheaded like her mother, the freckles squished together on her nose as she contemplated demanding more information. Knowing he'd never give it—never did.

He pulled Alyssa in when he didn't want to use CIA resources, which happened when he was working on his own—as he'd done with Sam and Eliza. And when he was breaking the rules.

Which he did too often.

Finally, Alyssa said, "PC? Mac?"

"It's a Mac, a pro, I think."

"Figures. Can you bring it by? I need to plug something—"

"I'm not in the States. I need to see what's on it now." When he didn't have an audience. Because once he hit US soil, the excrement would certainly hit the climate control device. The more information he had to share, the less messy and smelly the whole thing would be.

"Is there a USB port?" she asked.

He checked. "No, just one of those skinny—"

"You'll need a flash drive and a dongle. Any chance you have those?"

"I can get them."

"Fine. I'll email you a script. When you connect the flash drive, the script should do its magic. You have an email address for me?"

He gave her his private one, the one the CIA didn't have access to.

And yeah, it said a lot about him that he had a secret email address. Just like he'd had a secret girlfriend. And secret resources in the form of his super-secret hacker cousin.

And now he was on a secret—from the Agency—mission.

Which explained why it was inevitable that he'd eventually end up in trouble.

He really needed to examine his life choices.

"I'll have it to you in an hour," Alyssa said.

"Thanks, cuz. I owe you one."

That got a laugh. "Just one? I'll put it on your tab."

That morning before he'd left the hotel, he'd knocked on the unlocked door separating his room from the twins' and, when he got no response, peeked in—just to make sure Leila and Jasmine were there. He figured Jasmine would be, but he wouldn't put it past his girlfriend to go out for coffee or croissants, even though he'd expressly told her not to leave the safety of the room.

Probably should have *asked,* not *told.* He'd work on that. Hopefully, she'd work on not pushing back on his every...suggestion? Fine, order.

He could practically hear his mother's voice.

You order your girlfriend around? No wonder you haven't given me grandchildren.

If Mom knew enough about Michael's life to make the statement, at least she'd say it with a smile.

But Michael hadn't told his family about Leila. He'd become so accustomed to keeping secrets, he'd started keeping them even when they didn't matter.

Leila and Jasmine had still been sound asleep.

He'd left a note on the dresser closest to the door, suggesting they order breakfast from room service (translation: stay put) and promising to be back soon.

Not wanting to risk driving the pickup any farther, he'd rented a beat-up hatchback that might actually make it all the way to the northwest corner of the country.

After that, he'd stopped at a bazaar—a bizarre bazaar, considering how chaotic the place was, but he'd found almost everything he needed. It'd taken a few more stops to get the rest.

His burner phone rang, and he read the number, then looked around to confirm there was nobody within earshot. "Thanks for calling back."

"I'd have picked up last night, but...whose number is this?"

Derrick, Michael's youngest brother, sounded as happy-go-lucky as always.

"Long story." Michael had called the night before, then again this morning. Well, morning for him, but... "What time is it where you are?"

"It's about four."

"What are you doing up so early?"

"A flight. What's up?"

Michael's heart sank. "Are you out of town, or—?"

"I'm home. Just walked in the door and headed to bed. Your message said to call any time. You need something?"

"Any chance you can fly into Turkey?"

"Uh... Say that again? I think I heard you wrong."

"I need a ride. From Antalya."

"You're in *Turkey*?" Now, Derrick's pitch rose. "What are you doing—?"

"It's important. We need a ride out of here ASAP. Can you, or can't you?"

"Does this have anything to do with why you were acting so weird at the party?"

"I wasn't acting weird. I was fine."

"You were distant and distracted, and then you took off without a word."

Michael picked up a faint tapping in the background.

"Not that anybody else noticed," Derrick added, his voice taking on a dreamy tone. "But you know me, always watching you, trying to emulate your awesomeness. I can't help it. I idolize you."

"Whatever, idiot." Michael felt the grin as he hobbled toward the hotel. "Can you or not?"

The tapping stopped. "I'm serious, bro. What's going on?"

Michael didn't answer, just let his request hang in the miles between them.

After a minute, Derrick said, "You'll tell me soon?"

"Yeah." Not that he wanted to share his secret with another brother, but...

Actually, he did.

He hated hiding the most important thing about his life. Hated that nobody in his family—except Sam, after they'd spent so much time together a few weeks earlier—knew what Michael really did for a living.

"According to this," Derrick said, "the Turkish government needs at least forty-eight hours' notice before they'll give permission for a private plane to land. This forum I'm on, though... Looks like people wait a lot longer than that for clearance. I'm seeing suggestions that people apply a month in advance. Unless you wanna wait a month—"

"What about Mytilene?"

"Greece? Hold on." More tapping, then, "Yeah, I can do that."

"How soon?"

"Assuming I can get a copilot, tomorrow?"

Yes! Except... "Do you have to have a copilot?"

"It's four thousand miles, bro. Even if it wasn't the law, which it is—and I don't exactly want to lose my license—nobody in his right mind would try to fly that far without a copilot."

Which made sense, even if it increased their exposure. "I guess that'll—"

"Wait," Derrick said, "You said '*We* need a ride.' Who's we?"

"There'll be three of us. I'll explain everything when I see you." Well, maybe not *everything*. "Your copilot needs to be discreet."

"I'll ask Bryan. He's been bugging me to let him come along more."

What? "*Our* Bryan?" Michael's second-youngest brother worked at Bowdoin. He wasn't a pilot.

"He got his license awhile back. He's been helping me out."

"Did he quit his job?"

"Of course not. But it's not like professors work that hard. They get their TAs to do all the hard stuff."

Bryan would probably have something to say about Derrick's assessment of his career.

"He'll do it. Tomorrow works?"

"Yup. Gives us time to get there."

"You'll be safe till then?"

"Sure, no problem." He just had to figure out how to get Leila and her twin across the Med to the island of Lesvos, where the city of Mytilene housed a small airport. "This needs to stay between you and me. Meaning, don't tell anybody you're coming to get me. Don't even tell them where you're going. Not Mom and Dad, not our brothers, not even Bryan, not until we're on your plane. And not strangers. Definitely not strangers."

"I don't fly without filing a flight plan."

"But do you *have* to?"

"Not technically, but—"

"Then don't. Please. You can reach me on this line. If—"

"Should I have a codename? Maverick. You can call me Maverick."

"I'll call you Moron, like always."

"Ha. That would make you Putz."

Michael couldn't help smiling at the *Grumpy Old Men* reference. If Derrick could see him in his geriatric disguise, he'd roll over laughing.

"Oh," Michael said, back to business, "could you get your hands on a paper map of Munich?"

That earned a long pause. "Ever heard of GPS?"

"Can you order one off Amazon? Or go to a travel agency?"

By the time this was over, he was going to owe Derrick a lot more than the cost of a map. "We need it on the plane, if you can."

"Anything else, Your Highness? Tibetan sea salts to soak your feet? Peruvian pumice stones? A venti macchiato from Starbucks?"

He wouldn't say no to the last suggestion. "Let me know your ETA. We'll do our best to beat you to Mytilene, but we might not."

"Hey, bro?" All amusement leached from Derrick's voice. "Be careful. Mom and Dad don't need any more heartache."

"Always am. See you tomorrow." He ended the call and slid the phone back into his pocket.

Getting his little brother to fly his Cessna to Greece—that was the easy part. Telling Leila the plan...

Better hurry and rip off that Band-Aid.

A few minutes later, Michael let himself into his hotel room, closed and locked the door, and toed off his shoes, leaving the annoying pebble inside. Unfortunately, he'd need it again.

One thing he liked about Antalya—the prices. At less than a hundred bucks a night, he hadn't had high hopes for this place. Turned out to be a pretty fancy hotel, practically brand new, all modern and shiny with tile floors and lightly stained woodwork —nothing to distract from the view beyond the sliding glass doors and narrow balcony. From his sixth-floor room, he could see for miles. Sandy beaches, a marina, a few boats, some whizzing past, some meandering. Parasailing tourists drifted by.

Not a bad place to rest after driving all night. Before that, sleeping on a lumpy sofa in a dingy apartment in Baghdad. And in a crate.

And before that, collapsing in a cave, just lucky he didn't bleed out in his sleep.

Speaking of...

He hit the restroom, lifted his old-man style button-down plaid shirt, and removed the gauze he'd applied that morning after his shower. The stab wound was healing. He dabbed on more antibacterial ointment. There was no puffy red skin indicating an infection, and he wanted it to stay that way. He protected the wound with fresh gauze and wrapped the bandage around it again.

The injury hardly hurt, as long as he took ibuprofen every four hours.

He knocked a couple of tablets back now, washing them down with tap water.

Back in the bedroom, he plugged the flash drive he'd bought into his laptop, loaded it with the script Alyssa had sent, and shoved it into the port on the terrorist's laptop.

The light flickered, so it was doing something. Hopefully, eventually, it would give him access.

He knocked on the door to the sisters' room.

It swung open. At the sight of him, Jasmine gasped and backed away.

Whoops.

"It's me." He lifted his hands in the universal sign of *not gonna hurt you.* "It's Michael. Sorry."

Leila walked toward him from the far side of the room.

Both women studied him through narrowed eyes—like a lab specimen. Which made sense, considering he looked like an eighty-year-old man.

"Michael?" Leila said. "How did you...?"

He pulled off the hat and wig and rumpled his short hair. "Sorry. I should've warned you."

Jasmine backed up enough for him to step in.

He did and held out a shopping bag, which Jasmine took. "We need to leave soon. I have disguises for both of you." To Jasmine, he said, "Put on the skinny jeans and graphic T-shirt."

She peeked in the bag. "I am to be...what?"

"You're small enough to pass for an adolescent boy."

The women were still wearing the T-shirts and shorts they'd had on since they left Baghdad. They might not like the disguises he'd chosen for them, but at least the clothes would be clean.

To Leila he said, "You'll also wear jeans, but looser to make you look bigger than you are, along with a sweatshirt. I've got you shoes with lifts to give you a little more height. You also have a wig cap and wig."

"How will I be dressed?"

"Like your sister's older brother."

"I will pass for a man?"

"When I'm done with your makeup, you will. You two eaten?"

Leila nodded, her eyes narrowed. "What are we doing?"

He really didn't want to tell her. "Do you trust me?"

"I told you I did. I also told you I like to know the plan."

He took a breath. Braced for impact.

"They're going to be looking for us at the border." And not just Leila's father's men, either.

After calling the hospital and checking on Splat—he'd survived the night, and his prognosis was good—Michael had called the embassy in Baghdad to tell them where Splat was.

The embassy would send someone to check on him. And they'd run it up the chain, flagging Michael's name, which would alert Brock.

"What are we going to do?" Leila crossed her arms, preparing for bad news. Maybe she guessed because there really was only one way out now.

"Splat's recovering," he said. Avoiding the question.

"Oh, good." Her shoulders relaxed the slightest bit. "Thank God."

"Yeah." He took a breath and blurted it out. "We have to go to Lesvos—"

"No!" Her arms came down while her voice ramped up. "Are you crazy? On a boat? Do you know how many die crossing the sea?"

"It's just four miles. I've gotten you this—?"

"I do not swim." Leila grasped her sister's hand. "We do not swim. If we land in the water, we will drown."

They didn't know how to swim? He hadn't realized... "You'll have life jackets—"

"They stuff newspaper in the life jackets!"

Her words were practically shrill, her terror zinging through him. He'd known she'd be opposed, but he hadn't expected this.

"They do not care if we die. Don't you understand? The rafts *sink*. The so-called life jackets *sink*! Even if the people can swim or float, some are in the water for days. Others are discovered and pushed back to Turkey. And before that, the smugglers steal everything. They take and take."

He hated that she spoke from experience. She hadn't gone to Europe via Lesvos the first time she'd escaped Iraq, but she'd still had to depend on smugglers to get her there. He stepped toward her. "Did they? When you were traveling? Did they—?"

"They took everything. But this is not about that. We cannot. We will not."

"Sweetheart." He reached for her, but she backed away, bumping into the bed but not sitting.

Standing her ground.

"I am not going in the water. No."

"If there were any other way—"

"No. We are not going."

"You have a plan B?" He hadn't meant to raise his voice. But he didn't lower it. "Because I've been over this and over it, and there's no other way."

"We sneak across the border. We go over the mountains like I did last time."

"We'd have to go on foot. You think Jasmine can walk that far?" He flicked a gaze at the other twin, who'd slumped in a chair. Making his point. "I can have you in the US in forty-eight hours. How long did your way take? Weeks?"

Leila's gaze flicked around the room as if there might be a solution hovering just out of sight. "We cannot swim." Her voice was low, filled with fear.

"You don't have to swim."

"We will go in the water, and we will drown."

"You really think I'd let that happen? After everything?"

"I think...I think you are doing your best."

Which apparently wasn't good enough for her highness.

Fury sparked inside him. He turned, marched back into his own room, and slammed the door. It didn't latch, though, just bounced off the jamb. Stupid door.

Leila pushed it open. "You don't understand what the smugglers are like. You don't understand—"

"*You* don't understand." Did she really think he'd let some smuggler swindle them? Did she really think one would dare? He was strong and intimidating. He had weapons. Did he really seem so inept to her?

He could buy functional life jackets. He could pilot a boat. It was only four miles from the coast of Turkey to Lesvos. People made the trip every day. Yeah, smugglers couldn't always be trusted, but...

But what?

But smugglers would be too intimidated by him to give him a lousy boat?

Maybe. Maybe not, but even if they did, he'd be able to tell. He could demand better. But at what cost—in money, in time? In Jasmine and Leila's well-being?

He'd seen videos of boats dead in the water, their engines lifeless.

Others simply leaked out air until they sank.

He'd seen a movie about two Syrian teenagers. When their boat had started to sink because it was overloaded with refugees, they got out and swam to Lesvos.

Was Michael really going to subject Leila and Jasmine to that?

He sat on the side of the bed and dropped his head into his hands.

Wisdom, Lord. Please.

He couldn't exactly drag them through the water to the island, even if they did have life jackets on. If they couldn't swim, and if the boat sank or the engine died, then they'd be in trouble.

Dead in the water.

Maybe picked up by authorities.

They had to get to Lesvos. Being caught in Turkey would get him taken into custody and the women sent home to Iraq or to a refugee camp, assuming the men chasing them didn't find them first.

Whatever happened if they were caught, they would not be sent on the first flight to the States.

He had to face facts.

His plan wasn't going to work.

Leila sat beside him, hip to hip. She took his hand. "I am not trying to be difficult."

"I know." His voice was even. "Let me think."

The water route was the safest way. The only way, really. Except it meant he'd have to trust smugglers who made millions by profiting off refugees desperate to get to Europe. Smugglers who never had to answer to the souls lost, the bodies that sank to the bottom of the sea.

Smugglers who wouldn't care if their boat was seen by the authorities.

It was only four miles, though. Four miles.

He could swim it, for crying out loud.

"No smugglers." He looked at Leila, then at Jasmine, standing in the doorway.

The quieter sister said nothing, but by her terrified expression, she might as well have been shouting.

"Lesvos is the only way." He stood and nodded to his bed.

Jasmine took his spot while he paced, considering the problem. There was a solution, a rather obvious one.

"I'll buy a boat. How much more could it cost than what smugglers will demand?" It would probably cost less than passage for three people, now that he thought about it.

"But can you drive it?" Leila asked. "Do you know how?"

At that, he smiled. "My parents own a second home on an island in the Atlantic. I spent a lot of my childhood on boats. I'm pretty sure I can handle a four-mile trek across the Med."

The sisters looked at each other, then spoke in rapid Arabic.

"We must go," Jasmine said.

"But what if one of us falls in?" Leila still didn't sound happy. "Have you learned to swim?"

As if Michael wouldn't get them life jackets. But he said nothing, just listened.

Apparently, neither had ever so much as donned a bathing suit.

Leila was afraid of water after falling into the Tigris once when she was a child.

Jasmine remembered it well. She'd been terrified for her twin.

They went back and forth for another minute before he lost his patience. "You remember I speak Arabic, right?" He said the words in their language.

They both looked at him, blinking.

He sighed, then shifted to English. "If you're coming with me, this is how we're doing it. I promise not to let anybody drown." He'd storm out again, but this was his room. Instead, he bent to put his shoes back on, pebble firmly in place beneath the ball of his foot. "I'm going out to buy a raft." Hopefully, he'd be able to fit the thing in his tiny rental. If not, he'd return to the rental car company.

He was going to be bankrupt by the time this trip was over. Hopefully, he wouldn't be bankrupt and unemployed.

"Change your clothes," he said. "When you're ready, I'll do your makeup." He'd hated that stupid disguise class at the Farm. He was thankful for it now. "And then we're leaving." When he stood, he considered walking out, letting his commands stand.

But he really wasn't a tyrant. So he smiled and added, "Does that work?"

"Do we have a choice?" Leila asked.

He tried very hard not to let his frustration show. "You don't have to come with me." As if he'd leave them. If they refused, he'd have to drug them and carry them, *A-Team* style.

Yeah, right.

If they refused, Michael would be trekking over the border into Bulgaria, keeping the twins alive not across four miles of water but across hundreds of miles of rough terrain.

Assuming Derrick could land in Bulgaria. And who knew if he could?

Assuming they didn't get caught at the border, which they almost certainly would.

"I've already arranged for my brother to pick us up in Mytilene. You remember I told you about Derrick?" She nodded, so he added, "He'll take us back to America."

She straightened as if the thought of it infused her with courage.

"Private jet," Michael added. "Not a bad way to travel."

Leila swallowed. "We will have life jackets?"

"Obviously." He couldn't quite keep the frustration out of his voice.

Jasmine stood. "I will change and work on the wig." To Leila, she said, "Come, sister. He has gotten us this far."

Instead of following Jasmine back into their room, Leila stepped close to Michael, right into his personal space. She tipped her head back and reached up, sliding a hand around his neck.

Whatever anger he held onto dissipated at her touch. He bent and pressed a kiss to her lips, a light one because they did have to go. And Jasmine was standing right there. And he needed to stay focused.

"I'm sorry for my fear." Leila stepped back but kept a hand on his chest. "Thank you for listening to me."

"Sure." His voice sounded husky and deep and, wow, she could change the direction of his thoughts in a fraction of a second. He cleared his throat. "Next time, let's try to come to an agreement without all the yelling."

She smiled and followed her sister toward their room but stopped in the doorway and turned back. "Next time, come with a suggestion instead of a command, and we'll see what happens."

The door closed behind her.

Life with Leila was anything but dull.

～

Michael purchased an inflatable raft, a motor, a motor mount, a fuel container, and three life jackets. The items barely fit in the back of the rented hatchback.

Finally finished gathering all they'd need, Michael navigated to the hotel a little more than an hour after he'd left.

Because Michael had spoken to the station chief in Baghdad, Brock would know to look for him in Turkey. The longer Michael kept up radio silence with his team leader, the worse things would go for him once he was back in the States. If he reached out now, maybe Brock would listen to reason.

Deciding it was worth a try, he dialed.

"Brock here."

The only member of their team without a call sign—because the man rarely left the safety of his office.

"It's Wrong."

"Where are you?" The words were terse and angry.

"Trying to get out of Turkey."

"March yourself to the nearest consulate, and I'll get you out."

"I don't think so." Michael was careful to keep sarcasm out of his voice. "I rescued Leila and her sister, and I'll be bringing them to the US as soon as possible."

"Where they'll promptly be taken into custody."

"For what? Being kidnapped? Held against their will? That's against the law now?"

"Do you know who her father is?" Michael didn't, but Brock's tone told him he did, giving him an advantage.

"I know who Leila is, and I know she is not her father, or her family."

"You don't know anything," Brock snapped. "Her father is Saad Farad Fayad."

The name floated only a moment before landing on the proper peg in Michael's mind.

Fayad had worked for Saddam and then the new government.

Which tracked with what Leila had told him. He was the fence-sitter. But now that Michael had a name, he could picture the face. And remember what the Agency knew about him, along with what they'd suspected.

A man who looked like Fayad had been seen with top Al Qaida leaders—including bin Laden—in the years leading up to the attacks on September 11. After that, the same person had been seen with other terrorist leaders.

But that person couldn't have been Fayad because those sightings had occurred when Fayad was in Baghdad.

The counterterrorist experts had assumed it was a brother or a close relative, but Saad Fayad was an only child, and though he had cousins, none looked enough like him to be mistaken for him.

Agents in Baghdad had tested Fayad's loyalty, letting slip information to see if it was passed along.

Those secrets never got back to Al Qaida or, years later, to ISIL, the terrorist organization that had grown after the fall of Al Qaida in Iraq.

The powers-that-be in the Agency and in Baghdad had decided the man they'd seen through grainy satellite images had been Fayad's doppelgänger.

Even so, the Iraqi man had never been trusted, which had stunted his career with the new government—and maybe led to his early retirement. Based on Leila's description of her father, the Agency had been right to mistrust him.

Was Leila's father a terrorist?

And then an inconsistency rose to the top.

Leila had talked about an uncle, her father's brother.

But Saad Farad Fayad was an only child.

Apparently not.

A fact he would tell Brock, eventually. When he had more information.

"You didn't know." Brock's words were smug, the tone of a man who thought he had everything figured out.

"She promised to tell me everything when she's safe." Michael was careful to keep his tone even. "She's afraid, rightfully so, that her father and his men are going to catch up with her again. She wants to be able to honestly say she didn't tell me anything."

"Or there's a much simpler reason. It's time for you to face facts, Wrong. Your girlfriend is a terrorist."

"My girlfriend was being held in a locked third-story room in a compound in the middle of the Iraqi desert."

"How did you find her?"

He knew where Brock was going with this but answered truthfully anyway. "Her sister contacted me."

"Meaning they knew you were coming. Meaning they could have put her in that locked room to convince you—"

"She's not a terrorist. And she has information. Information you want."

"I am quite sure of that."

The man's arrogance set Michael's teeth on edge. "Leila saw a map of Munich in an office with some markings on it. As soon as I can get ahold of a similar map, I'm going to have her try to remember where the markings were. This is what we've been looking for. We knew Vortex was up to something in Germany. Now we'll be able to figure out where. And once I get the women out of Turkey, I can question them more thoroughly, find out what else they know. Leila's twin was trapped at that compound for a long time. It's possible she heard something that can help."

"All the more reason for you to come clean about your whereabouts. Maybe you can still walk away from this."

Going against orders might get him fired from the CIA, but it wasn't against the law. Neither was traveling to Iraq. Sure, he'd broken laws in-country, but Brock couldn't prosecute him for those.

But if Brock suspected him of conspiring with terrorists, he'd be taken into custody and questioned.

Leila and Jasmine would be too.

Michael had to protect them from that.

Somehow, he had to prove the women were on the right side of this battle. And he had to do it before Brock caught up with them.

"I have a name for Vortex."

The tension between them ramped up, nearly palpable across the miles.

"Where'd you get it?"

"Leila told me."

"What is it?"

He was tempted to keep it to himself, but lives were at stake. "Khalid Qasim. He's an old friend of her father's and a relative of her best friend. His family owns the compound where she was being held."

"We'll check it out," Brock said. "The longer you remain AWOL, the worse this is going to be for you."

"Considering you put me on leave yourself, I'm not AWOL. What did you expect me to do?"

"Tell your team what's going on, that's what I expected." The words were cold, angry. "Because you are part of a *team*, remember? A team that could've gotten in and out of Iraq in a matter of hours."

"You would've sent the team in?" Michael couldn't help the disbelief in his voice.

"We'll never know because you didn't give me a chance, just

went off on your own. From the looks of the so-called *friend* you dumped at that hospital—"

"I didn't dump him—"

"You could've gotten yourself and Splat killed. All because you don't trust us—me—enough to do what's best."

"Why would I? You think Leila is a terrorist."

"We'd have gotten her out. And questioned her, yeah. But if she's innocent, we'd have figured that out too. We'd have a lot more information now than you've managed to get."

Michael couldn't argue with his team leader's logic. Maybe he should've told Brock what he'd learned, let him send in the team.

If only he'd been certain Brock would. But if he hadn't, Leila would still be a captive. Jasmine, too. And they still wouldn't know who Vortex was.

He'd done what seemed best at the time, and so far, it'd worked out.

"This is why I didn't want you on my team," Brock said. "If not for your relationship with the White House, you'd be on some nothing assignment somewhere."

Michael clamped his mouth shut. Brock was wrong—Michael hoped, anyway—but arguing wouldn't help his cause.

"But there's no way you're slithering out of this one," Brock said, "even if you are friends with the chief of staff's son."

It always came back to his friendship with Travis Price. Michael wasn't sure if Brock envied it or if he really believed all of Michael's advancement had come because of Travis.

It hadn't, though. Michael was good at what he did. "I'm not trying to slither out of anything. I'm trying to keep my girlfriend safe."

"Right. What was it last time? Oh, yeah. Your brother's girlfriend—"

"His wife. And son. And about twenty other innocent women and children who were saved because—"

"How many laws did you and your team of merry men break that time? All of you would be in prison if not for Price."

That might be true. Travis had made a call, and the local sheriff hadn't charged any of them. Which they shouldn't have, considering Michael, his brothers, and some hired bodyguards had saved a lot of lives. "You'd have left them to die? To burn to death?"

"That's not the point." The tight tone of his voice told Michael he'd hit his target. "You're a lone ranger. No matter what happens when we catch up with you, you'll be off my team."

Michael cringed at the threat.

He hadn't wanted the assignment because he wasn't much for working with a team—that was true. But since he'd joined, he'd come to like the camaraderie. He liked knowing teammates had his back.

Except he didn't really believe it. If he did, he wouldn't be stuck in Turkey, alone, with no team members to help him out.

Brock wasn't wrong to want him gone. The fact burned like acid in his throat.

"Are you going to go to the consulate or not?" Brock demanded.

"I'll contact you when we're safe." Michael ended the call.

And tossed the burner phone out the window.

CHAPTER TWENTY-SIX

LEILA WAS SEATED on the edge of the bed in Michael's hotel room wearing the ugly clothes he'd bought her. The pants and sweatshirt were baggy and made her look chubby. Wearing the wig cap—it was already making her head ache—she looked ridiculous.

Her hair hidden, her makeup off, wearing the most horrible clothes imaginable, she felt vulnerable in a way she couldn't explain. As if her makeup and long hair were shields, and now that those shields were gone, everything she'd ever wanted to hide was scattered all around her, exposed, waiting to be picked up, studied. Judged.

Michael, who was setting all manner of tubes and powders and brushes on the bedside table, glanced at her, then looked again. "You okay?"

"Why wouldn't I be?" She hated her defensive tone. She hated more that she felt the need to defend herself.

But he grinned. "I'm not sure I have the skill for this. All this time, I thought you were just really good at makeup, but I was wrong. You have the most striking eyes."

And just like that, her defenses slid away. Michael was on her side. Why would she doubt him?

He went back to his pastes and powders. "What's your sister doing?"

"Resting."

"How is she?"

"Sick. You will make me look like a man?"

He chose a bottle and faced her. "Don't worry. You'll still be pretty."

Her cheeks warmed. It was silly that she cared.

He tipped her head up and rubbed something thick and pasty beneath her cheekbones. "I know you don't want to, but it's time for you to tell me everything about your family."

She ducked away. "When you tell me everything, I will do the same."

His eyebrows rose. "Will you?"

The way he said it, like a dare, had her ire rising. "Why do I have to share my secrets if you don't have to share yours?"

"Because I saved your life. More than once."

There was that, and she should let it go. But... "If we were not dating, that would be a good answer. We *are*, right? Together."

"I've made my feelings clear, Leila."

"Yes. As have I. So do I not have the right to ask what you really do for a living? And don't tell me you're a salesman."

"Tip your head back and close your eyes."

"Are you a spy?"

"Do what I ask, please."

"Fine." She did. With her eyes closed, she said, "Well?"

The soft edge of a sponge, cold with some product, dabbed her cheeks, her nose.

"Technically, I work for the CIA."

Her eyes popped open.

He was leaning close, just inches separating their faces. "Eyes closed, sweetheart."

The CIA. The American intelligence-gathering organization had been whispered about in Baghdad. People attached to the embassy were said to be CIA spies.

Not enemies of the new government but of people like Qasim and Hasan and Waleed, who hated all Americans, claiming they were enemies of Islam.

And the CIA, according to them, was the enemy's most powerful weapon.

She'd guessed that about Michael, but she hadn't really believed it. She certainly hadn't expected him to confirm it. "So...yes? A spy?"

"An agent."

She opened her eyes again. "What's the difference?"

He backed up, a makeup sponge in one hand, a bottle of what looked like foundation in the other. It was such a strange sight, this tough, dangerous man holding makeup. He held her eye contact, though she had the feeling he was forcing himself to do it. After a moment, he shrugged.

"It's a matter of semantics. Eyes."

Again, she closed them.

Semantics? She searched her memory but didn't know the meaning of that word. Before she could ask, he explained.

"It just means, you know, tomato, to-mah-to. You say spy. I say agent."

She didn't know what tomatoes had to do with it. Usually, talking to Michael wasn't so confusing. "But they are the same?"

"You could say so."

So, yes. A spy.

Her boyfriend was a spy.

"What do you mean by saying you *technically* work for them?"

"I'm attached to a covert group that operates outside normal CIA operations. We're assigned to special projects. I don't answer to the higher-ups in the CIA but to...someone else."

She heard the bottle being set on the wood. Then he was tapping her jaw with a fat brush.

"Who?" she asked.

When he didn't answer, she opened her eyes.

"Next question."

"You won't say?" she asked.

"I can't say."

"Why not?"

"It's a secret, Leila. Agents—"

"Spies."

"—have to keep secrets." He went back to...whatever he'd been doing on her jaw and chin. "It's the nature of the beast."

"What beast? The CIA is the beast?"

His grin stretched. "Just an expression. It means the normal course of certain...things. Like"—he looked around the space—"like working at fancy hotels involves dealing with people from all walks of life, right? It's the nature of the beast."

"I see. So being a CIA spy involves lying. That's the nature—"

"Not lying." His voice was cold. "Agents have to keep *secrets*."

"But you did lie. You told me you're a machine parts salesman."

"Eyes."

She sighed and closed them, though she wanted to watch his expression.

He jabbed at her brows. "I am a salesman."

She didn't respond to the obvious untruth, just lifted her eyebrows.

"Keep still. Please." After a moment, he added, "It's my

cover. I sell parts to factories, mostly in Germany, Poland, and the Czech Republic. I have customers. They buy actual parts which get delivered and installed on actual machines. It's the truth."

"But not the whole truth, which makes it a lie." He was tapping under her eyes, so she forced herself to keep them closed.

"Okay, *Nawra*. Let's talk about lies."

"I did not lie. I changed my name because I had no choice."

"You could have told me the truth."

She leaned away so she could watch his reaction. "Like you told me the truth, Michael Davis?"

He cringed.

She'd guessed the name was another lie. "Is it even Michael?"

"Yes, of course." But he looked away. "Davis is an alias. To protect the people I love."

The words were sharp and hit their mark.

"Not from you," he said quickly. "That's not..." He held his hands out, palms up, probably forgetting the makeup brush between his fingers. "I'm sorry. I'm sorry I couldn't tell you the truth. I wanted to. I planned to on our last date. Remember? We were coming back from Kitzbühel, and I told you I needed to tell you something?"

"But you didn't."

He brushed a hand down her cheek, the touch tender, then leaned in and resumed his work. "You spent the last half hour of our date on the phone."

"Because of a broken pipe. It was my job—"

"I know." He set the brush down and grabbed a different one, which he dabbed in blush. "The point is, I was going to tell you on the mountain, but we were having such a good day, and I didn't want to ruin it." He added the color to her cheeks, her forehead, the tip of her nose. "I was afraid you'd be angry—and you'd have a right to be. But I did plan to tell you before I dropped you off. Maybe not everything, but...some of it."

It seemed he expected her to accept without question that he would continue to keep secrets. "Do you mind if I ask why you decided to become a spy?"

"Agent," he corrected. After a long moment, he sighed. "It wasn't my plan. I wanted to serve my country and planned to join the Navy after college, but the CIA recruited me."

"It is good to serve. But to be a spy seems like a strange profession. Why were you drawn to it?"

He perched on the opposite bed. "When I was a teenager, I started hanging out with a bunch of boys. They were older, but they accepted me. They planned a prank one day."

"What is a prank?"

"A practical joke. Like, to trick somebody for fun."

That wasn't always fun for the person being tricked, but she didn't say so, just nodded for him to continue.

"They were going to break into the house of a girl one of the guys liked. At least, I thought Gary liked her. They told me they were going to break in, and he was going to leave a note in her room when her family was out for the evening. Looking back, I realize how creepy that is. But I was fourteen and the guys were older and I wanted them to like me. My job was to keep an eye on the road and let them know if anybody came. Like an idiot, I agreed to do it. I had no idea what they were really going to do.

"I was watching the road when the guys came running. Gary was laughing, but it was almost maniacal."

Leila hated to interrupt the story, but she said, "I do not know this word, maniacal."

"Out of control...and there was a hint of danger in it. That laugh gave me a very bad feeling about what they'd done—what

I'd helped them do. We were about to get in Gary's car when I smelled smoke."

"Oh, no."

"I don't think Gary planned to tell me, but the other two guys were mad. They were shouting at me to get in the car, and then they were shouting at him. Asking him why he did it. And I figured out that he set the girl's bed on fire."

"She wasn't home?"

"The house was empty, thank God. Gary threatened me, telling me to get in the car and keep my mouth shut. The other guys were yelling at him. All I could think about was that house, that poor family about to lose everything. We were way out in the woods, miles from town, and I was afraid the house would burn all the way to the ground before anybody even knew there was a fire. So I ran into the woods. I didn't know what I was going to do, but I wasn't getting back in that car with them.

"Gary followed me, but I was fast. After a few minutes, he gave up. I think he was scared of getting caught near the house, and they didn't think I'd tell on them."

Leila could picture the scene, a teenage Michael in the woods all alone while a house burned. "What did you do?"

"I thought about going back and trying to put the fire out, but I was afraid I wouldn't be able to do it. There was another house about a half mile away. I ran there and told the people what happened. They reported it. When the police came, I told them everything."

"Your friends must've hated you."

"They weren't *friends*. Friends don't make each other accessories to felonies."

"It was brave of you to go against them. Is that why you went to the CIA? To protect people? But you could have done that in the military, no?"

"Because I alerted the neighbor, the house was saved. I was

lauded as a hero. People acted like I'd done this huge act of bravery when, the truth was, I should never have been there in the first place. I shouldn't have helped them break into a house. I shouldn't have been friends with those guys at all. They were popular, sure, but Gary had a mean streak. In retrospect, it was more than that. He landed in juvenile detention—jail for kids—because of what happened that day. The other two guys straightened up, but Gary never did. Last I heard, he was in prison."

Leila knew too many men fueled by power and cruelty.

"It was worse than that, though," Michael said. "When I became friends with Gary and the others, I quit hanging out with Sam, who'd been my best friend all my life. But I made one good decision that night and was treated like a hero. I didn't deserve it."

Leila considered everything he'd said—and hadn't said. "You joined the CIA so you could be a hero, and nobody would ever know?"

He dipped his head from side to side. "I think that was part of the motivation. It wasn't completely altruistic, though." Before she could ask, he added, "Without selfish motives. The CIA sounded like an adventure, and I always craved adventure."

"Which is how you ended up with those boys in the first place, no?"

"Probably."

"Has it been the adventure you hoped?"

He grinned. "The last week has provided all the adventure I'll ever need." His grin faded. "I like what I do, but I am tired of the secrets. I'm sorry I didn't tell you the truth about myself. Can you forgive me?"

"What is your real last name?"

"I'm doing everything in my power to protect you. You

know that, right?" When she nodded, he said, "Telling you that could put my family in danger."

"You will tell me eventually?"

"When we're on US soil."

She could accept that. "Is there anything else?"

He licked his lips. "I did grow up near the ocean. My family does have property on an island off the coast. The things I told you about them are true. I have five brothers. My father is a physician. My mother teaches Bible studies at our church, volunteers at the food bank, and takes care of the house. Just like I told you."

She could feel it coming, so she prompted him with, "But?"

"But we didn't grow up in Maryland. I'm from New England."

Oh. She pictured a map of the US. New England was in the top right corner. Not a state but a group of states. "Where exactly?"

"I'll tell you, I promise."

But not now.

"It is cold there?"

"Not so different from Munich. It's beautiful. You're going to love it."

"I will see it? We will go there?"

"That's the goal. I'll tell you everything about my past, and anything I don't share, I'm sure my brothers and parents will fill in when we get home." The thought seemed to amuse him because he smiled.

The idea that she was going to meet his family had her nerves zinging. Would they like her?

Of all the things to fear, that seemed like the smallest. If this relationship with Michael was meant to be more, then it would be. She wouldn't allow herself to worry about what she couldn't control.

Michael's smile faded. "Now that we've covered my secrets, it's time to talk about yours."

And all the other fears rose again.

~

Leila braced herself for Michael's questions.

"Secrets are a part of my job," he said. "I've told you things about myself and my past that aren't true, and I've explained why. You can forgive me or not forgive me. I'm just telling you that I had reasons for being dishonest about my history. I was trying to protect my family. You understand that, right?"

"Yes."

"You lied to me about your family as well. Can you tell me why?"

She had a feeling he was expecting a much more interesting answer than she was about to give, but that was an easy question. "Before you asked me out, I had not dated."

He stood and grabbed a wig—short brown-and-gray curly hair. "Since you arrived in Germany?"

"Not ever."

His eyebrows hiked. "Ever?"

"I was not permitted when I lived with my father, and then there was the long journey out of Iraq and all the time spent in refugee camps. Other people dated and found...comfort, I think. But I saw too often those relationships torn apart when one would get a visa and the other wouldn't. Or one would leave Germany and the other would stay. After abandoning my family, my heart was already broken. I did not wish to expose it to more pain."

Michael plopped the wig on her head and adjusted it, then added a knit cap. When he had it like he wanted it, he slid a pair of black-rimmed glasses onto her face, then sat on the bed opposite her. "Go on."

"When I was in Germany and finally given a visa, I had no money and no idea what to do or where to go. I got a job cleaning at a hotel and worked many hours, just to survive. At church, I met a Christian couple, Iraqi refugees who have reached many Muslims with the truth of Jesus.

"They helped me find a place to live and get settled. They assisted me in applying for scholarships. I received one and attended college, which was a great blessing. But though my tuition was paid, I still had to work to survive—to eat and pay my rent. Between that and church and helping refugees, there was no time for dating. Even if there had been, nobody was interested in me, until I met you." Her cheeks warmed.

"That's very hard to believe," he said. "I mean you're..." He gestured toward her, then chuckled. "Usually gorgeous."

"I am not still gorgeous?" She infused her words with shock, and his grin broadened.

"Go look."

She walked into the bathroom and started at the face in the mirror.

It was a man's face.

She touched her jaw, surprised when the place that looked covered in whiskers was smooth.

"Don't touch." Michael stood in the open door.

She dropped her hand. "They teach you this in CIA school?"

"The goal is to change every descriptor you can. Instead of a woman with long, silky black hair, now you're a man with curly brown hair. Instead of being five feet tall in heels—"

"I am taller than that. Almost five-one."

He grinned. "I'll put lifts in your shoes, and you'll look five-two or...almost five-three." He added that last bit like it was funny. "Still short for a man, but believable."

She gave herself a long look, then batted her eyes at Michael. "You do not think I'm beautiful?"

"You are beautiful inside and out. Mostly, right now, inside." He took her hand and led her back to where they'd been seated. Once she perched on one bed, he leaned against the other. "I was interested, and I guess you were too because you agreed to date me. But you didn't tell me the truth about yourself. I still don't know why."

"I have told you about my friend Sophia before, yes?" At his nod, she continued. "Sophia has volunteered with refugees for years and has seen the way many are harmed or targeted. I heard stories, too, but it's easy to forget, to trust men with handsome faces and pretty words.

"Sophia told me to never tell strangers, certainly not men, that I was alone. There are people who prey on those who have no family, who have nobody who will care if they disappear. Or if they live or die. Like you, I had a story I told to strangers, a story about parents who expected to hear from me every day and would search for me if I didn't contact them. I didn't lie because I was hiding something terrible. I was trying to protect myself from being a victim."

"We've been dating since January. Did you really not trust me enough, even after all that time, to be honest?"

"What is that expression about the teapot and the...other pot? They are both the same, yes?"

He laughed. "The pot calling the kettle black?"

"It is not so easy, after you have lied, to be honest. I think this is something you understand?"

"I wanted to tell you the truth."

"I wanted to tell *you* the truth," she said. "But I was afraid you would not understand. Perhaps you feared the same?"

One short nod, and then, "What's your full name?" Before she answered, he added, "The name your parents gave you."

The thought of telling him raised anxiety inside her. "If I tell you, and if they catch me again—"

"I'll do everything I can to protect you. The more I know, the safer you'll be."

Perhaps. But what if, after she told him who she was, he no longer wanted to protect her? What if the information changed how he felt about her?

Asking the questions would raise his suspicions.

So she said nothing.

"You still doubt me, Leila?" His words were laced with surprise—and hurt. "After everything?"

"No. Not you. I am only saying..." She swallowed and looked away, ashamed to admit what she'd been thinking. "I am afraid. Afraid they will capture me..." If Waleed captured her, he would demand to know everything she'd shared.

She wanted to be able to honestly tell him she didn't betray her family. It would go better for her if she could. But...only by degrees. Because if Waleed caught up with her, her only relief would come in death.

"Okay then." Michael's words brought her back from that dark, frightening place. He licked his lips, then pressed them together until they turned white. "Wright. Michael Wright. My name is Michael Wright. Now, if they capture you, I have as much to lose as you do."

"I did not expect... I will try to forget, Michael *Davis*. I am Nawra Saad Fayad."

He didn't look surprised at all.

"You knew?"

"Called Brock earlier. He did his homework."

"Then why did you make me tell you?"

"I wanted you to confirm."

"Brock is...?"

"My team leader. I was hoping he'd get us out of here, but that's not going to work out. I'm confused, though. Our intel tells us Saad Farad Fayad—that's your father, right?" She nodded, and he continued. "Our intel tells us he doesn't have a brother, but you said..."

His words trailed.

He looked from her to the door separating his room from Jasmine's and back. A moment passed, and then he said, "They're twins?"

She had been warned never to say this.

It had been ingrained in her from childhood to never tell anybody.

But Michael already knew. If Waleed captured her, her life would be over. Why should she be loyal to the father who would give her to such a man?

Why should she be loyal to the uncle who'd had her kidnapped and imprisoned? What kind of misplaced devotion was that?

She straightened her shoulders. "His name is Hasan."

"Hasan Farad Fayad?"

"No." She swallowed, looked away. This was hard. It shouldn't be, but it was.

She appreciated that Michael didn't press, just waited, watching.

"He has always been a secret in our family, one my sister and I were warned never to tell. To do so feels like a betrayal. But I owe them nothing." She straightened her shoulders. She could do this. She would. "My uncle is Hasan Mahmoud."

Michael's eyes widened. He shuttered the expression, but she'd seen the shock.

Obviously, he'd heard of Hasan. Her uncle was a terrible,

terrible man. He had known bin Laden. He had worked with the leaders of the worst terrorist organization in the world.

"I don't understand," Michael said. "All our intelligence tells us your father is an only child. How did that slip by us? How are there no records of his existence?"

"Hasan wishes to be invisible. I don't know how he did it, but I wouldn't be surprised if he destroyed records and perhaps threatened people who knew the truth about him."

"As an adult, yeah, but when he was a kid? How could he possibly have orchestrated that? There's no record of him where your father went to school or university."

"I don't know the whole story." Leila had only heard whispers over the years about Hasan as a child, and none of them had been good. "In Islam, twins are considered a gift from Allah, but my grandmother said that Hasan was a curse, that he was..." She couldn't think of the word. "I think maybe... instable?"

"Unstable," he corrected. "You mean...mentally ill?"

She dipped her head side to side. "Bibi—my grandmother—told Mama a story once, that my father as a boy had been feeding a stray dog and had become attached to it. In our culture, dogs are unclean, but Baba liked them. Later, when Yasamin and I were girls in Baghdad, he would feed strays, even though Mama wouldn't let them in the house. There was a litter of puppies once." She could still remember the fluffy little balls of fur. "They were very lovable. We begged Mama and Baba to keep one. I believe Baba would have, but it was not done."

Michael didn't look amused. "Your father fed stray dogs but denied you food for days?"

She shrugged, unable to explain.

"Go on."

"When Baba and Hasan were boys. Baba became attached

to a stray dog. He loved it and wanted to keep it. Hasan killed it."

Michael straightened, the shock slight but unmistakable. "Did your grandmother know why? Was the animal dangerous or diseased?"

"No, I don't think so. Mama suggested perhaps Hasan had been jealous, but Bibi said it was only cruelty. She was afraid of him. Afraid he would harm Baba. So she and my grandfather sent Hasan away."

"This was their mother, yes?" At her nod, he asked, "To where?"

"I think a family friend, though I don't know more than that. Baba and Hasan were not raised together after that. Baba went to school in Baghdad. Hasan...I do not know."

"Do you know how old they were when that happened?"

"Maybe nine or ten?"

Michael's face was blank, but she got the impression he was trying not to react. "They're close now? Your dad and your uncle?"

"They were before I left, a decade ago. Now? Jasmine will know, I think."

"When did Hasan come back into your father's life?"

"I don't remember a time Hasan wasn't part of our lives. He visited more when I was a teen than when I was young. We saw him every month the last few years I lived in Baghdad. Before that, maybe a few times a year."

"Did your grandparents try to keep them apart?"

"If they did, they failed. Which is not surprising. They are not only brothers but twins. There is a connection, one that defies distance."

She'd felt a chasm in herself after she left Jasmine in Iraq. A few moments with her sister and the chasm was gone. Even though they had lived drastically different lives for a decade, they were twins, and the connection didn't fade.

She doubted Baba and Hasan's had, either.

"So Hasan was in your life, but you weren't supposed to tell anybody about him."

"He always arrived at night, always unexpectedly, and if someone came to visit when he was there, he would stay out of sight. He usually wore a thobe and would cover his face with a keffiyeh."

A thobe—the long robe-like garment many men in her culture donned—wasn't unusual, nor was the keffiyeh, or head scarf.

But to cover his face—that was unusual. Effective in hiding his identity.

"If he was seen in Baghdad by someone who mistook him for Baba, he would not correct the assumption. There were times they would tell funny stories about being seen by the same person on the same day, but in different clothes. They would laugh about people's confusion."

"Nobody ever put it together?"

"Who would assume there was a hidden twin?"

"Do you know where Hasan lives?"

"I do not."

"What can you tell me about him?"

Just thinking about her uncle had anxiety bubbling in her stomach. "He is not...normal. He is charming, I think, to those who don't know him. But even in kindness, there is cruelty about him."

Michael held her gaze as if searching for a lie. "Did he ever hurt you or your sister?"

"Nothing like that. When he was with us, it was like...like he brought a darkness with him. I think Baba would have let us live our lives as we chose, if not for Hasan. When Mama told me not to tell anyone that I'd become a Christian, it wasn't Baba she feared, but Hasan. He is the younger brother by a few minutes, but in his cruelty and anger, he is more powerful. When my grandfather was alive, he had some sway over Hasan. But he died many years ago."

"Did you see Hasan in the last few weeks? Was he at the compound?"

"The afternoon before you came, Hasan and Waleed arrived."

"Waleed?" Michael asked.

He still wore the makeup that made him look like an old man, but she saw past that now. He was just Michael, the man she'd known and trusted for nine months.

"Waleed... Shehab?" he asked.

How did Michael know?

He must've seen her surprise because his eyes sparked with anger. "He was the man who tried to take you? The one who shot Splat? How do you know him?"

"How do *you* know him?"

"You first."

"He is my uncle's... I don't know what to call him. Assistant, maybe. Waleed thinks everything my uncle does is good and worthy, and because he feels this way, my uncle thinks he is also good and worthy."

"Waleed's a sycophant."

"What is...sycophant?"

"A flatterer. Someone who fawns on a superior, usually for selfish purposes."

"I think, yes. A sycophant." She repeated the word in her head to commit it to memory. "I don't know how Waleed met my uncle or what he does, only that he has been at his side for many years, since he left school, I think."

Michael tilted his head to one side. "Did you know him in school?"

She didn't know how Michael guessed that. "He attended where Jasmine and I went."

"You didn't like him." He must've seen that in her expression. "Why?"

"When I was eleven, there was a boy a year ahead of me. He was different, I think maybe with autism or...how do you say it? Maybe not fully autistic, but—"

"On the spectrum?"

"Yes. He was socially...not adept. Waleed and his friends started picking on him one day. They surrounded him and were pushing him between them, calling him names."

"Waleed was the same age as the boy?"

"He was six years older than I was, so five years older than the boy, and much bigger. Other kids just watched. I waited for somebody to stand up to him, but nobody did. I wanted to get a teacher, but there were none nearby. So I pushed my way into the middle of the circle and confronted him."

Michael didn't look shocked by that revelation. He looked angry.

"It was...very scary and very stupid." Leila pressed a hand to her stomach, remembering the moment. "I was afraid. But I didn't run. I stood between Waleed and the boy, stuck my hands on my hips, and looked up at him."

"Way up, I assume."

"He was tall, yes. And I was a child. I told him to leave the boy alone."

She could still hear Waleed's response. *Or what?* He'd been laughing, and his crowd of followers had too. *What are you going to do? Glare me to death?*

She explained that, adding, "I had no good answer. While I distracted Waleed, the boy ran away." She let a smile tug her lips up. "I said, 'What? Are you going to hurt a little girl?' I think he thought I'd cower. So I pressed on. 'I suppose someone like you is only strong enough to pick on small boys and little girls. Perhaps if you were a real man, eh?'"

"Oh, Leila." Michael dropped his head and shook it. "Please tell me you didn't say that."

"I was young. And not very wise. Waleed was no longer laughing."

"You had no way to defend yourself. You were completely vulnerable. You ever get into a situation like that again, be agreeable. Be compliant."

"I will not!"

"I'm not saying..." He sighed. "Fake it, sweetheart, until you find a way to defend yourself. Why egg on a bully if you can't beat him? Just...let him think he's won. Let him think you respect him. Get him to let his guard down. Meanwhile, find a way to fight back."

His words were wise. She wished she'd known Michael back then. Maybe she'd have learned to be wise too.

She could still see the look on Waleed's face in that schoolyard. He wasn't angry, but it wasn't a good look, either. "I didn't know what to call it at the time. When he looked at me like that, I was more afraid than I had been before. Thank God teachers pushed into the circle. One took me away, and it was over."

"Was it, though?" By Michael's tone, he doubted it.

"I tried to avoid him, but often I felt him watching me. I was very happy when he graduated."

"And then he got to know your uncle. Did you see him a lot after that?"

"Not again until I was sixteen or seventeen. He tried to make friends with me, but I was not interested."

"Friends?" Michael's old-man-bushy eyebrows hiked.

"I think more than friends."

"Mmm-hmm. You're an adult now. Can you go back and see the look on his face? Can you name it?"

"I would say maybe...hunger."

"Yeah. That's what I thought." Michael walked away, shaking his head.

She spoke to his back. "You are angry with me?"

"No. With me. I had him in my sights. He moved at the last second, and I missed." Michael paced in front of the window. "He's a terrorist. According to our intel, he was behind that bombing in Baghdad last year, the one that killed eight people, mostly Iraqis, and injured dozens more."

She hadn't known that, but she wasn't surprised.

"He and Vortex—Qasim—work together." Michael didn't seem to be asking her, just processing what he'd learned. "Qasim found you and brought you back. But Waleed's the one chasing you." He stopped pacing and returned to sit across from her. "Why? Why is he spending time and resources to get you back? Do you know something? Don't take this the wrong way, but why are you important enough for all this effort?"

She could see no good reason not to tell him the truth. Even so, the thought of it frightened her.

"Waleed." She took a breath and blew it out, bracing for Michael's reaction. "He is the man Baba planned for me to marry."

CHAPTER TWENTY-SEVEN

"LET'S TAKE A BREAK." Before Leila could respond, Michael stood and marched to the door and into the hallway. He had to get away.

To think.

He closed the door behind him and walked to the elevator, then thought better of that and headed for the staircase. He needed to burn off his pent-up rage.

The thought of Leila being forced to marry a terrorist—not just a terrorist, but *that* terrorist, a man who picked on the weak and vulnerable.

A man who'd looked at her with *hunger* when she was eleven years old.

A man who'd latched onto her uncle. A flatterer and flunky to a psychopath.

The night Michael had broken the women out of the compound, he'd heard the cultured voice of an educated man demanding that Nawra be returned. *She will be ready tomorrow. As planned.*

He'd wondered...ready for what?

Now he knew the answer.

A wedding.

He tried to shake off the fears. God had protected her, and Michael needed to focus on that. And on the information he'd learned.

The staircase was deserted, his footsteps echoing on the concrete walls as he jogged down.

How had Vortex—Qasim—found her to begin with? Michael had been watching the man for months. Had Qasim figured that out?

Had the hunter become the hunted? And if so, had Qasim found Leila because of her relationship with Michael? Had her location been the collateral damage of Michael's activities?

He didn't think so. He'd been trained well and was very good at what he did.

So maybe Qasim—or her father or uncle or Waleed—had somehow tracked her to Munich. Was that the reason for the map Leila had seen? Had they been looking for her, using the map in their quest?

That didn't make sense. If she'd been spotted, they'd know where. If they'd known the hotel where she lived and worked—which they obviously had, considering they'd snatched her outside of it—then there'd be no need for a paper map of the city except maybe to come up with a getaway route.

But their phones had GPS, just like everybody else's.

And anyway, the map had been laid out on the office desk weeks after she'd been snatched. So, it probably had nothing to do with Leila.

He shoved his way out of the stairwell into the small lobby, and then out into the bright sunshiny afternoon. As long as he was moving, trying to work off his anger—fine, fear—he might as well grab food. He walked to a corner restaurant, where he ordered a family-sized salad, three bowls of soup, an assortment of dolmas—meat and vegetables wrapped in grape leaves—and a köfte dish. He loved the spicy meatballs that were a specialty in Turkey.

By the time the friendly man behind the counter handed over his sacks of food, Michael's temper had cooled. A little.

As long as he didn't think about Waleed Shehab.

Leila was gone when he got back. He knocked on the door between the rooms. "I got lunch."

It opened, and Jasmine stood on the other side in the skinny jeans, graphic T-shirt, and zip-up hoodie he'd bought her, along with the wig cap.

"You hungry?" he asked.

"Not very." She turned to Leila, who was seated on her bed looking like a middle-aged man. "Sister?"

"A little, I guess."

"I'd like us to eat before we leave so we don't have to stop until we get to the coast." He carried the food into their room, where the three of them sat at a small table by the window. The food was good, perfectly spiced. While he ate, he checked the laptop, but Alyssa's script hadn't unlocked it yet.

As soon as Jasmine was finished, only a few minutes after she'd begun, he said, "Let me get your makeup on."

She stepped past him into his room, and he spoke to Leila. "Give us a few minutes."

He didn't miss the suspicious look she shot him as he closed the door. He was tempted to lock it, but that would make both sisters nervous.

He got Jasmine settled on the edge of the bed. "Mind if I ask you some questions?"

He'd expected fear, at least hesitation, but she barely reacted. "What do you want to know?"

An open-ended question indeed. He dabbed on paste to camouflage her high cheekbones. There wasn't a whole lot he planned to do with her face, but he needed to stretch their time out. "Your sister told me about Hasan and Waleed—what she knows about them, anyway. She's been gone a long time, though. I wondered what you could add about them—or about Qasim."

"They are evil men."

She seemed finished, as if she'd said it all.

"Can you tell me more about that?"

"Hasan is a madman. Waleed is his...I do not know how to say in English. He is...not a puppet. More like...imitator? He tries to be like Hasan."

"In what way?"

"He does whatever Hasan says. I think, if Hasan tell him to go two miles, he would go four. You see?"

"Like he's trying to impress him?"

"Maybe impress. Maybe outdo." She shrugged. "I do not wish to get into the minds of evil men."

"But you know a lot about them."

"Only what I saw."

He grabbed an eyebrow pencil. "Close your eyes." When she did, he asked, "Did they come to the compound often?"

"It is their...base. Where they make their plans."

"It's a family home?"

"Not our family." She leaned away, covering her mouth with her hand.

He knew that look. He backed up, and she rushed to the bathroom and vomited.

She was wasting away, and no matter how much he fed her, it wasn't getting better. He couldn't figure out how she could still walk, considering the lack of nutrients.

"There's some mouthwash in my dopp kit," he called.

A moment later, she returned and sat across from him. "Sorry. Thank you."

Her breath, spicy before, was minty now.

"Do you know why you're sick?"

"It is nothing." She didn't hold his eye contact. And by her tone, her evasiveness, he knew she was lying.

He thought about pressing the issue, but it wasn't as if he could cure her.

"You need some more lemon juice?"

"If it's no trouble."

He made a mental note to stop on their way out of town. "My father's a medical doctor." He worked on her eyebrows with a pencil, making them look darker, bushier. "When we get to the States, you can tell him what's going on, and he'll be able to help. He'll keep your confidence. Your secrets," he added, in case she didn't know what he meant.

She didn't react at all.

"Why were you there, at that compound?"

"I did not have a choice." Defensiveness tinged her response.

"I understand that." He changed tack, coming at the question from a different direction. "According to my research, the place is owned by Iyad Assad, your friend Heba's father—"

"Yes, yes. But Khalid is Heba's uncle, the brother of Heba's mother. They are family. The compound is where they stay and plan."

"Headquarters?" he suggested.

She mouthed the word silently, nodding.

"That explains why Qasim was there," he said, "and Waleed and Hasan, if they're working together. What I don't understand is why were *you* there?"

"I did not wish to be."

He smiled and sat back. "Let me rephrase. Why was your father there? Why did he take you there?"

One shoulder lifted and fell. "Once Mama died, her parents and sisters stopped speaking to Baba. They know who he is, who his people are. Who his brother is. They want nothing to do with him—or with me. My grandparents are gone. Baba has nobody but me and Hasan. I think Hasan wanted him nearby, and Baba was lonely. He didn't want to be alone."

"But you said it's Qasim's property. Hasan doesn't live there, right?"

Jasmine looked beyond him. It was meant to be a casual gesture, but her hands were clenched together, her knuckles white.

He was poking a nerve, causing her distress. He could sense that. He could sense that she wasn't being forthright with him. The problem was, he didn't know what nerve he'd pressed or why she was lying or what she was holding back.

"When Hasan is in Iraq," she finally said, "he is usually there."

But he wasn't usually in Iraq?

Her makeup was done, but she seemed more comfortable when her eyes were closed. He picked up a brush and dabbed some translucent powder on it. "Close your eyes." When she did, he brushed her skin with the soft bristles. "Was your father having financial troubles? Is that why he's living with Qasim?"

Her hands unclenched. So his guess was way off. "I do not think so."

Unsure where to go next, he asked, "What do you know about Khalid Qasim?"

Her eyes popped open. "Why do you ask?"

That reaction needed to be examined later. But he just shrugged and smoothed his expression. "He's the man who found Leila. Close your eyes."

She did, and said nothing.

"How well do you know him?"

"He owns the property where I live. I see him often. He is connected to Hasan."

True, true, and true. Yet she lied. He could sense it.

He backed up and grabbed the wig he'd bought for her—curly and brown, longer than Leila's and without the gray. He settled it on her head. They weren't good wigs but the cheap kind people wore to costume parties. If anybody touched them, it would be obvious they weren't touching real hair. He didn't intend to let anybody get that close.

He shifted it this way and that, ensuring it was straight. A guise to watch her reaction. "What are they planning?"

She shrugged.

"Anything you can tell me will help. You said they're evil. I want to stop them. Do you want to stop them?"

Emotions flickered across her face. Fear. Hope. Rage.

Rage?

"They work together," she said. "Qasim, Hasan, Waleed. What they do, I do not know." She waved a hand toward Michael as if to brush him off. "I am not involved."

He smiled, hoping the expression conveyed kindness. "I didn't think you were."

And yet her gaze fell away.

"Would you say Qasim works for Hasan, or Hasan works for Qasim, or are they equals?"

"I do not know."

"Do you know if they're planning something?"

She nodded, the movement slow but unmistakable.

"Can you tell me what?"

"Something in Europe."

"Something bigger than finding your sister?"

"Yes."

"Where in Europe?"

"I would guess Germany?" By her tone, she wasn't sure. "Qasim traveled there often."

"Just Qasim, or Hasan and Waleed as well?"

"I do not know."

"Where else did Qasim travel?"

"I do not know."

"Come on, Jasmine. You must've heard them mention something. Cities, countries—"

"Munich and Berlin. And London, though not as frequently. I heard them discuss Brussels. Waleed mentioned Amsterdam. So many places. But did they go there? Were they passing through? I do not know."

"What did they do in these places?"

"I only hear conversation as I serve them. Nothing important, no business. I am not invited to listen. Not to hear and certainly not to speak."

Bitterness tinged the words, plopping them like mud pies on the floor.

"If you *had* felt free to speak," he asked, "what would you have said?"

"What would it matter? He wouldn't listen to me."

He. Not they. *He.*

"Your father?" Was Saad Fayad more involved than Jasmine had led him to believe?

By the way she blanched, she hadn't been referring to her father but to one of the others.

"My opinion is irrelevant."

"I don't think so." Michael chose a soft tone, careful not to let it slip into patronizing. "Your opinion is relevant to me."

Her gaze flicked past him, and now only one emotion filled her eyes. Fear.

She was dying to get away. From him, right now. To run and hide.

He didn't say anything, but he didn't back off, either.

"They think they can force loyalty." The words came fast. "They do not understand the word. Worshipping a god who harms and then expects devotion is as irrational as men who think they can hurt people to get them to willingly follow. They are not good people. They are not like the Christians I have met, the people who risk their lives to tell others about the One True God. Allah is not like Jesus, who loves first, last, and always. Who is compassionate even when we fail. These men you asked me about—they follow a liar and live by lies. They are fools. *That* is my opinion, but I am *not* a fool, so my opinion stayed with me. Not that they asked. Or cared."

Those were the most words Jasmine had strung together in the entire time he'd known her.

He'd definitely hit a nerve.

"What are they planning, Jasmine?"

"I don't know."

"Guess."

"Something. Some...retribution." She gestured toward the window, toward the men they'd left behind. "It is about Iraqis, refugees. People who betrayed Allah."

"Iraqi Christians?"

"I do not know."

"How do you think they found your sister?"

"I do not know."

"What about your father?"

Jasmine's eyes narrowed. "What about him?"

"Is he involved?"

The door between the rooms—behind Jasmine—inched open, and Leila poked her head in.

Jasmine had no idea her sister was listening.

Michael was tempted to shoo Leila away, but that would only irritate her and silence Jasmine. Instead, he willed Jasmine to hurry and answer the question before her sister's presence distracted her. Or shut her up.

"Before Mama died," Jasmine said, "Baba went against Hasan, sometimes. Since then"—again, her hand flicked as if to brush away a fly—"he is weak."

Leila paused just inside the door, behind Jasmine.

Michael didn't glance her way. "Did you know your father was going to force Leila to marry Waleed?"

By the way Jasmine's jaw dropped, that was news to her. The expression shuttered quickly. "Hasan's idea. Baba..." She shook her head quickly. "Baba's promises died with Mama."

"What promises?"

Leila moved.

He didn't meet her eyes but lifted a finger to silence her.

But since when did Leila ever do anything he asked?

She stepped toward them. "Baba promised to not choose our husbands or force us to marry." She sat beside her sister on the bed and took her hand. "I'm glad we escaped before he could do it."

"Yes." Jasmine's closed-lipped smile lacked any trace of joy. "I am happy to be here with you."

"Leila, would you mind waiting in your room, please?" He phrased it like a question, but he needed her out.

"Why?"

"Because I asked you to."

"That is not—"

"Leila."

She turned to Jasmine, who said, "It is fine. We are fine."

Leila huffed and returned to the doorway. She stepped through, and the door closed.

But not fully.

She was listening.

Michael cursed the circumstances. He needed to get Jasmine alone to figure out why she was lying to him. Was she a terrorist? Had she been working with Hasan, Waleed, and Qasim?

By the disgust he'd seen in her expression and the vehemence he'd heard in her words, he guessed not, but some people were good at deceit.

The twins' father and uncle looked identical but were opposites, good and evil. Or at least *good-ish* and evil.

Was Jasmine the evil twin?

He let the idea float in his mind, but it wouldn't take root. If she was lying, she was very, very good at it.

"Leila saw a map in an office at the compound," he said.

Jasmine's lips showed true amusement, and he realized how seldom she smiled. "Yes, that is how I discovered she was there. I saw her scaling the wall like Spider-Man. It was quite something."

"I'm sure." Michael tried not to picture his petite, fragile girlfriend hanging from tiny handholds three stories up. "What are they planning in Munich?"

The door between the rooms inched open. He couldn't see Leila there, but he could sense her. He willed her to keep quiet.

Jasmine licked her lips. She looked terrified. "I do not know."

"Why are you lying to me?"

"I'm not—"

"You are. You're lying about this and other things."

From the corner of his eye, that door opened wider.

Stay there!

He issued the command in his head, not looking but feeling his girlfriend's anger.

"Yasamin." He used the name her parents had given her,

plucking an authoritative chord. "I risked my life to save yours. Because you let me believe you were your sister, I almost got killed. I had to send you two off on your own, and *you* could've gotten killed. All of this"—he gestured to the room, the country, the days since their escape from the compound—"all of it happened because you lied to me."

"Michael." Leila's tone was sharp.

He ignored her. "There's something you're not telling me, and I need to know what it is."

"I am not..." Jasmine's gaze flicked everywhere but at him. "It is nothing you need to know."

"I need to know everything."

"Michael!"

"Don't." He didn't spare Leila a look. "Either be quiet or get out. Jasmine, you can tell me the truth, or you can tell interrogators at a black site. Do you understand that? You'll be treated like a terrorist."

"I am not a terrorist!"

"Michael, stop it." Leila's voice was loud and demanding.

"Jasmine, tell me what you're hiding. What are they up to?"

"I don't know! I don't know anything! They never talked about anything when I was there. They didn't trust me." She slapped her hand over her mouth.

She'd probably vomit all over him, but he couldn't stop now.

"You know something, Jasmine. Tell me."

Her eyes were wide, and for an instant, he saw something there. Not just terror but resolve.

He willed her to speak.

But Leila was crossing the room.

His raised finger didn't stop her this time. "Don't!" he barked.

Jasmine blinked and turned to her sister.

"Stop it!" Leila grabbed Jasmine and pulled her to her feet.

Jasmine took the opportunity and fled to the bathroom, then slammed the door between them.

"What is wrong with you?" Leila demanded.

His frustration nearly boiled over.

He'd been so close. So close. Didn't she see that? Didn't she understand—?

"You will not talk to my sister again."

"I'm trying to protect her."

Which was true. Just not the whole truth.

Because he needed to know what she knew.

"You are making her out to be a terrorist." Leila's words, no longer loud, were low and seething. "You are acting like she is your enemy."

"For all we know," he said, matching her tone, "she is."

He expected Leila to snap at him, but she didn't. She stepped back. The look she gave him left a chill.

Jasmine came out of the bathroom, and Leila faced her. "Are you all right?"

She nodded, her gaze lowered to the floor.

"Go rest. I'll be in in a minute."

Jasmine hurried through the door and closed it behind her.

Michael glared at his girlfriend. "You should have stayed in your room. I was almost there."

"Yasamin is not your enemy."

"She knows things I don't know. She has information that I *need to know*."

Beneath the makeup, he saw the woman he loved. He saw the way her expression closed. The way her eyes hardened.

She barely moved, but there was a shift, a monumental shift.

A wall rising between them. No, not a wall. A wall, he could climb over or break down.

This was a chasm, dark and empty. And suddenly, he realized something he should have understood much, much sooner.

Something Brock and the rest of the team had likely guessed all along.

Michael could either be loyal to his country or loyal to this woman.

But, if Jasmine had been compromised, then he could not be loyal to both.

CHAPTER TWENTY-EIGHT

IN THE MIDNIGHT DARKNESS, Leila stared at a glow in the distance—the faintest light rising from the black horizon. Michael had told her those lights came from the city of Mytilene on the island of Lesvos. Their destination.

So far away.

Between here and there, deep and dangerous water. Crashing surf, loud and close, only heightened her fears.

Michael was below her on the steep, rocky shore. He'd already inflated the boat. He needed to attach the engine and add fuel.

Jasmine had walked away to find a place to relieve herself, though how she had anything inside her that didn't come back up, Leila didn't know.

It had been a long, uncomfortable ride from Antalya. Eight hours of tension, and there'd been no getting past it. With Jasmine in the car, it wasn't as if Leila and Michael had been able to talk privately. Even if they had, what was there to say?

Leila knew her sister wasn't a terrorist.

Michael suspected she was.

She'd heard whispers of the CIA's tactics. Everyone in Baghdad had heard those whispers.

Torture.

Was that the kind of man he was?

Surely not. Everything in her demanded she discard the idea out of hand.

But he was a spy. Was she a fool to believe in him?

He walked up the hill. Despite the darkness, she made out his shape and the hair of the ridiculous wig poking out beneath his hat.

They were all still disguised, but nobody was watching from the buildings that lined the water here. Not homes and hotels but shops, all closed for the night.

Michael reached her side and faced the water.

In a sudden wind gust, she clamped a hand onto the knit cap and wig to keep them from flying off. It was much cooler here than it'd been in Antalya. Leila wasn't sure if the climate was different or if the weather had shifted.

"My sister is not a terrorist. You need to stop treating her like she is."

"I'm only asking her questions." His voice was kind and gentle. Maybe because the man was. Maybe because he was very good at getting people to trust him.

She didn't know what to believe about him, and it didn't matter right now. He'd gotten them this far, and he was their only hope. So she tried to believe him. She needed to make him understand.

"I know Jasmine," Leila said. "If she knew what they were planning, she would tell us."

"You haven't seen your sister in a decade. Anything could've happened since then. She was alone, Leila. You weren't there."

His words stabbed, even if Michael hadn't meant them to.

"Your mother died," he said. "Jasmine had nobody but your

father and those men. People who are alone and lonely will do whatever they have to do to not feel alone, to connect. How do you know they didn't turn her against you? Against your faith? How do you know—?"

"I would know."

"Maybe." The word was barely audible above the water that seemed to be inching closer with every wave. "She's hiding something. This is what I do for a living, Leila. I read people. I ferret out their secrets. She's lying. And I think you know that."

Leila wanted to argue, but she'd gotten the same impression, that her sister was keeping secrets. "She is sick. I think there's a story, but that doesn't make her a terrorist."

"I have to know everything, including what's going on with her health."

Leila opened her mouth to argue, but Michel spoke over her.

"It *is* my business because she spent the last ten years of her life with terrorists. For all we know, she's sick because she's been in contact with some kind of a biological or chemical weapon."

"My sister would have nothing to do with that."

"Maybe. Maybe they're being built on the property. She could have brushed up against something and not realized what it was. The point is, I need to know." He turned and took Leila's hands.

The warmth of his touch, and his gaze, threatened to melt her guard.

"I love you, Leila."

Oh.

It was the first time he'd said those words to her.

Michael paused, perhaps expecting her to confess her own feelings.

She wanted to. But there was still so much she didn't understand. She wasn't sure anymore what they were.

When she said nothing, he continued. "I would not have risked my life and my career and my future to get you out of Iraq if I didn't love you. If everything I've done so far hasn't proved that to you, then I don't know what will. Your sister is an unknown. My love for you cannot blind me to the fact that she may be on the side of terrorists, and everything she's saying and everything she's doing is because of some larger plot."

The very idea of it seemed so outlandish that Leila nearly laughed. Sweet, innocent Yasamin, a terrorist?

Michael was a fool if he thought so.

But she didn't laugh.

Because Michael was deadly serious.

"Qasim, the man who owns the house where she lived, *is* a terrorist," he said. "He's also a brilliant tactician and strategist, and it's possible he's set this entire thing up for a purpose, for *his* purpose."

"They tried to stop us leaving. They shot at us."

"Yeah. And maybe we got away because God protected us. Maybe we got away because that was the plan all along."

"But they came after us. They were going to take us."

"I know. Which is why I tend to believe her."

"You should believe her. Jasmine could not do such a thing."

"I'm not saying you're wrong. I'm saying you have to trust me. I have to protect my country. And innocent lives. Whatever these terrorists are planning, it's going to involve death and destruction. It always does with Qasim. Do you know how many major terrorist attacks have been carried out in the US since September eleventh?"

She shook her head.

"None. There've been small ones, committed by home-grown terrorists, but nothing large scale. And it's not because the terrorists quit trying. It's because of men like me. It's because we're better than they are. *I'm* better, and I have to stay that way. And one way I do that is by not being ruled by my emotions. I love you. I hope you're right about your sister. But I'm not certain that you are. I will find out all Jasmine's secrets. If you can't accept that…"

His words trailed, and with them, her hopes. Her dream of America floated overhead and popped, proving to be as tenuous and flimsy as a soap bubble.

Just like her relationship with Michael.

Because if he forced her to choose between him and Jasmine…

She'd choose Jasmine. Her twin. Her other half. How could she not?

But if Jasmine was a terrorist…?

No. No, she wouldn't believe it. She couldn't.

Michael bent toward her. "Let's get to Lesvos and then talk about it again. And maybe, between now and then, you can get your sister to trust me."

Mention of Lesvos had her turning toward the distant island.

"See how close it is?"

Close?

They defined that word differently.

The Greek island was only four miles from the coast of Turkey—at the shortest distance. But that route would land them, Michael had explained, on the north side. They needed to head for the eastern edge of the island so they'd land between the city and the airport south of it. That route would also take them farther from the coast guard who, if they spotted them, would assume they were refugees and push them back into Turkish waters.

At least, that was Michael's reasoning. Not that he'd ever done this before.

The moon shone between the clouds, its light wavering and

inconsistent. Even so, Michael had promised he'd have no trouble navigating them to the island.

But the water looked menacing. Black and angry, reaching toward her as if to pull her in.

So different from the river that had almost killed her years before.

Different, but deadly.

She could still feel the warmth engulfing her, dragging her to the bottom. Her panic as she'd tried to claw her way to the surface. Knowing she'd never make it. Knowing the murky water would take her life. Her lungs nearly exploding in pain.

But her father grabbed her and pulled her up. Seeing the moment through the eyes of an adult, she understood that his anger had only been a mask for fear.

He'd told her to stay away from the river's edge. She'd defied him—and almost died for it. Maybe she should have learned to be an obedient daughter after that, but the only lesson she'd taken from the incident was to stay far, far away from water.

Michael squeezed her hand. "I'm not going to let anything happen to you."

"I know." She looked up at him and found him watching her, eyebrows lifted.

"Do you?"

"You have gotten us this far."

He kissed her forehead, the gesture tender and disarming. "I wish there were another way."

Jasmine returned, stepping to Leila's other side.

Michael let go of Leila's hand and grabbed one of the orange life jackets he'd purchased that morning. He dropped to the water and rested it on the surface. It floated, bobbing on the gentle waves. "See?"

"It will hold our weight?" She had to shout the question.

"An eagle could hold your weight." Grinning, he included Jasmine in the remark.

He was trying to be funny.

Leila tried to smile.

They both failed.

He sighed, put the wet life jacket over his own head, fastened it, and waded in. He plopped down and lifted his booted feet above the waves.

The life jacket kept him afloat.

"You believe me now?" he yelled.

She nodded, unable to speak for the fear clogging her throat.

Jasmine called, "Thank you." As frightened as she'd been before, and as demanding as Michael had been of her, Jasmine wasn't holding a grudge.

Leila shouldn't either.

Michael splashed back out of the water, grabbed a dry life jacket, and eased it over Leila's head.

It was thick and, while not uncomfortable, not exactly a cozy sweatshirt. She squeezed one of the compartments, just to be sure, and felt the hard foam beneath. Not newspaper. Of course. Michael knew what he was doing.

He attached the clips and tightened them, his hands moving deftly, tenderly. "How's that? Okay?"

"It's fine."

"There's a strap that goes between your legs. I'll let you reach for it." He tugged an open clip. "It goes here. It doesn't need to be too tight. We just want it to keep the jacket from coming off."

"I can do it."

He turned to Jasmine, who'd already donned her own orange accessory. He ensured all the straps were snug.

Leila was surprised that he continued to wear his. "I thought you said you can swim?"

"I'm a strong swimmer," he said. "But there's no sense not wearing something that'll keep me above water. If we go in, I'll be glad I have it."

Leila's heart raced. Would they go in?

Again, she flashed back to that day in the river.

Michael must've seen the alarm in her expression, because he added, "It's just a precaution."

She would swear the waves had grown taller since they'd arrived on the coast. From the hotel room in Antalya, the rhythm of the surf had been soothing, but now, to try to float atop it...

This was madness.

But Michael tossed his pack into the gray raft, then dragged the boat away from the rocks, where it bobbed and bounced.

She tried to get up the nerve to follow but couldn't make herself move.

Jasmine linked her arm with Leila's. "We can do this. He will deliver us safely."

"I know." She did. At least, her brain did.

Her stomach had other ideas.

And her feet were telling her to run.

Jasmine started forward, but Leila pulled her back. "Don't. We will be washed away."

Before Jasmine could argue, Michael called, "Stay there. I'll get you." He splashed back to shore, holding a rope extending to the death trap. He stopped in front of Jasmine. "Ready?"

Jasmine unhooked her arm from Leila's, and he scooped her up and carried her to the raft. He plopped her inside. It looked barely large enough for one person, much less three. Jasmine crawled to the front and sat with her back to the rounded side, facing shore. She and Michael spoke, but Leila couldn't hear above the splashing water.

Or maybe it was the fear rushing through her mind.

Michael returned and stopped in front of her. "You got this."

"I don't."

He reached out and drew her close.

She should argue, push him away. She was still angry with him.

But he wrapped his arms around her and lowered his head and kissed her, long and lovely and, *oh my*.

All her anger faded away.

She slid her arms around his neck, lifting to her tiptoes to get closer, wishing there wasn't so much puffy orange life jacket between them. His wet clothes were cold, but the contrast with the heat inside her only felt good.

He scooped her into his arms, not breaking the kiss.

Nestled against his chest, she felt protected and safe.

He walked so slowly and carefully that she was only vaguely aware they were moving.

And then he pulled his lips away and stared down at her. His face was in shadows, but she felt his look, his smoldering gaze. Or maybe she only assumed what she'd see on his face would reflect what she felt in her heart.

That she never wanted the kiss to stop.

He leaned forward and set her down. In the raft.

Oh.

"You good?" She heard amusement in his tone.

"You tricked me." The words pitched up when the raft rose and fell.

His chuckle was low as he moved to the back of the raft and pushed. "Hang on."

All those warm feelings Michael had generated blew away on the wind as she searched for a handhold, then slid her fingers around a rope and gripped, her fingernails digging into her palm.

Jasmine was right behind her, her legs tucked to one side. Leila pulled her own knees up so Michael would have a place to sit.

When he hopped into the raft, it dipped to one side so low she thought she'd be launched out. She couldn't help the little yelp that escaped.

He sat on the raft in front of her, facing her, facing freedom. "Don't make me kiss you again."

She faced the land she was happy to leave behind.

And the man she loved. The man she might very well have to let go.

"If you kiss her every time she is afraid," Jasmine said from behind her, "we will never leave Turkey."

They were joking? Now? When they floated only millimeters from death?

But the inflatable craft didn't capsize or sink, just bobbed on the water.

He started the engine. Its rumble drowned out the sound of waves crashing on rocks.

Jasmine leaned close and spoke into Leila's ear. "Turn, sister. See where we are going. To Greece now. And then to America. Like we always dreamed."

They had dreamed it, as little girls, listening to American music and wearing American clothes and sipping American sodas while American soldiers filled their city. Scary with all their guns, but then they'd smile, sometimes wave.

There was kindness there, in those soldiers' eyes.

And now...now she was with one of those Americans. Maybe not a soldier, but a warrior, a protector.

She didn't need to fear. Michael would get them to Greece. He would get them to America.

But what would happen then? To herself? To Jasmine?

No, she couldn't credit Michael with this, couldn't let

herself see him as her savior. She had a Savior. Maybe God had sent Michael, but He was behind this.

When this was over, she might lose Michael, but she would never lose God.

The boat bounced over a wave that had Leila and Jasmine lifting from their seats.

But they held on.

More waves. More bouncing. Finally, they were past the surf and motoring across the water toward lights.

Leaving behind Turkey, Iraq, and the men who'd pursued them.

And for a moment, for the first time since she'd been kidnapped off the street in Munich, despite the fear still churning within her, Leila felt free.

CHAPTER TWENTY-NINE

MICHAEL AIMED the raft toward Lesvos, trying not to think about the kiss that had calmed Leila enough that she let him put her in the boat.

It'd done the opposite to him. Probably a good thing he'd had to wade through cold water to get her settled.

Kiss or no kiss, the chasm yawned between them, and it would stay there until Jasmine decided to trust him—or Leila did.

Ticked him off that, after everything, they still didn't. Especially Leila. Sure, Jasmine was her sister, but he'd risked his life to save Leila. He was still risking his life to save her—and her twin. Why couldn't the woman he loved at least try to see the situation from his perspective? Was that too much to ask?

Cold seawater splashed him, not soothing the itchy thought. Images of his brothers came to mind. Daniel, Sam, Grant, Bryan, and Derrick. Five men he'd trust with his life.

And defend to the death.

So yeah, maybe he got it. He could cut her a little slack for defending her twin.

Would it kill her to reciprocate?

Though he hadn't shared his assessment with Leila, the sea wasn't calm tonight but choppy and angry. The raft's engine was weak and sputtering, and the current fought them all the way. Michael kept a lookout for boats, fearing being seen by Greek authorities. A ship floated in the distance—a coast guard vessel, if his guess was correct. It was lit up like the town square at Christmastime, making it easy to avoid.

Michael had chosen a gray raft, not one of the bright yellow ones meant to be seen from a distance. They'd be hidden unless the vessel got close.

He couldn't help but think about the refugees on similar boats just a few miles north. He'd seen enough photos and videos to know their trip across this stretch of water was very different from the one he, Leila, and Jasmine were taking. Smugglers would provide a raft made for ten, not three, but they'd cram it with twenty or thirty people. If the refugees managed to bring belongings, often those items would be thrown overboard during the journey in order to keep the raft afloat.

Treasured possessions tossed aside, worthless when faced with the possibility of death.

Some of the rafts provided by smugglers wouldn't make it all the way. They'd leak. They'd sink.

Life jackets filled with newspaper only weighed precious souls down into the sea.

Engines petered out, leaving a boat full of refugees dead in the water.

If the Hellenic Coast Guard saw them, they'd push them back to Turkey, forcing the refugees to start all over.

For those who reached European soil, whether in Lesvos or elsewhere, a new trial would begin. They'd be herded into a refugee camp, where they'd wait, and wait, and wait—most for months, some for years—for visas that would allow them to settle in Greece or elsewhere in Europe.

In most cases, only the wealthy or at least the middle-class could come up with the money to escape their countries. Most of these once well-to-do people, by the time they reached their new adopted homelands, would have spent every penny they had. They'd have lost—or had stolen from them—all their worldly goods. And many would have lost loved ones along the way.

Some had lost so much that they regretted ever having left their homes.

Some never recovered.

Michael looked to the north, to those right now making their way to freedom. *Protect them, Lord.*

Protect us.

The problem was so big. The solutions, impossible. The cause...

Men like Qasim and Hasan and Waleed, evil men motivated by power and greed who ruled with cruelty, who took everything and gave nothing in return.

The engine grumbled as they motored toward the lights in the distance.

Leila and Jasmine had turned to face Greece, the life ahead of them. God willing, Michael would get them to safety. But what about the rest of the refugees? The thousands, the hundreds of thousands, desperate for freedom?

Two hours after they motored away from Turkey, they reached a dark beach south of Mytilene's city center and north of the airport. Houses dotted the opposite side of the road that ran the length of this stretch of coast, but at almost three in the morning, the shore was deserted.

Nobody saw them approach. As far as Michael could tell, nobody witnessed him hop out and pull the raft in or watched him lift Leila and then her sister—both damp from sea spray but otherwise unscathed—and carry them to land. Nobody saw him drag the raft up and leave it at the foot of a little tree like an offering, then toss three life jackets inside.

And probably nobody noticed when he lifted his face to the sky. *Thank You, God. Thank You for getting us here.*

They trudged south for a couple of miles until they reached the edge of the airport property. At that point, there was nothing to do but wait.

He found a copse of trees jutting up against a retaining wall between the sand and the road. It wasn't secluded, but it was hidden from passersby. "Let's try to get some rest."

Jasmine said nothing, just sat with her back to the wall.

Leila looked around as if there might be a better option, maybe a Holiday Inn.

He waited for her argument, but after a moment, she joined her sister.

Progress.

He shrugged off his pack, dug out a thin blanket he kept for such occasions, and laid it over them. He guessed the temperature was in the low sixties, but it would drop before the sun rose. In his wet clothes, and thanks to the wind coming off the water, he was cold.

He took off his drenched boots and socks, hoping they'd at least dry a little by morning, and tugged on his sweatshirt before leaning against the wall a few feet away from the twins.

"Sit with us," Leila said. "We'll all be warmer."

He wouldn't mind that, but he didn't want to intrude.

"Please." Jasmine scooted away from her sister, leaving a Michael-sized gap in the middle. "We would like it."

Jasmine was a forgiving soul. Or maybe conniving.

He was too tired and chilled to care.

He settled between them, made sure the blanket covered all three, and leaned his head back against the rough stone wall. Not that he'd sleep, but it wouldn't hurt to get some rest.

He tucked Leila against his left side, his arm around her back. She laid her head on his chest. They'd solved nothing, and his future with her felt more tenuous all the time, but they'd put off all the difficult questions until later.

Jasmine was stiff on his other side. He didn't put his arm around her, instead tapping his shoulder. "Go ahead. Get comfortable."

"I am okay."

But within a few minutes, Jasmine's cheek was pressed against his upper arm.

Yeah, he wasn't exactly battle-ready, and if an enemy came, he'd be at a disadvantage.

But he felt at peace.

Give me notice if someone comes, Lord. Hide us here.

He wasn't the kind of guy to get visions, but his mind filled with an image of himself and these two precious women tucked beneath the feathers of a giant goose.

Weird.

But he knew where it came from. He'd memorized Psalm 91 years before, back when he'd first joined the CIA. Because what he did was dangerous, and calling on God as Protector was never a bad idea. Now, he recited one verse in his head. *He will cover you with His feathers, and under His wings you will find refuge; His faithfulness will be your shield and rampart.*

God had gotten them this far. He had their backs.

Michael hated that he didn't have a better plan, but Lesvos had been the only way out of Turkey.

The problem was, if he'd come to that conclusion, no doubt others had too. He doubted Brock had bothered to try to head him off, not after their conversation the morning before, but Leila and Jasmine's enemies were close. He could feel it.

The only fast way off this island was by flight. The longer Michael, Leila, and Jasmine could avoid being seen between here and the airport terminal, the better.

He didn't sleep, but the sisters did for a few hours. Even after they all woke up, they stayed hunkered out of sight until Michael got a text from Derrick around nine thirty in the morning.

We're on the ground.

How long before you can take off again?

About an hour. There's a wait to refuel.

Any food on board? We're starving.

I'll call Dominos.

Michael wasn't in the mood for jokes but tapped back the standard "Haha," then added,

Text when you're ready to go. We're thirty minutes out. We need to be wheels up as fast as possible once we're on board.

The three dots flashed, telling him Derrick was considering a reply. But after a few seconds, Michael got a thumbs-up. Good thing, because he wasn't about to explain.

Michael, Leila, and Jasmine shared the last protein bar and tried to get cleaned up without the benefit of running water. Not such an easy task while still wearing the makeup and wigs.

Derrick texted again less than an hour later.

We're ready.

> Walk to the door to the terminal and send me a pin. Wait for us there.

Because Michael had never been to this airport and didn't know exactly where to go, and he sure didn't want to pause to ask for directions. Again, those three dots danced. Michael was tapping a quick explanation, as if he had time for that, when Derrick's reply came.

One sec.

Michael shouldered his pack and stood. "I'm going to get us a car. You two stay out of sight but be ready to go."

Seated with her back against the wall, Leila yawned and stretched. "Any chance you could grab coffee on your way back?" By the humor in her voice, she was kidding. But also a little serious.

"They'll have some on the plane. And food." Probably not pizza, but he'd take whatever his brothers could rustle up.

He left the twins to gather their few belongings and brush sand off each other. At a break in the traffic, he hopped over the low retaining wall and walked toward the airport. He hadn't put a pebble in his shoe to cause a limp—he might need to run—but used the cane he'd bought in Antalya as he meandered south toward the airport, just an old man out for a walk.

Which might look a little more authentic if not for the clouds that'd moved in overnight. The wind and scent of rain. Michael wasn't that familiar with the weather in this part of the world, but he'd lived on the coast enough to recognize the signs. A storm was coming. He prayed it would hold off until he, Leila, and Jasmine were aboard Derrick's Cessna and winging their way toward freedom.

It was a small airport. Tiny by most standards. From the road, the entrance veered off to his right and led to the terminal maybe seventy-five yards away. Cars were parked along both sides of the road. He saw no people, but even so, he had the distinct impression somebody was watching him.

Just an old man out for a walk.

Which a stranger might believe, as long as they didn't watch him too long.

He figured Leila and Jasmine would expect him to return in a taxi or an Uber, but those weren't really options. Instead, he searched for something suitable—meaning old.

He wasn't exactly the grand-theft-auto type, certainly not twice in the same week. But was it really stealing if he returned it when he was done? Or was that more like borrowing-without-asking?

In any event, it wasn't as if he had a lot of choices.

He found an old—very old—Volvo in the tiny lot near the airport and, after making sure nobody was looking, broke in and hot-wired it.

This was risky in the bright morning sunshine, but nobody stopped him as he got the car started and moving out of the lot. He turned north, drove the half mile to where he'd left the women, then pulled over and got out.

He walked to the retaining wall and glanced over.

Uh-oh.

They weren't there.

He looked around, fighting anxiety that rose in his midsection. He'd been gone seven minutes. How in the world...?

"We're here!" Leila's voice carried on the wind. She emerged from behind some thick bushes, her sister behind her. "There was a family walking a dog. We were trying to stay hidden from them and the road."

"Smart." When she reached his side, he almost leaned down to kiss her but stopped himself. They were still disguised as father and son.

He helped Leila and then Jasmine over the short wall and to the car.

"This is a rental?" Jasmine asked.

"Something like that." He opened the doors for the women, slid in behind the wheel, and took out his phone to see the pin Derrick had sent.

Half a mile. A two-minute drive.

He tapped a text to Derrick, telling him his ETA and confirming he was still at the door, getting a thumbs-up reply.

When there was a break in the traffic, he did a U-turn and sped up.

They reached the turnoff, and he veered right toward the terminal.

Almost there.

One minute. It would be less if not for the slow car in front of him.

There was Derrick, standing in the wind, gazing at the approaching cars. He wore a short black jacket over jeans and, in those aviator sunglasses, looked like a taller version of Tom Cruise in *Top Gun*, all cool and collected.

Michael couldn't help smiling at the image as he pointed him out to Leila and Jasmine. "See him?"

Leila follows his gaze. "He looks like you."

How could she tell what he looked like behind those sunglasses?

But...yeah, he could see it. His little brother was tall like he was. His hair was lighter and longer, but he supposed they were similar enough. "If anything happens, run to Derrick and go with him."

"We should stay together."

Michael managed to stifle his sigh. "Or you could just trust me and do what I ask."

After a slight pause, she said, "Sorry."

Progress. He liked it.

Soon they'd be wheels up, off the ground and headed far away.

Leila and Jasmine would be safe.

Knowing how close they were, fear tingled in his fingertips. Because this was the most dangerous part of the mission, showing up where their enemies knew they would be.

But he and the women were in a strange car, disguised. This should work.

This should work.

Unless his enemies had seen him earlier.

He should have walked the other direction to steal the car. Stupid move on his part.

But he was disguised.

This should work.

The words were still resonating in his mind when he caught movement to his left. A white Mercedes van moved out of a parking space.

Right at him.

He slammed the brakes.

Realized his mistake a second too late.

The van stopped in his path.

Its doors slid open.

Men streamed out. Guns raised.

"Down, down!" Michael grabbed Leila beside him, shoved her to the floorboard as he ducked as low as he could get. He checked the rearview mirror, thinking he'd reverse, but there was a car behind them.

They were trapped.

He rammed the car, desperate to get them out of there. But there was nowhere to go.

A gunshot boomed.

The windshield exploded.

The women screamed.

Michael grabbed his gun and shifted it into his left hand, then grabbed Leila's arm with his right. He was going to hang onto her, no matter what happened.

He would not lose her again.

He risked a look, searching for an enemy to take out. Aimed.

Before he could get a shot off, a bullet whizzed by his ear.

Shouting in Arabic, too fast for him to translate.

He waited for a guard to show himself, gaze flicking from window to window. He was ready. He'd shoot them all if he had to.

If he could.

He wouldn't lose her.

He couldn't.

A head popped up to his left. He swung his weapon that direction.

His window exploded.

Searing pain.

A door opened. Sounds, muffled and close.

But Michael couldn't see. Couldn't do anything. Couldn't move.

His grip loosened.

Leila's arm slipped away.

Screams and shouts and words in a language he should be able to understand but didn't.

And then...silence.

Emptiness and silence.

CHAPTER THIRTY

ONE MOMENT, Leila was comparing her boyfriend's features to his brother's, thinking how similar they were, wondering if all six of the Wright boys looked alike.

The next moment, armed men were coming from every direction. Firing guns. Yelling instructions.

And Michael...

Shot.

Blood, everywhere.

Before she could process it...

She refused to consider that Michael was...

Gone.

He was gone.

She was grabbed. Pulled out of the car.

Carried over a shoulder like a sack of animal feed.

Screaming. Fighting and pounding and yelling for help. Desperate.

People watched, mouths wide.

One person ran toward them.

The brother. Derrick. But he was too far away.

Stay there! Because if they saw him, if they knew who he was, they'd shoot him. He'd be dead.

Like his brother.

Michael. Oh, Michael.

She was dumped in a van, dark and cold

Her sister landed beside her.

Jasmine wasn't moving. She wasn't fighting.

No. No, no, no.

Leila bent over her, desperate for a sign of life.

And was yanked away by brutal hands.

The van's doors slammed.

And they were moving.

Leaving the airport. Freedom. Safety.

Michael.

Leaving them all behind.

CHAPTER THIRTY-ONE

"MICHAEL! MICHAEL!"

The words came from a million miles away.

Millions and millions of miles from the oblivion where he'd landed, in darkness and peace.

"Michael!"

He pushed his way back, back toward the voice. Toward a reality that had just exploded.

"I need an ambulance!"

Michael forced his eyes open, but the world was a blur.

"Thank God, thank God! Bro, come on. Are you with me?"

"Are they... Do you have them? The women? Are they safe?"

"What women?"

What women?

What was happening?

He was lying on his back, Derrick leaning over him, his face hard to make out even in the dim overcast day. But his voice was clear, terrified.

Michael tried to push himself up. "Help me."

"Stay down until the ambulance gets here."

"No." He struggled, pushing a hand against rough asphalt.

"All right, all right." Derrick lifted his shoulder. "Who were those guys?"

"Guards. Terrorists."

"Why did you have terrorists in your car?"

Huh?

Michael was confused.

"The men, in your car. Who were they?"

Men. Not men. Women.

In disguise, but not very good disguises, obviously. They'd been seen. Recognized.

"They're gone?"

"Yeah. Alive, I think. The first for sure. The other one looked... I don't know."

The wail of sirens seeped into his consciousness.

"Help me up."

"Dude." Derrick shifted in front of him, and Michael got a better look. The jacket he'd worn was gone, his button-down smeared with blood.

Blood?

Who was...?

Oh.

He reached toward the wound on his head. Now that he thought of it, it pulsed with pain. He felt...nylon. His brother's jacket.

Derrick grabbed his hand. "Don't. You were shot. I wrapped my jacket around it, but it's gonna need stitches."

Shot.

In the head?

The sirens got louder.

He didn't have time for cops or paramedics.

"Get me out of here." He grabbed his brother's wrist. "Take me inside, now. Grab my pack from the backseat."

Derrick didn't argue, just helped him up and reached into the car while Michael fought dizziness. His brother supported Michael into the warm building, straight to the men's room.

It was a three-staller, bright and clean. Michael said, "Lock that door."

Derrick did, then dropped the pack on the counter. "What are we doing? This is nuts. You need a hospital."

"You're just a bystander. A stranger who helped me to the bathroom. That's what you're going to tell them. I'm an old man, sixty-five or seventy. Got it?" Michael unwrapped the jacket from his head and looked at the wound.

The bullet had cut a gash starting a half inch from his eyebrow and forging a gully a centimeter wide that disappeared beneath the wig.

If the shooter had had a better angle...

Nausea rose so fast he didn't have a second to think before the contents of his stomach came out, landing in the sink.

"What can I do?" Derrick's voice was pitched high, but he wasn't panicked. Just worried.

Michael turned on the water, washing the sick down the drain, then cupped some water into his lips. "Go to the plane and wait."

"Yeah, that's gonna happen."

"I have to disappear. I have to find them." He yanked off the wig, wet a paper towel, and scrubbed off the makeup.

Derrick wasn't leaving.

Not that Michael had expected him to. "Grab me different clothes from my pack. Don't care if they're dirty."

Derrick tapped on a cell phone.

"Who are you texting?"

"Bryan. He's worried."

Oh. Right. Bryan was there too.

"There's a first-aid kit in my pack. And I need a hat."

Derrick lowered the pack to the floor, flung clothes and other items out of it, then held out the first-aid kit. "If you think I'm leaving you alone—"

"Tell me what you saw. Cars, license plates. Men. Everything."

While Derrick did that, Michael cleaned the wound, glued it shut, added clotting gauze, and spread tape over it.

"I don't understand what's happening," Derrick said. "Who were those men with you?"

"Women. They're women. Sisters. Disguised." Leila, in the hands of...

Had Waleed Shehab been there? He shook his head, then froze as pain shot clear to his toes.

A knock came on the door.

"Whoever that is, tell him to go away."

But Derrick opened the door, and Bryan stepped inside holding a small backpack. He froze. "What happened? Are you all right?"

Derrick said, "He was shot—"

"—I'm fine. Close that door." Once he did, he asked, "What's in the bag?"

"Clothes," Derrick said. "Clean ones. Who were the women?"

"My girlfriend and her twin." He reached for the bag.

Derrick didn't hand it over. "Your girlfriend? I didn't know—"

"Now's not the time." He leaned his hip against the counter, fighting a wave of wooziness, and held his hand toward the bag. "Give me that."

Derrick fished out a pair of black sweatpants. "Let me help."

"What women?" Bryan asked.

"They were with Michael," Derrick said. "And were taken by...terrorists?"

"Yeah." Michael nearly fell over trying to get his still-wet, sandy jeans off.

His brothers took over, holding him up, getting his dirty clothes off him, the clean ones on.

Michael thanked God for dry, loose pants, warm socks, and a clean T-shirt.

When they were finished, he reached for his wet boots.

But Bryan yanked off his tennis shoes. "I'll wear yours."

Michael didn't have the energy to argue and was too grateful for words when he put on the dry sneakers.

He added a baseball cap, wincing as it pressed on his wound, then slid on sunglasses he kept in his pack. He looked in the mirror. Gone was the old man who'd been shot.

Now he looked like a fortysomething American. Which was exactly what he was.

The thought had him turning to Derrick. "How did you know it was me, in the car?"

Derrick shook his head, and Michael saw what he'd missed before. His brother's red-rimmed eyes. Pale skin. Fear and worry etched in the lines around his mouth. "I don't know." He rubbed a hand down his jaw. "I just... You were acting so weird on the phone and in your texts. When I heard the gunshots, I just knew... And then I saw you in the car, slumped over and gray, and everything about you was wrong, but I... I don't know how. But I knew it was you. And I thought you were dead." His voice cracked.

"I'm okay, man." He grabbed his brother's arm. "I'm okay. Thank you for being here and for...all this."

Derrick nodded, shaking off emotion he'd not quite managed to hold at bay.

"I have to go," Michael said.

"What?" Bryan's voice was too loud. "Dad would kill us if—"

"Dad's not here. I have to get her back." He breathed through his own emotion, tamping it down. He needed to think. "I can't lose her now."

Bryan bent to retrieve the items Derrick had scattered all over the floor. The blanket. Clothes. Weapons. Two laptops. Multiple burner phones. He shoved them into Michael's backpack. "We'll help you." Bryan shot Derrick a look. "Right?"

"Of course. What do we do?"

No way was Michael putting his brothers in danger.

But right now, he needed a place to think. He needed quiet and food and water—and to avoid the police he figured were swarming outside.

"Can we get on the plane, maybe...park it for a while?"

"I'll claim mechanical trouble." Derrick wrapped a hand around Michael's upper arm. "Thing is, there's a storm coming. If we wait too long, we're not going to be able to take off."

"You two should go. I'll get the girls and find another way off—"

"Forget it—!"

"—Are you crazy?" Derrick asked.

He would argue, but if circumstances were reversed, he wouldn't leave them either, no matter what they said. "Okay, then. You two go—for now. Just mill around outside for a minute. If anybody asks if you saw the guy who was shot, tell him you tried to help him"—Michael gestured to Derrick's bloody shirt—"but he took off."

"What are you going to do?" Bryan asked.

"People had to see us come in here," Derrick added.

And yet, nobody had followed. This airport was small, and there hadn't been very many people when they'd walked in, which, he assumed, was the private aircraft portion of the terminal.

So, probably not. But they'd have seen Derrick with the gunshot victim.

"Tell them I left," Michael said. "Point...them some direction. Tell them you tried to help the guy, but he refused help and took off. You went to the bathroom to get cleaned up."

"Yeah, okay." Derrick and Bryan left, Bryan carrying Michael's huge backpack for him.

Michael closed himself in a stall and sat on the toilet.

Not the most sanitary place to rest, but standing, talking to his brothers, and pretending to be fine had taken its toll. The room was spinning.

He waited five minutes, praying for strength. For wisdom and guidance and Leila and Jasmine and help.

He needed help.

And to think straight.

He washed his hands and stepped out of the bathroom.

Into chaos.

Police and paramedics and security everywhere.

He acted mildly interested as he followed the directions his brother had given him, catching sight of Bryan at a rear door. He approached, holding out his hand as if they'd never met, as if they were pilot and client. Bryan shook it, not missing a beat, and they walked into the windy day to the waiting Cessna.

He climbed the steps to the cabin. And collapsed onto the first seat.

Leila should have been with him. Leila and Jasmine should be seated across from him, marveling at the luxurious accommodations.

But the women were in the hands of men who'd pursued them for a thousand miles.

Terrorists. Psychopaths.

And Michael had no idea how to find them.

CHAPTER THIRTY-TWO

LEILA DARED NOT SPEAK.

She was seated, cross-legged, on the floor, her back to the rear door, using her hands to keep herself from sliding or tipping with the movement of the van.

Her sister was lying beside her, head on Leila's lap. But she was awake. She'd looked up, her eyes full of fear, a few minutes earlier.

Leila didn't recognize any of the four men in the back, watching her with rage-filled eyes, all armed. The windows had been painted black, so the only light came from the deeply tinted windows in the front, where two more men sat.

She couldn't see either of them very well. The driver was young, based on the higher-than-normal pitch of his voice. He was talking like his words were footsteps and he was in a race, his free hand gesturing as he recalled the ambush at the airport. He sounded jubilant. "Shot him right in the head, man. Did you see the blood? That was awesome." He sounded eager and excited.

But she wasn't buying it, the crazed, over-the-top glee. The kid was trying too hard to convince himself that taking a man's life was *awesome*. Not fearsome. Not gruesome.

She couldn't think about what man he was talking about. Michael.

How could he be dead?

But she'd seen the blood. Felt his grip on her loosen and fall away.

Seen him slump.

And that boy driver, acting like it was all some big game.

She wanted to scream at him, let out all the fury inside. The man she loved was dead—dead because he'd tried to rescue her.

But the guards seemed to be waiting for an excuse to take out their wrath on her. How many of their number had died since she and Jasmine had escaped? How many had Michael killed at the compound? How many had he and Splat killed in Turkey?

She could hear Michael's voice in her head. Maybe, now that he was dead, he was with her there. Weren't there stories about such things, people hovering between life and death? Watching?

She'd never believed it, but now...now she wanted to believe that the voice so clear in her mind was more than a memory and a vapor and a hope.

Don't fight them until you have a chance to win.

Don't weaken yourself. Stay strong. Stay vigilant.

She'd never been good at following his commands in life. But now, she would do what he said. She would make him proud.

The van had been traveling fast on a straightaway. Now, it made a series of turns that had her bracing herself to keep from slamming into the metal walls.

She bounced on the hard floor, wincing as they hit bumps.

They went up a hill, around another corner, and then down, down into darkness.

The van backed up and parked. The driver, still babbling, seemed proud of himself for his maneuvering.

The man in the passenger seat twisted toward the back, his face barely visible in the dim light.

She gasped.

Waleed.

"Not much longer before you're mine. You'll be sorry for all the trouble you put us through." The words had started conversational but turned threatening at the end.

He clamped the shoulder of one of the men in the back, who was watching her with vitriol. "Hands off. Unless she gives you trouble, in which case... Just don't leave any bruises." He handed the man something she couldn't see in the darkness. To her, he said, "Get that makeup off your face and take your hair down. It is shameful for you to pretend to be a man."

She held his gaze, refusing to let him see the terror that bubbled inside.

Like that stupid, stupid eleven-year-old girl who'd stood up to him, embarrassed him in front of his friends.

Eighteen years later, he was going to get his revenge. By the anticipation in his eyes, he'd been looking forward to it for a long time.

CHAPTER THIRTY-THREE

MICHAEL SUCKED down the bottle of water Bryan had given him, then took the second and drank it as well.

The water helped, as did the chocolate croissant. Food and hydration.

Neither of which Leila and Jasmine had.

Bryan was seated in the chair opposite him, a table between then. "What now?"

"I need the laptop."

Derrick, in the leather seat facing his direction across the narrow aisle, unzipped Michael's pack and pulled two laptops out, holding them toward him. They were similar, but his was dark gray. The other was silver.

He reached for the silver one and opened it.

The script Alyssa had sent had worked the afternoon before, getting Michael past the password far enough that he was able to change it to his own highly secret one.

He typed *password123* into the box, and the home screen came up.

He'd had no time since they left Antalya to dig around, figuring he'd just hand it over to the tech guys at the Agency.

Now, he prayed there'd be something on here to tell him... something.

A clue.

Anything.

He aimed the pointer toward the email program and perused the messages, confirming what he'd guessed.

The laptop belonged to Waleed Shehab.

An icon in the dock caught his attention.

Americans texted. But in much of the world, people stayed connected with friends and colleagues through What's App. And Waleed Shehab, like Michael himself, had connected his laptop to those messages.

He clicked the app, and all the messages came up, along with the numbers associated with them.

He tapped his pockets, but his cell wasn't there. "I need a phone."

Derrick checked his own pockets, then set one on the table. "This was in the car."

"You grabbed it? Thank you." Using his own cell, he dialed Alyssa's number. It was evening in Maine. Was she on a date? Working out?

Please, please answer...

By the fourth ring, he was losing hope. And then, "Did it work? The script? I never heard—"

"Sorry. It's been..." Indescribable. "It worked. I need another favor."

"Of course you do." Her tone—sardonic, slightly sarcastic— might make him smile under different circumstances.

"I have a list of phone numbers. I need to know if any of them are on the island of Lesvos. In Greece."

"You have the weirdest requests." She was probably waiting for him to explain, or at least laugh. But he didn't have it in him. After a pause, she said, "Go ahead."

He read off the top ten phone numbers.

The messages were in Arabic and would take some time to translate. He doubted they'd texted their current whereabouts or plan, so he'd leave the translating to others.

When he was finished, Alyssa said, "I'll get back to you."

"It's important."

"Isn't it always with you?"

She wasn't wrong, but he needed her to understand. "It's about the woman I love. She's been taken."

"Oh." All humor gone. "Five minutes." She clicked off.

He set the phone down.

"Who was that?" The way Bryan was looking at him, Michael worried he'd recognized her voice.

Alyssa liked to keep her extracurricular activities private.

"Doesn't matter." He pulled up a map of Lesvos, zooming in on Mytilene. There were only two ways off this island, by air and by sea. According to his search, this was the only airport. "You guys didn't happen to see any other private jets hanging around, did you?"

"No," Derrick said. "But one is expected soon. That's why they had me move when I told them we had engine trouble."

"Any idea who's landing?"

"They didn't say."

Didn't matter. Even if Shehab and his cohorts had come by air, they'd have landed long before Derrick and Bryan.

"I could take a look around," Bryan suggested. "See if there are any other private jets nearby."

"No, don't do that." Waleed, if he had left a plane, would also have left the pilot, who could be armed.

Leila thought Michael and Derrick looked alike, and surely she'd say the same about himself and Bryan. He wasn't going to do anything to put his brothers on Shehab's radar.

"I'm gonna need a car. Could one of you rent one?" He reached for his pack. "My wallet's—"

"I'll put it on your bill." Derrick stood and headed for the exit.

He didn't even want to think about the size of that bill. And it was only going to get larger. "Thanks, bro."

Derrick disappeared down the steps.

Michael's phone rang, and he snatched it up. "Well?"

"Three are on Lesvos," Alyssa said, "all at the same place. Texting you the location."

His phone dinged, and he tapped the address, then typed it in the laptop's browser.

It was a four-star hotel in the heart of Mytilene, only eight kilometers away. Not even five miles.

"Thanks. I owe you." He was going to owe everybody by the time this was over.

"Anytime." Alyssa, always snarky, sounded serious. "Go get her, cuz."

"That's the plan." He ended the call and pushed to his feet.

"What are you doing?" Bryan asked.

"I have to go after them."

"You got a location?"

"They're just up the road."

Bryan pushed to his feet. "You have weapons for Derrick and me?"

"You'll be safe here."

Bryan's eyebrows hiked. "You think you're going to go after them alone? Wounded? I don't think so."

"I'm not putting you in danger."

"Then you're not leaving."

Michael couldn't help it. He smiled. "Look, bro, I appreciate—"

"You think I can't stop you? You're wounded in a couple of

places." He nodded at Michael's side, where he must've seen the bandage earlier. "You could outrun me, sure, but here? No way."

Michael could get past him, but he thought it would be rude to say so.

"When it was Sam's girl we were saving," Bryan said, "you had no problem calling us in to help. You think this is going to be easier than that was?"

"You thought that was easy?" Michael flashed back to the burning building, the smoke, the screams.

"We knew what we were getting into. What do you know now?" Bryan barely paused to give him a chance to answer. "How many are there? They already tried to kill you once, probably assume you're dead. When they see you're alive, you think they'll hesitate to shoot you? I'm guessing they won't miss twice. How are you going to save your girlfriend if you're dead, Michael?"

All those questions, and Michael had no answers.

He only knew he had to go. He'd figure it out as he went.

Like he usually did.

Like he'd done when he'd flown to Iraq without telling his team leader.

And how had that ended? He'd almost gotten himself—and Leila and Jasmine—killed. More than once. If he'd told Brock, the team could've gotten in and out in a matter of hours.

It'd taken Michael days...

And now he'd lost them both.

He'd feared Leila had been taken because of him. That assumption had propelled him onto this journey. And that assumption had been wrong.

But in his arrogance—and his fear—he'd gone it alone. As he so often did.

And because of that, he'd lost...everything.

If Jasmine died, Leila would never forgive him.

If Leila died, it would be all his fault.

And he'd never forgive himself.

"You can't do this alone," Bryan said. "Let us help."

Michael plopped back into the seat. He couldn't risk Bryan and Derrick to save Leila and Jasmine.

But his brother was right. He couldn't do this alone. This time, he'd do the right thing. He snatched his phone again and dialed.

This was going to hurt.

"Brock here." A hum carried through the phone, some kind of an engine.

"It's Wrong."

"You bet your life you're Wrong!" Michael endured his boss's response, so peppered with obscenities that he moved the phone away from his ear.

Earning raised eyebrows from Bryan.

He waited until Brock paused to take a breath, then jumped in.

"I need your help." Quickly, he gave his team leader a rundown on what'd happened that morning, including his guess that Waleed Shehab was behind the most recent ambush and kidnapping. "I can't get them back by myself."

"You finally figured that out?"

"You were right, okay? Is that what you want me to say?" Anger infused his words, but he wasn't mad at Brock.

He was mad at himself for proving Brock right.

And for messing everything up.

"You were right. About all of it." Michael's tone sounded harsh and impudent. He took a breath and started again. "I was an arrogant jerk who thought I didn't need help, and because I disobeyed you and broke all the rules, I've gotten the woman I love kidnapped—again. And myself shot. I'm lucky to be alive. And I need your help. Please."

He held his breath. No matter what Brock said—no matter what cruel words, or arrogant tone, or snide remarks—Michael would control his tongue. He'd be humble. He'd beg if he had to.

"They're with Shehab now?" Brock asked.

"I think so. I have a location. And Shehab's laptop, by the way, which I'll hand over. Any chance there's a team nearby? Athens or Turkey, someone who can be here—"

"Hold on." The connection was muffled, but he heard Brock shout, "How long?" A moment later, he came back to Michael. "We land in four."

"Where?"

"There. Of course."

"What? Why are you—?"

"Been watching your brother's plane."

Oh.

Of course Brock knew about Derrick's charter business. He was one step ahead of Michael. Even so... "Here? You're coming here? In four...hours?"

"Minutes. Figured you might need our help. Would've been there sooner, but we had an op."

Relief washed over him. *Thank You, God.*

But...they'd had an op? "Everybody okay?"

"Considering we were a man down?" Brock didn't even try to keep the scorn out of his voice, and Michael winced at the implication.

Had someone gotten hurt because he hadn't been there? Had the op gone sideways?

Brock didn't explain. "Text me the address, and we'll start working up a plan. I've got an SUV waiting, but if you're up for it, we'll need a second vehicle."

"On it. And Brock...sir?"

"Sir?"

Yeah. Michael had never been a yessir kind of guy. "Thank you. For coming, and—"

"You're still on my team. This is what we do for teammates." He ended the call before Michael could think of a response.

He'd barely set his cell down when the roar of a jet had him looking out the window.

Sure enough, a small charter touched down and turned for the terminal.

Derrick stepped through the door and into the aisle. "Got your car." He tossed the keys, and Michael snatched and pocketed them.

"What are we doing?" Derrick asked.

"I got some friends here to help." If anybody could get Leila and Jasmine out of Shehab's grasp, they could.

And take the terrorist into custody in the process.

For the first time since he'd seen those armed men, a spark of hope lit. Maybe, with God's help, they could actually do this.

CHAPTER THIRTY-FOUR

LEILA PULLED the wig and cap off while Waleed was gone, then wiped off makeup with tissues and hand sanitizer the guard had handed her.

The men in the cargo van had nothing better to do than watch. The four of them sat with their backs to the walls. The one closest to her had moved to his feet and now crouched as if preparing to launch. He seemed to be trying to take up as much room as possible, so that every time she shifted, she risked touching him.

She was very, very careful not to allow that.

When she was finished removing her own makeup, she wiped her sister's away. Jasmine had already removed her wig and brushed her fingers through her long hair.

The makeup and wig had been hot and confining.

And, in the long run, useless.

Leila settled against the door again. "How did you find us?" She directed the question to the guard closest.

"We saw the man walk by this morning. Didn't pay him any attention until he drove away. Waleed had a feeling, but we weren't sure until you got near the terminal. You make a better woman than a man."

The door behind her jerked open. She tipped backward, windmilling but unable to stop her fall.

Waleed caught her and swung her to the ground, pulling her against his chest.

It happened so fast, she barely uttered a gasp before she found herself face-to-face with the man Baba had decided would be her husband.

Waleed held her there, his body hot against hers, his smile cruel and tight. He tugged at her hair. "That's better." He plucked at her sweatshirt. "You will be lucky if you don't spend your life in a burka after this. Assuming you are ever allowed in public again."

He leaned toward her, his breath smelling of garlic and fish, and she feared he was about to kiss her. She would fight—and be punished—but how could she not? How could she let this murderer kiss her? Touch her?

This man who'd caused the death of the man she loved?

She'd take her own life first.

"Ah, not yet, my pet. But soon." He pushed her, and she stumbled and would have fallen if not for a guard behind her. He gripped her arm and dragged her away from the van and toward a car.

They were in a tiny parking garage, barely large enough for the eight cars crammed in there. She aimed for the backseat, but the trunk popped open.

"In," the guard said.

And if she'd thought of arguing, the words were stolen as he swept her feet out from under her and dumped her, head-first, into the tiny, cramped space.

A second later, Jasmine was deposited beside her. The lid slammed, leaving them in darkness.

Bringing to mind the escape from Baghdad, the crate.

And Michael, who'd held her close and kept her from falling.

Tears pricked her eyes, but she wouldn't cry for him now. Not when Waleed and his thugs were so close.

Jasmine's arms slid around her. "We must pray, sister. God sees us." Despite the weakness in her voice, Jasmine was right.

Hope seemed lost, but God was a God of hope, wasn't He?

Leila prayed aloud, her voice low enough that the men wouldn't hear her mumbled words. She sprinkled in some of the Scriptures she'd learned in the years she'd been in Germany, like the promise that God was their strong tower. That the righteous could run to Him and be safe.

"Make us safe, Lord," Jasmine said.

The car moved, jostling them, Leila's hip banging on the hard floor when it hit bumps. But she kept praying.

How much time had passed since she'd sat beside Michael, comparing him to his brother?

She doubted even an hour.

It felt like a lifetime. A lifetime since she'd held his hand. A lifetime since their long, passionate kiss right before he'd put her in the raft. A lifetime since she'd demanded he quit questioning Jasmine, when she'd erected a wall between them.

She should have been more understanding. She shouldn't have made demands of the man who'd risked so much for her. Who'd given everything for her. Given his very life for her.

Rather than savoring their time together, she'd made it awkward and strained.

Staring down a lifetime as Waleed's wife—his *slave*—she'd give anything to have those hours back with the man she loved.

They weren't on the road five minutes before the car parked again.

The doors opened and slammed. A few muffled words.

And then the trunk opened.

One of the men lifted her to the ground, and another lifted Jasmine out and set her on her feet.

Leila took in the surroundings. They'd parked in a narrow alley of crumbling concrete. A giant pile of trash leaned against the building nearest, carrying the stench of decaying food.

There was a second car, a small hatchback, which explained how all the men had gotten here despite the small vehicles.

A guard asked Jasmine, "You can walk?" He sounded concerned, almost human.

"Yes," Jasmine said. "Thank you."

Thank you?

But Jasmine was polite. Smarter than Leila, who wanted to scream at them all. During all those years alone with only Baba, Uncle Hasan, Qasim, and Waleed, in a compound full of guards, Jasmine must have learned that fighting back was futile.

"Come." Waleed walked into the tumbledown building.

She followed, guards on both sides, into a damp space littered with old carpet, cracked tiles, and broken furniture.

Something skittered along the floor, a sooty shadow that disappeared into a crevice.

A shudder worked its way up her spine. She gripped her sister's hand.

Waleed was already on his way up a dilapidated staircase, so she and Jasmine followed. She didn't dare touch the flaking wrought iron banister for fear it wouldn't hold her weight.

The rest of the men came behind them, the only sound the thumping of boots, so loud she worried someone might bang right through the rotting wooden steps.

But they made it all the way to the fourth floor.

The roof had collapsed on one side, letting in dim light—along with years of rain and filth. The space stank of musk and urine and death. Waleed pushed into one of the rooms, and she followed. She guessed this had been an apartment building at one time, based on the stained toilet beyond an open door and a counter separating a small kitchen from what must be a living area.

Waleed approached a wall of floor-to-ceiling windows, all cracked and dingy, their exterior shutters hanging lopsided and blocking part of the view.

"This'll work." He found an empty bucket and turned it upside down in front of one of the windows. Settling on it, he pointed toward the corner in front of him. It was the only place in the room without a view. "Sit."

As if she were a dog to be commanded.

Everything in her wanted to tell him what she thought of his command.

Fake it until you find a way to defend yourself...let him think he's won. Michael's voice was in her head again. *Meanwhile, find a way to fight back.*

So she didn't argue, just sat where Waleed had directed, gazing around the foul, ruined space for something, anything to use as a weapon. She saw nothing, but she felt something sharp beneath her bottom.

Jasmine sank to the floor beside her, linking their arms.

They were in this together. They'd come into the world together. They would fight together, try to escape together.

And maybe, today, they would die together.

CHAPTER THIRTY-FIVE

FORTY MINUTES after Michael's team touched down—forty long minutes—Michael directed Stone to pull up in front of a coffee shop within walking distance of the marina. He handed his phone between the seats.

Bryan took it. "This guy's a terrorist? He looks like an insurance salesman."

Michael had pulled up a photo of Waleed Shehab, which he'd gotten from a CIA database. "Don't let his looks deceive you. He's a psychopath and a murderer."

"Okay if I forward this to my phone?"

Michael glanced at Stone, who shrugged.

"Go ahead."

A moment later, Bryan whistled, and Michael guessed that he'd swiped to the next photo, this one of Leila taken in the Alps on their last date.

The majestic Eiger, snow-covered and formidable, rose in the background while she stood in the middle of a field of wildflowers.

"She's gorgeous," Bryan said. "*This* is your girlfriend?"

He didn't mind his brother's appreciation. He was a little annoyed by the shocked tone.

"If you see either her or her twin—"

"She's a *twin*? There's another one who looks...just like that?"

"Try to focus, man."

"I'll call you if I see any of them. Forwarding this photo too."

"Which you'll delete once we get her back."

"Of course." But there was humor in his voice, like this was all a joke.

Michael managed to keep his frustration behind his lips.

Bryan opened the door and started to get out. Before he did, his hand dropped on Michael's shoulder. "Be careful."

"You too."

"I'm just having a cup of coffee."

"If he sees you—"

"I got it. See you soon." He climbed out and slammed the door.

His brother limped away, heavy on the cane he'd been using a lot since the ambush at the campground a couple of weeks before.

"He'll be fine." Stone shifted into drive and turned toward the hotel.

Alyssa had been monitoring the phones associated with Waleed Shehab. According to her, they hadn't moved.

The guards should be there. Waleed should be there.

Please, God, let Leila and Jasmine be there, unharmed.

Just in case, Bryan would keep an eye out for the Mercedes van that'd cut him off at the airport. He'd be watching from the coffee shop near the entrance to the marina.

Derrick remained at the airport, seated where he could observe those coming and going, ostensibly reading his phone while keeping an eye out for Shehab, Leila, or any of the other guards.

Not that anybody thought they were going to grab a commercial flight off the island, but maybe there was a jet on airport property they hadn't seen.

Meanwhile, Brock had directed a satellite to watch the air and water around the island. Michael didn't assume the satellite they were using had the newest technology, meaning it would only be helpful if the clouds broke up or at least thinned out. If anything, though, they were only getting thicker.

All that surveillance should prove overkill because he and his team would rescue Leila and Jasmine in the next few minutes. *Please.*

He glanced at his friend, who was focused on the narrow cobblestone roads. "Tell me about the op."

"It was a target Tile found."

Tile was one of their teammates. As in *projectile*, as in projectile vomit.

Made Michael thankful for being called *Wrong*.

"What prompted it?"

Stone shot him a glare. "You wanna know? You should've been there. With your team."

Huh.

Stone was his closest friend on the team. If Stone was ticked at him...

"My girlfriend was kidnapped."

"You didn't have to join our team, *Wrong*." The name, usually said with humor, came out vitriolic. "You could've kept working alone. But you decided—"

"I wasn't going to, but—"

"We all know about your buddy at the White House."

Michael flinched at his friend's cold words.

If Stone knew about that, did he also know Michael hadn't

wanted to join the team? He'd liked his role working out of the Berlin office, alone. But the chief of staff's son, Travis Price, had been a friend in college. He was their contact at the White House and he'd appealed—no, he'd had his father appeal, on behalf of the president of the United States—to Michael to join the team.

What was Michael supposed to do? Say, "No, thank you, sir. I'm happy where I am"?

As if that'd been an option.

And even if it had been, it was an honor that Travis recruited him. In fact, his friend had insisted Michael join the covert team, wanting someone he could count on to tell him— and by extension, the president—the truth.

Michael didn't know everything about the political maneuvering that'd gone on before the inauguration, but obviously, the president didn't think he could trust the establishment. That fact alone said a lot.

Michael had never mentioned Travis to Stone or any of the guys. As far as he'd known, Brock was the only one who'd been aware of the connection.

"It means something to be on a team," Stone said. "You'd have learned that if you'd served." He yanked the small car around a corner.

And there it was. The thing that separated him from his teammates.

His lack of military service. "Brock sidelined me."

"While your team searched for your secret girlfriend."

Yeah, well... It sounded bad when he put it like that.

"You should have told us what you were doing. You should have trusted us."

"Trusted you when you showed up at my hotel room in London in the middle of the night?"

Stone shot him a glare. "You were there."

"Got out a second before you burst in."

"We knocked, man. We needed to find out what you'd learned."

"At two o'clock in the morning."

"Which happened to be about thirty minutes after our flight arrived. You should have trusted us."

Michael had learned a lot of things at the Farm. How to kill. How to stay alive. How to find bad guys and watch them. How to blend in.

He'd never quite mastered the *trust other people* thing.

Especially when it looked like they were betraying him.

Stone drove along a maze of streets so narrow and hilly it was a wonder a normal-sized car could traverse them.

Voices sounded in his earpiece, scratchy at first but growing stronger. The rest of the team had gone straight there. They were already searching for the van—and the terrorists.

The hotel was in the heart of the city, not far from the café where they'd left Bryan. The old stone building looked like it'd grown right out of the soil, as if it'd always been there.

Driving slowly, they passed wide steps that rose on both sides around a fountain and led to a small courtyard. Unlike the seemingly ancient exterior, the glass doors that must open to the lobby looked brand new.

Stone parked on a side street. Together, they approached the hotel from the back, keeping their eyes open for threats.

Inside the lobby, inlaid ceilings were painted with fancy scrolls, and intricate chandeliers hung over the kind of furniture that looked both fancy and well-worn. An eating area at the back held six café tables, all empty now.

His mother would call it charming.

His father would be impressed by the architecture.

Michael only wanted to know its secrets.

Despite the luxury the building might offer, he doubted very much that Leila and Jasmine were comfortable.

Beyond the glass doors he'd seen from the street, the hotel's wings rose on two sides, rooms with narrow balconies overlooking the water feature and courtyard.

He and Stone approached a middle-aged woman behind the counter. "Afternoon, ma'am," Michael said.

"You checking in?"

"We're looking for someone." He flashed a picture of Shehab.

She barely glanced at it. "We don't share information about our guests." Her tone was polite, almost bored.

"Even if they're terrorists?"

She took a step back, looking behind her as if for help, but there was nobody in the small room beyond the desk.

"This man and his friends took two innocent women hostage." He showed the photo of Leila. "We're trying to free them."

The woman's chin rose, glaring at Stone, then him. "Refugees?"

"Human beings," Michael snapped. "Friends of mine." This woman clearly shared the locals' disdain for refugees. Lesvos used to be a tourist haven. Now, most of the visitors came uninvited, by raft. And then there were humanitarian workers who weren't known for dropping fistfuls of cash. Tourists chose other islands for their beach vacations.

At Michael's harsh tone, the woman's attitude shifted. She glanced at the picture on the phone, then lifted one shoulder. "I haven't seen her."

He scrolled to Shehab's image again and angled it to face her.

"I haven't seen him."

But there was something in her tone. He didn't pull the phone back, didn't move, and didn't speak. Just waited.

After a moment, she added, "There are men who resemble him." Her eyes flicked around the space, but nobody was watching or listening.

She nodded out the doors toward the building on the left. "Second floor. Second door."

"Did you see them with women? Or very small men?"

"I don't watch who comes and goes."

She seemed exactly the type of woman who would, but he didn't challenge her.

"What about a car? What do they drive?"

Her lips pressed closed as she tapped into the computer on the desk. "They drive a white van. I saw it return not long ago. It's parked in the garage."

Stone walked away and spoke into his earpiece.

Michael heard the question, and the response, in his own ear.

The team confirmed that the van was there.

Michael held out his hand, palm up. "Key?"

After a slight hesitation, she tapped on her keyboard, then slid a plastic card through a machine to code the door lock into it. She slapped it into his hand. "You stole that."

He smiled. "I've never seen you before in my life." He leaned in and whispered. "God bless you."

He and Stone took the same side door they'd used to enter, keeping out of sight of the hotel room windows in case one of the guards looked out.

Stone was talking to Brock. Making a plan.

Michael listened through his earpiece.

Two men would come down from the roof and access the room via the balcony.

Two more would enter through the hallway.

Two would watch the doors on both sides of the building to make sure nobody escaped.

The goal: Disarm the terrorists and secure the hostages. Take Waleed Shehab into custody.

They could do this. With the element of surprise—and their advanced training, not to mention body armor—they'd be successful.

Their team had eight people.

But only jobs for six.

Brock would "direct traffic," as he liked to put it. Meaning he'd stay away from the fray.

Michael wasn't a bit surprised when Brock ordered him to wait in the car and "let the big boys handle it."

He managed to keep his response from slipping out.

If the team saved Leila and Jasmine, Michael would have nothing but gratitude for all of them.

They knew what they were doing, and in his state, with his wounds and his emotional connection, he'd probably be more of a liability than an asset. Not that he'd ever admit that out loud.

"I mean it," Brock said. "Do not interfere."

"Headed to the car." Michael got the keys from Stone and walked back to the rental, where he settled in the driver's seat to listen. And pray.

Only a few minutes passed before he heard the bang of a door through his earpiece. The one on the balcony, he guessed.

No gunshots.

Very few shouts, all in English.

And then... "They're not here." Stone's voice.

Michael tapped his earpiece to speak. "Who? The men? Leila and—"

"Room's empty," Stone said. "No targets, no hostages." A pause, then, "No luggage. Empty."

Stifling a curse, Michael sent Alyssa a text, just to be sure, even though Brock would be watching the location of the phones now.

She responded immediately.

Cells haven't moved.

At the same time, Tile's voice came through. "Phones are here. They left them."

Meaning, Shehab had figured out that Michael could track them.

And had led them right here. Wasting their time and diverting their focus.

Leila and Jasmine were gone. He'd lost them. And, if the guards weren't carrying those phones, he had no way to figure out where they'd been taken.

CHAPTER THIRTY-SIX

WALEED WAS GOING to kill Leila.

Or make her wish she were dead.

He squeezed her throat, cutting off her air.

The pain was unbearable. Silently, she begged Waleed to finish it. She knew where she was going. Heaven would be a place of peace. Jesus would welcome her. Michael would be waiting for her. The pain would be over.

She'd be able to breathe.

Things had been tense before. She'd huddled with her sister in the corner of the ruined apartment while the men stared out the window. Leila had no idea what they'd been looking for or what they'd seen.

At one point, she'd leaned forward toward the edge of the glass to try to get a glimpse, but Waleed had lifted his foot as if to kick her like a dog.

She'd scrambled out of his reach.

"Don't move again."

She settled against the wall as if she couldn't care less.

"There," the young driver said. "See?"

Suddenly, they'd all been so engrossed in what they saw outside that none of them paid her or Jasmine any attention.

She shifted slightly, moved her hand around on the floor to find the thing that'd jabbed her when she first sat. By the shape of it, she guessed it was a nail, maybe three inches long. The tip felt sharp, certainly sharp enough to break skin.

She shoved it into the pocket of her baggy jeans. Maybe she would get the opportunity to use it. Maybe it could help them escape.

This would be the perfect time, while the men looked out the window, except for the one who was guarding the door, arms crossed. Glaring at her as if she'd personally harmed him.

"There's another." The driver had narrated events as if all the men couldn't see. "They're like ants. Look at them. I count... four? Five?"

"There's two more," one of the guards said.

Leila hadn't known to be worried. She hadn't known what they were talking about.

She'd been stupid.

Because, suddenly, Waleed launched himself at her, yanked her to her feet by an arm. He shoved a hand against her throat.

Pressed her against the wall.

Squeezing. The pain was like nothing she'd ever experienced.

But worse was the terrifying, desperate need for air. She got just enough to stay alive. But if he squeezed any harder...

She was going to die.

And she didn't even know why.

Waleed's face, only centimeters from hers, contorted with rage. "Tell me everything you told them."

Leila tried to speak, but no sound came out.

"He already knew." Jasmine's words were rushed, frightened. "Leila did nothing. We told him nothing. The man who took us already knew."

"Lies!" Waleed punched Leila in the stomach.

Sharp and shocking, it would've doubled her over if Waleed hadn't held her against the wall. Her legs jerked up, coming out from under her, but Waleed tightened his hold.

She scrambled to stand lest he snap her neck.

"I'll kill her. I swear to Allah—"

"The man was CIA," Jasmine shouted. "He'd been watching Khalid. That's how he found us."

What? Jasmine hadn't known that, had she?

Jasmine's words were close to the truth, though it was possible she wasn't aware of that as she spun a story.

The room was getting darker. Closing in.

The pain...the pain was exquisite, narrowed to two small spots on Leila's neck until nothing existed but that place where thumb and forefinger squeezed, squeezed her windpipe.

Now, Lord. Take me now. To Yourself. To Michael. Please...

Suddenly, Waleed let her go.

She collapsed on the floor, her legs too weak to stop her fall.

She drew in a breath of the stale, rank air and thanked God for it. Her throat still felt tight, too small.

Jasmine crawled close and leaned over her, brushing her hair away from her face. "Are you—?"

But Jasmine gasped—and was gone.

Leila tried to focus on what was happening, but the world was still dark and blurry.

"I should kill you." Waleed seemed angrier and more dangerous than she'd ever heard him.

"But you will not." Jasmine's voice was no longer afraid. She sounded confident. "If you hurt me, you could hurt him. And he will kill you."

What?

Leila's throat screamed in pain. Her ankle ached where she'd fallen.

And she was confused.

The lack of oxygen must've affected her because her sister made no sense. Leila had no belief that Jasmine's crazy claim would change anything.

But Jasmine knelt beside her again. She lifted Leila's head and shoulders onto her lap, leaning down to whisper in her ear. "It's going to be all right. God is with us."

Was He?

Leila wasn't sure anymore. She wasn't sure about anything. Because the world was fuzzy and her throat was throbbing and her sister was confident and Michael was dead, and nothing made any sense at all.

Waleed spoke to the guards in low tones by the door.

Leila didn't even try to listen. She hurt too much to care what they said.

Most of the guards left, their pounding footsteps on the staircase fading until the door slammed three stories below.

Waleed, the young driver, Jasmine, and Leila stayed in that disgusting fourth-floor room for ten more minutes before making their way back down the stairs. Unlike on the way up, this time, Jasmine supported her.

She still felt weak as a newborn, every breath burning, her ankle throbbing—she must've twisted it when she fell, though she hadn't felt that over the desperate need to breathe. She was grateful for every inhale of the acrid air.

Jasmine seemed strong. The confrontation with Waleed hadn't cowed her but had, strangely, infused her with courage.

Would that Leila and her sister could both be strong at the

same time. To what end, though? They weren't getting out of this. Any hope she'd held onto had been squeezed out of her by Waleed's fingers against her windpipe. What could one pathetic rusty nail do to these men?

Leila and Jasmine would be returned to Iraq. Or they would die.

Leila would prefer death over a lifetime with Waleed. What would he do to her when she refused him on their wedding night?

What pain did she have to look forward to?

Why would God leave her here? *Why didn't You take me?*

At least she hadn't been murdered in front of her sister. For now, she and her twin still had each other. When Leila was alone with Waleed, she would pray for death.

They approached the sedan, where they were certain to be tossed in the trunk again.

But Jasmine froze a few feet from it, stopping Leila as well. "We will not be treated like baggage."

Waleed spun and bent to get in her sister's face. "You will do as you're told, or I will tie you up like a pig."

"I'll tell him. And he'll kill you."

"You overestimate your value, Yasamin."

"You overestimate yours, Waleed."

Leila ducked away, overcome with shame for abandoning her sister.

Jasmine wasn't cowering.

But Leila wouldn't survive another show of Waleed's strength, and he wouldn't let Jasmine's words go unpunished.

He glared. Then spoke over her head. "Yasamin will ride in the front seat with you. My bride will sit with me." To Jasmine, he said, "If you try anything, I will hurt her." Waleed swiveled and marched to the car.

Jasmine whispered in Leila's ear. "Are you all right, sister?"

"I-I..." Her throat wouldn't work. She had no sound, no voice.

Jasmine glared at the back of Waleed's head as he walked away.

The young driver hovered behind them, the flow of his words finally cut off.

With only two men to guard them, there probably wouldn't be a better opportunity to try to escape. But Leila didn't have the strength to fight, and thanks to Jasmine's illness, she wouldn't be able to run. To attempt it now would be suicide.

Or worse, they would survive and be punished.

Leila had to hold onto hope that there would be an opportunity.

Even if that hope felt as elusive as fog.

She settled in the backseat beside Waleed. He wasn't as big or broad as Michael, yet he took up far too much room.

She leaned against the door, as far from him as she could manage.

Jasmine sat in front of her, the driver taking his place behind the wheel. "Straight there?"

"Everything should be set up and wired."

The driver dipped his head. Gone was his exuberance. He looked pale and nervous. Was he afraid of what was to come? Or had the events—Michael's murder and whatever they'd seen out that window—caught up with him?

Now that she thought of it, she recalled what the men had said right before Waleed attacked her.

What had been *like ants*?

Soldiers? Police?

They'd been close to where they'd left the van. Had they been watching that place? That parking garage? Maybe the structure attached to it?

Were there men looking for her and Jasmine? With Michael gone...

She couldn't dwell on that. If she dwelled on it, she'd crumble and be useless.

Were Michael's people here? His...special CIA team?

If he'd called them, he hadn't told her about it. Would he have kept that from her?

She didn't think so.

She didn't understand and couldn't make sense of it. Nevertheless, against her better judgment, against all logic, hope gathered strength inside her like an injured bird, flapping its wings.

Trying to fly.

She watched the world outside the window. Tiny, narrow roads lined with restaurants and shops. People hurried along sidewalks, casting gazes at the gathering clouds above. A storm was coming, the world getting darker by the second.

She wished with everything in her to be one of those people. Worried about a little rain. Trying to decide what to eat for dinner. What to wear on a date.

She longed for the everyday worries of an everyday life.

But she'd traded her everyday—completely controlled—life in Iraq for freedom in Germany.

And then she'd had both normalcy and freedom snatched from her. Her hope of a happy life and a happy home were gone forever like the man she'd hoped to share those things with.

Oh, Lord. Forgive me. If she could do it all over again, she'd do exactly what Michael said, every step of the way. She wouldn't argue with him. She wouldn't distrust him.

This was her fault. She and Jasmine should have gone straight to Baghdad on that motorcycle. She should have stayed in the truck at the hospital in Diyarbakir. Michael had done everything in his power to protect her, and she'd gone against him and argued with him every step of the way.

Her foolishness had brought her and Jasmine here.

And sent Michael to his grave.

Forgive me, Father. I should have trusted him.

And then she knew something she hadn't understood before. It wasn't lack of faith in *Michael* that'd had her demanding to know—and have her way—in every step of their journey. Michael wasn't perfect, but he was intelligent and capable and trained. She couldn't have asked for a better rescuer.

He was...had been...following God's lead, praying for guidance and wisdom and strength all along.

It wasn't that she doubted Michael.

She doubted God.

Help me, Lord. Help me learn this lesson.

Let my sister not pay for my sins.

The way Leila would, knowing she'd caused the death of the man she loved.

The way his parents and brothers would when they learned their second-born was gone.

The driver reached a busy road and stopped to wait for a break in the traffic.

The close buildings gave way to space and air. Between the scattered buildings on the far side of the street, the Mediterranean churned, meeting the dark, stormy sky. A flash of lightning on the horizon was followed by a low rumble of thunder.

They turned right, and she looked at the shops and little sidewalk cafés. The sidewalks were emptying.

But sitting at one café...

She gasped.

Michael?

No. Not Michael. And not Derrick.

But that had to be the other brother, Bryan, sipping coffee and reading his phone like a tourist—despite the coming storm.

It had to be him. It had to be.

She tried to scream, desperate to get his attention, but barely a sound rasped out.

Waleed gripped her arm. "What is wrong with you?"

She ignored him, reaching forward to pinch her sister's hip.

Jasmine jumped.

"What are you doing?" Waleed said.

She didn't care what he said or did to her now. Because Michael's brother wasn't there to enjoy the scenery. He was looking for them. He had to be.

She banged against the window.

Waleed yanked her away.

But Jasmine screamed, the sound high-pitched and deafening in the small car.

The man at the table looked up, saw the car. But he gave no indication that he recognized them. Just settled back in with his phone.

Waleed twisted to look out the rear window. "Who is that?"

She tried to speak, but words wouldn't come out her swollen throat.

"Who!" he shouted.

"Leave her alone!" Jasmine snapped. "We thought it was Michael. The man you killed."

But it wasn't. And it wasn't Michael's brother. It was just a tourist who happened to be tall and dark-haired.

Tears filled Leila's eyes, dripped down her cheeks.

Smiling, Waleed settled beside her again. "You thought that was your boyfriend? I deprived you of oxygen too long, eh?" He chuckled, utterly confident.

And why shouldn't he be?

There was nobody looking for them.

The only one besides Jasmine who'd cared if she lived or died was Michael, and he was gone.

CHAPTER THIRTY-SEVEN

MICHAEL HAD SPENT the first ten minutes after the failed raid trying to get information on what vehicles had left the hotel property and where they'd gone.

It hadn't taken long to realize the satellite hadn't caught anything but the movement of clouds.

Leila and Jasmine had disappeared.

And he had no idea where to find them.

He'd already sent the rest of the phone numbers from Waleed Shehab's laptop to headquarters—and Alyssa—to try to find locations.

Nothing, nothing, nothing.

No leads. No sightings. Nothing.

While his team searched the hotel room for some indication of where Shehab might've taken them, Michael studied a map of the island. There weren't that many options.

Twenty minutes had passed—twenty long minutes while Leila and Jasmine moved farther and farther away—when his cell rang. Bryan's number displayed on his screen. He barked into the phone, "What!"

"I saw them." Bryan was huffing. "They passed the marina

and turned on a road beside it. There're a bunch of buildings. I can't tell exactly where they went. I'm walking that direction now."

Hope had Michael's heart thumping. "You sure it was them?"

"Identical twins. One of the women screamed. She was looking at me. It was them."

"She screamed? So they know you saw them? The terrorists?"

"I played it cool."

"Okay, good." Who knew what Bryan had done—or given away—in that moment. Or if Leila and Jasmine had given it away. He couldn't count on the element of surprise. "Don't get closer. And stay on the line. Calling it in." He tapped his earpiece. "Bryan's got 'em. They're near the marina. I'm going."

"Hold up." Brock, of course.

"I won't engage. I'll just see what's going on."

He shifted into drive, ready to gun the car back toward where they'd left Bryan.

But he didn't.

Brock hadn't said no. He'd just told him to wait. Not exactly Michael's strong suit.

Going it alone hadn't worked. He needed his team. "Come on, Brock. We need to know—"

"Report what you see," Brock said. "Do not engage."

"Yessir." He tapped the earpiece to silence his end. "I'm on my way," he told Bryan. "Send me a pin, and then go back to the café. Better yet, get an Uber to the airport and wait with Derrick, on the plane."

Where his brothers would be safe.

His phone dinged with the location, and he aimed toward it.

"You sure you won't need my help?" Bryan asked.

Not that he wouldn't take all the help he could get, but he

wasn't putting Bryan in danger. "We got it. Thank you. I can't even..." Emotion welled in his throat. He waited until it passed. "Thank you."

"Anytime. Be careful."

Michael ended the call.

One minute later, he squealed around a corner onto the four-lane road that hugged the coast. He passed Bryan, who was walking on the sidewalk, slowly. Across the street, a narrow road led to a couple of buildings all tucked up beside each other. Behind them, nothing but churning sea.

He continued past a small parking lot in front of a hotel.

Fat raindrops plopped on his windshield. Any second, the skies were going to open up.

Michael parked in an alley and fast-walked in the rain back to the lot. He hopped a fence and approached the hotel from the side, keeping close to bushes and trees that, with the help of the stormy darkness, would hide him from lookouts.

The hotel was bed-and-breakfast-sized, three stories high and probably held no more than four rooms per floor. The crumbling and dilapidated exterior told him this was no four-star property, but he doubted Waleed and company had chosen it for luxury.

As Michael reached the back of the property, his suspicions were confirmed. It wasn't the rooms Waleed had wanted but the private dock. Sailboats, fishing boats, and a few personal watercrafts—Jet Skis or WaveRunners or the like—bobbed on the choppy swells.

His gaze snagged on the vessel at the far end. It was larger than the rest but too short to be considered a yacht—maybe thirty feet from stem to stern. Beneath the deck, Michael assumed there was a galley and perhaps a bedroom. Perched a few steps above the deck, a small glassed-in cockpit.

Unlike the rest of the boats, lights glowed from within this one. And it was crawling with men.

He sent a pin to his team and tapped his earpiece. "They're on a boat at a private marina, preparing to leave."

"Don't engage," Brock said.

Michael counted four men on the deck, one more in the cockpit—all armed, he assumed. He could be rash sometimes. But he wasn't stupid.

"How far out are you?"

"Rain and traffic are slowing us down," Brock said.

Stone added, "Five minutes."

But the men on deck were unwinding ropes. Pulling buoys into the watercraft.

The engine rumbled to life. Water bubbled behind it.

The boat backed out of the slip.

"They're moving!" he shouted. "You're gonna need a boat. A fast boat." He scanned the private marina once more. "There's nothing here that'll work."

Which wasn't exactly true. But there was nothing large enough for the whole team.

Staying low, he jogged toward the dock, looking at the only options faster than the boat now motoring away. Jet Skis.

He bolted toward the hotel's rear door.

"We're headed to the marina," Stone said. "We'll secure a boat there. We'll contact the Hellenic Coast Guard. I know you like to go it alone, but—"

"Call in all the help you can get. Call the US Navy if you want. We have to stop them."

"Uh, not sure the Navy's anywhere nearby, but—"

"I'm getting a Jet Ski," Michael said.

"No!" Brock's command was sharp. "Stay there."

Michael reached the hotel door and yanked. It was locked.

He muted his earpiece and pounded until a clerk yanked it open.

Michael had no idea what the man was shouting at him in Greek. "I need the keys to one of the Jet Skis. Now."

"No, no. We don't rent in storms—"

"It's an emergency. I don't have time to explain."

The man stepped back, only then seeing the Glock Michael had pulled from its holster. His eyes widened and his arms went up like this was a stickup from an old Western.

Michael lifted his own hands. "I'm not going to hurt anyone. I need those keys, though. Now."

Blinking rapidly, the man seemed to be slipping into full panic mode.

"It's okay." Michael forced a calm tone. "Just get me the keys, and I'll leave. I'll bring it back."

Maybe. More likely, he'd be writing a check to cover the cost.

He was about two seconds away from aiming the Glock when the clerk swiveled and ran toward a check-in desk. He opened a drawer, chose a key hanging from a bright pink chain with a clip, and held it out.

Michael snatched it and ran back out into the now pouring rain.

"Answer me, Wrong!" Brock cursed. Michael had tuned him out for a few moments. "If you disobey me, I swear—"

"I'm here," Michael said.

"Stand down. Wait for your team."

Wait for his team.

That had been his problem all along. He hadn't waited for his team. He hadn't trusted his team.

But Shehab was getting away.

He and his team needed to take him into custody. They

could find out from him everything his little band of terror was concocting. They had to stop him.

But he didn't say any of that because, honestly, he couldn't have cared less about Waleed Shehab and his information at that moment.

All he wanted was to rescue Leila.

Michael watched as the boat got smaller and smaller in the distance, nearly disappearing in the sea spray and darkness.

"I'm not going to engage." Michael kept his voice calm and steady. "In this weather, if we lose them, we might not find them again. Let me follow. At a distance. I'll share my location." He pulled out his cell and did. "Now you'll know where I am. And where they are."

"You're going to take a Jet Ski out in a storm?" Brock's voice rose with disbelief. "Are you insane? You'll get yourself killed, and how will that help anybody?"

"I can handle it. I've been riding these things all my life. I grew up on the ocean, remember?"

"Stand down." Brock sounded determined. And he never reversed a decision.

But a boat the size of Shehab's would have a hundred-gallon tank, maybe larger. Even if the vessel only got five miles per gallon, that would give them a five-hundred-mile radius. They could make it to Antalya, or Cypress. Or any of a thousand other ports scattered across the Mediterranean.

Waleed would disappear.

Leila would be gone forever.

Michael couldn't lose her now. He wouldn't.

"Please, Brock." He reached the dock and climbed onto the first Jet Ski he came to, jamming the key in the hole.

Hoping, praying that Brock would change his mind.

The key didn't fit. Michael moved to the next Jet Ski.

Brock still hadn't answered.

"Please." Michael would beg if he had to. "I won't engage. I'll keep my distance."

The key didn't fit the second. He moved to the third and last.

Either this would work, or the clerk had tricked him to get him out of the hotel. Either way, he'd called the police. If this didn't work, Michael would probably end up in jail.

He shoved it in the keyhole and turned it.

The dashboard lights came on.

Based on what he heard in his ear, his team had reached the marina. They were discussing the different vessels they could procure. But they'd need to find an owner or figure out how to get one started without permission. It would take time.

"Brock, I'm begging you. We're going to lose him."

The voices in his ear silenced. Muted.

He imagined his teammates discussing it. Considering it. While he pulled the ropes off the Jet Ski and tossed them onto the dock.

Please, please.

The longer Brock waited, the smaller the boat got in the distance.

Finally, they unmuted their end. "Keep your distance," Brock said. "Do not engage until we're there. And don't drown."

"Yessir! I'll let you know what I learn."

He started the engine and blasted out of the marina, aiming for the speck on the horizon. The speck that was getting smaller and smaller.

CHAPTER THIRTY-EIGHT

TERROR CLOGGED Leila's swollen throat as the boat bounced over waves, pitching and roiling on the angry sea.

Leila had never been on a boat like this before—had never been on a boat at all except for the blow-up raft Michael had purchased. Whereas that one had been flimsy but new, this one felt solid but ancient.

She and Jasmine had been forced down the stairs into a tiny room. The bench where they huddled together was upholstered with faded red, orange, and green plaid that looked like it'd come from the previous century. The wood-paneled walls were worn and gouged, even separating in some places. The floor was cracked linoleum.

She hated to think of the condition of the...what was it called? The bottom of the boat? The...hull?

Was it also cracked? Was it taking on water?

She wasn't sure what frightened her more, the horrific death that would come if the boat sank, or the horrific life that lay ahead if it didn't.

Jasmine had vomited twice, probably not the result of whatever illness plagued her but seasickness. Now she laid her head on Leila's lap, curled up, arms wrapped around her middle.

Leila's stomach was churning, too, as she stroked her sister's long hair, trying to offer comfort despite her fear.

They'd been brought down here a few minutes before the engine roared to life. Most of the men were above, but two guards stayed with them as if they might try to escape. One was seated at a table near the stairs they'd come down, which led to a closed door above. He was eating a sandwich he'd pulled from a small refrigerator.

The other was on a chair adjacent to Leila and her sister, sipping a Coke.

There were other men above, in the pouring rain or perhaps in the little room above the deck. Maybe they'd all get swept away. Maybe the storm would take them.

Leaving her and her sister alone with these two.

Not alone, though. No matter what happened with Waleed and his cohorts, God was here. He was watching out for Leila and her sister. Whatever their future held, the One True God would never leave them or forsake them.

He'd promised.

No matter how bleak things get, I will trust You.

Rather than allowing herself to be overwhelmed with hope-lessness, she bent close to her sister and prayed, her raspy voice barely audible over the engine's rumble, the thunder, the men's footsteps, and the pouring rain.

She begged God to rescue them. To send help. To get them out of this.

Only God could save them now.

CHAPTER THIRTY-NINE

MICHAEL HAD LOST his connection to his team awhile back, and a glance behind showed no sign of them. But they were back there, somewhere.

Between the darkness from the heavy cloud cover, sea spray, and drenching rain, the boat was barely more than a smudge on the horizon.

Michael was gaining on it, but the choppy water and high waves made the ride treacherous. He had to be careful, hang on tight. Not let himself get thrown.

If he got thrown, he'd be separated from the Jet Ski, and in these waters, he might not be able to find it again, much less swim back to it. He wore no life jacket. He'd end up treading water, praying for his own rescue.

Useless to Leila and Jasmine.

So, though he itched to go faster, he didn't dare.

Cold seeped through his sodden clothes, chilling him through and through. His hands were frozen on the handlebar.

He feared he'd run out of fuel before he caught up, and all this would be for nothing.

Help, Lord.

He transferred all his questions and fears into prayers, never taking his eyes off his target.

Thirty minutes. Forty-five. An hour. Driving straight into the storm.

It didn't let up. If anything, it got worse. The swells higher. The rain heavier.

Growing up near the Maine coast, Michael had heard stories of ships in storms. All the modern advancements weren't a guarantee against shipwreck. Only a fool would be out here in the elements on a personal watercraft.

But the shadow got larger and larger until the boat took shape.

If Michael caught up with it, what was he going to do? Board it, try to take on all those men by himself?

How would getting himself killed help anything?

Brock and the team wouldn't announce their presence. They had to be moving in, using the darkness to their advantage.

Finally nearing his target, Michael slowed, not wanting to be seen. He maintained his distance, praying somebody would come along to help soon.

And then from the north, a boat moved in fast.

Not the team. No, this boat was lit up like...

The town square at Christmastime.

The Hellenic Coast Guard, on track to intercept.

Shehab must've seen it because the boat turned south.

Michael heard a crackle in his ear.

"Wrong." Stone's voice. "You there?"

Yes! He tapped his earpiece. "Quarter mile west of the target."

"We're intercepting from the south," Stone said.

"Coast guard's coming from the north. Shehab just turned toward you."

"We got him on radar. We're about two clicks out."

Two clicks. A little over a mile.

"Plan?" Michael asked.

"Stand by."

Michael moved closer to Shehab's boat, holding himself less than fifty yards away. He figured the men on board would be focused on the giant coast guard vessel and, when it came into view, the boat Stone and the team had procured. Even if they were looking toward Michael, he doubted they'd see him through the pouring rain.

"I can board it and disable it," Michael said.

"Stand by." Brock spoke this time.

Michael's team would put together a plan. If they used him in it, fine. If not...

He'd trust that they knew what they were doing. There weren't a lot of options. Waleed would aim for a port where he'd feel secure, where American soldiers weren't welcome. The team had to intercept the terrorists and rescue Leila and Jasmine before they came close to land.

"Okay," Stone finally said. "Listen closely."

It was simple—if not easy. The coast guard was going to come around from the east.

Brock and the team would head Shehab off on the west.

"We need you to approach from the north," Stone said. "Without being seen."

Michael gunned the engine and circled that way.

The plan should work. Assuming the men on board were rational and cared about their lives, it would work.

But terrorists weren't rational, and they didn't care about human lives—their own or anybody else's.

He'd seen firsthand the damage they could do.

Early in his career, one of his confidential informants had been granted entry into the US, where Michael had assured him he'd be safe from the people who'd discovered he was passing information to Michael. The man had barely gotten settled when homegrown terrorists, having learned about what they considered his treachery, found him.

They took the man hostage.

Because it happened on US soil, Michael called the FBI. The problem was, the FBI hostage negotiator assumed the hostage-takers were rational and would act in their own self-interest.

He negotiated while the terrorists plotted and lied, making deals they never intended to keep.

When the FBI moved close, believing the kidnappers had been convinced to give up their hostage and turn themselves in, the terrorists started shooting.

FBI agents were killed. Terrorists were killed.

And Michael's CI was killed.

The guilt had nearly destroyed him. He'd never been the most trusting soul, but after that, he found it nearly impossible to rely on anybody but himself.

This time, Michael had to trust his team. Even so, no matter what Brock and Stone planned, anything could happen.

But the alternative—losing Leila to these madmen, maybe never finding her again—was unthinkable.

Time dragged.

Or maybe it was the cold that made Michael feel like he was moving in slow motion.

Though he didn't check his watch, dared not take his eyes off the target, Michael thought at least half an hour had passed by the time he'd circled and reached the rear of the boat.

As he'd hoped, none of Shehab's men seemed to notice his

approach. They were all focused on the giant military vessel heading them off from one side and the smaller speed boat they surely saw by now, coming in fast from the opposite direction.

Shehab or whoever was at the helm hadn't slowed. If anything, he was going faster than before, the boat hitting the swells hard.

The Jet Ski got air more than once as Michael worked to match its speed. When he was close, he said, "Two minutes."

"Copy."

He aimed for the starboard side, bouncing over the larger vessel's wake and breathing thanks for the howling wind and downpour that covered the noise of his approach. When he was alongside, he matched the boat's speed, getting near enough that someone would have to look straight down from the deck to see him.

Now came the hard part. He had to figure out how to get from the Jet Ski to the boat without landing in the water. At thirty-plus miles per hour.

Lord, I'm gonna need some help.

To his team, he said, "Boarding."

"Copy," Stone said, adding, "Careful."

Yeah.

He took a breath. Held the throttle with his right hand and lifted his right foot onto the seat.

A big wave nearly bounced him off the watercraft. But he managed to keep his grip, only dropping behind a little. He sped up again.

A waist-high metal bar surrounded the swim platform at the stern. He reached out with his left hand, let up on the throttle.

He launched himself toward the bar, shoving the Jet Ski away in the process.

He gripped the bar.

It was wet and cold and slippery, and his fingers slipped.

He managed to swing his other hand up and held on.

That was close. Too close.

He dangled, his feet dragging in the freezing surf. He swung them onto the swim platform and ducked under the metal bar.

Once on the slick surface, he tucked himself against the low wall beside a short ladder that led to the deck.

"You on?" Stone must've been watching through binoculars.

"On." He kept his voice low, unholstering his Glock.

And listened.

At first, he heard nothing but the engine and the surf and the wind.

Lightning flashed. Seconds later, thunder roared.

He'd seen two men on the deck near the stern when he'd approached but had no idea where they were now. Even if they'd looked behind, they probably hadn't seen Michael. If they knew he was there, bullets would already be flying. He needed to keep his presence hidden as long as possible to give the team the opportunity to close in.

And him the chance to get the twins into the water.

He didn't want to think about what that might require.

As he calmed and focused, he heard voices. They carried not above the other sounds, but below them, nearly concealed in the low-pitched roar.

Two men, speaking in rapid Arabic. Too fast and too distant for Michael to translate.

But not so far away that he could get by them without being seen. Which meant he'd need to take them out.

But how, without alerting everyone else on board of his presence?

Lightning burst in the sky, and he had his answer. He counted one, two, three...

Thunder cracked.

Michael scrambled up the ladder, stopping below the level of the deck to avoid being seen.

He whispered, "Next thunder, I go."

"Copy," Stone said.

He waited, waited.

Come on.

He both cursed this stupid storm for its cold and waves and thanked God for the darkness and noise.

Come on...

A flash.

One...Michael popped his head up.

Two...sighted the man to the port side.

Three...

Thunder crackled.

He fired. The man went down.

The other man turned when his friend collapsed. Confused.

Michael fired again, getting the shot off an instant before the thunder faded.

Keeping low, he scrambled onto the deck and to the first man. He opened one of the bench seats surrounding the deck, then lifted the man and dumped him inside. A moment before he closed the lid, he spied something. A waterproof bag, the kind used to protect food and cell phones.

Perfect.

He grabbed it, opened a second bench seat. There were only two life jackets. He grabbed them and dumped the second body inside.

The rain was already washing away the blood.

With the life jackets and the bag looped over one arm, he settled in front of the hatch that led belowdecks, breathing. Thinking.

The sisters were probably in the cabin. He wanted to get them off the boat, but he had to disable the engine first. Which meant the terrorists were probably going to know he was there before he could rescue Leila and her sister.

He hated that, but there was nothing for it.

Much as he wanted to check on them, he had to assume they weren't alone, and the guards with them wouldn't wait for the cover of thunder to shoot.

He'd have had no choice in the matter if not for the second hatch just a few feet away. This one was built into the deck floor right beside the stairs that led up to the cockpit. If the pilot or someone with him were to look down at just the right moment, they'd see him.

A risk he'd have to take.

He pressed his hands against the cold door behind him, imagining Leila on the other side. Terrified of the water and the waves. And the men who'd snatched her. *Soon, sweetheart. Just hang on.*

He considered waiting for another blast of lightning, but the storm seemed to be moving off. Staying low, he hurried to the hatch, pulled it up, swung down, and lowered it over his head.

He froze in the pitch-black room. No movement. No alarm.

The howl of the wind, the crash of the waves, the pummeling of the rain—all of it faded in the roar of the engine.

In his ear, Stone said, "You're in?"

"In. Hold."

Michael turned on his phone flashlight and scanned the small, hidden space. The engine wasn't much bigger than the one that'd been on the boat Dad had when they were kids. Daniel, Michael's older brother, had never had any interest in learning how it worked, but Michael and Sam had helped Dad tinker with it. It'd always needed repair or maintenance.

Dad had told them that understanding how engines worked would come in handy someday.

Right again, Dad.

Before Michael did what he came to do, he angled the flashlight to the wall on the opposite side of the closet-like space, seeing a hatch that must open into the cabin. This was a small enough boat that he doubted there were multiple rooms belowdecks. Meaning the twins were most likely right on the other side of that door.

He scanned the ceiling again, and the walls, but there were no other ways in or out of the engine room.

Two entrances. He'd only be able to defend one. But he'd need to get to Leila and Jasmine. So...

He searched the floor. Dad had always kept tools in their boat's engine room. Sure enough, Michael found a tool box and, inside, a long screwdriver and a small pry bar.

He stuck the pry bar into his back pocket, then wedged the screwdriver through the handle in the ceiling hatch and against the ceiling. That should keep the hatch closed for a few minutes.

Maybe it would be long enough.

He found a spot to wedge his phone, aiming the flashlight out so he'd be able to see.

"Starting now," he said.

Stone's response: "Moving in."

He slid the waterproof bag off his arm.

There were two ways to disable a diesel engine. The first was to cut off the fuel. Problem with that was getting it running again would be a simple matter of reconnecting the fuel line.

Well, first shooting Michael and then reconnecting the fuel line, which would give the terrorists a chance to escape.

The second method caused more damage. It wouldn't render the engine unfixable, but it would take some time and expertise to get it going again.

He doubted any of the men on board had the expertise.

Even if they did, with the team so close, they definitely wouldn't have time.

He found the air intake and shoved the waterproof bag in front of it to block it.

Only a few seconds passed before the engine sputtered and died.

Bringing profound quiet.

Voices rose from above, Arabic, but loud enough that he caught most of what they were saying.

"What happened?"

"I don't know."

Someone else shouted, "Go check!"

Cursing and footsteps, easy to make out as the boat slowed, pitching this way and that on the waves.

Michael hurried to the cabin hatch, gun at the ready, and inched it open.

He peeked into the room.

Heard a gasp.

Leila slapped her hand over her mouth.

A man moved into Michael's line of sight from around the corner.

Michael fired, and the guard lurched backward.

Another guard was there. He must've been in the galley behind the women.

The man shoved Jasmine out of the way and yanked Leila up from the couch, putting her between Michael and himself.

Blocking Michael's shot.

Jasmine crouched as if she might attack the guard, which could have him firing the gun he held to Leila's head. Killing her.

He shook his head. *Please, don't.*

Jasmine didn't move, just looked between Michael and Leila.

Leila's eyes went from wide and afraid to something else. Determined.

Her hand came down, hard, against the man's leg.

Blood spurted.

The man cried out and pitched to one side. Leila ducked to the other.

Michael fired, drilling the shot in the center of his forehead.

The man collapsed.

Footsteps and shouting came from above and then on the steps.

A man burst into the room.

Michael fired, and the enemy tumbled into the cabin and fell.

"Come on. Hurry!" Michael gestured to the tiny space behind him.

The twins bolted past him and inside.

He closed the hatch and jammed it with the pry bar.

"I have them," Michael said. "We're in the engine room."

"Copy." Brock this time.

The cabin hatch rattled, along with shouts and curses and demands that they open up.

Someone must've gotten the bright idea to shoot their way in, based on warnings not to.

So the terrorists weren't all stupid. Firing at an engine was rarely a good idea. It probably wouldn't explode—this wasn't the movies, after all—but it could cause the engine to seize up.

Which meant, as long as the pry bar held, Michael and the twins would be safe from that direction.

No sounds came from the hatch overhead.

Did Waleed and his men even know it was there?

"You two all right?" Michael slid the life jackets off his arm and handed them to the sisters. He started to help Jasmine with hers.

"I can do it," she said.

The steadiness in her voice surprised him. Despite the illness, she seemed strong. "Don't forget the strap between your legs. You'll need that."

At her nod, he shifted to Leila. She'd already started clicking her life jacket in place. He checked, making sure it was tight enough. Mostly, just wanting to be near her. "What'd you stab him with?"

"A nail." Her voice was low and raspy. "I waited, like you said."

"Well done." He wanted to pull her close. He wanted to tell her he loved her and he was sorry and he was never going to let her out of his sight again.

But not yet.

There'd be plenty of time for that later.

"How are you here?" she asked.

Her voice sounded like she'd come down with laryngitis since he last saw her.

"How are you alive?"

"Bullet grazed me," he said. "And dazed me for a few seconds. Long enough for them to get you." He held her shoulders and leaned away, straining to see her face in the dim light. She looked not like the man he'd made her up to be, but like Leila. Lovely, vulnerable Leila.

He pulled her against his chest, whispered, "I'm sorry. I love you."

"You do not apologize. You are our rescuer. Again."

He hoped she felt the same way after he told her the plan.

The cabin hatch was rattling against the metal wall. By the multiple voices, lots of men were trying to gain access.

"How many?"

"There were six at the airport, but when we came on board, there were more. I do not know."

"You hear that, Brock?" Michael asked.

Brock said, "Copy."

"Listen." He shifted to address both women. "You remember before we got in the raft, I showed you how well the life jackets work?"

"Yes," Jasmine said.

Leila nodded, but even in the darkness, he saw fear in her eyes.

"They'll pull you above water. You just have to hold your breath when you go in."

The wall hatch was about to give. They had seconds.

He climbed the ladder to the ceiling exit.

Maybe the men were all in the cabin.

Or maybe some were on the deck, hoping to trick him into the open. Where they'd shoot.

"Brock. Any men on deck at the stern?"

"One, port side, watching the coast guard."

"Copy." To the sisters, he said, "I'm going to open this and provide cover. While I do that, run to your left." He pointed toward the rear of the boat on the starboard side, to be sure they both understood. "And jump."

"What?" Leila's question came out ragged.

He'd never heard so much terror in a single word.

"I'll be right behind you." He kissed her forehead. "Trust me."

They were out of time.

If Leila and Jasmine didn't do as he said...

This would end very badly.

CHAPTER FORTY

LEILA WAS STILL TRYING to make sense of what Michael had said.

Jump? Into the sea?

Was he insane?

But killers were coming. Almost in.

Michael shoved the door over his head open, rose up, aimed. Fired. "Go!"

Everything in her screamed.

No!

But she didn't try to come up with a plan B.

She scrambled up and out into the cold, damp air.

Jasmine followed, right on her heels. They bolted to the side of the boat.

Reached the railing.

Climbed up.

Inhaled.

And jumped.

Into the abyss.

Water covered her, frigid. It had waited, waited all those

years for the life that had been snatched from its jaws when she was a child. It swallowed her now, pulling her down, down...

She tasted salt and death and knew this was the end.

But then she rose, just like Michael had promised she would.

Someone gripped the life jacket and yanked her back to the surface.

She sucked in blessed air.

"I got you," a man said. "Stop fighting me. I got you."

Was she fighting? She was fighting—fighting death and terror. She forced her limbs to be still.

"That's better." The man kicked, taking her along with him. "I'm Stone. A friend of Michael's."

"Where's Yasamin?"

"We got her. So that makes you Leila? Michael's girlfriend?"

"Yes."

"Nice to meet you."

The words were friendly, spoken as if they were meeting over coffee. How could the man be so calm?

"Where is Michael?" She looked around. Surely, he'd jumped right behind her. "Is he drowning? He wasn't wearing a life jacket." She strained to see another body in the water.

"Don't worry," Stone said. "He's all right."

But how could he know?

Before she could ask, hands pulled her up and out of the water. Onto another boat.

Michael had come for her. And this time, he'd brought his whole team.

Once she was on the deck, the man let her go and reached over again. He dragged Jasmine up.

The two rescuers swam away, back toward Waleed's boat.

Shouts rose above the fear rushing in her brain.

Shouts and gunshots.

She and her sister were safe, but this was far from over.

CHAPTER FORTY-ONE

MICHAEL SHOT two men while Leila and her sister jumped overboard.

He wanted to check on them, to be sure they were safe.

Instead, he hurried out of the engine room and closed the hatch.

No way to lock it from up here. And no time.

His team swarmed over the side of the boat. Engaging the hostiles in the cabin and on the deck.

Michael was closest to the stairs leading to the cockpit. He crouched low and climbed. When he reached the door, he looked inside.

The room was large enough for a couple of captain's chairs and all the equipment needed to maneuver the boat.

He didn't see anybody.

But a bullet whizzed by his head.

That was a little too close. "Missed me again, Waleed."

He expected expletives. Or at least an angry retort.

But the hidden man inside only chuckled. "*I* did not miss you at the airport," Shehab said. "That was my young friend. I shouldn't have trusted him with the job."

Shouts below. A few scattered gunshots.

"Hard to get good help these days," Michael said.

"Indeed."

This was the cultured voice he'd heard at the compound.

This was the man he'd almost killed in Diyarbakir.

The man who'd looked at eleven-year-old Leila with hunger. And now planned to force her to marry him.

Over Michael's dead body. Which, of course, Shehab would be happy to bring about.

Below and in his ear, he heard his team calling to each other.

Clear.

Clear.

Clear down here.

"It's all falling apart." Michael kept up the conversational tone. There was no reason to rush now. It was just a matter of time before he and the team got Shehab to surrender. Surrender and give up all his secrets. Or commit suicide, which Michael wouldn't put past him. But the team would move in. While Michael distracted him, one of them would find a way to disarm him.

"The women are safe. You're on your own. How many of your people have I killed in the last week? I've lost count." Though he said the words casually, the images flashed through his mind. Enemies falling onto the desert floor.

At the van.

On the boat deck.

For every moment Michael remembered, did Shehab see a face? A friend?

Did he care?

He didn't have a snappy comeback, which made Michael think that, despite the terrorist's penchant for violence, he had at least had a little regard for the men who followed him.

Tension stretched between them.

A bullet ricocheted off the wall beside Michael's head, inches away.

"Close," Michael said. "But even if you shoot me, you're not getting out of this. I've got my whole team here. And of course, if you look to the port side—that's your right, if you're facing me—you'll see the coast guard. Pretty sure you can't defeat us all."

"I don't have to defeat you all," the terrorist said. "Only you."

Ah. This was personal for Shehab.

Well, it was personal for Michael too.

As much as he'd like to make the man bleed, to hurt him for what he'd done to Leila—

He could still hear her ruined voice. There was only one thing that could've caused that.

How close had she come to death?

How afraid must she have been?

Yes, he wanted to kill Shehab like he'd never wanted to kill anyone in his life.

But they needed him alive.

"Throw your gun out here, at my feet," he said. "Then put your hands on your head."

He didn't think the man would do it. He'd prefer no more bullets to fly, but Shehab wouldn't make it easy.

And then a gun skidded down the stairs.

Huh.

"Your hands are over your head?"

"Why don't you look and see?"

Right. And get shot. But somebody had to check.

Michael got low, very low, and stuck a hand out, then yanked it back fast.

No gunshot.

He dared to look.

Waleed was standing in the center of the cockpit. Arms up. One behind his head.

The other held...not a gun. But...

Shehab smiled.

"Bomb!"

Michael screamed the word. Jumped down the stairs.

He was nearly to the railing. Almost there...

The world exploded.

CHAPTER FORTY-TWO

THE THUNDERING BOOM.

Fire billowed up, up in a haze of black smoke.

A wave of hot, dry air rolled over Leila.

She couldn't make sense of it.

And then she did.

She screamed. Screamed past the pain. Screamed as loud as her ruined throat would allow. She wasn't sure if the sound she heard was her own voice or Jasmine's, only knew it was nothing, nothing compared to the pain.

He had been with her. Only minutes before. He'd promised he'd be right behind her.

She'd trusted him. She'd believed him.

She was vaguely aware of arms wrapped around her, pulling her back, back from the edge of the boat. She was so close to him. Some small part of her wanted to climb over. To follow.

Michael was in the abyss, somewhere. Gone.

How could he be gone?

"Inside, ma'am. You need to get inside."

The one who'd pulled her into the boat now dragged her toward a door. But she couldn't take her eyes off the flames still rising.

And she thought of the friend of Michael's who'd brought her to this boat. And the other one, the one who'd rescued Jasmine. Both of those men had swum back to Waleed's boat and climbed aboard.

Joining the team already there.

She and her sister were alive at the cost of all those lives.

Jasmine tugged her arm. "Please, sister. We must."

Leila lost all her fight. She backed into the small glass-enclosed space and sat on a bench near a table.

A simple dining table, where people would eat lunch and plan excursions and play games. And live their lives happily unaware of the evil everywhere.

Where was God?

Was Michael in His arms now?

How could she lose the same man twice in one day?

Jasmine held her close. "It's okay. They're going to find him. Listen to me, sister. They're going to find him."

Who was they? There was no *they*. There was Jasmine and Leila and the one man on the boat with them.

Even if some of those men had survived, they would only find Michael's body. Maybe. But he'd worn no life jacket.

He would sink. Sink to the bottom of the sea.

Leila was sinking too. Losing hope. Because evil had won. Evil always won. And no matter how she tried to escape, it always found her.

Jasmine was praying aloud for all those men, her words rattling off in Arabic. "Rescue them, Lord. Bring them all home. You are able. Bring them up from the sea."

Leila wanted to join the prayer. She couldn't make herself

speak past her clogged and swollen throat. But she tried to focus on the prayer.

Yes, Lord. Please.

A voice outside the small room. A shout.

She looked past the glass as the man in the boat helped another onto the deck.

And then another. And another.

Not all dead, then. Thank God for that.

But none of them would be Michael.

She closed her eyes, unable to watch, unwilling to be sorry at the sight of every face that wasn't that of the man she loved. Each one of them mattered. Each one had risked his life for her and Jasmine.

Forgive me.

Save them, Lord. Save them all.

A wet hand wrapped around hers.

Water dripped onto her head.

"Sweetheart?"

Her eyes popped open.

Michael?

He crouched in front of her. "Are you all right?"

Her hand covered her mouth. Tears stung her eyes. It couldn't be. And yet, here he was.

"How?" But her voice was barely audible.

Men had filed into the space. Alive, talking, some laughing. Recalling what'd happened.

Michael heard her—or read her lips. "I saw the trigger. We had just enough time. Thank God, nobody was belowdecks."

Nobody? Meaning all the men survived?

Jasmine voiced the question.

Michael smiled past Leila at her sister. "The team survived. Are you okay?"

Jasmine's hand slid down Leila's arm. "We are glad to see you."

Leila could only nod, overcome. There were no words.

Michael pulled her into his arms. "It's over, sweetheart. You're safe now."

CHAPTER FORTY-THREE

IT WAS a long ride back to Mytilene, and Michael savored every moment. Leila was tucked up beside him, her head on his chest, her arms around his torso like she might never let go. They were covered with a blanket, as were the rest of his friends scattered around the small cabin. Some were talking. Some were resting.

Some were probably replaying those last few terrifying moments. The bomb. The flames. The heat.

Shehab's final act had been an attempt to murder Michael and his entire team. But God was bigger than a small-minded terrorist. Michael still couldn't believe they'd all survived, propelled by the blast off the boat and into the blessed water.

Except the man himself, who'd been trapped inside the cockpit.

If the explosion hadn't killed him, the water that filled and sank the boat certainly had.

Michael could go over the events in his head a thousand times. Maybe what had happened could be explained logistically. But Michael knew the truth.

God had saved them. Simple as that.

Leila shifted away to smile at him. Maybe to confirm, again, that he was really there.

He kissed her forehead. "How's your throat?"

She shrugged and laid her head down again.

Eventually, he'd find out exactly what the monster had done to her.

Right now, he'd just savor her warmth.

Jasmine was lying on a sofa on the other side of the room, an IV trailing from her arm. Michael had told the team medic that she needed fluids, explaining the nausea that had dogged her since Iraq.

He wasn't positive, but he had a guess about what was causing it. He understood her reluctance to tell her sister, but he knew something else.

The cause was definitely not *nothing.*

His suspicion that Jasmine might be a terrorist plant had dissolved. Obviously, Waleed and his men had been determined to get her back, which convinced him they'd never intended to let her go.

She needed protection.

Until she had the courage to tell them all the truth, he would ensure she was cared for. He'd do everything in his power to convince Jasmine that she was safe with him and his team. That she'd be safe in the US and protected from the men who pursued her.

If his guess was right, he was certain that at least one of them would continue the search.

There was plenty of time to worry about all that later.

Time for all the questions that would come. The reprimand he was certain to receive. Maybe even an invitation to leave the team.

Would he lose his job?

Maybe.

But he'd saved Leila and her sister.

God had brought them to this place. He had their future in His hands. Michael didn't need to figure it all out. He'd just trust the One who'd proved Himself trustworthy over and over.

Michael stretched out under the covers on a twin bed in a tiny room at the hotel where Shehab and his team had been staying.

Michael and Leila hadn't had a moment of privacy on the boat. As soon as the boat docked, he'd been separated from her and her sister—and they'd been separated from each other. As if they were all enemy combatants.

Michael was too tired to get worked up about it. He'd whispered to Leila during their long ride back to Mytilene that she and her sister shouldn't give Brock any information until they'd been promised asylum in the US—and had the paperwork to prove it.

He'd nearly told Leila to insist that the paperwork be signed by Travis Price, Michael's friend in the White House. But he hadn't. Instead, he'd decided to trust Brock to do the right thing.

Michael could always get in touch with Travis later, if necessary.

He wasn't going to let Leila and Jasmine be dumped off at some refugee camp in Europe to fend for themselves. After everything that'd happened, and considering all the information the twins could provide, they needed to be in the US.

For now, all of that was out of Michael's hands.

He'd showered and changed into warm clothes someone had left on the bed for him, thankful to wash away the previous forty-eight hours—filth and sand and salt water and blood. Now that he was clean and dry and warm—and the twins were safe—he felt like himself again.

Outside the window, the clouds had blown off, leaving a gorgeous pink-and-orange sunset.

Michael was just starting to drop off to sleep when the door opened and Brock stepped in. He carried a notebook. "Time for you to tell me everything."

Michael sat up on the side of the bed, registering his team leader's aggressive and angry tone. Rather than respond to it, he stood and approached him with his hand outstretched. "Thank you, sir. I can't thank you enough."

Brock glared at his hand, then at him.

Maybe there was the slightest softening of his features when he shook Michael's hand. "Since when do you call me sir?"

"Should have been since always. Sir."

"It's not going to be that simple."

"I know." Michael had had a lot of time to consider everything he'd done—and done wrong. And all the ways it could've gone sideways. "I want to apologize again. You were right about everything. I should have trusted you and the team. I shouldn't have gone after Leila by myself."

Brock's jaw dropped, and Michael worked to stifle a smile. Not because he didn't mean the words but because, obviously, Brock had never expected him to say them.

"Whatever happens now," Michael added, "even if you kick me off the team, even if you get me fired from the Agency... Whatever happens, I want you to know that you were right, I was wrong, and I'm sorry." He stood straight, inhaling a breath for courage. "What do you need to know?"

"What can you tell me?"

Michael nodded to the chair against the wall. "Have a seat."

It was a subtle attempt to get control of the interview.

But Brock was too smart for that. His eyebrows rose, and Michael smiled and settled back on the bed.

"You already know that Leila and Jasmine are Saad Farad

Fayad's daughters. What you don't know is that Saad Fayad has a twin brother. His name is Hasan Mahmoud."

"Huh. But Fayad..." He clamped his lips shut, backing up to the chair Michael had indicated earlier. He sat, letting the information take shape in his mind.

Michael saw when Brock came to the same conclusion he'd come to. "When we saw—or thought we saw—Saad Fayad, it was actually..."

"Hasan Mahmoud."

"How did they keep that secret?"

"Leila and Jasmine can tell you more. Apparently, they weren't raised together because their mother feared Hasan."

"Feared him why?"

"I don't know for sure, but from what they said, he sounds like a psychopath."

Brock was nodding slowly. "That explains...a lot."

"I already told you Vortex is Khalid Qasim. He's an old friend of the family. The head terrorist on the boat was Waleed Shehab."

"They're all working together? Shehab, Qasim, Mahmoud, and Fayad?"

"The sisters don't think their father is involved, but..." Michael shrugged. "You'll have to question Jasmine. She knows more than she's said."

Brock was nodding. "Do you trust them?"

"Leila, definitely. I wasn't sure about Jasmine before. I considered the idea that we escaped because that was the plan, that Jasmine might be a plant—as you suggested."

"But?"

"But you saw what Shehab did to get them back. Obviously, she was not intended to escape. Even so, I think there's more to Jasmine's story."

"Exactly what?"

"You need to ask her."

"I'm asking you."

Michael kept his tone friendly. "I'll tell you everything I know and everything I've guessed, but let's give them a chance to tell you first, okay?"

"The thing is, your girlfriend has ties to terrorism."

Any friendly feelings he'd felt toward Brock dissipated. "She has no control over who her family is."

"You wouldn't be the first spy to be taken in by a pretty woman."

"Not all pretty women are working for the enemy."

"Doesn't explain why she went willingly with Qasim. She didn't fight and made no effort to alert anybody at the airport she was being taken against her will."

"Qasim threatened her sister."

"She told you that?"

"Yes. And it makes sense. She probably couldn't have gotten away even if she tried. And if she had, her sister would have paid the price."

"Maybe," Brock said. "If you'd told us when you found out where she was, we could have assembled a team. Made a plan."

"You would have gone into Iraq and rescued her?"

"Maybe."

But not because she was Michael's girlfriend, not because of his feelings for her, but because she was seen with Vortex. They'd have rescued her to get information.

"If I'd shown up twelve hours later," Michael said, "Leila would have been married—against her will—to a terrorist."

"Who?"

"Shehab. And then she'd have been taken away. She'd be gone, and with her, all the information."

"You didn't know that before you went after her."

"True. But let's be honest about something. If it was the

wife or girlfriend of any other member of our team, we would have gone in immediately, no question about it. The only reason you sidelined me is because she's Iraqi."

"The only reason?" Brock's voice rose, but he tempered it. "Or was it because you didn't tell anybody about her? You kept her a secret."

Right. There was that. "Is it so wrong to want a little privacy?"

"You gave up your right to privacy when you joined the CIA. Look, Wrong. Your training is good. Your instincts are good. Your skills are second-to-none. But you're a lone wolf, and lone wolves get the rest of the pack killed."

He wasn't sure that was true of real wolves in the wild, but he saw Brock's point.

"That's why I didn't want you on my team from the start," Brock said. "Because you always think you know better. You always think your way is the right way. What did you learn about Qasim's plans?"

"Nothing, yet. Once they have asylum—"

"You think they're getting asylum?"

"Seriously?" Michael pushed to his feet. "Of course they need asylum. They just escaped terrorists. They have information we need." Jasmine did, anyway.

But he needed Leila to get asylum. He needed them both in the US with him.

"You got nothing out of them?" By Brock's tone, he wasn't buying it.

"They were afraid to talk, and I don't blame them. Take them back to the US, and I have no doubt they'll tell you everything they know."

Brock pushed to his feet. "Let's hope you're right."

"Am I in custody?"

Brock's smirk told him he'd love that. But the expression slipped. "No."

"Do I still have a job?"

"I don't know, Wrong. Should you?"

He didn't answer what he guessed was a rhetorical question. "Where are Leila and Jasmine?"

"Leila's with the team in the lobby. I'm going to talk to Jasmine now."

"I need to contact my brothers."

"They're waiting at the airport. They know you're safe."

Which meant...what? Was Michael going home with Derrick and Bryan, or with the team?

He was afraid to ask.

His boss started for the door.

"Hey, Brock?"

He turned, eyebrows raised.

"Jasmine's sick. Go easy on her." When he nodded, Michael added, "I meant what I said before. Thank you."

Brock walked out, leaving Michael alone with his thoughts —and worries.

What if the twins weren't offered asylum? Would Travis help?

Or had Michael used up all his old friend's goodwill—and favors?

CHAPTER FORTY-FOUR

LEILA SAT at a table by herself in the small hotel dining area. She'd refused wine and coffee but had accepted a cup of tea from the middle-aged, balding hotel manager, whose gaze flicked often to the five men seated at tables deeper in the room.

Michael's teammates had smiled at her when she'd walked in. One of them had approached, introduced himself as Stone— the one who'd pulled her to the rescue boat—and offered her food.

She wasn't sure where the meal had come from, but the counter, which she guessed was usually used for breakfast items, was covered with steaming dishes. She could see the selection from where she sat—meat, vegetables, falafel, rice. There was a container of Greek salad and a couple of bowls of yogurt and fruit for dessert.

The men ate like they hadn't seen food in a year.

She didn't join them. She wouldn't eat until she knew Michael and Jasmine were all right.

She watched the glass doors until, finally, Michael approached. Everything in her wanted to run to him, but she didn't. Maybe, with all his friends watching, he wouldn't want that.

Maybe now that he was back with his people, he'd want her to keep her distance.

He stepped inside, scanned the space, nodded to a couple of the guys, and then approached her, his hand held out.

She took it, and he pulled her to her feet and wrapped her in a hug. "You all right?"

"I think so." Her voice was all wrong, but being in his arms felt right. Her fears dissipated.

He backed up, brows lowered, lips pressed closed.

She felt strangely shy with him, despite everything they'd gone through. For the last...she'd lost track of the days, but since he'd rescued her from the compound, they'd been forced to be together. They'd talked about his secrets and hers. But they had talked very little about what would happen next.

Maybe...maybe this was all over.

His gaze traveled from her eyes to her neck.

She pressed her hands over the ugly bruises forming there. Bracing for the question she knew he'd ask.

But he surprised her. "Did you eat?"

"I was waiting for you and Jasmine."

"Your sister's going to be a while, but she's all right. She's being questioned. Come on." He led her to the food and handed her a plate. "I'm sure you're hungry. I know I am."

She felt she should wait, but her stomach growled.

Michael grinned. "Go ahead. There's no shame in needing food."

She filled her plate and grabbed a bowl of yogurt. She was very hungry, but it hurt to swallow. Maybe the yogurt would be the best choice.

Back at the table, Michael took her hand. "Okay if I pray?"

She nodded. She would speak if she had to but would avoid it when she could.

"Lord..." The word hung between them, filled with emotion. "Thank You for bringing us here. Take us all the way home. And bless our food." Another long moment passed before he added, "Amen." He smiled at her, then dug into his meal.

She tried to do the same, but the meat was too rough to get down. Even when she cut up the vegetables very small, they felt like razors when she swallowed.

She pushed the plate away and ate the yogurt and spoon sweets—fruit suspended in thick syrup. She swallowed a few bites, thankful when the calories hit her empty stomach.

"Be right back." Michael walked to the buffet, though his plate was still half full.

He returned with a second bowl of yogurt and syrupy fruit. "If that's all you can eat, you're going to need more."

She smiled her thanks.

"You're welcome." He took a few bites of his dinner before he spoke again. "Was Brock hard on you?"

She shook her head. "He was kind."

Michael's eyebrows hiked. "Kind? Brock? Are you sure?"

She grinned.

"Did he say anything about asylum?"

She shook her head, cleared her throat to answer.

"It's okay," he said. "He probably wanted to talk to Jasmine first. If he doesn't offer it, I'll go another route."

"Are you in trouble?"

It was probably the sound of her voice that had him wincing. "Whatever happens, it was worth it to get you free."

Oh. The words, so casual, meant more than she could express.

Tears filled her eyes, and he looked confused. "What? What did I say?"

She shrugged again.

Maybe he figured out what she'd been thinking because he leaned close and kissed her cheek. "I love you." He sat back and waved her off before she could respond. "I know, you love me too. How could you not?"

She smiled, wishing she could tell him exactly how she felt. That she did love him. That she owed him her life—and her sister's life. That she was sorry for ever doubting him.

She'd also tell him she was afraid of what the future would hold. Would they be allowed into the US? Or sent back to Germany? Or to Iraq?

Brock had made no promises. If she had more information, maybe he'd want to keep her close, but she knew very little.

"It's going to be okay," Michael said, reading her mind. He touched the sweatshirt she wore. "Where'd you get the clothes?"

She dipped her head toward the team, shrugging. Brock had handed her the sack of clothes after he'd put her in the empty hotel room and told her to shower, that he'd be in to talk to her in fifteen minutes.

Someone must've run to a store somewhere and bought the leggings and sweatshirt and socks and underwear. She was embarrassed that a stranger—a man—had picked out the things, but she got over that quickly as she'd dressed in the warm clothes.

Michael was wearing a new sweatshirt, too, so apparently, they'd shopped for him at the same time.

Silly the things that mattered. Warm clothes. A hot shower. Food.

Being with someone you trust.

Michael finished his dinner, then eyed hers.

She smiled and nudged it toward him.

"I'm not proud." He traded his empty plate for hers and ate while she finished the yogurt.

"You need more?" he asked.

She shook her head.

"Okay. I'll make sure we have soft food for you until that heals."

Obviously, he was thinking they'd be together. But what if they weren't? What if he was sent back to the US and she and Jasmine were sent elsewhere?

"Hey."

She blinked the questions away to look into his kind face.

"I'm not leaving you. Whatever happens, we're in it together. I promise."

"Okay." She rasped the word.

"What did...?" He shook his head. "I'm guessing he strangled you. Was it Shehab?"

She nodded.

"Why?"

"For information from Jasmine."

"Interesting." The single word held meaning she couldn't decipher.

The team member who doubled as their medic had looked at her throat and told her that she would heal in time.

The glass door opened, and Brock stepped through.

Michael stood, and Leila did, too, as he approached.

"You two ready?"

"For what, sir?" Michael asked.

"There it is again," Brock said. "You calling me *sir*. Not sure I'm going to get used to that."

Michael's smile was tight. "Where's Jasmine?"

"She's in the car. Tile's gonna drive you to the airport."

"What's happening?" Michael asked.

But Brock spoke to Leila. "Your sister had a lot of information, which she gave up in exchange for asylum for both of you."

"Oh." Leila pressed a hand against her throat and the pain the single word caused.

"Jasmine needs to eat." Michael, always considerate, glanced back at the table of food. "I can grab her a plate."

"I'm not a monster, Wrong." Brock shook his head and smiled at Leila. "She ate in the room before I questioned her. Did you get something?"

She nodded. "Thank you."

"That sounds painful. I think if Shehab weren't already dead, your boyfriend would hunt him down and kill him. Right, Wrong?"

"Yes, sir." Michael's words were grim—and deadly serious.

"You three are headed back to the States."

"And me, sir? Am I—?"

"I'll be in touch, Wrong. Get some rest." He passed them, continuing into the room and toward the food.

Leila waited, watching the man she loved say goodbye to his teammates. Shaking hands, offering thanks. Each one greeted him kindly, like a good friend.

Brock was angry, but even that seemed couched in respect. These men cared about him—as he cared about them.

Finally, Michael rejoined her and took her hand.

The team was watching, and she wished she could tell them how much she appreciated all they'd done for her.

Michael leaned down and whispered, "They know."

She lifted her hand in a wave.

Which brought smiles and waves in return. "See you soon," one called, while another said, "You ever get tired of Wrong—"

"All right, that's good." Michael turned her toward the door. "Let's get out of here."

She was ready. To leave Greece. To leave Europe and all the fear behind.

≈

Less than thirty minutes later, Leila stepped into another world.

A private jet with plush, cushy leather seats, six on each side of the aisle, some forward-facing, some rear-facing with tables interspersed between them.

Two tall men stood just inside.

The first smiled at her, holding his hand out. "I'm Derrick."

She recognized him, the man Michael had pointed out hours earlier when they'd arrived at the airport.

Behind her, Michael said, "Leila, meet my youngest brother." To Derrick, he said, "Her throat is hurting, so she's not talking if she can help it."

Derrick smiled. "No problem. Glad you're here."

As was she, though *glad* didn't cover all the feelings inside her.

Leila wasn't a hugger. She'd been raised to keep her distance from men, to keep her eyes down. But this man who'd come so far to help? She couldn't speak, but she could make her feelings known. She held her arms out and stepped toward him, emotion clogging her already pained throat.

Michael's brother wrapped her close. "Yeah," he said. "I'm happy to see you too."

He let her go, and she turned to the other brother. The one who'd seen her in the car. The one who'd pretended not to.

"That's Bryan," Michael said.

She hugged him. "Thank you."

He held her tightly. His voice cracked when he said, "My pleasure."

"All right." Michael's voice held a tinge of humor. "That's enough of that."

Leila stepped away, her cheeks heating at her forward behavior. But they didn't seem bothered by the hugs.

Jasmine spoke her thanks to the brothers.

"We'll refuel in the UK." Derrick stood in the aisle as he explained. "We'll be in Portland by morning. There's food and drinks in the back. Help yourselves. Those seats recline." He opened an overhead compartment and pulled out pillows and blankets. "I assume you're sleepy."

Michael took them. "Thank you. I can't even—"

"No problem. Get comfortable. We won't take off for"—he checked his watch—"about thirty minutes."

Leila sat across the aisle from her sister, and after grabbing bottles of water, Michael settled in the seat facing her on the other side of a small table.

He opened a bottle for Jasmine and another for Leila before twisting the cap off his own. He downed about half the bottle before he set it aside and focused on Jasmine.

"What'd you tell him?"

Leila was tempted to tell Michael to leave her sister alone, but Jasmine didn't seem bothered by the question. "I told him everything I know about what they're planning."

But how would she have any information?

Before Leila could ask, Jasmine reached across the aisle and gripped her arm. "Don't talk. I already know your questions." To Michael, she said, "I didn't lie to you. I was only with the group of men when they were together for meals, and Hasan and Waleed were very careful not to tell me anything."

Leila didn't miss the omission. What about Qasim?

She was confused, but Michael didn't seem to be.

Her sister had told him something he hadn't told her?

Jasmine said, "I think you have guessed, no?"

He didn't confirm or deny. "Why don't you just tell us."

Not a question so much as a suggestion. Or a command.

Jasmine slid her hand down to hold Leila's. "Baba arranged a marriage between you and Waleed."

She nodded. "We escaped in time." The words were thorns in her throat, but she felt such gratitude in speaking them, in the truth of them...

"*You* escaped in time," Jasmine said.

And realization dawned...or darkened.

"I am the wife of Khalid Qasim."

The words... Leila couldn't make them make sense. Her sister was married?

Her sister had been married—had been *forced* by their father to marry Khalid Qasim.

An old man.

A terrorist.

The man who'd snatched Leila off the street in Munich and threatened to hurt her twin if she didn't come.

Threatened to harm his own wife.

"Oh, sister." The words hurt, but that was nothing compared to what Jasmine must've dealt with. "When?"

"A few years ago."

Years. She'd been married for years.

Leila looked at Michael, expecting to see her own shock mirrored in his face. But again, he didn't look shocked. Only gentle and concerned.

"You knew?" She rasped the words.

"I guessed."

"How?"

His gaze flicked to Jasmine, who said. "I am curious as well."

"You called him by his first name a couple of times, and there was something familiar in the tone. In Antalya, when I asked about him, you became defensive. When I asked you what you would have said if you'd felt free to speak, you said, 'He wouldn't listen to me.'" Michael quieted, gave her a moment to speak, but she didn't. "At the time, I thought you meant your father, but then I started to put it together. Especially with…" His voice trailed, and he shook his head. "I wasn't sure I was right."

Jasmine's gaze held admiration, as if she were impressed he'd figured it out.

Leila might be, too, if she wasn't so annoyed. He'd guessed, and he hadn't told her.

Maybe he felt her annoyance because he said, "It wasn't my place to tell you. And I could've been wrong. I didn't want your sister to feel cornered." To Jasmine, he said, "I wanted you to tell me because you trust me."

"You should have trusted me." Leila sipped her water to cool the fire in her throat.

Jasmine squeezed her hand. "I did. I do trust you. You are my sister, my dear sister. I just wanted out, away from them. I was afraid."

Yes. Maybe she could understand that.

Jasmine pulled her hand back and settled it on her stomach. Was she sick again?

But she didn't look sick. And the way she rested her hand…

"I am not only his wife. I am the mother of his child."

Oh.

Oh.

That explained everything.

Again, a glance at Michael showed his lack of surprise.

"I guessed," he said. "And it wasn't my place to say." To Jasmine, "My father asked me if you were pregnant when I called him from Baghdad. I brushed off the question at the time, but the more time we've spent together, the more I wondered. I did a little research. It's called—"

"Hyperemesis gravidarum," Jasmine supplied, then spoke to Leila and said, "Extreme morning sickness. But…not nothing. I'm sorry I didn't tell you the truth. I do not wish to have

Khalid's child. Maybe this is why I am sick? Because I don't wish to be pregnant?"

"Don't take blame for things you can't control," Michael said. "I'm sure my father will have a solution." After a pause, he asked, "Does he know? Your...Qasim?"

She nodded. "I wish he did not, but yes."

Leila couldn't wrap her mind around it. Her sister was pregnant with a terrorist's baby.

She wasn't sure how to feel. Babies were gifts.

But this baby, this man's child, felt more like an anchor. One that would sink Jasmine to the bottom of the sea.

"He'll never give up," Leila whispered.

Jasmine's gaze flicked toward the windows and the night. They were still on the ground, and suddenly, the darkness outside felt terrifying, as if Qasim might materialize and take them both back to Iraq.

Because the man would never stop searching for his wife and child.

Never.

Michael reached across the aisle and gripped Jasmine's hand. "I promise, he won't find you." He took Leila's hand with his free one. "I promise, I'll keep you both safe."

Jasmine smiled. "I believe you, Michael Wright." She looked around as the plane taxied. "We are here, are we not? You have gotten us this far."

Jasmine was right. Michael had gotten them this far. Not Michael, though.

God had gotten them this far. He wouldn't forsake them now.

The jet raced down the runway and lifted off.

Leaving all the terror behind.

CHAPTER FORTY-FIVE

A WEEK LATER, Leila put the finishing touches on her makeup with shaking hands.

She wasn't ready.

But, as Michael had suggested at dinner the night before, maybe she would never feel ready. Maybe she had to do it even when the idea terrified her.

He'd seemed to find her fear amusing.

"You escaped Iraq when you were eighteen years old, all by yourself. You made it across Turkey and into Europe with nobody to help and nothing to count on except your own wits. You faced refugee camps, college, career—all alone. And when you were taken, you escaped again."

"With you," she said.

He shook his head as if that part were irrelevant. "But you're afraid of *this*?"

Not just afraid.

Terrified.

"What if they don't like me?"

Her question had only made him smile more broadly. He'd

leaned over a plate of seafood he'd brought with him and kissed her cheek. "I promise, they're going to love you."

Maybe.

She hoped he was right.

Now, she stowed her makeup in the drawer in Michael's guest bathroom and looked into the bedroom she shared with her sister.

Jasmine was lying on the bed nearest the window.

"You all right?"

Her twin sat up and swung her feet to the floor. "Are you?"

"Of course."

Jasmine wasn't fooled by Leila's overly bright tone.

They were speaking English. By an unspoken agreement, neither had lapsed into Arabic since they'd touched down in Maine.

Jasmine looked better. Not just better but healthy. She had color in her cheeks and had even, if Leila wasn't mistaken, put on a couple of pounds since her visit to Michael's father the day after they'd arrived from Greece.

Dr. Wright—Roger, he'd insisted they call him—had prescribed rest and small meals and a supplement.

Jasmine had taken his advice to heart, and what a difference. Fortunately, she was early enough in the pregnancy that Roger didn't think the baby had been harmed by lack of nutrients. Apparently, the nausea had only been bad for a couple of weeks before Jasmine discovered Leila at the compound. The activity and stress of escaping Iraq had worsened it.

Jasmine pushed up from the bed. "I'll be ready when Michael arrives."

Leila headed down the stairs. Michael's house had three bedrooms, all on the second story. The ground floor held a living room, an eat-in kitchen, and a dining room. He'd said his house was a Cape Cod—apparently, that was the name of the style.

Also, an area in Massachusetts, she discovered when she looked it up.

Strange. But so many things in America were.

Like the way people she'd never met before smiled at her as if they were friends.

The way the neighbors had come over to introduce themselves, guessing she and her sister were new owners or renters. Michael was there so infrequently that neighbors had thought the house unoccupied.

She might've guessed the same if she'd peeked in the windows. There was a little furniture, but it looked brand new and largely untouched. There were no family photos, no personal items. It was a house, not a home.

Which Michael had explained away easily. "I bought it a while ago, but I'm hardly ever here."

And he still wasn't. He'd moved Leila and her sister in, but he'd been staying with his brother Sam, who lived nearby.

Which was where Leila and Jasmine were going today.

To meet the family.

A knock had Leila glancing out the window. Michael stood on the front porch.

She opened the door. "Why are you knocking on your own door?"

He leaned down and kissed her lightly.

But the kiss turned into something else. He wrapped his arm around her and held her against him, deepening the kiss and almost making her forget her fear.

After a minute, he lifted his head. "Hey."

It took her a moment to recover. She stepped back. "You don't have to knock. This is your house."

"I'd better not get quite that familiar. Seems wiser somehow."

Yeah. She knew what he meant.

"You sound better today."

She took his hand and pulled him inside. It was chilly out there, a cold wind coming from the ocean. But the sky was bright blue, bluer than any sky she'd ever seen. And though most of the trees had lost their leaves, some still hung, bright yellow and orange and red. The rest skittered along the roads and sidewalks, their scent woodsy and comfortable.

Maine was so different from where she'd grown up. And different from Munich. It was beautiful.

She loved everything about it. Or maybe she just loved this man and, by extension, the place he called home.

He closed the door behind him. "You ready?"

"I am. My sister is coming."

"How's your throat today?" He'd been eager for her to meet his family, but he hadn't wanted to introduce her until she could talk without pain. Now, after asking permission with his gaze—which she granted, as she always did—he moved her turtleneck aside to look at the bruising.

The marks had gone from red to black-and-blue to purple. They were fading now, just a few purple smudges, barely noticeable on her dark skin.

He saw them, though, and scowled, like he did whenever he remembered what Waleed had done.

Far less damage than Qasim had done to Jasmine, whom Leila awakened many nights to pull out of nightmares.

It was probably wrong to wish a man dead, so she begged forgiveness every morning. But every night, at the sound of her sister's whimpers, she wished it again.

Even so, Jasmine seemed better in every way. Not just because she felt better. She seemed to have a different feeling about the baby she'd said she didn't want. Now, though her stomach was still as flat as ever, Leila had caught her often with a protective palm over the tiny baby inside.

They were both healing.

Leila gently removed Michael's hand from her neck. "If I tell you I'm not up for it, can we put it off another week?"

His concern quickly morphed into a smile. "Too late. They've gone all out for the party."

He must've seen her surprise because he added, "Not a party. Wrong word. Just a casual get-together."

"With your whole family."

At that, he shrugged. "They're going to love you."

"Hmm." So he kept saying. But she couldn't help her worry. "Any news from Brock?"

"Nope." He tossed out the word as if it didn't matter, but she knew better.

"I will not forgive myself if you lose your job."

He stood back, eyebrows lowering and scrunching together. "None of this is your fault."

"You are in trouble for rescuing me."

"I'm in trouble for not trusting my team. It was an error in judgment, and if I lose my job because of it, then I'll get another one. I'm actually pretty good at sales. It'll be fine."

"But you love what you do." She said the words confidently, but his head dipped to the side.

"Why do you think that?"

"Am I wrong?"

"I love serving my country, but I've been in the CIA since I graduated from college—almost twenty years. I've had some interesting assignments and gotten to do some amazing things. If it ends here"—he shrugged, and she could almost believe it—"so be it. I'll never regret rescuing you." But at the end, the casual tone turned dark. "The only thing is... I really want to finish this. Stop your uncle and Qasim, for your sake and your sister's."

His words were a balm to her frightened heart.

Jasmine had told them what she'd told Brock, that she believed Qasim was planning an operation in Munich. Michael guessed now that he'd seen Leila somewhere—on the street or perhaps even in the hotel she managed. Of course he'd have noticed her, a woman who looked just like his wife.

A woman who'd dared escape her family.

Jasmine didn't know much about what they were planning, and her information was inconsistent. She'd heard something about a bombing. But she'd also heard talk of ancient Islamic artifacts.

The two things were so opposed to each other, nobody knew what to think.

She'd mentioned a few locations, including the museum where Leila's friend Sophia worked. But also a refugee center nearby, and a government building.

Studying the map of Munich, Leila remembered what she'd seen circled in that office in the Iraqi desert. Intersections downtown, but that hadn't helped narrow targets.

They didn't have enough information.

Michael wanted to be part of taking Qasim and Hasan down. She understood that, but selfishly, she wanted him to be safe.

"You really wouldn't mind leaving the CIA?" she asked.

"I've had a good career. I hope to hang on until I reach the twenty-year mark so I can retire with my pension. At that point, I wouldn't mind hanging around home a little more."

"Even if your family doesn't like me?"

"You are a silly, silly woman." He looked beyond her, up the stairs. "You look better every time I see you."

Jasmine reached the landing. "I hate to think how bad I looked when we met."

"Not bad. I didn't mean... Just, you know..."

Jasmine giggled. "You are very easy to..." She looked at her sister. "What is the word? To believe my jokes."

"Tease?"

She nodded. "Yes, you are easy to tease."

"One of you was bad enough." He shook his head in mock seriousness. "Not sure I can handle two."

"You definitely cannot," Leila said.

"I love your confidence. You'll need that to meet my family."

Her face must've shown her worry because he kissed her forehead. "You're also pretty easy to tease."

The drive was too short. Not even ten minutes after they climbed into Michael's car, he parked in the driveway in front of a...mansion. "Your brother lives here?"

"Yeah." Michael gazed through the window. "He does okay."

Okay? Better than that, she thought. She realized he was using sarcasm or perhaps understatement. These things were clear to her in Arabic and in German, but though she spoke good English, she didn't always pick up on tones yet.

He came around and opened the back door to let Jasmine out, then opened hers.

She wasn't used to men opening the door for her, but he'd insisted she allow it, especially when his mother might be watching.

She'd barely stepped onto the driveway when the front door opened.

Panic had her adrenaline spiking as Roger, Michael's father, stepped outside and down the steps. Michael gave him a quick hug, and then the older man turned to them. He wasn't quite as tall as his son but seemed as strong and stable. He addressed Leila. "Thought I'd come out and greet you before the crowd." He waved toward the front door, and she glanced that way.

Maybe he saw her fear because he smiled, the expression

crinkling the skin at the corners of his eyes. "Don't worry. They can't wait to meet you." He turned to Jasmine. "How are you feeling?"

"I am better, thank you. And for what you said. I have decided to believe you're right." Again, that protective hand skimmed over her middle.

"About what?" Leila asked.

"He told me that this is not Khalid's baby, and it's not my baby. It is God's baby, and to carry a child of God is always a privilege."

Leila hugged her sister to her side. "I think Dr. Wright is very wise."

"Call me Roger." He repeated what he'd said when they'd last met him. Now, he stood to the side and gestured toward the front door. "Come on in. Time to face the firing squad."

She'd started to follow but froze.

"Dad," Michael said, "that's not helpful."

The man chuckled. "The most dangerous thing inside that house is caramel brownies."

She turned to Michael. "Brownies are dangerous?"

"Only to your waistline." He looked her up and down. "I think you'll be okay." He took her hand. "Let's do this."

Ready or not, it was time to face the firing squad...and the brownies. She prayed for courage.

CHAPTER FORTY-SIX

WHY WAS MICHAEL NERVOUS?

Leila's fears had infected him. Now that she'd planted the idea, Michael couldn't help worrying about what he'd do if they didn't like her.

As they walked into Sam's house, his hands tingled, his body tensing as if danger were imminent. Ridiculous, of course. He'd been staying here with his brother since he'd brought Leila and Jasmine to Shadow Cove, thinking it wise to give them privacy in his house. He was going to need to rent an apartment for the twins or himself soon. Staying here wasn't ideal, especially considering Sam and Eliza were newlyweds. Their lovey-dovey looks and stolen kisses were starting to get on Michael's nerves.

His emotionally reserved brother was over-the-moon in love with his bride.

Michael had an inkling how he felt. He felt a little more *over the moon* every time he saw Leila.

Mom hurried through the foyer toward them, a huge smile on her face as she approached Leila and Jasmine. She embraced them both like old friends.

"I'm Peggy Wright." She looked from one sister to the other.

"Oh, my word. You two are absolutely gorgeous! Which one is which?"

Michael stepped in. "Mom, I'd like you to meet my girl-friend, Leila." He took her hand so there would be no confusion, then smiled at the other twin. "And her sister, Jasmine."

Jasmine said, "Thank you for having us."

Leila's smile was shy. "It is a pleasure to meet you, Mrs. Wright."

"Call me Peggy, and I'm so glad you're here." Mom looked back and forth from one sister to the other. "It's going to take me some time to tell you apart."

Michael could tell them apart with a glance. They did look alike, but not as much as he'd first thought. How he'd ever confused Jasmine for Leila, he couldn't know. Leila's eyes were a little bigger, and there was a spark in them that was uniquely her.

Now that Jasmine had gotten some rest and some food in her stomach that didn't come back up, she was nearly as pretty as her sister.

The girls dressed differently as well. Michael had taken them shopping the day after they'd arrived in town and bought them clothes. Today, Leila wore a pretty teal turtleneck sweater that hid her bruises, along with black slacks.

Jasmine was still getting accustomed to Western-style clothes, having donned loose-fitting Iraqi garb all her life. She wore a flowing black dress that was probably meant to be knee-length but hit her about mid-calf. She'd added a brightly colored scarf.

Hopefully, the very different styles would help his family tell one sister from the other.

"Come on, ladies. Everybody's dying to meet you." Mom gripped Jasmine's hand, then hooked her arm with Leila's, leaning close and mock whispering, "Our Michael has been keeping secrets."

Leila peered at him over her shoulder as Mom led them away. "He is very good at that."

"Hmm." Mom shot him a scowl but said nothing else.

He and Dad followed the ladies into the kitchen, where the rest of his family had congregated.

He stood beside Leila and took her free hand. "Leila and Jasmine, meet the Wright family." He waved toward the two farthest back. "You know Bryan and Derrick."

The youngest brothers lifted their hands.

"Glad you made it," Bryan said.

Derrick seemed almost dazed. There was a protracted beat before he managed to focus on Jasmine. "You look good. I mean, rested."

Okay.

Michael moved on. "This is Sam." He nodded to the brother closest to him in age, who pushed off from the counter and approached, hand outstretched.

"Great to meet you both." He shook their hands, then indicated the brunette behind him. "This is Eliza, my wife." Did his whole face brighten a little with the word?

Eliza had cut her hair and wore jeans and a sweater that somehow, on her, looked like high fashion. Knowing Sam, they probably were high fashion. Her smile was wide as she shook their hands. "It's so nice to meet you. Have you been comfortable at Michael's house?"

"It is very nice." Leila's gaze flicked to him. "He has been kind to us."

Eliza said, "Of course he has—"

"—Michael? Kind?" Sam said.

Eliza fake-elbowed him in the ribs. "Be nice." She shook her head, clearly delighted by everything Sam said and did. "Our son is around here somewhere."

Sam called, "Levi!"

Four-year-old Levi burst into the room at top speed, dodged all the bodies, and slammed into Sam's legs. "Hi, Daddy! Did you call? Is it time to eat?"

Sam chuckled. "This is Levi."

The boy looked from his father to the twins, and his jaw dropped. "You look exactly alike!"

Leila laughed. "Do we?" She looked at Jasmine. "I guess we do a little, huh?"

Jasmine said, "I am so lucky to look like you!" But then she crouched down to Levi's level. "I'm prettier, though, right?"

He looked from one to the other as if it was the most important question in the world. After a moment's thought, he said, "I think you're being silly."

Everybody laughed.

Grant approached from the far side of the counter, scooping Levi up on his way and settling him on his hip. He held out his hand to Leila. "I'm Grant, fourth brother." He shook both sisters' hands, then introduced his wife. "This is Summer."

The tall blonde stepped forward and greeted them. "Welcome. Glad you're here."

"Thank you," Leila looked from Summer to him. "I knew you had a big family, but I didn't realize how very...big they all were."

He took in the sight of his tiny girlfriend surrounded by the tall Wright brothers. Even Summer was nearly six feet—almost a foot taller than Leila and Jasmine.

Mom stepped forward and stood between the twins. "We normal-sized humans have to stick together."

From behind Grant and Summer, a hand went up. "Don't

forget about me." Eliza managed to squeeze past them. "I'm normal-sized."

Mom looked her up and down. Eliza wasn't as tall as Summer, but she was a good half a foot taller than Leila and Jasmine's five feet.

Mom motioned her forward. "You'll do, I suppose."

In the next few minutes, typical Wright family pandemonium prevailed as everybody filled glasses and carried huge serving dishes into the dining room, all talking at the same time.

Was someone supposed to be listening? Poor Leila and Jasmine were trying, but who could keep anything straight?

Sam had lived alone in this house for years, but he must've had family dinners in mind when he bought the table. It was round, large enough to accommodate the twelve people who sat at it now—and there was room for more.

Leila and Jasmine stayed together. Michael sat beside Leila, and Derrick—Michael couldn't help but notice—hurried to Jasmine's side and pulled out her chair for her. "You look like you feel better."

"Thank you." She sat, and he pushed her chair in. "I have slept many hours since we arrived in Maine."

"I'm glad. Have you seen much of town? I'd be happy to show you around."

Michael didn't hear Jasmine's answer. It seemed like Derrick was developing a crush. But Jasmine was married. And carrying a child. Perhaps that was information the youngest Wright brother needed sooner rather than later.

Michael couldn't blame Derrick for his interest, though. Jasmine was the second prettiest woman in Maine.

The way Leila was looking at Michael now, eyes wide with wonder... She wasn't just the prettiest woman in Maine but maybe in the country. In the continent. In the world.

The joy in her expression spoke of not only delight but

surprise, as if his family were an amazing sight to behold. He thought so, but he was partial. Maybe it wasn't just the family, though. Maybe it was the family, plus this big, impressive house overlooking the Atlantic, and in this charming little New England town, and the perfect weather they'd enjoyed since they arrived from Greece—crisp, sunny autumn days.

Dad cleared his throat, aiming a look at Levi, who had already grabbed a piece of bread and was about to shove it in his mouth. "Let's pray before we start."

They joined hands around the table.

"Thank you for this family and this day," Dad prayed. "We are especially thankful that Leila and Jasmine are here—and Michael. You brought them safely through many obstacles, and we praise You for Your protection."

Michael had told his father the story, wanting his guidance before he shared everything with his family. Or maybe just wanting Dad's reaction first.

Dad had been supportive—right after he'd been angry that Michael hadn't told him the truth about his job sooner.

Now, it seemed that gratitude had won the day, and Michael felt exactly the same way. If not for God, he didn't want to think about where he, Leila, and Jasmine would be.

All glory to You, Lord.

Leila squeezed his hand, and he had the feeling she was thinking exactly the same thing.

"We thank You for the delicious food and the beautiful woman who prepared it."

"Amen!" Derrick said, eliciting chuckles around the table.

"And we thank You for the little ones represented here at this table, Grant and Summer's unborn baby, and Levi."

Michael heard what his father didn't say—his thanks for Jasmine's child.

"Bless our food and our conversation. Let it be sprinkled with grace."

Ah. And that was for Michael, for what he was about to do.

"In the name of our Lord and Savior Jesus Christ, amen."

Choruses of *amen* were followed quickly by clanking dishes and chattering Wrights.

Mom had been happy to let Sam host, but she'd done all the cooking. The family passed giant platters of spaghetti Bolognese and fettuccini Alfredo, baskets of crusty garlic bread, and bowls of crisp Caesar salad. There was an antipasto plate with olives, peppers, and fancy cheeses, and Eliza carried in a dish of bruschetta warm from the broiler.

All Michael's favorites, and he was pleased to see the sisters taking portions of everything.

He leaned close to Leila. "No pressure if you don't like something. Mom's not going to get her feelings hurt."

She looked at him with genuine confusion. "Is it not good? It looks very good."

"It's delicious."

"I thought so." She took a spoonful of pasta and passed him the dish. "I do not feel pressure. I do feel hungry."

Once the food was passed around, they dug in. For about thirty seconds, it was quiet. Michael enjoyed his food, but he enjoyed watching Leila taste hers even more. The way she seemed to savor every option. The appreciative little moans of pleasure.

Yes, she fit right in. What had he been worried about?

Conversation started again, chatter here and there.

And then his youngest brother pointed a fork at him and raised his voice above the din. "All right, Michael. It's time for you to tell us what's going on." Derrick's eyes were gleaming, like he thought he was so funny. But beneath that, Michael saw concern. Which made sense, all things considered.

The rest of his family quieted, all looking at him.

Dad knew the high points. Sam knew he was a CIA agent, but nothing about what had happened the last couple of weeks. Even though Michael had been staying with him, there'd been little opportunity to talk, with Eliza and Levi around all the time.

Bryan and Derrick knew he'd had to escape terrorists, but little of what had come before that.

Now, it was time for everybody to know...everything.

The little bit of food he'd managed to toss down turned inside him. He was used to keeping secrets. Secrets made him feel comfortable.

Sharing secrets made him feel exposed.

But these were his people, and they deserved to know.

He set down his fork.

Under the table, he felt Leila's hand touch his, and he held it, thankful for the connection. "I guess I should start by telling you that I'm not only a machine parts salesman. I do that, but it's not all I do."

Mom went very still. She wore a look on her face he hadn't seen in a long time, not since he was a kid. Disapproval, disappointment. Because he'd lied to her.

He hated that, but he hadn't wanted to worry anybody. And...it was easier to keep secrets than to be honest. It was easier to let people only see his mask, never the real man. It was easier to pretend than to be genuine.

Years before, way back when he'd thrown over his little brother—his best friend—for a bunch of loser high school kids, he'd gotten a glimpse of the real Michael Wright. The ugly person behind the veneer.

He hadn't liked who he'd seen.

He never wanted anybody to see the real him again. He'd

wanted to control what people knew about him—and thought about him.

It came back to that, his need to control everything.

Over the years as he'd grown closer to God, he'd learned that, yes, his flesh could be pretty ugly. But the man God had created him to be wasn't, and the more he walked with God, the less ugly he became.

He didn't have to hide anymore. And he didn't have to control what people believed about him. He could be honest, let people in, and live with whatever conclusions they came to.

"You guys remember when I was in college and interviewed with the CIA?" At a few nods, he plowed ahead. "I got the job. I've been working for the CIA since I graduated."

"Whoa." Grant sat back. "I knew it was something, but—"

"I knew it." Derrick leaned out and spoke to Bryan. "I told you."

"You called it," Bryan said.

Sam smiled at Michael, supporting him.

Dad wrapped his arm around Mom's shoulders.

Mom didn't look happy, not at all. "Why did you lie to us? Is that how you really got that—" She waved toward him, and he touched the wound on his head.

"It's a long story." Not one he planned to tell his mother. Fortunately, she knew nothing about his other wounds.

"You've been lying all these years?" Her face turned red as she pressed her hands against the table as if she planned to storm away. But she dropped them to her lap. "Why?"

It would be so easy to claim he'd had no choice. "At first, I was afraid I wouldn't be able to hack it. I didn't want you to know if I failed. And then I didn't tell you because, even though it sounded like an exciting job, mostly I was doing boring analysis at Langley. I loved what I did, but I couldn't really tell you anything about it. It seemed easier to stick with the fib."

"Fib?" Mom echoed. "Is that what it was?"

"That's what I told myself. And then I went into the field, and I was glad you didn't know. I didn't want you to worry about me."

"Grant was a Green Beret. You think I didn't worry about him? I managed to survive."

"I know. You're right." He scanned the room as a painful silence settled. "I hope you can forgive me."

Sam spoke into it. "You don't need my forgiveness, bro." He took Eliza's hand. "I owe you...everything."

"You don't owe me—"

"Not that it's okay," Grant said, "but I understand the desire not to tell anybody what you're doing. You can't share most of it. Sometimes it's just easier not to say anything."

"That's true."

"And you sometimes want to just leave it at work, not bring the worry with you." Grant focused on their mother. "There were plenty of things I didn't tell you. There are things I still haven't told you—and never will."

"That doesn't make me feel better." But she was softening, the tight skin around her mouth loosening the slightest bit.

Leila cleared her throat, a tiny sound that had the table quieting. "I am sure it doesn't help, but he didn't tell me the truth at first, either, not about what he did for a living or where he was from, or even his last name."

Mom's gaze flicked from Michael's girlfriend to him and back. "And you're okay with that?"

"He said he kept those things secret in order to protect his family. He never wanted anything he did to harm any of you."

"Oh. Well..." Mom sat back.

Michael squeezed Leila's hand but spoke to his mom. "A lot of agents don't tell their families what they do for a living. It's not because we're ashamed. I wanted to protect you"—he focused on Leila—"and you from the people I've been tracking."

"Who was that?" Grant asked.

Thankful for the subject change, Michael said, "I can't really get into it."

"Really?" Mom said. "You're going to almost tell us everything, but not quite?"

"National security, Mom."

"Convenient," she said. "Can you at least tell us about how Leila and Jasmine came to be here? I get the feeling there's more to the story than we've heard."

Michael looked at Leila and her sister.

Jasmine shrugged.

Leila said, "It is up to you. We do not wish to hide anything."

"None of this can go past this room," he said. "And, speaking of, you can't post pictures of them—or me—on social media. They need to remain hidden."

At the nods around the room—and the looks of concern on many faces—he started at the beginning. How he'd met Leila in Munich and they'd begun dating. How she'd been kidnapped and he'd gone to rescue her.

He told the story in broad brush strokes, skimming over the scary parts, though Grant, his special forces brother, was likely reading between the lines.

He told about being smuggled out of Baghdad, then out of Iraq.

He skimmed over the attack in Turkey and explained how they'd taken a boat to Lesvos.

"Which was terrifying," Leila said.

Michael couldn't help smiling. "Leila's afraid of the water."

Grant laughed. "Summer's afraid of boats."

"I'm not afraid." She smiled across the table at Leila. "I just happen to like more space between myself and freezing cold water than a quarter inch of metal."

"Very wise," Leila said. "We agree on this."

"Not afraid?" Grant's tone was teasing—and a little unbelieving. "Those of us who've been on boats with you might disagree."

She elbowed him in the side, and he faked pain.

Actually, Summer was pretty tough. Maybe Grant didn't have to fake it.

"I called Derrick," Michael said, "and he and Bryan came to Mytilene to fly us home." He focused on the charter pilot. "You need to let me know how much I owe you for that."

"Take it up with Sam," Derrick said, causing everyone to turn his way.

Sam glared at their youngest brother. "That was necessary, right now?"

"He brought it up." Derrick sounded very much like the baby in the family. "Was it a secret?"

Sam shook his head, turning to Michael. "I took care of it. It's nothing."

"It's not nothing." Michael had no idea what it cost to charter a jet, and even if Derrick only charged him for expenses...expenses on a jet were a lot.

"You saved my family," Sam said. "I'll never be able to repay you for that."

"That's not how families work," Michael said. "We don't keep score."

"Unless it's pool." Bryan's best sport because it didn't require the use of two strong legs.

"Or ping pong," Grant added, winking at his wife, who was very good.

Sam said nothing, just held Michael's eye contact.

Michael couldn't comprehend it. The debt was paid?

Just like that?

"Thank you."

Sam dipped his head. "It's the very least I can do."

They resumed eating while Michael told them about how he'd rescued Leila and Jasmine from the boat in the middle of the Mediterranean. Most of the story up until now, he'd downplayed, but he didn't downplay this part.

Maybe he wouldn't mind if his brothers were a little impressed.

When he was finished, though, Bryan said, "That's almost as cool as when Grant took down those drug dealers all alone."

"Almost," Grant said, smiling, looking smug. "You helped, though."

"A little."

Michael had no idea what they were talking about, but sheesh. What did a guy have to do to get some respect in this family?

Mom was looking from Bryan to Grant and back, and she was not happy. "What happened?"

"You should've seen it, Ma," Bryan said. "Grant swam out to this yacht off the coast of York, climbed up the outside—"

"Okay, I think we've had enough horror stories for one family dinner." Dad shot Bryan a *shut-up* look.

He lifted his hands in mock surrender. "Just don't want Michael to get the big head."

"Apparently," Michael said, "the size of Grant's head isn't a problem."

"What?" Grant feigned offense. "I'm the humblest man here."

Michael lifted his garlic bread, prepared to throw it across the table.

"Don't you dare," Eliza said. "Some of us are trying to teach table manners."

Levi looked so excited that Michael almost did it just to see the kid laugh.

But he set the bread down. "I guess I'll have to be the bigger man."

～

Michael wasn't sorry when the meal was finished and everybody stood to help clean.

While most carried dishes into the kitchen, he took Leila's hand and tugged her into the living room, away from his nosy brothers—and nosier mother. They walked to the slider and gazed past the trees—some still hanging onto their colorful leaves, but most bare. Soon enough, snow would fall. There'd be trips to the family camp, bonfires and table tennis tournaments and Christmas. The future looked beautiful from where he stood.

There'd be storms coming, no doubt about it. But today was perfect, the water in Shadow Cove smooth as glass.

"It's beautiful," Leila said.

"I'm sorry about my crazy family."

"They are..." Leila's gaze flicked past him toward the noise and chaos in the next room. "Amazing."

"You think so?" Because after the inquisition he'd just endured, his family seemed far from amazing to him.

Leila took his hands, looking up at him with her big, beautiful eyes, dark as onyx. "I hope you know how blessed you are to have a family that can talk freely. They can disagree without fighting. They can tease and make jokes. Not only that, but they show genuine kindness to one another, not because it's expected but because they choose to be kind. This is a beautiful thing. Your family is beautiful. And if your mother is angry with you for lying, can you blame her? She only wishes to know the truth."

"I didn't want to worry her."

Leila shook her head. "It is more, and you know that, and she knows. Perhaps she would have prayed for you differently. And perhaps those prayers would have made a difference. To not tell her the truth is to rob her of the opportunity to be a part of your life."

Huh.

That made sense.

He lifted her hands and kissed her knuckles. "You're very wise. And very beautiful. And my family likes you."

She smiled, the expression shy and hopeful. "Do you really think so?"

"No question."

"I like them too."

It meant so much for her to say it. She barely knew them, but over time, they could all get to know each other better. As different as Leila was—in looks and culture and background— she could fit in with them.

"I have no idea what's next for me," he said. "I want to finish what we started, find out what Qasim and your uncle are up to. But then... I might be out of a job."

"I didn't fall in love with Michael Wright, CIA agent. I fell in love with *you*. I don't care what you do. I would be happy for you to get a nice, boring job."

Maybe he would, eventually. He was halfway decent at sales. Maybe he could find a real sales job somewhere.

"I need a job as well," Leila said. And a place to live."

"We'll figure all that out."

"My sister has never worked, and now she is with child and sick—"

"Please, don't worry. She's your sister. She'll be cared for. I promise."

"You are a very kind man."

"Selfish. I want to keep you, and Jasmine is part of the package. Besides, I like her. I think there's a lot more to her than I've gotten to see."

"She is unique."

"As are you." He held her hands to his chest. "You and I need to get to know each other, without all the secrets between us."

"I would like this."

"So, we'll go back to dating?"

"Yes. If..." Leila lowered her face, then peeked up at him through her long eyelashes, looking almost bashful. "You don't feel obligated because you brought me here?"

Obligated?

Was she crazy?

There was nothing Michael wanted more than this woman.

Unable to come up with an answer that wouldn't scare her away, he wrapped his arms around her and kissed her.

And he'd have kept kissing her if not for the not-so-subtle clearing of a throat behind him.

"Sorry," Eliza said. "I wanted to offer dessert, but—"

"Okay." Michael didn't look at his sister-in-law. "We'll be right there."

After Eliza walked away, Leila said, "We should probably help with the dishes."

She started toward the kitchen, but he took her hand and pulled her back. "I'm not done with you yet. I need to ask... Can you see yourself here? In Shadow Cove?" But that wasn't the question. He took a breath and started again. "With me?"

Leila backed away to look up at him. "When we were girls, Jasmine and I used to dream of coming to America. We would go to university and get jobs and find an apartment. We would have friends and go to church and be free."

Right. America had been her dream.

He'd known that, and he was glad to give it to her. But was that what this was about? Was he just her ticket to America?

She pressed her hands to his chest, resting one right on his heart, which was suddenly beating like it wanted out.

"That dream was good. But this?" She didn't look out the window at the vista or beyond him at the beautiful, fancy home. She tapped his chest and looked into his eyes. "This is so much better than my childish dream. This is everything I ever wanted."

He lowered his forehead to rest against hers. "I never even knew to wish for you, Leila. But now that I have you, I will never let you go."

The End

Of this story, so far. However, there is one more (bonus) chapter, and you won't want to miss it. Check out the *Rescuing You Bonus Epilogue* for one more chapter. (Or go to https://www.subscribepage.com/rescuing-you-epilogue)

Okay, now... The End.

Of Michael's story, but we have some loose ends to tie up. Like...what are the terrorists planning? And can they be stopped?

While Jasmine recovers in Shadow Cove, antiquities professor Bryan Wright will team up with Leila's best friend in Munich, art exhibit designer Sophie Chapman, to discover what ancient Babylonian artifacts could possibly interest Hasan Mahmoud and Khalid Qasim.

Turn the page for more about *Finding You,* Book 3 of the Wright Heroes of Maine.

FINDING YOU
Wright Heroes of Maine, Book Three

One obscure Babylonian artifact in the hands of terrorists could bring down an entire city...

When antiquities professor Bryan Wright is tasked with discovering why a band of terrorists might target a museum in Munich, he teams up with the museum's attractive exhibit designer to study their ancient artifacts. Something in this collection holds special value to the terrorists, and Bryan must figure out which item and why—before enemies get their hands on it.

An American living in Munich, Sophie Chapman wouldn't have expected to be attracted to a musty old antiquities professor—but this guy is neither musty nor old. Even so, she's not ready for a new boyfriend, considering she hasn't figured out how to get rid of the old one. When her apartment is broken into, she has bigger worries than the ex who won't leave her alone.

The seemingly random break-in is anything but. Terrorists are closing in, and their plot will destroy more than the romance growing between Bryan and Sophie.

It'll destroy everything they hold dear.

ALSO BY ROBIN PATCHEN

The Wright Heroes of Maine

Running to You

Rescuing You

Finding You

Sheltering You

The Coventry Saga

Glimmer in the Darkness

Tides of Duplicity

Betrayal of Genius

Traces of Virtue

Touch of Innocence

Inheritance of Secrets

Lineage of Corruption

Wreathed in Disgrace

Courage in the Shadows

Vengeance in the Mist

A Mountain Too Steep

The Nutfield Saga

Convenient Lies

Twisted Lies

Generous Lies

Innocent Lies

Beautiful Lies

Legacy Rejected

Legacy Restored

Legacy Reclaimed

Legacy Redeemed

Amanda Series

Chasing Amanda

Finding Amanda

ABOUT THE AUTHOR

Robin Patchen is a *USA Today* bestselling and award-winning author of Christian romantic suspense. She grew up in a small town in New Hampshire, the setting of her Nutfield Saga books, and then headed to Boston to earn a journalism degree. After college, working in marketing and public relations, she discovered how much she loathed the nine-to-five ball and chain. After relocating to the Southwest, she started writing her first novel while she homeschooled her three children. The novel was dreadful, but her passion for storytelling didn't wane. Thankfully, as her children grew, so did her writing ability. Now that her kids are adults, she has more time to play with the lives of fictional heroes and heroines, wreaking havoc and working magic to give her characters happy endings. When she's not writing, she's editing or reading, proving that most of her life revolves around the twenty-six letters of the alphabet. Visit robinpatchen.com/subscribe to receive a free book and stay informed about Robin's latest projects.

Made in United States
Orlando, FL
01 February 2025

58036934R00223